'Ko's unforgettable narrative voice is a credit to the moving stories of immigration, loss, recovery, and acceptance that feel particularly suited for our times'
Nylon

'[E]ngaging and highly topical ... Ko deftly segues between the intertwined stories of the separated mother and son and conveys both the struggles of those caught in the net of immigration authorities and the pain of dislocation'
The National Book Review

'[A]n impressive literary debut ... Ko does a wonderful job of crafting sympathetic characters. *The Leavers* is never sentimental or cloying'
South China Morning Post

Lisa Ko is the author of *The Leavers*, a novel which was a finalist for the 2017 National Book Award for Fiction and won the 2016 PEN/Bellwether Prize for Socially Engaged Fiction. Her writing has appeared in *Best American Short Stories 2016*, *The New York Times*, *Brooklyn Review*, and extensively elsewhere. Lisa has been awarded fellowships and residencies from the New York Foundation for the Arts, the Lower Manhattan Cultural Council, the MacDowell Colony, the Helene Wurlitzer Foundation, Writers Omi at Ledig House, the Jerome Foundation, Blue Mountain Center, the Van Lier Foundation, Hawthornden Castle, the I-Park Foundation, the Anderson Center, the Constance Saltonstall Foundation, and the Kimmel Harding Nelson Center. Born in Queens and raised in Jersey, she lives in Brooklyn.

Visit Lisa on her website lisa-ko.com or on
Twitter @iamlisako #TheLeavers

THE LEAVERS

LISA KO

dialogue
books

DIALOGUE BOOKS

First published in the United States in 2017 by Algonquin Books
of Chapel Hill (a division of Workman Publishing)
First published in Great Britain in epub by Dialogue Books in 2017
This paperback edition published by Dialogue Books in 2018

10 9 8 7 6 5 4 3 2 1

A CIP catalogue record for this book
is available from the British Library.

ISBN 978-0-3497-0052-6

Typeset in Berling by M Rules
Printed and bound in Great Britain by
Clays Ltd, St Ives plc

Papers used by Dialogue Books are from well-managed forests
and other responsible sources.

MIX
Paper from
responsible sources
FSC
www.fsc.org   FSC® C104740

Dialogue Books
An imprint of
Little, Brown Book Group
Carmelite House
50 Victoria Embankment
London EC4Y 0DZ

An Hachette UK Company
www.hachette.co.uk

www.littlebrown.co.uk

Sin Yao Tai

Like the sea, I am recommended by my orphaning.
Noisy with telegrams not received,
quarrelsome with aliases,
intricate with misguided journeys,
by my expulsions have I come to love you.

–LI-YOUNG LEE,
'The City in Which I Love You'

PART ONE

Another Boy, Another Planet

CHAPTER ONE

The day before Deming Guo saw his mother for the last time, she surprised him at school. A navy blue hat sat low on her forehead, scarf around her neck like a big brown snake. 'What are you waiting for, Kid? It's cold out.'

He stood in the doorway of P.S. 33 as she zipped his coat so hard the collar pinched. 'Did you get off work early?' It was four thirty, already dark, but she didn't usually leave the nail salon until six.

They spoke, as always, in Fuzhounese. 'Short shift. Michael said you had to stay late to get help on an assignment.' Her eyes narrowed behind her glasses, and he couldn't tell if she bought it or not. Teachers didn't call your mom when you got detention, only gave a form you had to return with a signature, which he forged. Michael, who never got detention, had left after eighth period, and Deming wanted to get back home with him, in front of the television, where, in the safety of a laugh track, he didn't have to worry about letting anyone down.

Snow fell like clots of wet laundry. Deming and his mother walked up Jerome Avenue. In the back of a concrete courtyard three older boys were passing a blunt, coats unzipped, wearing neither backpacks nor hats, sweet smoke and slow laughter warming the thin February air. 'I don't want you to be like that,' she said. 'I don't want you to be like me. I didn't even finish eighth grade.'

What a sweet idea, not finishing eighth grade. He could barely finish fifth. His teachers said it was an issue of focus, of not applying himself. Yet when he tripped Travis Bhopa in math class, Deming had been as shocked as Travis was. 'I'll come to your school tomorrow,' his mother said, 'talk to your teacher about that assignment.' He kept his arm against his mother's, loved the scratchy sound of their jackets rubbing together. She wasn't one of those TV moms, always hugging their kids or watching them with bemused smiles, but insisted on holding his hand when they crossed a busy street. Inside her gloves her hands were red and scraped, the skin angry and peeling, and every night before she went to sleep she rubbed a thick lotion onto her fingers and winced. Once he asked if it made them hurt less. She said only for a little while, and he wished there was a special lotion that could make new skin grow, a pair of superpower gloves.

Short and blocky, she wore loose jeans – never had he seen her in a dress – and her voice was so loud that when she called his name dogs would bark and other kids jerked around. When she saw his last report card he thought her shouting would set off the car alarms four stories below. But her laughter was as loud as her shouting, and there was no better, more gratifying sound than when she slapped her knees and cackled at something silly. She laughed at things that weren't meant to be funny, like TV dramas and the swollen orchestral soundtracks that accompanied them, or, better yet, at things Deming said, like when he nailed the way their neighbor Tommie always went, 'Not-bad-not-bad-not-bad' when they passed him in the stairwell, an automatic response to a 'Hello-how-are-you' that hadn't

Praise for *The Leavers*

'There was a time I would have called Lisa Ko's novel
     tifully written, ambitious, and moving, and all of
     is true, but it's more than that now: if you want
    understand a forgotten and essential part of the
     rld we live in, *The Leavers* is required reading'
Ann Patchett

[*The Leavers*] uses the voices of both [a] boy and his
 irth mother to tell a story that unfolds in graceful,
 ealistic fashion and defies expectations. Though it won
 ist year's PEN/Bellwether Award for Socially Engaged
 iction, Ko's book is more far-reaching than that'
 ew York Times

 .] dazzling debut . . . Filled with exquisite,
 artrending details, Ko's exploration of the
 en-brutal immigrant experience in America
 a moving tale of family and belonging'
 eople

 A sweeping examination of family . . . Ko's stunning
 ale of love and loyalty – to family, to country –
 , a fresh and moving look at the immigrant
 experience in America, and is as timely as ever'
 ublishers Weekly

 *k*ilfully written . . . Those who are interested in
 ly observed, character-driven fiction will want
 eave room for *The Leavers* on their shelves'
 *l*ist

'This timely novel depicts the heart- and spirit-breaking difficulties faced by illegal immigrants with meticulous specificity'
Kirkus Reviews

'Ko tells the heart-breaking story of a Chinese mother and her American-born son, who is adopted by a white couple after she disappears without warning and fails to return for several months. Ko is part of an active subgenre shining a light on an ugly truth about our country – that it is possible to come to America and be worse off as a result'
Los Angeles Times

'A must-read'
Marie Claire US

'Heart-wrenching literary debut'
Entertainment Weekly

'One of 2017's most anticipated fiction debuts . . . *The Leavers* feels as relevant as ever as the future of immigrants in America hangs in the balance'
TIME

'Touching upon themes such as identity, determination, addiction, and loyalty, the author clearly shows readers that she is an emerging writer to watch. Ko's writing is strong, and her characters, whether major or minor, are skilfully developed'
Library Journal

'Courageous, sensitive, and perfectly of this moment'
Barbara Kingsolver

yet been issued. Or the time she'd asked, flipping through TV stations, '*Dancing with the Stars* isn't on?' and he had excavated Michael's old paper mobile of the solar system and waltzed with it through the living room as she clapped. It was almost as good as getting cheered on by his friends.

When he had lived in Minjiang with his grandfather, Deming's mother had explored New York by herself. There was a restlessness to her, an inability to be still or settled. She jiggled her legs, bounced her knees, cracked her knuckles, twirled her thumbs. She hated being cooped up in the apartment on a sunny day, paced the rooms from wall to wall to wall, a cigarette dangling from her mouth. 'Who wants to go for a walk?' she would say. Her boyfriend Leon would tell her to relax, sit down. 'Sit down? We've been sitting all day!' Deming would want to stay on the couch with Michael, but he couldn't say no to her and they'd go out, no family but each other. He would have her to himself, an ambling walk in the park or along the river, making up stories about who lived in the apartments they saw from the outside – a family named Smith, five kids, father dead, mother addicted to bagels, he speculated the day they went to the Upper East Side. 'To bagels?' she said. 'What flavor bagel?' 'Everything bagels,' he said, which made her giggle harder, until they were both bent over on Madison Avenue, laughing so hard no sounds were coming out, and his stomach hurt but he couldn't stop laughing, old white people giving them stink eye for stopping in the middle of the sidewalk. Deming and his mother loved everything bagels, the sheer balls of it, the New York audacity that a bagel could proclaim to be everything, even if it was only topped with sesame seeds and poppy seeds and salt.

A bus lumbered past, spraying slush. The WALK sign flashed on. 'You know what I did today?' his mother said. 'One lady, she had a callus the size of your nose on her heel. I had to scrape all that dead skin off. It took forever. And her tip was shit. You'll never do that, if you're careful.'

He dreaded this familiar refrain. His mother could curse, but the one time he'd let *motherfucker* bounce out in front of her, loving the way the syllables got meatbally in his mouth, she had slapped his arm and said he was better than that. Now he silently said the word to himself as he walked, one syllable per footstep.

'Did you think that when I was growing up, a small girl your age, I thought: hey, one day, I'm going to come all the way to New York so I can pick gao gao out of a stranger's toe? That was not my plan.'

Always be prepared, she liked to say. Never rely on anyone else to give you things you could get yourself. She despised laziness, softness, people who were weak. She had few friends, but was true to the ones she had. She could hold a fierce grudge, would walk an extra three blocks to another grocery store because, two years ago, a cashier at the one around the corner had smirked at her lousy English. It was lousy, Deming agreed.

'Take Leon, for instance. He look okay to you?'

'Leon's always okay.'

'His back's screwed up. His shoulders are busted. Men don't work in nail salons. You don't finish school, you end up cutting meat like Leon, arthritis by the time you're thirty-five.'

It seemed disloyal to talk like this about Yi Ba Leon, who was so strong he'd do one-arm push-ups for Deming and Michael and their friends, let them punch him in the gut for kicks, though Deming stopped short of punching as hard as he could. 'Do it again,' Leon would say. 'You call that a punch? That's a handshake.' Even if Leon wasn't his real father – on this topic, his mother was so tight-lipped that all he knew about the man was that he'd never been around – he made Deming proud. If he could grow up to be like any man, he wanted to be like Leon, or the guy who played the saxophone in the subway station, surrounded by people as his fingers danced and his chest heaved and the tunnel filled with flashes of purples and oranges. Oh, to be loved like that!

Fordham Road was unusually quiet in the snow. Ice covered the sidewalk in front of an abandoned building, a reddish piece of gum clinging to it like a lonely pepperoni atop a frozen pizza. 'This winter is never-ending,' Deming's mother said, and they gripped each other's arms for balance as they made their way across the sidewalk. 'Don't you want to get out of here, go somewhere warm?'

'It's warm at home.' In their apartment, if they could just get there, the heat was blasting. Some days they even wore T-shirts inside.

His mother scowled. 'I was the first girl in my village to go to the provincial capital. I made it all the way to New York. I was supposed to travel the world.'

'But then.'

'But then I had you. Then I met Leon. You're my home now.' They started up the hill on University Avenue. 'We're moving.'

He stopped in a slush puddle. 'What? Where?'

'Florida. I got a new job at a restaurant. It's near this Disney World. I'll take you there.' She grinned at him like she was expecting a grin back.

'Is Yi Ba Leon coming?'

She pulled him away from the puddle. 'Of course.'

'What about Michael and Vivian?'

'They'll join us later.'

'When?'

'The job starts soon. In a week or two.'

'A week? I have school.'

'Since when do you love school so much?'

'But I have friends.' Travis Bhopa had been calling Michael and Deming cockroaches for months, and the impulse to stick a foot out as he lumbered down the aisle was brilliant, spontaneous, the look on Travis's face one of disbelief, the sound of Travis's body going down an oozy plop. Michael and their friends had high-fived him. *Badass, Deming!* Detention had been worth it.

They stood in front of the bodega. 'You're going to go to a good school. The new job is going to pay good money. We'll live in a quiet town.'

Her voice was a trumpet, her words sharp triangles. Deming remembered the years without her, the silent house on 3 Alley with Yi Gong, and saw a street so quiet he could only hear himself blink. 'I'm not going.'

'I'm your mother. You have to go with me.'

The bodega door slammed shut. Mrs Johnson, who lived in their building, walked out with two plastic bags.

'You weren't with me when I was in China,' he said.

'Yi Gong was with you then. I was working so I could save money to have you here. It's different now.'

He removed his hand from hers. 'Different how?'

'You'll love Florida. You'll have a big house and your own room.'

'I don't want my own room. I want Michael there.'

'You've moved before. It wasn't so hard, was it?'

The light had changed, but Mrs Johnson remained on their side of the street, watching them. University Avenue wasn't Chinatown, where they had lived before moving in with Leon in the Bronx. There were no other Fuzhounese families on their block, and sometimes people looked at them like their language had come out of the drain.

Deming answered in English. 'I'm not going. Leave me alone.'

She raised her hand. He jolted back as she lunged forward. Then she hugged him, the snowy front of her jacket brushing against his cheek, his nose pressing into her chest. He could hear her heartbeat through the layers of clothing, thumping and determined, and before he could relax he forced himself to wriggle out of her arms and race up the block, backpack bumping against his spine. She clomped after him in her plastic boots, hooting as she slid across the sidewalk.

They lived in a small apartment in a big building, and Deming's mother wanted a house with more rooms. Wanted quiet. But Deming didn't mind the noise, liked hearing their neighbors argue in English and Spanish and other languages he didn't know, liked the thuds of feet and the scraping back of chairs, salsa and merengue and hip-hop, football games and *Wheel of Fortune* spilling from the bottoms of doors and through ceiling cracks, radiator pipes clanging along to running toilets. He heard other mothers yelling at other kids. This building contained an entire town.

There was no mention of Florida over dinner. Deming and Michael watched *George Lopez*, followed by *Veronica Mars*, as Deming's mother folded last week's laundry. Leon was at the slaughterhouse, night shift. Leon's sister, Vivian, Michael's mother, was still at work. Deming lay against one side of the couch, legs stretched out to the middle, Michael on the other side, a mirror image, still recalling Travis Bhopa. 'He went down hard!' Michael's heels pounded the cushions. 'He had it coming to him!' What if the rooms were so big in Florida they could no longer hear one another?

His mother was rubbing lotion into her hands. 'You're my home now,' she said. Earlier, he had volunteered to get her cigarettes at the bodega and shoplifted a Milky Way, then gave half to Michael when she wasn't looking. 'Badass, Deming.' Michael chomped his half in one bite and looked at Deming with such admiration that Deming knew it would be fine. As long as Michael came with them, as long as he wasn't alone, they could move. His mother wouldn't find out about detention, and he and Michael could make new friends. He pictured beaches, sand, ocean. Wearing shorts at Christmas.

Late at night, early in the morning, Deming woke to a smack on the mattress across the bedroom, Leon and his mother whispering as Michael snored on his back. 'Go fuck yourself,' his mother said. The snow shovel trucks rolled down the street, scraping the pavement clean.

Despite his efforts he fell back asleep, and when the alarm rang for school Leon was still sleeping, Michael in the shower, his mother in the kitchen in her work clothes, black pants and black shirt, half-smoked cigarette on the edge of an empty jar. The ash grew soft and long, collapsed.

'When are we moving?'

The radiator pinged black dots. His mother's hair fuzzed up in a static halo, her glasses smudged and greasy. 'We're not,' she said. 'Now hurry or you'll be late for school.'

The day sustained its afterglow following the scrapping of Florida – no more beaches, though – even when Travis Bhopa said 'I'll kill you' in a vampiric accent outside the cafeteria, although he'd said weirder things to other kids, like I'll burn down your building and eat your ears. Travis lacked allies; he had no backup. After school Deming and Michael walked home together, unlocked the apartment with the keys their mothers had given them, exhumed a block of rice from the refrigerator and a package of cold-cuts, moist pink circles of ham. They were adept at making meals even their friends found disgusting.

Later, these meals would be the ones Deming missed the most: fried rice and salami showered with garlic powder from a big plastic bottle, instant noodles steeped in ketchup topped with American cheese and Tabasco.

They ate on the couch, which took up most of the living room, a slippery beast printed with orange and red flowers that made zippy noises when you attempted to sit and instead slid. It was also Vivian's bed. His mother hated it, but Deming saw worlds in its patterns, stared at the colors until he got cross-eyed and the flowers took on different shapes, fish tank, candies, treetops in late October, and he envisioned himself underwater, swimming against the surface of the fabric. 'When I manage my own salon, the first thing I'm going to do is get rid of that thing,' his mother would say. 'You come home one day, it'll be gone.'

Four to eight was the TV dead zone, talk shows and local news. There was a Geometry test tomorrow that Michael didn't need to study for and Deming wasn't going to study for unless his mother found out about it. He got sleepy thinking about the worksheet they had done in class today, on which he'd scribbled made-up answers next to triangles and other assorted shapes. *What is the measure of angle C? Fifty hotdogs.* When it was seven and his mother wasn't home, he figured she was working late, that he had been granted a Geometry reprieve.

Vivian came home before *Jeopardy* ended, trailed by the scent of ammonia. She sewed at the kitchen table, piecemeal orders from a factory, but lately she had also been cleaning apartments in Riverdale.

'Polly's not here? No one's made dinner?'

'We had ham,' Michael said.

'That's not dinner. Deming, your mother was supposed to get food on the way home.'

'She's at work,' Deming said.

Vivian opened the refrigerator and shut it. 'Fine. I'm taking a shower.'

When Leon returned it was eight o'clock. 'Your mother's supposed to be home already. Guess that new boss made her stay late.' He bought frozen pizzas for dinner, and the sausage balls resembled boils but were oily and delicious. Deming ate three slices. Mama never got bodega pizza.

Leon's cell phone rang. He took the call in the hallway, and Deming put away the dishes and waited for him to return. 'Was that Mama? Can I talk to her?'

'It was her friend Didi.' Leon squeezed his phone in his hand like he was wringing a wet towel.

'Where's Mama? Are we going to Florida?'

'Away for a few days. Visiting friends.'

'What friends?'

'You don't know them.'

'Where do they live?'

'It's late. You should get to sleep.'

Michael was sitting on their bed. 'Where's your mom?' With his glasses off he looked older and thinner, his stare wide, unfocused.

'Leon says she's away for a few days.' As Deming got under the blankets he couldn't shake the feeling that something wasn't right.

A week passed and he went to school once. When his mother and Leon had gone to Atlantic City for a night, she had called and reminded him to go to sleep on time, but now he stayed up late, ate M&M's for breakfast, played hooky with his friend Hung, whose father had died the month before. They watched DVDs in Hung's apartment on Valentine Avenue for so long they fell asleep and woke up and fell asleep again, cranking the volume until the car chases and gunfire soothed the cold horror skittering inside him. Where was Mama? She had no friends to visit. There was nobody to lie to for the following day's detention, to hound him about having a plan. Vivian never checked homework; Michael always did his.

Saturday, again. The tube of hand lotion was inside the bathroom cabinet next to her toothbrush. Tucked into the bristles was a green speck, vegetable matter she had brushed from a molar. Deming uncapped the lotion, pushed out a glob. A familiar fragrance, antiseptic and floral, socked him in the sinuses, and he rinsed his hands with soap and hot water until the smell faded. He found one of her socks at the foot of the bed and its partner across the room, lodged against the dresser, and bundled them into the ball shape she preferred. He sat in a corner of the bedroom with a box of her things. Blue jeans; a plastic cat for decorating a cell phone antenna, still sealed in its packaging; a yellow sweater she never wore, tiny hard balls of yarn dotting its sleeves. There was a blue button, solid and round, which he stuck in his pocket.

Her sneakers, her toothbrush, the purple mug with the chipped rim that she drank tea from: still in the apartment, though not her keys, not her wallet or handbag. Deming opened the closet. Her coat and winter hat and boots were gone – she had worn them to work that Thursday – but the rest of her clothes still there. He shut the door. She hadn't packed. Maybe she'd been the victim of a crime, like on *CSI*, and maybe she was dead.

Michael drank water from the purple mug and Deming wanted to smack it out of his hands. He didn't want her to be dead, never ever, but it seemed preferable, in a fucked-up way, to having her leave without a good-bye. The last words he said to her had been, 'When are we moving?' If he hadn't gotten detention – if he had left school at the usual time – if he hadn't resisted Florida – if he'd intercepted the fight she had with Leon – she would still be here. Like a detective inspecting the same five seconds of surveillance video, he replayed last Wednesday afternoon, walking the blocks from school to home. Again and again Deming and Mama crossed Fordham Road, waited at the light, slipped on the ice, hugged, Mrs Johnson forever watching. He zoomed in on the frames, slow-motioned their walk up University, then reversed it so they goose-stepped downhill, cars and buses groaning backwards. He picked apart the words she said, hunting for clues, the way his English teachers made them read poems and spend twenty minutes talking about a sentence, the meaning behind the meaning. The meaning behind her telling him about her life. The meaning of Florida. The meaning of her not coming home.

He heard a key in the door and hoped it was her, going, 'What, you thought I left you? Who do you take me for, Kid, *Homecoming?*' They had watched the TV movie where a mom left her kids at the mall and never came back, and he'd been more entranced by the mall, its sprawling, suburban emptiness. If she came home, he wouldn't play with his food or speak English so fast she couldn't keep up. He would do his homework, wash the dishes, let her kick his ass at Whac-A-Mole like she'd done at the church carnival in Belmont last summer, where Michael had barfed up cotton candy after riding the Octopus.

But it wasn't his mother in the door, only Vivian, shaking slush from her shoes. He ran to her and shouted, 'You need to find her, she's in danger.'

Vivian put an arm around him, her face round and wide like Leon's. 'She's not in danger.' She was warm and familiar but not the right mother, and instead of nail polish and hand lotion she smelled of sweat and lemon disinfectant.

'Is she in Florida?'

Vivian bit her lip. 'We don't know for sure. We're trying to find out. I'm sure she's okay.'

Snow melted. Pink buds appeared on the trees. One night Leon and Vivian spoke in the kitchen but when Deming walked in, they stopped and looked at each other. That week, Deming and Michael packed away their winter coats and took out their T-shirts. Deming saw his mother's spring jacket in the closet, the one she called her Christmas coat because the green was the color of pine needles, and turned away fast. He apologized to Travis Bhopa in hope that it would set things right, that by sacrificing his pride it would guarantee her safety. 'Are you crazy?' Hung said, and Michael looked like Deming had tripped him instead. Travis grunted, 'Whatever.' She stayed gone. The worse he felt, the more it would make her return. He decided to not eat for a day, which wasn't hard as Vivian and Leon were always out and dinner was a bag of potato chips, a cup of instant ramen. Bodega pizza four times a week. Now she would have to come home. He fell asleep in school, lightheaded from skipping breakfast. She would take him out for enchiladas but be glad he lost weight because she wouldn't have to buy him new clothes. She stayed gone. If he cracked an A in Geometry, she would come back. He pulled a B-minus on a quiz and doubled down for the next one – B-plus. She stayed gone. Vivian was right. She'd left for Florida and left him, too.

CHAPTER TWO

A decade later, Daniel Wilkinson stood in a corner, hoping no one would notice his shoes. They were insulated hiking boots, clunkers with forest green accents, necessary armor for upstate winters but aesthetic insult in the city. With his Gore-Tex coat, wool hat, and puffy gloves stashed in a back room with his guitar – a butterscotch Strat he'd bought off of Craigslist – his jeans and black T-shirt didn't seem too blatantly suburban, yet the other guys' feet were clad in stark white sneakers or dark leather boots, and the old fear bucked up that he'd be exposed, called out, exiled. *You're a fake. What's your real name? Where are you really from?*

He dug his hands in his pockets and rubbed the fabric between his thumbs and index fingers. How did you sew the inside of a pocket, anyway? He saw a roomful of sewing machines, women guiding denim beneath darting needles, and thought of his mother.

The show was in a loft apartment on the last remaining industrial block in Lower Manhattan. Windows lined one wall, edged with late February frost, and the concrete floor was tacky with spilled drinks. Closer to where the bands played, it was as hot as July. The current act, math rockers whose set sounded like one thirty-minute-long song, dull grays and feeble angles, the singer's head shaved bald around the sides while the hair on top sprouted up like a fistful of licorice, reminded Daniel of being stoned for days in his dorm room at SUNY Potsdam, hitting repeat on the same song until the notes separated and unraveled.

Thank God he was no longer at Potsdam. He drank vodka in his plastic cup, let the warmth spread into his belly, sandpapering his nerves until the music soaked down to his toes. When he and Roland played, the audience would be incredulous, admiring. Not like earlier, when this dude Nate had been talking about Vic Sirro and Daniel had blurted, 'Oh, you mean the blue backpack guy?' and Nate had made a face like he'd noticed a stain on his pants.

Oh, you mean the blue backpack guy. Daniel mentally punched himself. Nate was so tall and skinny he had a premature hunchback, and his long, thin face was giraffe-adjacent, but even he thought Daniel was a loser. After tonight, no one would turn away from him in the middle of a conversation or look over him as if he was invisible. The band would play sold-out shows, be profiled on music blogs, his picture front and center. Roland had been telling people that this new project was his best yet, reunited with his original collaborator, with Daniel's insane guitar. Hearing this made Daniel nervous, like they were tempting fate. All week he'd been waiting for someone to tell Roland to shut up and stop bragging. But half the room was here because they wanted to cheer Roland on, and Daniel was trying hard to absorb the excitement.

He poured himself another vodka, downed it, poured another. He wandered out to the rooftop, the city spread wide like an offering, though he knew better than to admit he was impressed by the view. Upstate, snow was everywhere, the season in a deep coma. Yet in the city there was minimal snow, heat lamps on the roof and bridges in the distance lit up like X-rays, and there was music, wordless and thumping, bulbs of gold and green, and dancing, arms and legs moving in slow motion, like animals stalking their prey. There were girls with geometric tattoos up the insides of their forearms, hair bundled up like snakes, eyeliner packed on so thick it looked like it had been applied with a Sharpie. One of them had played a set earlier, creeping yowls and crashing keyboards, violin, theremin, melodica, each instrument creepier than the next. Daniel glanced at his hiking boots and moved toward the eye of the dancing, the music an underwater dream.

Years before these transplants dared to venture out of their suburban hometowns, Daniel had been a city kid who memorized the subway system by fourth grade. Yet he still felt like he didn't belong. Post-Ridgeborough, it had never been easy for Daniel to trust himself. Not like Roland, who could give a party direction simply by showing up. When Roland asked if anyone wanted to eat at Taco Bell, which would elicit silence or even derision if anyone else suggested it, people said sure, cool. If Roland proclaimed a show boring, people agreed to bounce. Daniel was malleable, everyone and no one, a collector of moods, a careful observer of the right thing to say. He watched other people's reactions before deciding on his own; he could be fun or serious or whatever was most strategic, whoever you wanted him to be. Sometimes it backfired, like when he'd overheard these guys talking about a band named Crudites and said, 'Yeah, I've heard of them, nineties pop punk, right?' and one of them had said, 'It's not a real band. It's a joke.' How quickly he'd stammered that he must have misheard. Or the other night, when he and Roland were hanging out with friends who were talking about how much they loved *Bottle Rocket*, Daniel had nodded along. 'But you hate Wes Anderson,' Roland said later.

'I'm allowed to change my mind,' Daniel said. He wondered if his annoyance at the preciousness of Wes Anderson movies was misinformed, if he had overlooked a hidden brilliance obvious to people more schooled than he was.

If only he had the right clothes, knew the right references, he would finally become the person he was meant to be. Like Roland – self-assured, with impeccable taste – but less vain. Deserving of love, blameless. But no matter how many albums he acquired or playlists he artfully compiled, the real him remained stubbornly out there like a fat cruise ship on the horizon, visible but out of reach, and whenever he got closer it drifted farther away. He was forever waiting to get past the secret entrance, and when the ropes did part he could never fully believe he was in. Another door materialized, another rope to get past, always the promise of something better.

He gripped his empty cup. He'd torn it apart, bent the rim back and forth until the plastic split in a single line. The math rockers had been playing for forty minutes. Inside, he didn't see any familiar faces, so he got a new cup and poured one last vodka. He found Roland standing against the wall in a black blazer, dark hair buzzed close to his scalp. From the neck up Roland reminded Daniel of a nineteenth-century mobster, with his furtive features and disarming smile. In high school, both of them had been too different to receive attention from girls (or boys, whom Roland also dated these days), though Daniel liked to think it didn't matter now. Roland was still short, compact but hard, his pointy face hawkish, his movements clipped and sharp. His manic energy no longer seemed as freakish as it had been in Ridgeborough, nor did the deep croak that had been slightly spooky on a twelve-year-old.

'We've got this,' Roland said. 'These guys are so derivative.'

Daniel laughed, letting the room blur at its corners. How

great it was to be back in the city, playing music with Roland again. They had been playing together for nearly half their lives, Daniel on guitar and vocals, Roland on vocals and beats and production and sometimes bass, shows at Carlough College house parties or the Ridgeborough Elks Lodge or in a barn out in Littletown. In high school there'd been a thankfully brief electroclash experiment, a power trio with their friend Shawn as the drummer, and an art-punk duo called Wilkinson | Fuentes, in which Daniel had tried and spectacularly failed at playing his white Squier with his teeth, Hendrix-style.

'These guys sound like they're jerking off to their dads' Yes albums,' he said.

'Too many derivative acts,' Roland said. 'Not like that set with the theremin.'

The truth was, Psychic Hearts was derivative, a nü-disco nightmare, like Roland was trying to mix hair metal and *Dracula* with a thinned-out noise pop sound, jacking the title from an obscure Thurston Moore album. All that fronting and polishing only to be purposely stripped down. It was over-manufactured lo-fi, not the kind of music Daniel would choose to play, not his own music. He found Roland's drum-machine beats pre-dictable, the lyrics vague and murky, the eighties stylings too self-conscious. There had always been something distasteful in Roland's stage strutting, how naturally the performance came to him, how effortlessly the crowd ate it up. But if Roland wanted to make music like this, Daniel wouldn't let him down.

Roland had called last month and said he needed a guitarist for a new project. 'Our couch is yours as long as you need it. What's the point in being all the way up there by Canada?' Roland had moved down to the city right after high school, worked until he could afford to go to college part-time, and Daniel hadn't seen him, had barely talked to him, in over a year.

'Nobody can do music with me like you can,' Roland said, and the next day Daniel charged a one-way ticket and rode down to the city on a bus that smelled like diapers. It wasn't as if he had any plans after getting booted from Potsdam. Like his parents said – like they'd remind him again tomorrow – he had thrown his future away.

With gray curtains stapled crookedly to the walls and graffiti crayoned across the bathroom door, this was an invite-only party where the bookers of venues like Jupiter, where Roland longed to play, came to check out bands. Roland knew the girl who managed the secret e-mail list, who had booked them on the basis of his past projects. If the Jupiter guy was into Psychic Hearts, he might book Daniel's solo act one day.

Daniel scanned the crowd. A man with a mustache and white baseball cap was in the back by himself, wearing enormous brown hiking boots with orange laces. Daniel looked again at his own shoes. 'That him? The Jupiter booker?'

Roland rolled his eyes. The math rockers had stopped playing. Anemic applause rippled through the front of the room and one of Roland's friends looked over, gave a thumbs up. 'You ready for this?'

'Always,' Daniel said.

The fourth vodka had been the mistake. By the time they finished the sound check, Daniel felt like he was seeing the room through another person's glasses. He blinked at a spray-painted drawing of a cat on the far wall and returned to tuning his guitar, plucking the same string over and over. He wished more people were scrolling through their phones rather than looking at him, waiting for him to screw up. Roland played the first notes of the first song, started a beat on his Akai MPC60. Daniel produced a chord, sleek and assertive, and the song began to leak its colors, dark blues and lighter browns, like gut notes being forced through a tube. The six-song set list, scribbled at his feet, drifted up at him. He played a C, an E minor. Roland sang the first line. The notes sounded sad and clashing, deeply wrong, like the time he bit into a yellow square he thought was pineapple but turned out to be a very sharp cheese.

Roland kept going. They'd screwed up plenty at shows, and whoever was at fault would eventually right himself. It was their unspoken pact, like what parents said to kids – in case we get separated, return to the place we started from. But this time, the notes did not return. They had only practiced a few times, cocky with their years of history, and when Daniel squinted at the set list none of the titles were familiar. It wasn't nerves – despite his age, he was no amateur – but more self-sabotage. *You mess everything up.* He lunged for a chord, then another. A riff came to him and he played it. It was his melody, a melody, and he wanted to play it louder, so he did. Bright orange pinwheeled around him. Feedback squealed. He saw people grimace, cover their ears.

Roland stopped singing and said, 'This is a song called "Please, Show Me Your Fangs".' He began the next song, but Daniel didn't recognize this one either. It was like he'd woken up in a foreign country where everyone spoke a language he had never heard of, and was required to give a speech. 'Learn to play,' one guy yelled. Daniel couldn't see the Jupiter booker anywhere. The room grew hotter, narrower, and he could no longer hear anything except a rapid acceleration of agitated drumming, a scurry of horse hooves, vicious brushstrokes of gray over black. Danger, the drumbeat signaled. He had to fix it – he had to right himself – he was slipping so fast he could do nothing but tilt, like clicking the button to bet in No Limit Hold'em despite knowing his hand was crap, clicking again, watching the money dip lower, clicking again, unable to do anything but pursue this singular impulse toward ruin. He knew it was the worst thing he could do to Roland, that Roland might never forgive him and he would never forgive himself, but he couldn't bear to be onstage any longer.

He unplugged his guitar and pulled it off. The beats continued. 'What are you doing?' Roland whispered. Daniel lurched off stage, shoving his way through the crowd. He heard Roland calling his name, laughter as he ran out of the room.

He stumbled onto the street, cold air punching him in the face. He had left his coat upstairs. On the Bowery, passing Jupiter, a crowd lined up on the sidewalk. He imagined his name on the sign out front and looked away, then crossed at whichever light came on first, wandering south. He should give up music, go back to school, make his parents happy. Hanging a sharp left, he took Mott down to Canal, passing noodle shops and bodegas, everywhere signs in Chinese. He could make out one character and piece it to the next: LICENSED ACUPUNCTURE. INTERNATIONAL CALLING CARDS. Deciphering Chinese was a welcome distraction, and he walked faster, sliding in the snow, wiping his runny nose with his knuckles. Upstate, he had occasionally formed the sporadic outlines of a word in Fuzhounese, sensed the shapes it might make in his mouth, recalled a Sh or a Tze, but trying to find the right word was like wrestling with air, the meanings there but the sounds long lost. There wasn't anyone he could speak to, even if he could.

After years away, he was shocked at how many people there were in Chinatown, streets in places he couldn't remember, storefronts packed upon storefronts. Being surrounded by other Chinese people had become so strange. In high school, kids said they never thought of him as Asian or Roland as Mexican, like it was a compliment. He wasn't that

Chinese-or-Japanese-or-Korean-or-whatever kid with the professor parents but the guy who played guitar, who was in all those bands, who scowled in the back rows of Honors classes but always passed (everyone assumed, despite his test scores, that he was great at math). At Potsdam there had been a few other Asian students in his lecture classes, exchange students that clumped together or other lone wolves he'd see at parties surrounded by their own non-Asian friends. He avoided them; it was mutual. But he wasn't at Potsdam anymore. There was only the city and its long, Lost Weekend: dancing at a party on a barge; a cab ride over the Williamsburg Bridge with Manhattan shining in the distance, five of them crushed into the backseat, a random girl on his lap, Roland in the front gabbing to the driver about intestinal flora or mushroom foraging; watching *A Clockwork Orange* late at night and stepping out into a Saturday sunrise. Nights like these, the past and present and future rolled out in a sugary wave, everyone he'd ever known riding alongside him on a merry-go-round to a soundtrack of whistling calliopes.

He tripped over his shoelace and bent down to retie it. Was all that gone, after tonight? Maybe there wasn't so much to lose. There were mornings he would wake up on Roland's couch, another solitary day stretching out in front of him, and he would trudge around in the cold for hours, not wanting to go back to the empty apartment, convinced he had made a fatal mistake. And now he had. He'd messed up in front of the people he longed to impress.

He rubbed the goosebumps that had formed on his arms, teeth chattering, and passed a cell phone store with signs in Chinese taped to the windows. Junior year of high school, he had seen a Chinese woman in the Littletown Mall. Thin, with permed hair, gripping plastic bags with the handles twisted around each other. She'd honed in; there was no hiding his face, and when she spoke he understood her Mandarin. She was lost. Could he help? She needed to make a phone call, find a bus. Her face was scared and anxious. Two teenage boys, pale and gangly, had watched and mimicked her accent, and Daniel had said, in English, 'I can't speak Chinese.' Afterwards, he tried to forget the woman, because when he did think of her, he felt a deep, cavernous loneliness.

He thought of her now, wishing he had his headphones, wanting a song to soothe him, noise and a smoke to blot out the night. A man, in the kind of glossy puffer coat Daniel remembered seeing crammed on the racks of Fordham Road, eyed him, curious. 'What are you looking at?' he shouted at the man's back.

His phone buzzed. A text from Roland: *you ok??* He checked his e-mail. There were messages from music mailing lists, an article on unemployment rates and college degrees forwarded from his parents that he erased without reading. There was the message from a Michael Chen, the one he had received more than two months ago, which he still hadn't replied to but hadn't deleted either. Instead he read it again, then closed it, keeping the words simmering inside him at a near constant boil:

Hi Daniel,

I'm looking for a Daniel Wilkinson who used to be named Deming Guo. Is this you?

HI!! It's Michael. You and your mom used to live with me and my mom and my Uncle Leon in the Bronx. My mother got married a few years ago and I live with her and my stepfather in Brooklyn. I'm a sophomore at Columbia.

I know we haven't talked in years, but if this is the right Daniel, can you write me or call me at 646-795-3460? It's important. It's about your mother.

If this is the wrong Daniel Wilkinson, can you let me know too so I don't bother you again?

Hope to hear from you soon!

Michael Chen

'Fuck,' he said. 'Motherfucker.' As if Michael and Leon and Vivian could come back ten years later, as if all of a sudden he mattered to them. They'd let him go, given him away. He couldn't think of anything Michael could tell him about his mother that he wanted to know. Wherever she was, she was long gone.

He turned his phone off and walked uptown. His hiking boots chomped at the pavement. Crossing Canal, he stepped into a puddle and felt liquid splash the back of his jeans. He would never sell someone out like that. He wouldn't quit or disappear, not like his mother or Leon. He'd go back to the apartment and apologize to Roland, learn all the songs, play until his fingers were sore, practice until he was absolved and good again, until he was perfect.

'I don't know why they have to make this menu so hard to read.' Peter squinted at the jagged lettering, which was printed to look like handwriting. His legs hit the underside of the table and the silverware jumped. 'And this chair. It's sized for an infant.'

The waitress, who had a chunky nose ring between her nostrils, was already shouting over the jazz standards, but Peter asked her to repeat the brunch specials as Kay asked questions about the dishes. *Is lemon curd very sour? I don't like sour. What are pepitas? What is LaFrieda beef, why do they have to name the cow?* The floppy velvet cushion on Daniel's chair kept sliding out beneath him, and he bunched up the fabric, tucking it under his knees.

Daniel's parents were in the same sort of clothes they'd been wearing for as long as he had known them, Peter in his rumpled khakis and earth-tone cardigan, Kay in her pastel turtleneck and wide-wale corduroys. After ten years he had stopped noticing how different they looked from him, but he hadn't seen them in two months, had been working and riding the subway and walking the streets with all kinds of people, and now they were the ones who seemed different – quieter, diminished, out of touch. This role reversal was unexpectedly fulfilling.

'Controversy's brewing at the college,' Kay said. 'Excuse the coffee pun.'

Daniel drained his cup. 'At Carlough?'

'The minority students have been protesting.' Peter placed a hard emphasis on *minority*. 'They want the administration to establish an Ethnic Studies department.'

'So what's wrong with that?'

'Well, it's not that we don't agree with them,' Kay said. 'I mean, we do value diversity.'

'But the level of vitriol,' Peter said. 'Frankly, it's not helping their cause. I've had students walk out of my lectures. It's simply disruptive.'

'It's the white students, too, of course,' Kay added. 'All this focus on trigger warnings, political correctness. I'm afraid we're breeding a generation of coddled children. I'd like to think that we've raised you to not have that sort of entitlement, Daniel.'

'Of course, Mom.'

The waitress returned with their food and Peter ordered a coffee refill. Kay removed the teabag from her cup and pressed it against her spoon. Neither of them taught on Fridays, and they had gotten up at six in the morning to drive five hours to the city, planning to drive home right after lunch, refusing Daniel's offer to stay the night in Roland's apartment. 'We are not sleeping on Roland Fuentes' sofa,' Peter had said, as if the mere suggestion was absurd.

'Another coffee for me, too, please. And water.' Daniel had chugged two glasses of water when he woke up, but his mouth was still dry.

Kay studied him. 'Were you out late last night? Did you just get up?'

He shook his head.

'Sure. Like I remember you getting up at the crack of dawn over summer vacation.'

'You know me,' Daniel said. 'I like to rise with the sun.'

'Get a head start on the farm, right?'

Peter stirred sugar into his coffee. 'How is Roland doing these days?'

When Daniel had woken up, forty minutes ago, after a few hours of negligible sleep, his coat was folded at the foot of the couch and Roland's bedroom door was closed. They hadn't seen each other since he had run out of the show.

He spoke through his teeth, tilting his sentences upwards. 'Great! We played a show last night.' As he cut his omelet, his elbow bumped against Kay's.

'Last night. Was it in a bar?'

'Mom. I haven't been doing anything. A beer or two now and then.'

'You know what they say, temptations can lead to relapses. You should be at home with us, going to meetings – you are going to meetings, aren't you?'

She asked him the same thing each time they spoke, and he always lied. 'The one near Roland's place. I told you about it.'

He'd seen the letter that had arrived from the dean at the end of last semester, the bold print detailing the terms of his academic dismissal. After his spring semester GPA fell to a 1.9, the school had put him on probation, and in October, he stopped going to classes. Peter had installed blocking software on Daniel's laptop, though the poker sites had already banned him after he overdrew too many accounts.

His knee knocked against the table, sloshing Kay's tea out of its cup, and Peter watched as he mopped the liquid with his napkin. 'I'm doing good here. I'm making decent money at my job, not using my credit card, and Roland's roommate is moving out in May so I'm going to take his bedroom. It's not like Potsdam, where there's nothing to do. I'm too busy to get distracted by that stuff here.'

'Nothing to do in Potsdam, he says.' Peter huffed. 'It's school. You're supposed to be studying, that's what you're supposed to be doing. Not all this – stuff.'

'I don't know,' Kay said. 'These addictions, I've been reading about it, they go beyond self-policing, and New York City is so full of temptations.'

'Trust me, Mom.'

'There are bad elements everywhere, yes, but there are more people in New York City, more chances to run into bad elements.'

'Working in a Mexican restaurant like a common laborer,' Peter said.

'Don't be racist,' Daniel said.

'What, it's racist now to say Mexican? Well, you serve tacos and refried beans. If that's not Mexican, I don't know what is. Call a spade a spade.'

'A spade? Are you serious? The owners are rich and white, so you have nothing to be worried about. All kinds of people work there, all races and ages. Why, I even have an Indian co-worker who's at FIT, and a Black co-worker who's going to NYU. And the owners didn't go to college and they're fucking millionaires. I haven't met them because they don't even live in New York. One guy lives in a tree house in Washington state, his brother's surfing in Costa Rica, and the other guy's in Berlin.'

Peter said nothing, scooped up forkfuls of eggs Benedict.

'Daniel,' Kay said. 'Don't talk to your father like that.'

'Enough of this,' Peter said. 'No more beating around the bush. We didn't drive five hours to listen to his sarcasm.'

'We have good news,' Kay said. 'Great news. Carlough College is willing to take you as a student, starting this summer. You can make up the credits you missed. It'll be on a provisionary basis, of course.'

Peter and Kay had wanted Daniel to go to Carlough, where they could get him a faculty tuition cut, but had relented to his choice of SUNY Potsdam as long as he promised not to take music classes. His financial aid and work-study income had been enough to cover tuition when his grades were decent, and Potsdam had been far enough upstate that Daniel could hide out, not be solely known as Roland's friend.

'But I'm here now. I have a place to live.'

'Roland's sofa is not a place to live,' Peter said.

Daniel took a long sip of water. 'I don't want to go to Carlough.'

'You should have thought of that before you got expelled from Potsdam.'

'I don't want to go anywhere. I want to be here.'

'Your mother and I have put ourselves on the line for you. We succeeded at getting you into Carlough despite the misgivings of the dean, which were, honestly, quite warranted. She saw the dismissal, your transcript. We had to bend over backwards to convince her you deserved another chance. Your ingratitude is simply astounding.'

Kay placed her palm on Daniel's wrist. 'I know it's been a

difficult time. But you cannot quit after two years of college. What are you going to do without a degree?'

'Play music.'

'Play music!' A flush spread across Peter's forehead. 'Don't be foolish. Is music going to pay your rent, buy your groceries?'

Peter had been saying the same thing since Daniel was twelve years old. 'Roland didn't finish college and he's doing fine,' Daniel said, neglecting to mention that Roland was taking business classes at night. 'His roommate Adrian's in his third year of college and already has a hundred thousand dollars in student loans.'

'This is madness.' Kay rummaged through her tote bag, removed a bundle of papers, and passed them to Daniel.

'March 15,' Peter said. 'Three weeks away. That is the deadline for you to fill out this application in order to matriculate at Carlough for the summer. The website for the online form is printed out here. I would write the statement of purpose for you myself if it wasn't ethically wrong. Don't think I haven't considered it. But do not mistake this for a choice.'

Peter had already filled out the first page with Daniel's name and their address in Ridgeborough. Daniel folded the forms and put them in his pocket.

'What if I enroll in Carlough in the fall, or transfer to a school in the city? There are more job opportunities here, networking opportunities. I need a few months off. When I do go back to school, I'll be healthy. Focused.'

'I don't think so,' Kay said.

'One semester off is already too much,' Peter said. 'You're in danger of falling behind. Now, if it were up to me, we would be taking you home with us after this meal. But your mother seems to believe that you can take care of yourself.'

'Well—' Kay said.

'I can. You have nothing to worry about.'

'We'll get the forms from you next weekend. A copy of your statement of purpose. And after that, you will send us a confirmation of your submitted application.'

'Next weekend?'

'We'll be in the city again,' Kay said. 'Jim Hennings is turning sixty and having a party on Saturday night. Angel will be there. You'll join us, of course.'

Daniel's muscles contracted. So Angel hadn't gone to Nepal. If they were still friends, if she was still talking to him, he would tell her about Michael's e-mail, about Peter's accusation of ingratitude, how torn he felt between anger and indebtedness. If only Peter and Kay knew how much he wanted their approval, how he feared disappointing them like he'd disappointed his mother. Angel had once told him that she felt like she owed her parents. 'But we can't make ourselves miserable because we think it'll make them happy,' she had said. 'That's a screwed-up way to live.' Daniel had known her since they were kids, but their long, insomniac phone calls had only started last spring, and for most of last year she had been his greatest consolation. Her sincerity was contagious, and he liked hearing about her friends and crushes, her plans for the summer, the classes she liked and the ones she didn't, how living in the Midwest was calmer and quieter than Manhattan – sometimes the silence still spooked her – but God, she would kill for a decent slice of pizza, a lamb shawarma in a pita.

Kay motioned to the waitress for the check. 'We love you. We want the best for you. I know it doesn't seem like that right now, but we do.'

'He'll see it someday.' Peter pushed his chair away from the table. 'Where's the bathroom?'

Daniel watched Peter walk across the restaurant, a new

stiffness in his shoulders and legs. Guilt sank through him; they wanted him to succeed in the ways that were important to them because it would mean that they had succeeded, too. Roland had been too busy to talk to him for a year, but Kay and Peter called each week. How could he hurt them more than he already had? He could never return Michael's e-mail.

He turned back to Kay. 'I'll fill out the application, Mom.'

After a seven-hour shift at Tres Locos, Daniel's wrists were sore from bean scooping, pepper chopping, and burrito wrapping. On Roland's kitchen table was an empty box for a Neumann microphone, and Daniel picked up the receipt and let out a low whistle. The mic had cost two thousand bucks. He removed the Carlough College forms, now crumpled after being in his pocket, and left them on the counter.

The couch pulled out into a bed where he slept, his backpack and guitars stashed at its feet. Roland's roommate Adrian was either working or at school or at his girlfriend's place, and Roland was mostly out as well, taking classes, transporting art, working on a construction crew for gallery installations, modeling for a designer friend, helping friends in other bands. Daniel sank onto the couch and took his guitar out. Despite his sore wrists, he wanted to work on a song.

He heard keys in the door, and before he could put his guitar away, Roland came in. 'What are you playing?'

'Just fooling around,' Daniel said.

They looked at each other. 'Listen.' Roland shifted his weight from one foot to the other. 'I want you to know I'm not mad or anything.'

'I didn't say you were.'

'We'd barely practiced.'

'I'm sorry.'

'Come listen to something I did today.'

Daniel sat on Roland's bed as Roland opened Pro Tools on his computer. A line trickled out, Roland's voice, a Psychic Hearts song. Roland pressed a button. It was the same line, but altered with plug-in effects to sound scratched up, scuzzified. Daniel didn't get it. It was using cheesy CGI effects in a historical film, a bad vintage photo filter.

'Hutch, the Jupiter booker, is into this shit,' Roland said. 'After you left last night, I ended up talking to him about the bands he's worked with. You know he helped Jane Rust blow up, right? And Terraria. Brutal percussion, guitars in overdrive. Now they're huge. I'm thinking Psychic Hearts should go in this direction.'

'You want to change the band for Hutch?'

'I want to play Jupiter. I want to get signed.'

'What about your own music? You don't even care?'

Roland shrugged. 'Art evolves.'

'Oh, give me a fucking break.'

'We don't have to.' Roland hit pause. 'But we should.'

'It's not like Hutch is going to book us after last night anyway.'

'Nah, I talked to him. And Javier's playing a show in a few weeks, nothing big, but we can have one of the opening slots.'

'With the new sound. That Hutch likes.'

'Yeah, of course.'

Still, Daniel was closer to it than ever before. The oldest burrito wrapper at Tres Locos, a red-haired white guy named Evan who dropped frequent mentions about how New York had been so much cooler and more dangerous in the nineties, was thirty-six and still trying to get his band off the ground. Daniel had gone to see Evan open for four other acts on a Tuesday night, and the guy could barely sing. At work today, when Daniel mentioned he'd played the loft party, omitting the part where he had run away, Evan had said, 'Get the hell out of here' and plopped down a spoonful of pintos with such force, bean juice had splattered his chest. If Psychic Hearts played Jupiter, he would be sure to invite Evan. In high school, Roland used to tell the other kids, 'You have to see Daniel play,' and if they did a show and no one said anything, Daniel would fall into a funk, consider tossing his guitar in the trash. But when people called him amazing he basked in it, couldn't sleep, reviewing the compliments over and over in his mind.

He wanted to be complimented again, to be called amazing. 'Okay,' he said. 'The new sound.'

'We should record at Thad's studio, the one that does cassette demos. This summer, after we have a few more songs. Or even before.' Roland had ferried a crate of his parents' old eighties tapes down from Ridgeborough, the ones he and Daniel had once studied like they'd been unearthed from a Paleolithic cave and were now as bewilderingly valuable as the rarest, most pristine vinyl. Daniel had to admit there was an oddly comforting quality about tape's crusty, decaying sound, a sincerity, a depth that digital couldn't reach.

'Sure,' he said. This summer, he would be going to classes at Carlough, living in his old room in Ridgeborough. He wouldn't be playing music at all.

'Where'd your parents go, to a hotel?'

'They went home.' By now they would be back in that big, cold house, reading in bed. He fiddled with his sweatshirt. 'Oh, I got a strange e-mail a while back. From this guy I'd grown up with, when I lived with my mother – my birth mom. Before I came to Ridgeborough.'

'What did it say?'

'He said he had something to tell me about my mom. I didn't write him back, but I'm a little curious.'

Daniel knew what Roland's response would be before he even said it.

'Don't do it. You'll regret it.' On the topic of parental ghosts, Roland was dependable, unwavering. His own father had died when Roland was too young to remember, and he'd never shown interest in learning more. Daniel craved Roland's decisiveness for himself. He had always wished he could be so sure.

He picked up the Carlough application forms and put them back down. He returned to his guitar, played the refrain that had been bouncing around earlier, reshaped it, scribbled a few lines, then pictured Kay's face, teary, as he told her he had found out what happened to his real mom. The song slipped away. Thinking of his mother brought a low, persistent ache in a spot he could never get to. He put his guitar away and picked up his laptop. Just a quick search; Peter and Kay would never know. In junior high, he had done these searches every few months, until the urge to know more had fallen away. He had stopped searching after realizing he was averting his gaze while scrolling through the results, relieved to never find the right one. Not knowing more excused him from having to change the life he had gotten accustomed to, and it had been years since he had searched for Michael Chen – Michael's name had always been too popular, with nearly half a million results – or Polly Guo, or Guo Peilan, in English or even in Chinese characters, which never brought up anything matching his mother. He had never found the right Leon or Vivian Zheng.

But tonight he typed in 'Michael Chen' and 'Columbia' and pulled up a website for a university biology lab, scrolled down the page and saw Michael's name and a headshot of a lanky guy, smug and happy in a dark shirt. Michael's face was longer and he didn't wear glasses anymore, but Daniel could see the kid version there, the wide-eyed ten-year-old who would go anywhere with him, the closest thing he'd ever had to a brother. Someone who had known Deming.

He shut the laptop screen as if it were on fire. If Michael had information about his mother, it wouldn't change the fact that she had left him. Roland was right. There was no need to stir up bad memories.

He paced the living room, the kitchen, toyed with the box for the microphone, imagined Roland onstage at Jupiter as he sat in a college lecture hall. He couldn't make Roland and Peter and Kay happy at the same time, but he might as well try.

CHAPTER THREE

She promised she'd never leave him again on the day they found their doppelgängers. Back then, six-year-old Deming and his mother were still strangers to each other, but formed a satisfying pair. The same wide noses and curly smiles, big dark pupils underlined with slivers of white, a bit of lazy in their gaze. Her hand was foreign in his; he was used to his grandfather's warmer grip and more deliberate walk. His mother was too fast, too loud, like the American city he'd been dumped back into, and Deming missed the village, its muted gradients of grass and water, greens and blues, burgundies and grays. New York City was shiny, sharp, with riots of colors, and everywhere the indecipherable clatter of English. His eyes ached. His mouth filled with noise. The air was so cold it hurt to inhale, and the sky was crammed with buildings.

He'd sought comfort in something familiar. He heard melodies in everything, and with them saw colors, his body gravitating to rhythm the way a plant arched up to the light. Crossing Bowery he felt the soothing repetition of his feet hitting the sidewalk, his left hand connected to his mother's right, his two steps to her every one. She launched into the crosswalk. It was her one day off in two weeks. Deming examined the sidewalk droppings, cigarette butts and smeary napkins and, exposed between chunks of ice, so much gum. Who chewed these gray-pink wads? He had never chewed gum and neither had his mother, to his knowledge, or any of her six roommates in their apartment on Rutgers Street. This was before they moved in with Leon, before the University Avenue apartment in the Bronx.

They stood before the subway map with its long, noodley lines. 'So what color should we do today?' she asked. Deming studied the words he couldn't read, the places he'd yet to go, and pointed to purple.

He'd been born here, in Manhattan Chinatown, but his mother had sent him to live with his grandfather when he was a year old, in the village where she had grown up, and it was Yi Gong who starred in Deming's earliest memories, who called him Little Fatty and taught him how to paddle a boat, collect a chicken egg, and gut a fish with the tip of a rusty knife. There were other children like him in Minjiang, American-born, cared for by grandparents, with parents they only knew from the telephone. 'I'll send for you,' the voice would say, but why would he want to go live with a voice, leave what he knew for a person he didn't remember? All he had was a picture, where he was a scowling baby and his mother's face was obscured by a shadow. Each morning he awoke to *cht cht cht*, Yi Gong sweeping the front of their house on 3 Alley, Yi Gong's wheezing, silver smoke rings dissolving skyward, until the morning Yi Gong didn't wake up and then Deming was on a plane next to an uncle he would never see again, and a woman was hugging him in a cold apartment full of bunk beds, her face only familiar because it resembled his. He wanted to go home and she told him the bunk bed was home. He didn't want to listen, but she was all he had. That was two weeks ago. Now he sat in a classroom every day at a school on Henry Street, not understanding anything his teachers said, while his mother sewed shirts at a factory.

Two transfers later and the purple line was running above ground, and Deming and his mother looked out the window at signs in languages they didn't recognize. 'This one's for socks,' he said, pretending to read, 'that one's for dogs.' Near the end of the line the signs switched to Chinese, and his mother read each one out to him in a funny voice, deep and low, like a radio announcer. 'Going Out of Business!' 'Immigration Troubles?' 'We Cure Bunions!' He liked her like this; he could trust that she was his. He kicked his legs in the air as she slapped her thighs in a giddy beat.

They had traveled to Queens, from one Chinese neighborhood to another, and when they emerged from the subway the buildings were lower and the streets wider, but the crowds and the languages were similar, and despite the cold air Deming could smell familiar aromas of vegetables and fish. It was a frigid, hard bite of a winter afternoon. Stopping at a corner, she introduced a new game. 'There could be a Mama and Deming who live here, too, another version of us.' Like a best friend but better; like a brother, a cleaved self. They chose the building this Mama and Deming would live in, a short one with a flat front like theirs on Rutgers Street, and watched mothers and children walk along the sidewalk until they found a boy Deming's age and a woman his mother's height, her hair also cut so it settled in wisps against her chin. Like his mother, she wore a navy blue coat, and could be mistaken for her son's older sister.

'Can't we ask them to come over?'

'We shouldn't disturb them, they're busy. But let's watch them, okay?'

She steered him into a bakery and he begged for an egg tart. In those days you could buy three for a dollar, but she refused, said it was a waste of money, and they sat at a table without buying anything, examining their doppelgängers through the window. The boy leaned up to his mother and she bent down to talk to him as they crossed the street. In the boy's palm was a glazed, puffy object. A flaky yellow pastry.

'Can I have an egg tart? Please?'

'No, Deming.'

He pouted. Sometimes Yi Gong had let him guzzle Cokes for breakfast, but she never bought him anything.

'I want to meet them.' He stomped his boot on the floor. Again she said no. He tore down the sidewalk after them. 'Wait!' he yelled.

They turned around; they knew Fuzhounese. The Other Mama was older and skinnier, and the Other Deming was eight or nine and not five or six, square-faced and squinty-eyed like the kind of boy who might light bugs on fire for kicks. A fat crumb of pastry dangled from his bottom lip. In the moment before his mother yanked him away, Deming met the Other Deming's eyes and the Other Deming said, in English, '*Hi?*' Then they walked off, fading into a sea of winter coats.

'They're gone,' Deming said. 'They left.' Frightened, he longed for Yi Gong. 'Are you going to leave me again?'

'Never.' His mother took his hand and swung it up and down. 'I promise I'll never leave you.'

But one day, she did.

By July, Deming's mother had been gone for five months. Ever since the February day she disappeared, he had been waiting for a sign that she'd be back, even a sign that she was gone forever.

The summer was one big dead-end sign. The city had been too hot for weeks, the sofa's upholstery sweaty against Deming's thighs during the long, overheated afternoons. He and Michael batted their faces against the rattling plastic fan and sang *la-le-la-le-la*, the vibrations taking their words and spitting them out in a watery brown croak. They melted ice cubes in glasses and sucked on them, dug into cushions to search for forgotten change for Mister Softee runs, the ice cream always a letdown, soggy orange sugar that soaked into its cardboard shell before Deming even got his tongue in.

The rest of the school year had been a derailing. Principal Scott said Deming could go on to sixth grade if he went to summer school and made up the subjects he had failed, but Deming didn't feel like going.

'If you don't go, you'll be left back,' Michael said.

They sat on a metal railing, a row of benches below. Even Crotona Pool, which they'd gone to last summer with their friends, had lost its appeal.

'Fuck this summer,' Deming said, tasting the pleasing heft of the words. 'Fuck you.'

'Fuck you, too.' Michael's consonants were resonant with spit. 'Don't you want to graduate high school?'

That was not my plan, Deming heard his mother saying. Fuck a plan. He contemplated the drop-off to the street. An odor of rot mingled with more familiar scents, flatulent exhaust and sweet garbage, searing pavement and grass. Pot smoke and perfume. Somewhere, a barbecue.

'Dare you to jump down,' he said.

Michael laughed without making a sound. 'It's not far. I'll make you jump.'

Deming sat with his knees bunched up, jabbing his chin into the air like Leon did when he knew you were full of shit. 'No one's making me do anything.'

'We'll all be in sixth grade and you'll be stuck in fifth.'

'Shut up.' Deming slid off the railing. On W. 184th, Michael trotting alongside him, they passed Sopheap's building, the same as all the others on the block, squat and brown or taller and gray, the windows full of other families, the sidewalks noisy with other kids. They paused and observed the window where the same plastic blinds hung, the ones they had seen so many times from the inside of Sopheap's apartment. But that summer it seemed like their friends had never existed, that they, like Deming's mother, had vanished with no guarantee of return.

Elroy was visiting his aunt in Maryland, Hung was at a relative's upstate, and Sopheap, that traitor, had promised he'd be home all summer but had decamped at the first opportunity to outermost Queens, where his cousin allegedly had a large-screen television and lived in a building full of hot chicks. Last time Michael and Deming had seen Sopheap, four days or six weeks ago or whenever it was, Sopheap had described the peek-a-boo bra strap exposed on the shoulder of the hottest chick, how close she had sat to him while they watched TV. She smelled, he said, of bubblegum and pepperoni pizza, and Michael and Deming had hooted and said Sopheap was full of crap, how come he never invited them to outermost Queens. Instead of hot chicks Sopheap might be spending the days with his grandma, who had moley arms and a long yellow tooth that caused her to fling saliva as she barked away at the boys in Khmer, slapping her slippers against their shoulder blades to get them to sit up straight.

Everything was suspect. Had Sopheap's family ever lived there in the first place? Would Elroy and Hung even show up for school at the end of the summer? What happened to his mother? Nothing, no one, was certain anymore.

Michael and Deming stood in the space beneath the overhead tracks and hurled curse words into the subway's rattle. A car bumped past blaring a bass line in rich, glossy maroons, and a slow ache spread in the center of Deming's chest. Before his mother disappeared, he and Michael had been united in the secrets they kept from their moms, like filching a can of beer from Leon's twelve-pack. Michael had grimaced and belched as they drank, and Deming had knocked back more. They had giggled, teetered. Another time, they stole a pair of panties out of a cart at the laundromat across the street from Elroy's building, and in Elroy's room ran their hands over the tiny cotton panel where an actual girl's actual crotch had actually nestled. Held it to their noses, sniffing exaggeratedly, saddened yet relieved when they smelled only detergent. Hung laid the panties on the bed and the boys stared at the scrap of pinkish fabric until Elroy plucked them up and smuggled them into his closet. 'I'll keep them here,' he said, 'for safekeeping.' Deming said they might not even belong to a hot girl but to the woman who sat in front of Elroy's building and rubbed her fingers into her ponytail after scratching her hairy armpits. The other boys yelped in horror, Michael's shriek the loudest and highest.

Now the only mother in the apartment was Vivian, and the fact that Deming's mother was gone was no secret. It was a car alarm cutting through an empty street in the middle of the night. He could curse as much as he wanted, but the words tasted like they had gone rotten in his mouth. He tried to remember as much as he could about her. Such a brief time when she had belonged to him alone. She cuffed her jeans twice so they wouldn't drag on the ground. She pulled the sleeves of her sweaters down like oversized mittens. The pleasing incongruity to her cackle, how she'd pinch the fat under his arms and call him a meatball, the delicate prettiness to her features. You had to hunt for her beauty, might not even catch it at first. There was a sweetness to her mouth, her lips lightly upturned, lending her a look of faint amusement, and her eyebrows arched so her eyes appeared lively, approaching delighted.

He looked away so Michael wouldn't see the tears that came so fast he almost let them fall.

They turned the corner. 'Deming?' Michael sounded hesitant, like he was talking to a teacher or a friend's mom. 'Did you hear? Travis Bhopa's moving to Pennsylvania.'

'So?' Deming didn't know where Pennsylvania was.

'His mom left his dad for another man and now he's got to go live with his grandma.'

'What other man?'

'Some neighbor.'

Deming dug his fingernails into his arm, ten sharp half-moons sparking pain. But what if she wasn't dead? 'That sucks,' he said. 'For Travis.'

They ate dinner at the folding table in the kitchen, the plastic top printed to look like wood, a corner peeling and exposing a foamy underlayer. Deming snatched a piece of chicken from Vivian's plate.

She tried to grab it. 'Stop it. Bad boy.'

Vivian's fat was rearranging itself. Her belly and arms were thinner but extra skin had appeared beneath her chin and around her mouth, like plaster hastily slapped on top of an existing structure. She huffed when she walked upstairs, no longer danced to music on the radio, and fell asleep at the table, gave the boys food and claimed she wasn't hungry. Deming had seen her look in her wallet and curse, and when he opened the refrigerator she yelled at him to shut it. He heard her and Leon fighting about the rent, who would watch the kids.

He licked the chicken before she could get to it, ran his tongue up and down the salty skin. Leon glared at Deming and passed Vivian the rest of his food.

Leon looked like hell, reminded Deming of pictures of

cavemen in a school textbook, standing straight and de-haired into upright Homo sapiens. Leon after Mama was reverse-order evolution; he had developed a stoop, a paunch, a spotty beard specked with gray. It scared Deming, like Leon had aged a hundred years while other people remained the same.

Once, riding the Staten Island Ferry with his mother and Leon, the wind had stung his face but he felt warm, as if nothing could go wrong. His mother had said, 'Do you like this boat, Kid? Isn't it better than Yi Gong's fishing boat?' And Leon had laughed, a belly chuckle that made Deming feel like he'd outrun the other kids at the playground. Now he couldn't recall the last time he had heard Leon laugh. Had Mama left, refused to marry Leon, because Leon got ugly? Deming chewed chicken. They had a lot of neighbors. Mrs Johnson, Tommie Not-bad-not-bad-not-bad, Miss Marie with the baby girl. There was the bodega owner, Eduardo, who'd been asking, 'Haven't seen your mother lately, how's she been?' Deming would say good, busy.

'Eduardo's always asking how Mama is.' Deming watched Leon for a reaction.

'Who?'

'The guy at the bodega.' Leon's face was blank. Deming tried again. 'I saw Tommie the other day.' No answer. 'Yi Ba? Can we go to Florida?'

He had never referred to anyone but Leon as his father, and when his mother had first told him he could call Leon 'Yi Ba', it had seemed a little illicit. In school, spacing out as the teacher chalked the multiplication table, trying to ignore the other kids who were hyped on sugar and rocking back and forth, busting out in Tourettes-y curse strings (one particularly restless kid liked to chant *Balls, titties, balls balls titties* all day), Deming would mouth his own words: *Yi Ba, can you come here? Yi Ba, can I watch TV?*

Leon looked up. 'Florida? Why?'

'If Mama's there, we're not trying hard enough to find her. What if she's in danger?'

'She's not in danger.'

'But how do you know?'

'I know. She'll call soon.'

'Mom?' Michael asked. 'Can we go to Florida?'

'No,' Vivian said.

'I want to go to Disney World,' Michael said.

'No, no, no, no.'

As Deming scooped rice out of the pot, a clump fell on the table.

'Don't waste food!' Vivian swept the spilled rice onto her plate and took his bowl away. 'Maybe your mama left because she was tired of feeding such an ungrateful boy.'

She took Deming's plate to the sink.

'Don't listen to her,' Leon said. 'She didn't leave because of you. We're all going to stay together, you and me and your mama. We just have to wait.'

Vivian said, 'I'm going to the store.'

Leon went to work. Michael fell into the couch like it was eating him. Deming didn't know what he was doing here. Leon wasn't his real Yi Ba, Michael and Vivian not his real cousin and aunt. If his mother ran away with another man, he had to let her know that she couldn't get rid of him that easily. He grabbed clothes and stuffed them in a plastic bag.

'Stop blocking the TV,' Michael said.

'I'm going to Florida to find my mom.'

Laughter from the studio audience rattled out. Michael stared at Deming, his eyes enormous behind his glasses. 'Then I'll go, too.'

'Are you serious?'

'Of course. We're brothers, right? Like brothers.'

'Okay, then we have to hurry.' Deming dumped a ball of Michael's clothes into the bag. 'We have to go now.' He took his keys, tossed Michael's shoes at him, and they moved out the door.

'How are we going?' Michael shouted as Deming ran up University, taking a right on 192nd. He didn't know which store Vivian had gone to, which block she'd take back to the apartment. 'My shoelace!'

'I have a plan,' Deming said, though he didn't. As they neared the subway station they heard a train pulling away, and they ducked into the stairwell, panting.

'I don't have a MetroCard,' Michael said.

Deming swung the bag of clothing against his leg. It was heavier than he'd expected. 'Me neither.'

'I'm going to tie my shoelace now.' Michael bent down, tied one loop, then another.

'I don't have any money,' Deming whispered.

'We can ask my mom maybe.'

'She won't let you go if you ask her.' Michael looked so serious, so trusting. He couldn't ask Michael to leave Vivian. Then they would both be without mothers. 'Let's go home.'

'What about Florida?'

'Another time.'

They turned back. 'I'm hungry,' Michael said. Inside the bodega, Deming lingered in the aisles, fingering a candy bar, but Eduardo's bushy white beard kept catching his eye.

'Whoo,' Eduardo whistled from behind the cash register. A giant metal fan batted warm air around. 'This stinking heat.'

'It's a heat wave,' Michael said.

'How's your mama doing? She all right?'

'She's great,' Deming said. 'And we're late for dinner.'

They walked out with nothing. By the time they got to

their building, his arm ached. He asked Michael, 'You seen Tommie lately?'

'Not for a while.'

They paused outside Tommie's door. Deming wanted to kick it, but it didn't sound like anyone was inside. 'Where's Pennsylvania, anyway?'

'Real far.'

Deming could see the relief in Michael's face when they got home. He brought the bag of clothes to the bedroom, unpacked as quietly as he could, and heard Michael saying, 'We went for a walk, Mom.'

Mom. Deming fell asleep on the couch, woke to drool caked on the side of his face. Much later, after Leon came home, the sky cracked open and it rained, drops splattering against fire escapes, running down rooftops, giving the air conditioners a free bath. A slow, humid breeze trickled into the bedroom, Michael's limbs flailing in a distant dream. Deming watched Leon sleep, the rise and fall of Leon's chest, pressing his arm against Leon's back. He needed Leon to stay.

But they were safe, for now, humbled and seething. They were two men without her.

Leon said it was no big deal: that his woman had split and nobody knew where she was. He made a little laugh, a joke – She left me! Isn't that crazy? – but Deming saw how the skin on his neck was droopy and crinkled, deep brown circles blooming under his eyes like a wet cup on a paper plate. 'I'll get another woman, you hear?' Leon said, sitting at the kitchen table in the dark.

The summer dragged on. Deming heard Leon and Vivian talking, hid in the other room so they wouldn't know he was listening: At work, a falling hog had smacked Leon and he skidded on the slick floor, coming to on his back. Got probation. He sliced the wrong veins, let an animal drift on by like a graceful ocean liner, large crooked knife slashes against the meatgrain. He was given the second of three strikes, his hours docked. The landlord had already given two extensions for late rent; the loan shark's men were less understanding.

Mama's co-worker Didi – Leon's buddy Quan's wife – had called screaming about the nail salon, how the boss had been involved in something shady. 'Do you think she went to Florida?' Vivian said. But Didi had tracked down the number of the restaurant, and when Leon called, the owners said Mama never showed up.

Didi had called the police, Immigration, and they said there was no record of her. So Mama was okay, not in danger like Deming had feared, just took off on her own. Leon told Vivian he'd gone to a lawyer, one Quan had found, whom Quan had to help translate. Back home Quan would be a freak, an American-born Vietnamese Chinese who could only speak a drop of Chinese, but here Quan was a big shot, because of his English, and here Leon was a nobody, because of his Chinese. It drove Leon crazy that he needed Quan, a little guy with a big voice who spiked his hair into mini spears.

Leon had wanted to belt the lawyer when he asked, 'Did she know anyone? Any other men? You might think you know a woman and you don't.' When Quan translated, Leon said, 'Tell him to go suck his own cock.'

Vivian said they couldn't keep bothering the police, not without papers. All they could do was wait to hear from her. Deming heard Leon say how he was wiring the loan shark Mama's payments, almost double what she'd been able to afford. At dinner, he snapped at Deming. 'Playing with your food again, no respect.' But the next day, he took Deming out for donuts at the Vietnamese coffee shop, offered up maple-glazed, powdered-sugar, Boston cream. 'I spent three months on the boat coming over from Fujian,' he said. 'Washed with seawater. Slept on soggy cardboard. Think about your bed. Think about your bathroom. *You* can sleep.' Deming concentrated on his donut. The cream oozing out – where was the Boston? – like something obscene. On the boat, Leon said, the enforcers had nearly beaten a man to death for stealing a packet of instant ramen from the captain's quarters. One man had tried to stop the crew from doing something bad to a woman, and the enforcers kicked him in the face and threw him into the ocean. Leon could still hear that woman's screams.

Deming licked cream off his fingers. 'Mama came on a plane, not a boat.'

That night, Leon didn't come home until morning. Deming couldn't sleep, waking up every few hours to find the other side of the mattress still empty. When he heard Leon's voice in the hallway, he got up.

'Yi Ba, where were you?'

'Get out of the way. I need to go to bed.'

'You smell like a bar,' Vivian said. 'Must be nice to stay out all night doing whatever you want. Wish I could do that.'

'Go out all you want,' Leon said. 'I don't care.'

'You don't care? Who cooks the meals? Who cleans up your garbage? Who washes your clothes? Who takes care of your Polly's son while you stay out all night drinking and pissing money away?' Vivian picked up a pair of Leon's underwear and threw it at him. 'Wash your own panties! Find another girl to take care of this child!'

'Will you be quiet?'

Vivian slammed the bathroom door and opened it so she could slam it again. Leon pushed past Deming and fell onto the bed, landing on Mama's pillow.

*

Ten days later, Leon was gone. Left in the middle of the night. Vivian said he had gone to China.

Michael started to cry. 'Is he coming back?'

'Not for a while. He found a job there, in our cousin's business. Lots of people going back these days.'

'We're not going, too, are we?' Michael asked, and Vivian shook her head.

It was like the time he fell off a swing and the wind got knocked out of him: boom. Deming wanted to cry, but held it in, kept his face as still as possible. There was a rock inside him, a boulder.

'He would have said good-bye,' Vivian said, 'but you and Deming were sleeping.'

Deming knew this was bullshit. Leon had left because he was a coward. He hadn't said good-bye because he knew he shouldn't have left, and he had left because he felt bad. As Deming watched Vivian comfort Michael, a wall hardened around him.

Three weeks later, Vivian announced that she and Deming were going out, the two of them. They were going to buy new clothes for school.

'Why can't I come, too?' Michael said. 'I want new clothes.'

Ever since Leon had left, Michael and Deming no longer bothered to walk past Sopheap's apartment or try to find change for Mister Softee. They stayed inside, despite the heat. In the shower, Deming balled his fists up and hit his thighs. He had to pretend things were normal.

'This is Deming and me time,' Vivian said. 'We never spend time together, right, Deming?'

'Michael should come, too.'

'I'm coming, Mom.'

Vivian told Michael to stay inside the apartment. 'I'll be back soon.'

'No, don't leave.'

'Put the deadbolt on right away. I'll make you a nice dinner tonight.'

Michael was crying again. 'Please don't leave.'

'I'll be back very soon.'

'I'll? What about Deming?'

'We'll be back.'

Michael stopped crying. Vivian and Deming waited in the hallway, Vivian holding a plastic bag, until they heard the lock click shut. Deming heard a loud sniffle from inside the apartment and wanted to go back in, but Vivian was already walking toward the staircase.

They got on the Bx12 bus, taking a pair of seats near the front. Deming wondered which stores they would go to.

'Face it,' Vivian finally said. 'Your mother isn't coming back, and you need a good family. I can't provide for both you and Michael right now. I'm sorry, Deming. I don't have the money. I'm going to have to move to a smaller apartment, get roommates. I'm getting people to look after you until Leon makes enough in China so he can come back to New York. You'll be okay, and when Leon returns, we'll see each other again.'

The wall tightened. He could barely breathe. 'When?'

'Soon,' Vivian said.

'*How* soon?'

Vivian didn't answer.

'I'll get a job! I'll be twelve in November.'

They got off on the Grand Concourse and entered an office building. He sat in a chair near the door as Vivian spoke to a woman in awkward English, her voice much softer than usual. He heard her say, 'I have his birth certificate.'

The woman came over to him. She was tall and black; her glasses had gold frames. 'Deming? Why don't you wait in here while I talk to your aunt.' She led him into a smaller office, with a folding table and ceiling fan, gave him crayons and a stack of coloring books, then reached into a drawer and handed him a box of apple juice and a bag of chips. 'Here's a snack. You can draw if you want.' The woman's smile was small but kind. 'I'll be back.'

Deming opened a coloring book. It was for younger kids, with large outlines of animals, and most of the pages were already filled in. The crayons were all snapped in two. He scratched large X's over the faces of the animals and told himself Vivian would have the address of wherever he was going, that she and Michael would come get him in a few days. Maybe he'd get to go somewhere exciting, with video games.

When the juice and chips were long gone, the woman came back, holding the plastic bag Vivian had been carrying. 'You're going to come with me now. We have a place for you to stay tonight, in Brooklyn.'

He rode with the woman in a van, sitting up front, the bag on his lap. Inside were his clothes and toothbrush. They drove on a highway and across a bridge, and the woman asked him about school and his friends. She gave him another juice box and asked about his mother. He said he hadn't seen her since February.

They drove to a neighborhood where the people were Chinese, and there were Chinese stores and restaurants, but it wasn't Manhattan Chinatown. There were more trees here, houses with aluminum siding, children riding bikes on the sidewalks.

The woman parked the van on a side street. They got out, walked to a three-story house, and rang a bell. A man and a woman answered the door, both Chinese and with graying hair. The four of them walked upstairs to an apartment, and the black woman spoke to the Chinese woman in the kitchen but Deming couldn't hear their words, while the man sat with him on a couch in the cool front room, saying 'Relax, be good' until Deming fell asleep on the cushions, drained from the heat and the car ride. When he woke up, the black woman was gone.

'How long will I stay here?' he asked the man.

'A while,' the man said.

They fed him vegetables and beef stew, big bowlfuls of it. He asked if he could call Michael, and they said not now, later. They turned up the air conditioner and let him sleep and watch TV.

Days passed. Deming lost track of time. He slept on the couch and watched TV. Afternoons, alone in the apartment, he roamed the small rooms, opening empty drawers and cabinets, eating Chef Boyardee that he heated in the microwave. The couple's bedroom remained locked. There was no telephone. He wanted to go outside, but the front door was locked, too.

One morning, when the doorbell rang, it wasn't Vivian and Michael but a white man and woman, who spoke to the Chinese woman in English. The white woman said Deming's name first. 'Dee-ming, Dee-ming.' She drew the vowels out so the word was unrecognizable. The Chinese woman said 'Deming' and he sat up, still sleepy. The white woman tried again, closer this time.

They approached on tiptoe. 'Hello, Deming.' The man's voice was reedy, gently nasal. His hair was floppy with light yellow strands, and his eyes were a diluted blue, surrounded by lines. The white woman's hair was short, blonde with chunks of brown. Her cheeks were a pale pink.

'Hello, Deming,' she said. They sat on either side of him. The woman's arms touched his. The man's legs pressed against his. He had only been so close to white people on the subway before.

'Who are these people?' he asked the Chinese woman in Mandarin.

'These are your new foster parents,' she said in English. 'Peter and Kay Wilkinson.'

Deming jumped up. Peter and Kay Wilkinson were tall, but he was fast. He made it halfway down the carpeted stairs before he felt hands on him. 'Stop, Deming.' It was the Chinese woman. 'The Americans will take good care of you. They have a big house and lots of money.'

'I already have a family.'

'Your old family isn't here anymore. This is your new family. Relax. Everything will be okay.'

Peter and Kay Wilkinson squatted on the steps. 'Deming,' Kay said. 'We're going to take care of you. It's going to be okay.' She put her arms around him. Her shirt smelled like laundry and soap. His mother had been gone for half a year. And now Leon and Vivian were gone, too. Nobody wanted him.

Deming leaned against Kay and she stroked his hair. 'There,' she said, victorious, and she laughed, a peal of delight, a flag unfurled in the sun. 'It'll be okay.'

He followed the Wilkinsons out of the house. On the drive upstate he fell asleep and missed his last glimpse of the city, woke up in a car parked in front of a large white house with a wraparound porch, tall trees looming. In the city it had been one of those steam-chamber August afternoons that felt like dying, but here, in the shade, it was cold.

Peter turned off the engine. 'Welcome home.'

CHAPTER FOUR

One week later, tucked into a double bed sheathed with red flannel, Deming Guo awoke with the crumbs of dialect on his tongue, smudges and smears of dissolving syllables, nouns and verbs washed out to sea. One language had outseeped another; New York City had provided him with an arsenal of new words. He'd bled English vowels and watched his mother's face fall.

He wrapped the blankets tighter around him, cold even in late August. The white clapboard house in Ridgeborough, New York, population 6,525, five hours northwest of the city, was nearly two hundred years old, Peter said, an antique. Five times the size of the Bronx apartment, seven times the size of the house on 3 Alley. Three big bedrooms: one for Kay and Peter, one for Deming, and the third for *guests*, a bed chubby with quilts and pillows in which nobody ever slept. Two bathrooms and two floors and a whole room for eating, another for studying and working on the computer.

A breeze snaked in through the oversized windows. The beanbags that lay across the bottoms of doors could not ward off this draft.

I am Daniel Wilkinson.

He shivered. He had never slept alone before, never had a room to himself, all this vast, empty space.

Deming heard a *toot-toot* of a whistle. Peter was in the doorframe, hands on hips. He liked to whistle tunelessly.

'Good morning, Daniel.'

It always took a second to realize they were talking to him. When school started, they said, it would be easier with an American name. Though it wasn't official. His birth certificate, Kay explained, still said Deming Guo.

'Time to get up now. We'll be leaving for church in an hour and a half.'

From downstairs wafted breakfasty odors, eggs and sausage in salty grease. Deming's stomach rumbled.

In those early days he called them nothing, spoke to them without saying either Kay and Peter or Mom and Dad. When Kay leaned in for hugs, Deming wiggled away, her hold too tight, the Wilkinsons smelling like cheese and flowers, bitter and sugary sweet. But other times he lingered. 'We're glad you're here, Daniel,' she would say in English, then perform shapeless approximations of Mandarin words. She had learned some Chinese phrases, taken Mandarin classes and bought a Chinese–English dictionary, but her tones were so off-kilter that Deming couldn't understand what she was saying.

'I don't know who you are,' he'd respond in Fuzhounese.

When he spoke Chinese, Peter's leg would bounce and Kay's lips would press even thinner, as if they were being sucked into her body, her mouth consuming itself. 'English,' Peter would warn, concerned that Deming wouldn't be fluent enough for school, as if the English he spoke was tainted. His mother used to swat at his shoulders in a way that looked playful but felt serious when he spoke too much English and not enough Chinese; his weapon of choice had been the language that made her dependent on him. Whoever she was with now would have to translate.

The giant windows. The yard outside with its large, gnarled trees. No sidewalks on Oak Street. Hours could pass without a car going by, the absence of overt sound a trickle of gauzy peach. Deming would stand at the window and listen to the languid chirp of birds, the dim roar of a distant lawnmower. The air maintained a steady, nearly indiscernible buzz. Peach-brown gauze swept over his eyelashes.

In a corner of his new room was a pile-up of plastic games, action figures of muscular men with swords, sturdy fire trucks and police cars with miniature sirens, toys Peter and Kay said were his. (Playing cops didn't interest him. There was nothing fun about screeching sirens.) On a shelf by his bed was a row of books, Condensed Classics for Children, paperback versions of *The Count of Monte Cristo*, *The Last of the Mohicans*, and *Oliver Twist*. The word *condensed* reminded him of the cans of milk his mother had bought as a treat, a drizzle of sugared glue atop his breakfast oatmeal. Like him, she had a sweet tooth, but didn't give in to it often. Eduardo would offer her damp muffins encased in plastic wrap, the blueberries reminiscent of pigeon poop, but she would buy bananas instead. Occasionally there had been condensed milk, Tootsie Rolls, a package of Twizzlers.

Full of omelet, Deming fidgeted in the pews of St. Ann's. The collared striped shirt, a hand-me-down from a nephew of Kay's, made his neck itch. Stand, sit, pray. The priest droned on and Deming gripped the blue button from his mother's box. He had found it inside a pair of shorts Vivian had packed. Now he slept with it under his pillow.

He rubbed the button's hard upper lip, the rounded center, and remembered the subway as it shot out of the underground at 125th Street and his mother with her arms around him, saying

'Look!' He dreamt of dashing up University with Michael, where the street curved and the buildings slapped hands with the sky, legs swinging, backpacks bouncing, sharing a bag of Funyuns with Elroy and Hung, shoving Sopheap around in the park. The pizzeria, the donut spot, the Chinese takeout, the shop selling rows of stiff blue jeans and dresses for $4.99. In the city, far, far away from St. Ann's Church and the town so small you could spit on a map and rub it away, there had always been the warm press of bodies, Vivian ladling bowls of soup, the chatter of the television, chugging soda, burping contests with Michael, his mother talking on her cell phone. Sharing a bed, it had been warm enough to not need flannel blankets or wool socks.

He tried to tuck away the Bronx in scraps and shards. Once he had read in a book, an ancient science textbook still being passed off as useable at P.S. 33 – one day, man will walk on the moon, it said, more than a quarter century after the fact – that people could have tumors inside them for years, harmless cysts, and these cysts could grow teeth and hair, even fingernails. A person could carry this alien being and never know. A monster twin. A hairball double. So many things could be growing inside him, inside every person. He carried Mama and Leon, Michael and Vivian, the city. Reduced to a series of hairs, a ball of fingernail clippings and one stray tooth. A collection of secret tumors.

Deming kicked the pew. A little girl in the next row turned around and looked at his face until her mother elbowed her.

The minister mumbled a prayer. Deming had never been to church before, so he did what everyone else was doing. He stood. He sat. He recited lines from the heavy book and stifled a yawn. Thank you God, amen. He tried to ignore the people around him as he walked with the Wilkinsons to their car.

*

Ridgeborough Middle School was two blocks from downtown Ridgeborough, which consisted of one main street and a park with a big American flag. Deming sat in the front seat of Kay's silver Prius on the drive down Oak Street, then Hillside Road, across the railroad tracks and into the west side of town, where the houses were closer together and the yards were smaller.

'Daniel might be better served if he does the fifth grade over again instead of going into the sixth. Across the board, his grades were very poor.' Principal Chester, a man with tufts of white nose hairs that protruded from his nostrils like grassy tusks, pointed to papers on his desk. 'It seems that this school, this Bronx school, also recommended him for special study.'

'I did summer school,' Deming said.

'We'll need the records for that, then.' Principal Chester looked through the papers. 'They didn't have the same classes we do here. What kind of math and science did you take at your old school, young man?'

He wondered how Principal Chester could breathe through the nose hairs, and wished Michael and his friends were here so they could joke about them. 'Just math.'

'Geometry? And what about language arts, what did you study at your old school?' He looked at Kay. 'Where is he from? Originally?'

'I already told you,' Kay said. 'New York City.'

'But originally?'

'His mother, I guess, was Chinese.'

'China. Interesting. And you and your husband are his adoptive parents?'

'Foster,' Kay said.

Principal Chester shuffled papers. 'His English may need a little brushing up on, but I'm afraid we don't have enough foreign students in this school district to warrant an English as a Second Language class.'

'His English is perfectly fine. He was born here.'

'It would be beneficial to let him be with the fifth-graders. Kids can get discouraged easily. We don't want to get him started off in his new country on the wrong foot.'

'As I mentioned, he was born in the United States,' Kay said. 'And you can hear him talk, he's fluent. I don't agree with holding him back. It will only impart low expectations. Kids are adaptable, they learn fast. He belongs with the other kids his age, in the sixth grade.'

'And your husband? Does he agree with all this?'

'Excuse me?'

'Certainly your husband has an opinion as well,' Principal Chester said.

'Developmentally, Daniel is academically above grade level. If you can recall Vygotsky, as an educator like yourself surely can, then you are aware that social interaction is fundamentally tied to a child's cognitive development processes. Even if your school employs a transmissionist model, we can take into account that scaffolding teaching strategies among Daniel's peer group will ensure that he can, and will, thrive in the appropriate sociocultural context. In other words, in the sixth grade.'

Principal Chester looked at the papers again. 'Well, let's not get ahead of ourselves.' He chuckled. 'All that talk about models. I'm not sure I'm as well-versed in models as you are, Mrs Wilkinson.'

'Dr Wilkinson. I teach at Carlough.'

In the end, Principal Chester put Deming in sixth grade.

'That man's a complete idiot,' Kay said, as they left the school.

Deming's first weeks in Ridgeborough were like sleepwalking, murky and addled, as if he'd wake up and be back in the Bronx with a finger snap. The bag of clothing Vivian had packed was the only thing he had left from the city, clothes Kay had washed and folded and placed in the dresser in his room. She took him to the mall to buy what she called a proper back-to-school wardrobe, the parking lot a wide expanse of blacktop bigger than any lot he had ever seen, its size more apparent because of its emptiness, only a few cars parked in the myriad spaces. They walked past stores as soprano saxophone trilled over the loudspeakers, and like at church, like the few people he'd seen on Oak Street, everyone else was white.

They passed stands selling jewelry, watches, baseball caps. 'Let's see,' Kay said. 'What would an eleven-year-old boy wear?' She stopped in front of Hollister, Abercrombie & Fitch. 'Do you like these stores?'

'I don't know,' Deming said. Inside Abercrombie & Fitch were life-sized cardboard teenagers romping on a beach, girls with sun-streaked hair laughing in bikinis and boys holding surfboards against their muscled torsos. His mother had bought his clothes on Fordham Road, he and Michael getting two of the same shirt in different sizes and colors.

'Look.' Kay pointed to the cardboard cutouts. 'It must hurt to smile like that.' She bared her teeth and struck the same pose as one of the bikinied girls, thighs lunging, arms raised. Deming watched her, not sure if he was supposed to laugh.

Cargo Pants. Boys' Shorts. Classic Tees. Chinos, Polos, Hoodies. Kay held up clothing and Deming said, 'Okay.' In the dressing room he removed his green shorts and gray T-shirt, took off the Yankees cap Leon had given him. Michael had the same pair of shorts in blue and a striped version of the gray shirt. Did Michael miss him, or was he was glad to have the bed to himself? Leon might have called from China. If Vivian moved, his mother would have no way of getting in touch with her, to let him know where she was.

Heart pounding, he zipped on cargo pants. He looked in the mirror and felt weird, misshaped.

'Can you come out here and show me?'

Kay gave him a brief once-over. 'Do you like them? Do they fit?'

'Yeah.'

'So, do you want them? And these shirts here, I guess, too?'

'Okay.'

Kay handed the cashier a piece of paper and said she had a clothing voucher for foster children.

'We don't take these,' the woman said. 'Try Walmart or Target.'

'Oh.' Kay laughed. 'It's okay.' She put the paper back in her purse and took out her credit card. After signing the receipt, the shirts and pants folded inside a bag, she asked Deming, 'Do you need anything else?'

Deming was puzzled at the enormity of the question. 'What about sneakers?' he finally said.

Kay's hand flew to her forehead. 'Come on, Kay, get it together. Shoes, how could I forget about shoes? Can't go to school barefoot, Principal Chester would not approve.'

At the Athlete's Foot, Deming picked the most expensive pair of Nikes on the shelf, with puffy tongues and red and black stripes. Kay handed over her credit card and signed. What else could she buy him – a motorcycle, a computer? They wandered upstairs to the food court. Kay held the clothing bags, Deming the box with his new sneakers, and they shared a plate of cheese fries. He licked the hot yellow sauce from between the ridges of each fry. Crinkle-cut, they were called.

'Did you go to malls in New York City?' Kay's skin had become pinker, perhaps from the heat of the fries. Deming looked at families eating at other tables, old couples walking arm in arm, teenagers counting change and pouring sodas.

'Why am I here?'

Kay picked up a fry. 'Because – we have room for a child in our family. And you needed a family to stay with.' She grew even pinker. 'Are you nervous about school?'

'Not really.'

At a nearby table sat a mother with two boys around his age, all of them soft and oversized – even their teeth were big – doing diligent damage to a pizza. He accidentally made eye contact with one of the boys, who glanced at his brother and snickered. Their mother stared at Kay and Deming as if they were standing on the street with their butts exposed.

He grabbed more fries and tried to ignore the family at the other table. He wanted to like Kay's laughter, its bursting crescendo, and the easy way she bought him things.

She kept talking. 'I know it's scary, being the new kid. My family moved once when I was in the seventh grade, just two towns over, but it was a new school and I thought it was the end of the world, literally, that my world was going to end. It wasn't that I liked my old school so much, not at all, but I was scared it would be worse. But you know what, I ended up making friends. Which was a miracle in itself. I mean, I was such a nerdy kid, a bespectacled bookworm. I loved reading so much I'd stay up all night with books and fall asleep in class the next day. I'd even stay inside during recess to read. As you can imagine, that didn't win me any popularity awards. But you're going to be okay, Daniel. You're going to be fine.'

On the first day of fifth grade at P.S. 33, Mama and Vivian had walked Deming and Michael out the door of their building. All along the block were kids streaming out of their own buildings, big kids, little kids, sisters and brothers, and at the light was a crossing guard, a Puerto Rican lady who always said, 'Good morning, sweethearts' in a sugary alto.

Ridgeborough Middle School seemed miles away from Kay and Peter's house.

He heard them talking on the other side of his bedroom wall.

'It sounds horrible, but maybe a younger child would've been easier,' Kay said. 'More of a blank slate.'

'We waited years for a younger child,' Peter said. 'Even when we were still thinking about China.'

'I know. But I can't figure out how to act around him sometimes.'

'Be yourself. Aren't children supposed to know if you're not being natural?'

'You're at school all day. Are you sure you can't work here at least part of the time? We have a study, you can write there.'

'Let's not go through all this again,' Peter said. 'You know this is an important semester for me.'

'It's not like they're going to decide to not make you department chair because you come home early once in a while. Work–life balance. You've been there forever, they know you and your work. That's not about to change.'

'Not with Valerie in the running. She has no kids to worry about and one more book than I do. I have to work more right now, not less.'

'Honey. Really.'

'There's no work–life balance when it comes to academia. You of all people should know that. But it could be different for women. There aren't the same expectations, the same drive.'

'Right.' Kay laughed. 'We don't have drive! We're expected to do all of the childcare and all of the cooking and go to work and teach and do research and write our own books. We're expected to support our husbands, make sure they're taken care of so they can do their very important work. And lucky me, I get to be an adjunct forever.'

'Well, you wanted this. And now you have it.'

'Oh, that is not fair. You wanted it, too.'

It was quiet. If Kay left Peter for another man, would Deming have to go back to the city?

'You did want it,' Kay said. 'Right?'

'Of course.'

'Do you think we're going to be okay at this?'

'Of course,' Peter said. 'That's the advantage of fostering. We can try it on for size, see what happens.'

'I'm afraid to get too attached. The aunt or the mother, they could come back for him anytime.'

'We'll take it day by day.'

'And not that I think that success in parenting is biological, but it's hard. It doesn't come naturally, though I hate to use such an essentialist term.'

'It takes time. It'll be better once he goes to school. He'll make friends. You'll see.'

'I want him to open up to me. Tell me about his mother or the city or anything.'

'He's been through a lot. Don't push it.'

There was another silence, and Deming was backing away from the wall when he heard Peter say, 'Maybe it's cultural, why he's more reserved?'

'Maybe. Maybe. Oh, are we crazy? Having him live in a town with no other Asian kids? I wouldn't blame him if he hated us.'

'I'm not going to say it'll be easy,' said Peter. 'But white, black, purple, green, kids of all races have struggles with belonging. They're fat, or their parents don't have a lot of money.'

'That's true,' Kay said. 'I was a bookworm with glasses. I never belonged in my hometown.'

'Issues are color-blind.'

'If things work out, we'll have to make sure we connect him with his culture. I'll talk to Elaine about that summer camp.'

'We'll take care of him. That's all that matters, and he knows that.'

Deming pressed his ear against the wall, but Peter's words faded into mush.

He slipped into bed. His mother was short and round and nothing like Kay. *Don't think about her.* His mother talked with her hands and let him watch as much TV as he wanted. *Don't think about that.* Kay and Peter only allowed three hours of TV per week. They preferred PBS.

The kitchen smelled like milk farts and meat. Kay heaped Deming's plate with meatloaf, gravy, and brussels sprouts and filled his glass with cold skim milk. Milk gave Deming stomachaches but Peter said it was good for him, so he drank a glass at every meal.

He made sure to set the dinner table the way Kay taught him, forks and knives in the right order, no spoons, napkins and place-mats centered, glasses in their proper corners. The other night, he saw Kay move the glass he'd placed in front of her placemat from the left corner to the right. *Right, not left! Don't screw up again.*

'One more day of summer and it's back to school for all of us,' Peter said. Classes started tomorrow at Ridgeborough Middle and Carlough College, where Peter taught economics and Kay taught political science.

Deming wedged meatloaf against the side of his cheek. If he gave in to the Wilkinsons he would be stuck here with them, his real family forever lost.

Kay turned to him. 'Daniel?'

Peter's gaze joined hers. 'Are you looking forward to school tomorrow?'

'I guess so.'

'Daniel, please look at us when we're talking to you,' Peter said.

Kay's lips pressed and creased. 'We love you, Daniel.'

He forked another chunk of meatloaf. His mother said she had wanted big things for herself, but then she had him. If he could love Peter and Kay, they could leave, too. They had been waiting for a younger child who would have been easier, whom they had wanted more.

Late at night, Deming crept downstairs to the kitchen telephone. He remembered his mother's cell phone number, though he'd never memorized Leon's or Vivian's, and there was no landline in the Bronx apartment. He lifted the receiver, pressed the numbers, and heard an automated message tell him he needed to dial a one. He tried again with a one. There was a pause, another announcement. *This call cannot be completed at this time.* He called again, switching the order of the last two numbers, and the phone rang but went to a strange man's voice mail. The first number was the right one; he hadn't forgotten, but his mother wasn't there.

Upstairs, the toys in the corner of his room formed a shadow. Deming made out the shapes of a fire truck, a police car, and put one vehicle in front of the other and pushed them across the rug. He rammed the fire truck into the police car and whispered the sound of sirens.

On the first day of school, Kay made a special breakfast, blueberry pancakes with maple syrup. She dropped Deming off on her way to Carlough, and he summoned his best don't-mess-with-me face, walked into Mrs Lumpkin's homeroom class and found a seat. The classroom was bigger than the ones in P.S. 33, and instead of sitting at tables in groups of four, kids in Ridgeborough sat at individual chairs attached to desks.

Mrs Lumpkin called roll and Daniel Wilkinson was the last name called. 'Here,' he said. Twenty-four pairs of eyes looked over. Mrs Lumpkin, who was skinny despite her name, double-checked the roster.

At P.S. 33 there'd been thirty-two kids in his homeroom, but at Ridgeborough Middle, there were only fifty kids in the whole sixth grade. Deming sat through History and Science and Language Arts. Alone at a cafeteria table, he ate the turkey sandwich, celery sticks, and hard, crisp apple Kay had packed. Everyone he saw was the same color except for him, and their silence seeped into the air like a threat.

At home after school, Deming stared at the noiseless street, heard the same blank buzz, and felt a sickening loss. He punched the wall as hard as he could – *You call that a punch? That's a handshake!* – until his knuckles were screaming and he was screaming, too. The house was empty; Peter and Kay were at work. When they were home, he was forced to keep a straight face, but it felt like he was being skinned alive.

On the second day of school, Deming decided he had been imported from another planet to come to Planet Ridgeborough. He was not aware of the length of his assignment, only that one day, he would be sent home. This was how he got himself through the hours. He studied Amber Bitburger, who sat in front of him in homeroom and whose long blonde hair had white strands interspersed throughout, a yellow-brown closer to the scalp that lightened progressively toward the ends, her skin visible beneath, pink and soft, like a baby animal before the fur comes in. Her eyes were a gray-green, her face a range of hills – nose, chin, cheekbones.

They were big. Deming was big, too, he'd been one of the biggest Asian kids at P.S. 33, but they were different, had never noticed the way they looked to other people, because there were no other people present. Here, they paid too much attention to him (at first) and later, they would pay no attention to him. It was that kind of mindfuck: to be too visible and invisible at the same time, in the ways it mattered the most. Too obvious to the boys who wanted to mock him, yet girls would only notice him when he was walking around with his fly down.

He studied their noses. Some were pointy, others drooping like overripe fruit. Some nostrils flared up and out, while others were pinched and narrow. The boys and girls separated into distinct clusters at recess, with the crumbs, the leftover kids who didn't belong to any group, scattered along the margins of the playground. Deming could see he was a crumb. Crumbs didn't want to be noticed but were as noticeable as an open sore, tucking themselves away to avoid the places of highest concentration: the jungle gym, the corners of the blacktop where girls congregated, the basketball court and soccer field that were home to boys who were good at sports.

If the crumbs were successful at hiding from others they weren't fooling each other. They lashed out at the nearest targets, happy to train that spotlight two feet over to the left. But Deming did not want to hide. Three Alley and the Bronx had prepped him, and Planet Ridgeborough was the ultimate test. He had been specifically placed on this mission by his superiors to test his strength and patience. When he fulfilled his mission he would be reunited with his real family. Who were his supervisors? He had that figured out, too. They communicated, telepathically, in Fuzhounese, the language he didn't have to try to hear. This mission made him brave. So he got out on the blacktop at recess, out there in the open, daring anyone to mess with him.

On the third day, a girl stopped at Deming's table in the cafeteria, clutching a box of apple juice with a scrawny straw, teeth marks flattening the tip. Her dark hair was pulled into a stubby ponytail. Her glasses had bright red frames.

'Where are you from?'

Deming cleared his throat. 'The Bronx. Where are you from?'

'I'm from here,' she said, and walked away.

On the fourth day, there was gym. In Ridgeborough, kids played sports. Football, soccer, basketball, swimming, baseball, tennis, volleyball, hockey. Ridgeborough boys were supposed to charge and ram. Deming observed the youth of Planet Ridgeborough in the boys' locker room as they changed into gym clothes, from the unformed baby limbs of short kids like Shawn Wecker, the crumbiest of crumbs, to the meaty paws and Frankenhead of Cody Campbell. He studied Cody's plump hands, thighs like pork roasts, the waggle and sweat of Cody's chins.

He took off his shoes, took off the athletic shorts Kay had bought. The crumbs stayed on the edges of rows, scuttling to change without being noticed, but the other boys joked and yelled out to their friends.

Shawn Wecker, his foot tangled in the fabric of his shorts, stumbled into a locker. He was a small boy with a shriveled face, so pale he'd been nicknamed Ghost. 'Fag,' one of the other boys said. 'Ghost is a fag.'

'Fuck you!' Shawn yelled back. 'Fuck! You!' The locker room's collective response was laughter, so much worse than anger, and Shawn slunk away. Then Deming felt the shove, a blow between his shoulder blades. He tipped forward.

It was Cody. 'What are you looking at? Chinese retard.' On the side of his face was a flying-saucer-shaped mole. He pushed Deming again, but this time Deming charged Cody and knocked him backwards. Cody stumbled, making a sound like *oofaa*. He was less graceful than even Travis Bhopa; he was big but lacked balance. This struck Deming as both comic and predictable.

There was a weight on him, a jab in his side. One elbow, then another. Deming cried out and the weight rolled off. Cody collected himself. Deming stood up. 'What the hell?'

The weight was Shawn Wecker, his face snarled.

Deming walked away. 'Retard,' Cody repeated. 'Chinese retard.' It sounded like a bawl, fleshy and raw, an animal turned inside out.

In gym they played kickball, a sport Deming had never played before. When it was his turn to kick, he heard a snicker and a voice go, 'Nice shoes.' He looked down at his new Nikes and the ball socked him in the gut. When he whirled around he saw a row of boys trying not to laugh.

After school, he walked home by himself. It wasn't that far, only a half hour, but the view was relentlessly unchanging, house after house, tree after tree. The tight streets unrolled into mini-fields, so vast that looking at them made him dizzy, frightened at the unendingness. As he got farther from school, the spaces between houses were bigger than the biggest houses themselves. He had grown so unaccustomed to hearing cars that when one drove past, he jumped.

Passing the railroad tracks, he heard footsteps behind him and tightened his stance, anticipating Cody and his friends.

A boy's voice said, 'Hey.' Deming lunged. But it wasn't Cody, it was a kid whom Deming had observed with curiosity, Roland Fuentes. He looked different than the other kids; he, too, wasn't one of them. Deming had heard people say Roland's last name with an exaggerated accent, drawing out the syllables like a mockery, though Roland never reacted. 'Hey,' he said now to Deming, 'I'm Roland. You're Daniel, right?'

Roland Fuentes was in the smart math class with the girl from the cafeteria, Emily Needles. He would've fit in fine in the city, but in Ridgeborough his speed and determination made him suspect. He jutted his chin forward as he moved, eyeballs darting like a nervous bird. His skin was browner than the bond-paper-white of Amber Bitburger and Shawn Wecker, and his dark hair was baby fine and thinning, or perhaps it had never filled in, if a boy could be balding before junior high.

Together they crossed the tracks, kicking up gravel. No trains, to Deming's knowledge, ever went through here.

'You in Dumpkin's homeroom?'

'Yeah.'

'I'm in Moore's.'

Deming knew that but wasn't admitting it.

'Where do you live? I live over on Sycamore.'

'Near there,' Deming said. 'On Oak.'

'Where are you from?'

It didn't seem as annoying as when it came from Roland. 'The city. The Bronx.'

'Cool.'

'Where are you from?' he asked.

'Mars!' Roland was small but his voice was the lowest out of all the boys', a scratchy, gravelly baritone. 'No. I'm from here. *Ridge* Burrow.'

Roland said he and his mom lived on the corner of Sycamore and his dad was dead. 'But I don't remember him. He died when I was three and a half. In a car accident.'

'My dad died, too,' Deming said. He suddenly wanted to be friends with Roland, to be friends with anyone. 'In China.'

'Did your mom die, too? Your real mom.'

The word came out before he could stop it. 'Yeah.'

At dinner Peter asked if Deming had a good day at school and Deming said yes, he made a friend. Kay asked if he liked his teachers and he said they were okay, a little boring. She laughed and said, '*Lump*-Kin.'

'What a name,' said Peter. 'The kids must go to town on that one.'

After dinner, Peter and Kay taught Deming gin rummy, and they sat together at the kitchen table and played cards until it got dark outside.

Upstairs, in the silence of his room, Deming spoke Fuzhounese to his mother and told her he was sorry for saying she was dead.

Roland and Deming had no classes together except for gym, but at recess they wolfed down their sandwiches and forsook the playground for the computer room, where crumbs and nerds of all grades played video games. Sometimes they'd see people in there they wouldn't have expected, like Emily Needles, or even once, Cody Campbell.

For two weeks they dominated the top scores for all the games, beating their own records. No matter what game you played, you'd only see two names, DWLK and RFUE. At first, Deming had typed DGUO, but Roland had asked, 'What's Dee Goo Oh?' and it was too complicated to explain. (He'd written 'Deming Guo' on his worksheet the first day of school and Mrs Lumpkin had called him up to her desk after class: 'Is there a problem? Is this a joke?') Whenever Deming won another game, Roland held a hand out and said, 'Who's awesome? D-W-L-K is awesome!' Deming returned the high five and glanced around the room, wishing Roland would keep it down. It wasn't safe to be bragging like that in Ridgeborough, and he didn't like how Roland jumped up and down when he typed in RFUE, pumping his fist in the air. But between games Deming returned to the top score boards to look at the repetitions of a name that was supposed to be his.

In math, Mr Moore drew obtuse angles and Amber Bitburger

chewed on the ends of her white-yellow hair. *Stay awake*, Deming told himself. *Stay alert*. The easiest way to make sure he wouldn't get comfortable was to remember he was on a mission, that gin rummy and meatloaf and flannel blankets were a part of his investigation. If he held everyone at arm's length, it wouldn't hurt as much when they disappeared.

After a few weeks, the wooden floors of the Wilkinsons' house no longer felt so slippery, and when people said 'Daniel' he answered, didn't think they were talking to someone else. No longer did Peter and Kay look as unusual to him, the shade of their skin and the shape of their noses as normal as the low buzz of the empty streets, and he didn't always remember to dial his mother's phone number at night. When he did he always got the same message: *This call cannot be completed at this time*. Now it was his face that seemed strange when he saw it in the mirror.

He told himself his mission supervisors could come for him at anytime, yank him out of class, drag him from the kickball game, approach him in the cafeteria as he ate PBJ on wheat, seemingly unaware. For he could never be unaware. There was always the possibility that one afternoon there would be his mother or Leon or even Vivian in the cafeteria, ready to pick him up and bring him home, or a rap on the door at homeroom, Daniel Wilkinson excused as the rest of the class murmured 'Oooo' like he was in trouble, and in the principal's chair would be Mama, her face a warm light, apologizing for taking so long, rolling her eyes behind Principal Chester's back. They would jump on the next bus to the city, and Deming could clear the lint from his throat, loosen his milk-coated tongue.

It wasn't his mother or Vivian who came to the Wilkinsons' house one Friday, but a freckled white woman with a button nose and a small cup of a chin, hair springing from her face in toast-colored coils. 'I'm Ms Berry,' she said, 'but you can call me Jamie.'

'Jamie is our caseworker from the foster care agency,' Peter said.

The woman turned to Deming. 'Do you want to show me your room?'

'Go ahead, Daniel,' Kay said.

Jamie followed Deming upstairs and sat on the floor, against his bed. She looked at the plastic trucks. 'Are these your toys?'

'Yeah.'

'Do you want to show me how they work?'

'Not really.'

'Okay, that's fine.' Jamie smiled. 'How's school going? Have you made any friends?'

'Yeah. Roland.'

'Do you want to tell me about him?'

'He's – a boy.'

'I know you've been through a lot of big changes recently. But whatever you want to tell me, it's between me and you. And you don't have to say anything if you don't want to.'

'Okay.'

'What's your favorite subject at school?'

'I don't know.'

'What about your least favorite subject?'

All of them? 'Math, I guess.'

In the empty playground, the weary swing had creaked as Deming's mother swayed. This was last November, three months before she left. *Eek-eek-eek*, it went, *eek-eek-eek*. Deming leaned, palms on her back, but he couldn't get her that high. Up, down, curving behind him and sweeping forward, her jacket a silver dollar against the gray sky, she had yelped into the clouds. *Ha! Ha.* He pushed her until she said, 'Enough. Your turn.' She lifted one leg, then the other, patting the saggy U of the rubber seat.

He sat, legs dangling. 'Ready?' Up he went, higher, swing squealing past the pockmarked asphalt, the slide flaked with curls of rust. A hot glob of lunch dribbled up inside him and the next thing he knew he was no longer clutching the chains but flying, soaring like a brick, and before he smacked into the asphalt he saw the pavement tilt sideways, blotting his vision, a concrete eclipse.

He'd awoken in a strange room with the worst headache of his life, lying on a cot next to another cot with an old man in a diaper and an IV drip, mold stains blotched across the ceiling tiles. He heard crying babies and saw white static. A sign on the wall said URGENT CARE.

His mother flipped through a magazine. When she saw him moving she jumped up, grabbed his hand. 'You're awake.'

'What happened?'

'You slipped, Kid.' She squeezed his hand harder.

'I did?'

'I was so scared. You were out for a minute. Seemed like forever. How are you feeling? Are you hungry?'

A nurse spoke about recovery, said Deming should rest. Here were white pills to take, and he needed to drink them with water.

He looked at his mother's pouched and tired face, the brown splat of mole on her neck, and his eyes filled with bright, stabbing light. When he closed them he saw dark stars, and he questioned what he remembered. Maybe she pushed him too hard, or maybe he'd jumped, heeding an urge to leap and flap. Superhero dreams.

Leon had said it was an accident, Deming was a big boy and big boys didn't get hurt easily. 'Got to be more careful next time. Boys are energetic. Hard to keep you still.'

At the apartment, Deming woke again to his mother, at the

edge of his bed, watching him in the dark. 'Mama?' In the yellowy shadows of the streetlights filtering through the curtains, he saw the outline of her nose and chin, hair matted and uneven from sleep.

She ran her nails against his scalp, scratching lightly. He heard her whisper: 'It's important to be strong.'

Deming and Kay watched the other moms across the parking lot of Ridgeborough Middle School, their baggy shin-length pants, mushroomy haircuts, and pastel cardigans. The other moms matched; their kids did, too. Other moms attended PTA meetings, had gone to one another's baby showers, were elated when they found out their sons and daughters would one day be classmates. Ridgeborough parents worked at the hospital or in the prison, and none of the other kids had a mother and a father who both taught at a college.

The other moms stood in a tight circle by their cars, their voices jigsawing across the asphalt. They talked about their husbands and children, made plans with one another's families for the upcoming weekend, and Deming noticed a hungry look on Kay's face as she shook her keys. 'They're probably discussing scrapbooking and cookie recipes,' she said. 'And voting Republican, for whoever their husbands vote for.'

Like him, Kay was a crumb, and like him, she didn't want to be friends with the mom equivalents of Cody Campbell and Amber Bitburger. But unlike Deming, Kay had no friends, aside from her and Peter's co-workers at Carlough. At least he had Roland.

Instead of friends, Kay and Peter had books they read in bed at night. They left articles for each other, clipped out of news magazines, on one another's pillow, with underlined paragraphs and notes in the margins: *Think you'd like this. Thought about you! Did you know??* The tall shelves in the living room were stuffed with hardcover books on subjects like war and economics and the electoral college. The most intriguing thing in the house was the stereo system from Peter's brief bachelor days, with mustard-yellow speakers, a silver hi-fi tuner, and the crowning glory, a record player with a turntable wrapped in a soft cloth. The cabinet below the record player housed a small record collection, along with an eraser-like object used to clean the records.

One afternoon, Deming was at home by himself. He knelt in front of the stereo and, simultaneously daring himself and accepting the dare, pushed the cabinet door open. The records' covers were throbbing and bright, bands he'd never heard of, and inside the cardboard pockets were hard black discs, slick and coated, with circular rings, what alien trees might be like if you sliced their trunks open.

When he saw Peter's car pull into the driveway, Deming closed the cabinet.

Peter put his bag down on the couch. 'How was school today, Daniel?'

Deming got up from the floor. 'It was fine.'

'Why don't you choose a record and we can listen to it?'

Conscious of Peter watching him, Deming opened the cabinet again. He took out the record he had been looking at, Jimi Hendrix's *Are You Experienced*, the words written in a psychedelic leer, as if the letters had fingers and feet. On the cover was a picture of a black man standing with two white men.

'Hold it by the edges. You don't want to scratch the surface.' Peter lifted the lid of the record player, Deming set the disc down, and slowly, the record spun, the needle lowering itself with a resolute crackle.

Peter turned the volume knob up in one circular motion. Then came the opening notes. The music filled the room with color, a punch with a grin. Deming hovered by the speaker. Peter twisted the volume knob higher, and they stood there, basking in sound.

'What—' Kay held her car keys, the front door open, and Deming felt a breeze stream into the house, as if the guitars were fanning him. 'It's really loud,' she said.

Peter turned the volume down, and when Kay left the room, he said to Deming, 'Your mother doesn't appreciate music the way we do.'

On Peter's old headphones, puffy, silver, with a curly black cord, Deming listened to *Are You Experienced* after school, lying on the living room floor. He counted the heartbeats during that little catch between songs, savoring the delicious itch as the needle dropped and the melody snuck its toe out from behind a curtain. The disc of a record was hardier yet more delicate than plasticky CDs. A record was to be treasured, its circle scratches a mysterious language, a furtive tattoo. Deming walked the hallways of Ridgeborough Middle with lyrics scrolling mad loops in his mind: *Hey Joe, where you going with that gun in your hand?* He translated the lines into Fuzhounese and snickered as other kids gawked. He repeated the line in Mandarin as a group of eighth-graders passed, looked at one another, and said, 'What the?' Headphones delivered shapes and notes directly to his bloodstream. A drumbeat's taut assault gave him a semi-boner.

How he had missed music, how he craved it! The city had been one long song, vivid, endlessly shading, a massive dance mix of bus beats, train drums, and passing stereos, and in Ridgeborough its absence was flagrant; before he found the records he would turn up the little clock radio in his room and point it toward the window to receive weak signals from a station that played scratchy techno music and another that played scratchy Spanish music, but the reception was spotty and the songs flashed in and out. In Ridgeborough there wasn't enough sound to produce any colors but the weakest, haziest ones.

Peter gave him a pair of tiny earbuds and burned a couple CDs. Kay gave him her old Discman and a pack of batteries. Deming preferred Peter's old headphones because they were a bigger buffer to the world. The blank streets and large trees became comical when paired with a soundtrack, made him an action hero instead of an abandoned boy, and Planet Ridgeborough blew up. Platinum flowers morphed into oscillating lines and dancing triangles, electric blue snare drums punctuated a chocolate bass line topped with sticky orange guitar, turquoise vocals whipped into a thick, buttery frosting. He played and replayed, played and replayed. As he walked down Oak Street he shut his eyes and pretended he was in the city with his mother. She looked like him, he looked like her, they looked like the other people they saw on streets and trains. In the city, he had been just another kid. He had never known how exhausting it was to be conspicuous.

He came home from school the next day expecting to find the house empty as usual, but when he unlocked the door, he heard voices. Kay was in the living room with the television on, scooping apple slices into a jar of peanut butter. The TV played a soap opera, an older woman scolding a younger woman in front of a window overlooking a beach.

'Television stunts development,' Deming said. He'd heard her and Peter say it before.

'At least someone's been listening to me, unlike my undergraduates. I couldn't handle office hours today, so I played hooky. Don't tell anyone.' Kay patted the couch. 'Look, these women are about to find out that they're married to the same man. Come watch with me. Eat apple slices and peanut butter. We'll stunt our brains together and become a pair of blathering idiots.'

Deming settled in, luxuriating in the noise. Jaunty keyboards on detergent commercials bathed him in rainbow waves. The couch was a forest green plaid, its cushions smooth and shiny.

'How's school?'

'Okay.'

'I'm going to talk to that Mrs Lumpkin about getting you extra help in math. After dinner, let's go over your homework.'

'I hate math,' Deming said.

'It's not that hard. I know you can do it. You need to get over that mental block, the one that says, "I hate math. I'm not good at it."'

'But I hate it and I'm not good at it.'

Kay picked up the peanut butter and angled her apple slice inside, scraping the sides of the plastic. 'My mother believed girls were naturally bad at math. Bad at school, even. She still doesn't really understand what I do. My father was more encouraging, but they assumed your Uncle Gary would be the one to go to college and work a respectable profession, like in accounting or pharmacy. But Gary barely graduated from high school. Now he works in a Home Depot outside of Syracuse. That's the city I grew up in, we'll go there for Thanksgiving. He's been divorced twice.'

'What's a Home Depot?'

'It's a big store, where you buy tools. And wood.' She crunched her apple. 'They were hard on Gary. Hard on both of us. You know, your father had it hard, too. He had a lot of pressure put on him at a young age. His father was a respected lawyer who wanted him to take over his law practice. Your father wanted to travel more, see the world. He got a scholarship to go to UC Berkeley, out in California. But his parents didn't let him go. They said he had to go to Dartmouth, because that was where his father went. His only rebellion was to go into academia, instead of law. His father never forgave him for that.' Kay recrossed her feet, right over left. 'Anyway. I guess what I'm saying is that you might have internalized, I mean, you might have been told that you aren't good at math. Or even that you aren't good at school. So you need to tell yourself, "Self, that's not true."'

Deming scooped a wad of peanut butter with his index finger. The soap opera switched to a commercial with bright, arching music, two children and their parents dashing toward a castle, giant animals and adults dressed like dolls skipping alongside them. Disney World, the screen said. The Magic Kingdom. Orlando, Florida.

The peanut butter dangled from his finger as he gaped at the screen. His mother had wanted to take him to Disney World.

'Do you want to go there?' Kay asked.

She could be looking at this castle right now, Tommie at her side. 'No,' he said. 'It's stupid.'

'Well, thank God.'

By October, he was a quarter of an inch taller since August, according to the growth chart Kay was marking with a pencil on the dining room wall. When he looked in the mirror his jaw-line seemed more pronounced, his eyebrows bushier. He didn't know if his face was still echoed in Mama's. He had no pictures of her, no evidence.

Roland's mother, Ms Lisio, worked at Carlough, too, in human resources, a phrase that confused Deming. She would leave out Food Lion brand cookies and jugs of fruit juice for Roland and him. They could have watched three hundred channels of cable TV at Roland's house, but instead they played *Grand Theft Auto 2*.

After Deming showed Roland his Discman and headphones and played him Hendrix, *Grand Theft Auto* was abandoned. They spent a month of Sundays listening to a shoebox of cassette tapes that the deceased Roland Fuentes, Senior, had left behind. In Roland's room, they rewound his father's life on an old tape player, debated whether they'd rather sing or play guitar, and which was better, Ozzy solo or Black Sabbath (ever the classicist, Deming was Sabbath all the way). Roland's parents were in their early twenties when he was born – they had met in college, moved to DC and Montreal, and somehow ended up in Ridgeborough – and Roland and Deming listened to tapes of Adam Ant, the Ramones, the Clash, AC/DC, Van Halen, the Pixies, New Order, Jane's Addiction. From there it was hours of web searching for related bands. Each song was theirs to discover; they had been previously schooled in nothing.

'That's so green,' Deming said, as they listened to a mixtape Roland's mother had made for Roland's father before Roland was born, with a collaged cover of magazine cutouts and a label that said HIGH LIFE.

'Yeah,' Roland said, 'so neat.'

'No, *green*. The guitar is the color of grass.'

Never had there been a time when sound, color, and feeling hadn't been intertwined, when a dirty, rolling bass line hadn't induced violets that suffused him with thick contentment, when the shades of certain chords sliding up to one another hadn't produced dusty pastels that made him feel like he was cupping a tiny, golden bird. It wasn't just music but also rumbling trains and rainstorms, occasional voices, a collective din. Colors and textures appeared in front of him, bouncing in time to the rhythm, or he'd get a flash of color in his mind, an automatic sensation of a tone, innate as breathing. The candy red of a Wurlitzer organ made him want to retch, yet it repulsed him to even consider the possibility of it being any other color. A particularly nefarious jingle for a used car dealer produced the most evil clash of greens, and there'd been one summer when he couldn't even turn on the TV, afraid the jingle would be ready to pounce. A two-line refrain he heard from a boom box on Fordham Road recreated the lapping blues of the river in Minjiang so completely that it would haunt him for years, until he tracked down the song and listened to it until it grew thin. He would learn how to create music, matching tones to shades to feelings and translating them back to melody. The purest and most inept form of communication. He'd craft songs that conveyed exactly what he wanted to say, yet he was the only one who could understand them. The rest of the world heard only sound. His efforts would always fall flat; the gift would always be his.

Deming chased after music with a hunger that bordered on desperation. Why didn't other people have the same need, how could Kay prefer the low, modulated voices of NPR in the car when she could as easily choose to blast the blowout world of Hendrix or the bright angles of Prince or the sun glare of Bowie (*water*, Deming would see when he listened to 'Sound and Vision', *water water water*)? When he was a grown-up with his own car, he'd never be so boring. Binge-listening to a good song was better than binge-eating a bag of Hershey's Miniatures in the pattern of Mr Goodbar–Milk Chocolate–Krackel–Special Dark (there had been one glorious, motherless Bronx afternoon when he and Michael had done exactly that). Music was a language of its own, and soon it would become his third language, a half-diminished seventh to a major seventh to a minor seventh as pinchy-sweet as flipping between Chinese tones. American

English was loose major fifths; Fuzhounese angled sevenths and ninths.

He made up band names on his walks home, sketched out their album covers and song lyrics: The Toilet Plungers, 'Floaters or Flushers'. Dumpkin & Moore, 'I Shot the Food Lion'. Necromania, 'Brains on a Spike'. Roland, delighted when Deming showed him the list, scribbled the fake band names onto the fronts of his notebooks, and when other kids asked about them he would feign shock and say, 'You don't know that band?' They'd shake their heads. 'Hey, Daniel, you get that new Necromania album yet? I like that first track, "Brains on a Spike".' In the middle of the hallway, around the corner from Principal Chester's office, Roland belted out the lyrics Deming had written: *Brains on a spike / Yum yum burp / Heart on a spike / Damn that hurt.* Deming wanted to correct Roland. It was heart on a *knife*, not *spike*. 'I heard they're playing at the Dunkin' Donuts next month,' Roland said aloud, to no one in particular. 'Necromania! I'm getting tickets. Don't want it to sell out.'

Cody Campbell, who played soccer with Roland, came up to Deming in homeroom and said, 'I heard about the band you're in. Roland's band. Necro . . . mania.'

'That's my band, not Roland's,' Deming said. 'I started it.'

In November, Peter and Kay asked Deming what he wanted for a birthday gift. 'An electric guitar,' he said. On the morning of his twelfth birthday he awoke to find an index card on his bedside table, with a note in Peter's handwriting: *It's time to play some Hendrix.*

'It's a treasure hunt,' Peter said, clapping his hands together. 'You go to the place you think is being referred to on the card in order to find the next clue, and so on. The clues lead to your birthday gift.'

'It's a Wilkinson tradition,' Kay said. 'Every year on our birthdays, we make treasure hunts for one another. On my last birthday, your father set up clues that led to a restaurant near Syracuse. Now it's your turn.'

Deming went downstairs and lifted the lid of the record player. On the turntable was another card that said *What word comes after 'surprise', alphabetically?* He took the dictionary down from the bookshelf, flipped through pages until the next card fell out.

After being led to the linen closet, the china cabinet, and the dishwasher, he followed a clue that said *Put your socks away* to the hamper, and opened it to find a box wrapped in silver paper, topped with a plastic bow. It was a big box, but not big enough for a guitar.

He brought it to his bedroom. 'Open it!' Peter cried.

It was a new laptop, white and glimmering. 'All yours.' Kay kissed him on the cheek. 'Happy birthday, Daniel.'

Deming pierced the plastic wrapping with his fingernail. The plastic clung to the cardboard, then slowly unfurled. He opened the box, lifted the lid of the computer, and plugged it in, wishing that Michael could be there so they could watch videos together, wanting to show it all to Michael: the laptop, the records, the tapes, the Discman, the town full of white people. Where was Michael, why wasn't he here? It was Roland he invited to his birthday dinner with Peter and Kay, at Casa Margarita in the strip mall on the highway, where they ate fajitas and drank virgin margaritas with paper umbrellas tucked in the slush. The waiters led the room in singing and Deming blew out the candles on his ice cream cake. When Roland saw the laptop, he whispered, with a reverence that made Deming proud: 'Your parents are cool.'

As long as he didn't think about his mother, Deming was not

that unhappy in Ridgeborough. Yet there was always this nagging, icy swipe of fear, a reminder that he needed to stay alert. At times the fear was so far in retreat he forgot its existence; at other times it was so strong he could barely stop himself from shrieking. These people were strangers. He couldn't trust them. Like when a Chinese maid had appeared on a TV show, a woman in a tight dress with garish eye makeup speaking a botched version of Mandarin, and Kay had stopped talking, the silence in the room was so loud it formed a dark red curtain, and Kay had flushed and quickly changed the channel, blabbing about winter and skiing as the TV played a commercial with a blonde lady putting a plate of fish sticks in a microwave. If Leon or Mama or Vivian had been there they would have all laughed at the Chinese maid together, made a joke about what province she was from, how could they get a job like that. Or the time Kay asked him to run into Food Lion and pick up a gallon of milk while she waited in the car, and Deming swore he'd heard someone make a noise like they did in kung-fu movies: *hi-ya!* When he told Kay about the sound, she had said, 'Maybe you misheard? Maybe they were singing a song, or telling a friend about a movie?' Or eating shitty Chinese takeout at Roland's house, gloppy chicken in nuclear red sauce, and Roland had poked at the meat lumps and asked what it was and his mother joked that it was cat or dog, was that a tail they saw there, and Deming felt chilled, implicated. *Be careful. They're not on your side. It's important to be strong.*

'Next year, can I get a guitar?' They were driving home after dinner at Casa Margarita, after dropping Roland off. If he had a guitar, he and Roland could have a real band.

'Let's not carried away,' Peter said. 'Music is fine to listen to as a hobby, but you need to focus on school.'

'But what if my grades get better?'

'You need to be more responsible, Daniel. Don't ask for more when you can't even be thankful for what you already have.'

'I am thankful.'

Kay turned around. 'Enjoy your laptop first. Live in the moment.'

They were talking in bed again. 'He's getting C's and D's,' Peter said. 'We should look into a tutor. A student from Carlough.'

'That's a good idea,' Kay said.

'He needs to work harder.'

'Oh, God, sometimes I look at him and think, what are we doing with this twelve-year-old Chinese boy? In Ridgeborough? Jim and Elaine, at least they're in New York City. How could we have considered bringing a child from China here? The other day, Daniel told me he'd heard something, I don't know, racist at the Food Lion. I was horrified. And now, whenever we go out, I'm suspicious. Are people looking at us because I have blonde hair and he has black hair? Or is it more nefarious? It's making me paranoid.'

'We're learning, we're learning.'

'I mean, should we cook Chinese food? Or start Mandarin lessons again? I don't want to be this, you know, this white lady—'

'You're not doing anything wrong. It's not easy, caring for a foster child. This has been a big change for us, a big adjustment.'

'Tell me about it. Some days I want to do one of those marathon writing days like I used to, but then there's this boy here who needs us, and I need to make him meals and buy him clothes and make sure I'm loving and caring and patient so I don't mess him up more than he already is. I'm afraid I'm too old to learn how to be the kind of mother who gives everything up to mom. Even foster mom. I'm using mom as a verb here, in case you can't tell.'

'Well, if you're too old, then I'm too old, too,' Peter said. 'You know, at a meeting the other day, Will Panov said Daniel was lucky to have us and we were brave to take in an older boy. I told him, we're the ones who are lucky that he's staying with us.'

Kay sighed. 'I know you're trying to be nice, but it's different for men. All those books and articles I read about the whole unrealistic American expectation regarding motherhood, the martyr-like aspect of it, the reality is so much worse than I'd even expected. You get to work all you want, but you never feel bad about it. You weren't brought up that way.'

'No? I think I know a little about familial expectations.'

There was a lengthy silence.

Peter finally said, 'This might sound callous, but honestly, whatever we do is going to be better than what he experienced before. You remember what the agency said, how the mother and stepfather both went back to China. We're the first stable home he's ever had.'

'I know, but I feel like I'm holding my breath. The aunt could still come back. I'll feel so much better when it's all finalized, one way or the other.'

'We'll know more next month at the hearing.'

'I want to treat him like he's my own son, not just a foster kid, but there's this chance it won't work out.'

'Remember, Jamie said it's unlikely there will be an appeal since there hasn't been any communication from his family. And after six months we can start proceedings.'

Back to China? Proceedings? Who were Jim and Elaine? If his mother had gone anywhere, it was Florida, not China. In his bedroom, in the dark, Deming held his breath, wondering if they would say more about her, if they knew things about her that he didn't. They were hiding things from him. He'd been right not to trust them.

'Did you read that article in the paper today?' Kay said. 'An abandoned baby in a bus station in Buffalo? I'm sure his mother had her reasons, whatever they were, mental health, financial hardship.'

'All that matters is that we're taking care of Daniel right now,' Peter said. 'Not whether we're Asian or Chinese or whatever.'

'But do you think we didn't prepare enough? Even if we'd been planning for years.'

'Oh, we could have read every single book out there and it still wouldn't have prepared us.'

'I think of his mother constantly, though I probably shouldn't,' Kay said. 'What did she look like? What was her name? It's not like I can ask Daniel about her. He doesn't say a peep. Sure, I know it's cultural, but it's also like he's scared of us.'

'He won't always be.'

'I hope so. We'll love him so much we'll make it all better.'

'Killing them with kindness, that sort of thing?'

'But no actual killing,' Kay said. 'I'm a pacifist.'

Deming waited for them to say more, but they had stopped talking.

Kay was wrong. He wasn't scared of her. He was scared of finding out what really happened to his mother.

Roland asked outright, said the word that no one else had. 'Is it weird being a foster kid? Are the Wilkinsons going to adopt you?' They were walking home from school, down Hillside Road, past the Ridgeborough Library and the Methodist church, the sidewalk bumpy with tree roots.

Adopt. There was a similar term in Chinese, yet Deming hadn't thought of his time with Peter and Kay to be anything but vaguely temporary, like the stay with Yi Gong had been vaguely temporary. Even the name Daniel Wilkinson seemed like an outfit he would put on for an unspecified period of time, until he returned to his real name and home planet. Where that real home was, however, was no longer certain.

'It's weird,' he said.

'Do you miss your real mom?'

'Yeah.'

'I kind of miss my dad, even if I don't remember him.' They stopped on the corner. 'Are you coming over?'

'I just remembered I have to help my mom with something.'

Deming ran the three blocks back to Oak Street. He knew he had a good hour and a half before Kay and Peter came home. He brought his laptop to the study and pulled up an online dictionary.

> *Foster child*: A child looked after temporarily or brought up by people other than his or her natural or adoptive parents.
>
> *Adoption*: A process whereby a person assumes the parenting for another and, in so doing, permanently transfers all rights and responsibilities from the original parent or parents. Adoption is intended to effect a permanent change in status, through legal sanction.

It took a minute to parse through the language, but when he did, it seemed like the computer was expanding.

Temporarily. Permanent.

He pulled open the drawer of the file cabinet next to the desk, a long, metal arm crammed with folders for taxes, property-related documents, and research for Peter's book on something called free trade. Sandwiched between KAY WORK and LIFE INSURANCE was a fat folder labeled ADOPTION/FOSTER. Deming tugged until the folder gave way and poured its contents onto the floor.

It had to be a joke. He sat on the rug and picked up a color pamphlet titled *Gift of Life: Your Child Is Waiting for You*. Blurry pictures of children with large, liquid eyes were placed throughout, as well as pictures of adults holding babies with darker skin. The children, the captions said, came from Ethiopia, Romania, and China. The pamphlet talked about how international adoption gave an unwanted child a home and blessed adoptive parents with a child of their own.

He dumped out the rest of the folder, listening for sounds downstairs, footsteps or the front door closing. He scanned a printout of an e-mail message, dated more than four years ago.

Dear Sharon,

I attended the Gift of Life informational seminar last Saturday with my husband Peter. After years of unresolved fertility issues, we are very interested in becoming parents, and soon! We've been married for over twenty years and are more than ready to make our family complete. Our loving home in Ridgeborough is ready for a child.

We have good friends who are parents to a Chinese adoptee, so we are familiar with the process, and are interested in adopting from China as well. I know there are sending countries that look down on 'older' first-time parents (Peter and I are each forty-six). We don't mind adopting a Chinese child who is older, as we know they can also (like us 'older' parents) be 'harder to place'. Peter and I have traveled extensively and both teach at the college level, so we have experience working with young people. We think international adoption would be a good fit for us.

I look forward to hearing from you.

Sincerely,

Kathryn S. Wilkinson

He saw medical records, criminal clearances and background checks, documents stating the Wilkinsons' home was safe for a child, and an e-mail from the Gift of Life director saying that with sending countries' new restrictions on international adoption, Kay and Peter might want to consider domestic adoption, or foster-to-adoption. He flipped through reports from social workers stating that the Wilkinsons were well-established professionals who were financially and emotionally equipped to become loving parents, and papers that said they had completed mandatory training classes and were court-certified to foster and adopt. When he saw a packet of papers labeled INITIAL PERMANENCY HEARING REPORT: IN THE MATTER OF DEMING GUO, he stopped. The report was dated two months ago. He had to read a few sentences over twice, but at the end, he understood, even if he wished he didn't.

Birth mother and putative father abandoned child six months ago and returned to China. Caregiver V. Zheng signed Surrender Form.

After interim care in Brooklyn, child was placed in foster care with the Wilkinsons due to K. Wilkinson's indication of Mandarin-speaking skills.

Foster parents plan to petition for termination of mother's parental rights on grounds of abandonment.

No current reunification plan with birth family.

Anticipated Permanency Planning Goal: Placement for Adoption

There were so many more e-mails and documents, bundles of legal papers and dense forms, but Deming couldn't bear to read them, and Peter and Kay would be home any minute. He stuffed the papers back into the folder, then wedged the folder in the file cabinet and pushed the drawer shut.

Termination. Permanency. His mother had abandoned him. She'd returned to China. He wanted to puke. He closed the browser window. The laptop seemed grotesque, too big and new.

At dinner, he asked them if he was adopted.

'Well, right now we're your foster parents,' Kay said. 'That means that you're living with us, like any kid lives with his family, because you need a safe place to stay. And we would like to have you stay with us for as long as you want. We would like to adopt you. Would you like that?'

Deming shrugged.

'It wouldn't happen right away,' Peter said. 'It might take a long time.'

'But what happened to my real family?' Deming asked.

'We are your real family,' Peter said.

Kay frowned. 'Your mother wanted to take care of you, but she couldn't.'

The table grew blurry, the food tasted dry. 'So she left me.' After he heard Peter and Kay talking in their room the other night, he had been waiting for them to say something to him about his mother. But they kept acting like everything was fine.

'She loved you.' Kay refolded her napkin.

'And we love you, too.' Peter exchanged a worried look with Kay.

'I saw that,' Deming said.

'Saw what?' Peter asked.

'Never mind.'

Mama had perminated him. Vivian had lied to him about coming for him soon. His skin burned and the kitchen lights were so bright, the floorboards so wide and wooden. The mix on DWLK was a single song on loop, a mash-up of *abandoned* and *permanent*. He felt faint, pulled back to the ammoniac odor of the hallways in P.S. 33, the blue-gray floors and dented metal lockers.

'Daniel, you look tired,' Kay said. 'Are you okay? Do you want to rest upstairs?'

Deming put one hand on the table to balance himself. Kay pressed her fingers to his forehead. 'Peter, he's really warm. It must be the flu or something. It's been going around at Carlough, half my students are out sick.'

Peter took another bite of his chicken. 'Daniel, go upstairs and rest.'

'He can barely stand up,' Kay said. 'You carry him.'

Peter put down his fork and knife. He stood and lifted Deming, one leg, then the other, and carried him up the stairs, grunting with the effort. Deming held his arms around Peter's neck, his legs around Peter's waist. Peter's footsteps were slow and unsure, each step a quiet struggle.

Eleven in the morning and they had been on the road for almost five hours. Peter slammed his hands on the steering wheel when the car came to an abrupt stop on the FDR, idling behind a potato chip truck and a yellow cab. In the backseat Deming counted exits. None of the highways they had taken from Ridgeborough were familiar, and he skimmed billboards for the furniture one he and Roland especially loved, a store called Sofa King.

The Wilkinsons were on their first family road trip to New York City, to visit the Hennings family, who had a daughter Deming's age. Kay said she'd be his friend. 'This will be a good trip for your father,' Kay had told him, 'he needs cheering up.' Valerie McClellan had been asked to take over as the chair of Carlough's Department of Economics in the fall, after Will Panov retired. The day Peter found out, Deming had seen him wheeling the plastic garbage bin up from the curb, his face red. 'Goddamn it!' he yelled when the bin's wheels caught on a branch in the driveway.

Deming tried to remember that first drive upstate with Kay and Peter, eleven months ago, when they were still strangers. First he had looked out the window, trying to memorize the roads so he could make his way back. Then he fell asleep. Now they were no longer strangers, they were Kay and Peter, Mom and Dad, and this was the last day he would see them. He had gotten used to having adults speak to him loudly and slowly, as if he was deaf, and it was less terrifying being the *only one*; the terror had become normal. He no longer fantasized that his mother would come for him, but as they drove deeper into the city he stared at the looming high-rises with a catch in his throat. Slick pavement, ferocious honking, spewing fire hydrants, fetid mystery puddles, wet steam expelled through sidewalk gratings as if the Earth was panting, firm thwacks of rubber against concrete on handball courts. That precarious dip when you walked over a metal door atop a restaurant basement.

It was July. Peter and Kay had filed an adoption petition, and when the judge approved it, they would all go to court to sign the papers. Last month, they had bought Deming a yellow dirt bike and matching helmet, and he and Roland had been biking around town, exploring little streets on the outskirts of Ridgeborough, still gravel, still unpaved, with names like Bajor Lane and Meeker Road, streets he would never see again. Deming had perfected a wheelie on his bicycle. He and Roland had created a stage out of a tree stump and taken turns jumping off of it into a crowd of invisible fans.

He turned away from the window but when they drove past signs for the Cross Bronx Expressway, turned back. After Kay told him they were going to visit the Hennings, he had called his mother's cell phone for the first time in over a month and got the same message. The call could not be completed. But he'd packed extra clothes.

The potato chip truck nudged up. 'Finally,' Peter said. Deming watched the brown buildings fade behind them, breathed a small circle onto the glass and wiped the moisture away with his finger.

In front of a gray apartment building on East Twenty-First Street, the sounds and colors came back. The squawk of a lowering bus. The soundtracks of passing cars. House music, an old track with twisting keyboards and words about getting your back up off the wall, a song sung in Spanish with shiny horns and the fattest tuba bass. Bright pastel smudges rapidly filled the sky. It was hotter here than in Ridgeborough, and Deming turned in a slow, clockwise circle, stricken by the tinkling notes of a nearby ice cream truck, hesitant and plaintive, reminding him of the rainbow sherbet push-pops he would eat with Michael, the sweet liquid that made their tongues blue. He could hear Michael's quaking laughter, Mama and Vivian snap-talking in Fuzhounese.

A woman on her cell phone bumped him as she walked by, and Deming rubbed his shoulder. 'Excuse me,' a man said, pushing past. Kay shrank back.

A white man with a booming voice and a receding hairline bounded out the front door of the building. He and Peter slapped each other on the backs as if they were trying to dislodge food. Deming had never seen Peter with a friend before, and he liked it.

'This must be Daniel.' The man kissed Kay on the cheek and extended a hand for Deming. 'Jim Hennings.'

'Mr Hennings and I were at school together,' Peter said. 'Freshman roommates.'

'Your father and I always made sure we studied all the time,' Jim said, and winked.

The doorman held open the lobby's glass doors. Deming

followed Kay into an elevator as Peter and Jim went to park the car.

'Twentieth floor,' the doorman said.

Deming pressed the button. The elevator made its journey up and finally opened into a large, sunlit room that smelled of brewing coffee. Empty wine bottles crowded a table and strung between two walls was a streamer of glittery letters: HAPPY GOTCHA DAY!

He scanned the room. The elevator was the only door he could see, and it dinged when it opened. He would have to wait until everyone was asleep.

A girl Deming's age skipped into the room, hair hanging past her armpits, eyes peeking out from behind a blunt fringe of bangs. 'Mom'll be out in a sec.'

'Angel, you've grown so much.' Kay bent down and hugged her.

To Deming the girl said, 'I'm Angel Hennings.' She was the first Chinese person he had seen in nearly a year.

'Tell Angel your name,' Kay said.

'Daniel,' said Deming.

A woman padded out in a T-shirt and jeans. 'Ka-ay.' Her dark wavy hair was laced with wiry white, and her voice was round and velvety. She reminded Deming of a cartoon cow in a milk commercial.

Kay hugged her. 'Elaine, it's so good to see you. And this is Daniel.'

Elaine enveloped Deming in a hug. Her hair smelled like apple shampoo. 'Daniel, call me Elaine. What grade are you in? Sixth, like Angel, right?'

'Seventh,' Deming said.

'Seventh grade?'

'Going into seventh in the fall,' Kay said. 'Ridgeborough Junior High.'

Elaine released the hug and studied him at arm's length. 'Junior high already?'

Deming's mouth was dry. He and Roland were supposed to be in the same class in September, but he wasn't sure where he'd be going to school now.

The elevator dinged. Deming heard Jim say, 'His English appears more than adequate.'

'Like a regular little Noo Yawker,' Peter said.

'Peter!' Angel flung her arms around him.

'Coffee, anyone? I'm blasted from last night. Mommy needs her caffeine fix now.' Elaine walked into the kitchen, still talking. 'Angel was so excited about her Gotcha Day party. So were we, of course, with all that wine. It's too bad you couldn't make it.'

'I know, I know, we really wanted to,' Kay said. 'It would've been a rough drive last night, with all the weekend traffic. But we can have a Gotcha Day party for Daniel, and you guys can come.'

'Oh, you must,' Elaine said, 'you absolutely *must*.'

'Oh, we *will*,' Kay said, talking like Elaine.

Deming glanced at Angel, but she was bouncing from foot to foot and looking at the Gotcha Day sign. 'Where am I sleeping tonight?' he asked. There was a couch that would make it easy to get to the elevator.

'Oh, we'll figure that out later,' Elaine said. 'Are you tired? Do you need a nap?' He shook his head.

'Elaine.' Angel tugged at her mother's T-shirt. 'Can I show Daniel my room?'

Her room was much smaller than his, with light pink walls, a bed with a pink bedspread and a heart-shaped headboard, clothes thrown across the unmade sheets and toys littering the floor, stuffed animals stacked four deep. Deming cleared a path through the center, pushing aside T-shirts and socks.

Angel held up a small pink iPod and white headphones. 'Want to listen?'

They each took an earbud and sat on the floor. Music swelled into Deming's right ear, a tinny electronic drumbeat and a woman singing crunchy, processed vocals.

Angel bobbed her chin. 'When's your birthday?'

'November 8.'

'I don't have a real birthday because I'm adopted, but we decided that my birthday could be March 15. When's your Gotcha Day?'

'What's Gotcha Day?'

'You don't know? All adopted kids have one. It's like a birthday but not a birthday. It's the day that you went home to your forever family.'

Gotcha sounded less fun than a birthday, more like he was being hunted. 'I'm not adopted yet. I'm a foster kid.'

'What's that?'

'It's like being adopted but it's more temporary.' Deming looked at Angel. Her skin was light brown, her nose wide and squashy. She had a missing tooth, one of the pointy ones. He took his Discman out from his backpack. 'You like Hendrix?'

'Who?'

'Jimi Hendrix. He has a song with the same name as yours.' Deming unplugged the earbuds and replaced her iPod with his Discman. He forwarded to 'Angel' and pressed play. The guitar and cymbals shimmered in their ears, and he sang along. *Tomorrow I'm going to be by your side.* Then he got afraid that Angel might think he was singing to her, that he liked her. He hit stop. 'You like it?'

'It's all right.'

'He's only, like, the greatest guitar player ever in the history of the universe.'

She flipped open a container, exposing a yellowing plastic U. 'Do you want to see my retainer? I have to wear it when I sleep. It's supposed to keep my teeth in place. It kind of hurts. I have too many teeth, I had to get one removed.' He was afraid she'd put the plastic U in her mouth, or even more terrifying, make him try it on, but she shut the container and tossed it onto the floor, where it landed on a stuffed parrot.

Deming wanted to tell Roland he had hung out with a girl, make it sound cooler than it was. He had Roland's phone number on a piece of paper; he would call later and explain. He would have to do the same for Peter and Kay.

'You should ask your parents about your Gotcha Day when you're adopted,' Angel said. 'That way you'll get gifts. I got a CD from my friend Lily and a T-shirt from my other friend Lily. I have three friends named Lily and a friend named Jade. We're all adopted from China.'

Deming got up. From the window he could see the rooftops of smaller buildings, a woman watering plants, a couple sunbathing.

'That's north,' Angel said. 'Where the Empire State Building is. See that tall one over there?'

'I know what the Empire State Building is. And the Bronx, that's north, too.' He couldn't see the Bronx from where they were, but Angel's confirmation of what direction they were facing helped orient him. He had a plan.

'The Bronx is far.'

'I used to live there.'

'With Peter and Kay?'

'Before I met them.'

'I thought you were born in China, like me.'

'I was born in Manhattan. I'm *from* here.'

Angel's eyebrows were too close together, sparse and dark and wiggly. Deming grasped for the lost Mandarin words and lunged. 'Did you think it was forever when you came here?'

She bunched up her face. 'I don't know Chinese.'

'Oh,' he said, crushed.

Kay insisted he hold her hand. It was his job to lead her through the city, to make sure she was okay. An old woman with a cane was overtaking them, and Deming tried to get Kay to walk faster. Peter lingered behind them. 'Come on, Dad,' he said.

Deming trudged on, a sour stench emanating from the garbage bags on the curb, and when he wasn't looking he stepped into a smear of dog poop. He scraped his sneaker against the pavement. On the corner, a guy with a blonde ponytail was letting his dog pee all over the sidewalk.

They were going to Chinatown for lunch, passing Chinese people who were following the paths from his face to Kay's hand to Kay and Peter's faces, from Angel's to Jim and Elaine's. Angel couldn't understand Chinese. 'Kay, this is where they have the best cakes.' She pointed to a storefront that Deming didn't recognize. They couldn't be far from Rutgers Street.

'There used to be a bubble tea place here,' he said.

'This is where I have lion dance,' said Angel. 'My sifu's name is Steve and our troupe is called the Lotus Blossoms.'

'They're something,' Elaine said. 'The lion dance and the fan dance, all the different dances, I can't keep track. It's *so* good for the kids to connect to their culture. That way they'll still know how to be Chinese.'

'Yes, it's *so* important,' said Kay.

'It's not too late to register Daniel for camp,' Elaine said. 'It's the last week of August. It would be great for him. They have all kinds of cultural activities for the kids.'

'E-mail me the info. I've been meaning to ask you about it.'

They passed a wet market with plastic buckets of crabs. Two ducks hung in a window, roasted brown and sticky with sauce. Peter took his camera out and fumbled with the settings. He aimed his lens, then frowned at the screen.

'Hey, how about a family shot?' Jim said, taking the camera from Peter. Angel ran in front of the window, hip stuck out into a pose.

'Work it, Angel, work it!' Elaine said. 'Come on, Wilkinsons!'

They assembled on the sidewalk beneath the roast ducks and sweaty window, a man in a white apron hacking meat inside as Elaine wrapped her arms around Angel, Peter and Kay's arms around Deming.

'How do you use this thing?' Jim shouted, and Peter broke away to assist. They passed the camera back and forth. 'Okay. Smile, everyone. One, two, three . . .'

Deming stood against Peter. People were staring. Jim pressed another button. 'One more. Daniel, smile in this one. Come on, you're on vacation. Vacation is supposed to be fun.'

'Smi-ile,' Elaine said.

Deming forced a smile.

'Cheese!' sang Angel.

Kay pulled him closer. 'It's okay,' she whispered, 'you don't have to smile.' But he did, glad that she was on his side.

At a restaurant on Mott Street, the waiter gave them English menus, looking at Deming and Angel. He started to dole out chopsticks, then paused and pulled out silverware instead. On the table in front of Deming he placed a glinting metal fork with a water stain on the handle.

'Chopsticks for me, please,' Elaine said.

'Me, too,' said Kay.

'Chopsticks for all,' Jim said.

The waiter put down chopsticks and took their orders, and as he walked away Deming heard him talking to another waiter in Fuzhounese about moving tables together for a larger group of customers. The words elicited zaps in a dormant corner of his brain. Soon, he would be speaking Fuzhounese all the time.

The dishes came out fast and were limp, reheated. Turnip cake, broccoli, shrimp dumplings. Angel stabbed holes into the side of a dumpling, and even the solitary curl of steam was lackluster.

'Delicious,' Kay murmured, scooping up food for Deming's plate. The meat tasted old. His mother would have never eaten food this bad.

'This is one of those off-the-beaten-path places,' Elaine said. 'We've been coming here for years.'

Jim turned to Deming. 'You must miss this, Daniel, having authentic Chinese food.'

'We went to Great Wall that one time,' Peter said.

Deming recalled the tempura and pad thai he'd picked at during a visit to the buffet table at the strip mall restaurant. The owners hadn't even looked Chinese.

'Come on, Great Wall doesn't count,' Kay said. 'Daniel knows that.'

'Okay, okay, Ridgeborough isn't exactly Manhattan when it comes to ethnic food,' Peter said. 'It's more like a cultural desert.'

'You have to reframe it,' Elaine said. 'Think of it as a cultural retreat.'

'A cultural siesta,' Jim said.

'But we've had terrific Chinese food traveling in Vancouver and London,' Kay said. 'Spoiled us for life.'

Peter nibbled a turnip cake. 'This is what we come to New York for.'

'And to see us!' Angel said.

'I was about to say that. That's the most important thing of all. Almost more important than dumplings.'

'Almost?' Angel said.

Elaine waved her hands. 'Guys, should we get dessert? Bean soup?'

The waiter stopped at their table. 'What would you like?' he asked in English.

Before Elaine could respond, Deming spoke in a rush of Fuzhounese. 'She says she wants to order the red bean dessert, you got that?' He'd forgotten the pleasures of flinging vowels, the exhilarant expulsions. He knew his tones were pure 3 Alley.

'Yeah, yeah, of course,' the waiter said.

'Great, bring it on. These American cows want a couple of bowls.'

'You got it.'

Elaine put down her chopsticks. 'He's fluent in Mandarin!'

Deming hated Jim and Elaine's outsized smiles and exaggerated speech, how they spoke to him and Angel like they were little kids, how Peter and Kay didn't seem to notice. He had the sensation that he was being mocked, that they all saw him and Angel as objects of amusement.

'It's not Mandarin,' he said. 'It's Fuzhounese.'

'You know, the local slang,' Peter said.

'Daniel,' said Kay. 'Don't talk like that to Mrs Hennings.'

'But she's wrong,' Deming said. 'She's stupid.'

'Daniel!' Peter said.

'But it's not local slang. It's a language called Fuzhounese.'

Jim laughed. 'It's all Chinese to us dumb-dumbs.'

'You don't know,' Deming said. 'You don't even care!'

'I'm *so* sorry, Daniel,' Elaine said. 'It's my fault for getting it mixed up. I mistook it for Mandarin because I studied it in college.'

'Daniel, say sorry to Mrs Hennings,' Kay said.

'Sorry.'

'He can be *so* sensitive,' Kay said to Elaine.

'It's okay. Obviously, that was in prehistoric times, when I was young and in college,' Elaine said. 'But I was an East Asian Studies major, so I should know better.'

'Oh,' Kay said, 'remind me, I need to ask you to help me with my terrible Mandarin. Daniel laughs and laughs when I talk to him with my Chinese.'

'I do not!'

'Of course.' Elaine smiled at Kay. 'We'll talk later.'

'I studied international finance in college,' Jim said. 'We've both always had such a strong fascination with Asia. So it made sense that we decided to get our little girl from there.'

'We didn't *get* her,' Elaine said. 'We were already bound by red thread.' She over-enunciated the words. 'You must know the story of the red thread, Daniel. It's an ancient Asian story.'

'Never heard it.'

'The red thread story! It says that the people who are destined to be with one another are bound with invisible red thread. And that's how Angel and Jim and I were all connected with red thread, and how we found each other in our forever family.'

'You don't know the story?' Angel said.

'I said I've never heard it.' He couldn't believe Peter and Kay were nodding along with Elaine and Jim. 'Can I be excused for a minute?'

In the bathroom, he washed his hands with a grimy soap bar and looked in the cloudy mirror. He saw skin like Angel's, eyes and nose like Angel's, hair like Angel's.

He could sneak out now. There was a subway station not too far away they had passed on the walk over, and in his pocket was a five-dollar bill, more than enough for train fare. He could sprint from Fordham and University, sneak into the lobby and rush upstairs, knock like crazy until the door opened. Whoever was there would screech when they saw him, they would all scream and scream. Vivian and Michael could still be there. Leon and his mother could have come home.

He slipped in with a family making its way to the exit, three generations of parents and children and a Yi Gong, matching their pace out the door and onto the sidewalk.

He heard Kay saying, 'He's upset, feeling left out.'

And Peter's forced whisper, which Deming recognized from listening through the bedroom wall: 'He's used to getting all of our attention.'

They must have left the restaurant while he was in the bathroom. Peter spotted him first. 'Daniel, there you are. Were you looking for us?'

Defeated, game over, he walked toward the Wilkinsons, let Kay steer him closer until he was sandwiched between her and Peter. 'Elaine and Jim are still inside getting change,' she said.

Angel came outside, pointing at him. 'You disappeared.'

There would be no Bronx, no having to call to explain. 'I went to the bathroom.'

Angel and Deming sat in Angel's room as the adults drank wine in the living room.

'What happened to your bio mom?' she asked.

'She was going to go to Florida and I was going to move there with her. She might've gone to China.'

'Elaine and Jim said I was found in an orphanage in China. They paid money and got me and I got my Going Home Barbie and my forever family.'

Deming had noticed Going Home Barbie, an unsmiling beige doll with long blonde hair and empty blue eyes, encased in plastic on a shelf next to Angel's bed. It held a doll baby out in front of her like it had a disease. The baby had a fringe of black hair and rectangular black eyes that he recognized as supposedly being Chinese, and the box had a drawing of a white house with a picket fence and a sign: WELCOME HOME!

'It's a collectible. My friend Lily doesn't have one because her parents stayed at a different hotel when they went to China. Her mom was so mad.'

Deming nudged a stuffed tiger with his toe. 'Do you really believe in that? The red thread, all that?'

'I don't know. I guess.'

'It's bullshit.'

'Yeah?' Angel deliberated.

'Bull-*shit*.' He squirmed under Going Home Barbie's deadened gaze.

'Are you hot? I can ask Elaine to make the air conditioning higher.'

'My real mother might be in the Bronx.'

'You mean she's there now?'

'My Yi Ba might be. Or my aunt, my brother – cousin.'

'Let's go.'

'How?'

'I know how.'

He reached into his pocket. 'I have five bucks.'

'Wait.' Angel kicked her way across the room and Deming watched her carefully. If she was going to tell on him, go fetch Peter and Kay, he was prepared to take her down. It wouldn't be hard; he was bigger than she was. He bounced up on his ankles, ready, as she rummaged through her closet and pulled out a pair of pink stockings. 'Daniel,' she said. 'Look.' Inside the stockings was a stack of twenty-dollar bills. Deming sat back on his heels, laughing. 'I steal them from Jim,' Angel said. 'He doesn't care.'

*

There was no guest room or study in the Hennings' apartment, so Kay and Peter had to cram onto an air mattress in Angel's room, while Angel and Deming camped out on the living room floor, waiting until Gotcha Day hangovers defeated Elaine and Jim and the early morning rise overcame Kay and Peter. When snoring could be heard from both bedrooms, they stuffed towels into child-sized shapes under their sheets and made their move. Angel pressed the code to disarm the alarm system, keys in her pink plastic purse, Deming close behind her, backpack in hand. He resisted the urge to whisper good-bye to Peter and Kay. They skipped the elevator and took the stairs down ten flights, dashing out the service exit. On the corner Angel hailed a cab. Deming had assumed they would take the subway but Angel said no, she had it covered.

'We're going to the Bronx,' Angel told the driver. 'Our parents gave us money.'

'University and W. 190th,' Deming said. 'My family is there.' As he said it he felt a cold lump inside him, growing. *This call cannot be completed*, the lump whispered. But she wouldn't have abandoned him. The cab driver fiddled with the radio. 'Can you turn the music up?' Deming asked, and the car filled with drums. Deming repeated *Mama, Mama, Mama*, and directed the driver as they pulled off the highway and entered the Bronx, and there it was, the glowing insistence of the Kennedy Fried Chicken sign, the shadows of subway tracks and the aching rise of the sidewalks up the bend in the block. The sneaker shop, the liquor store, the bodega. It all looked exactly the same. These past eleven months, everything had gone on without him. Forget Peter and Kay, forget Roland and Ridgeborough. He was home.

'Want me to wait?' the cab driver asked, but Deming was already out the door.

'Wait five minutes.' Angel unzipped her purse and passed the driver two of Jim's twenties.

Deming couldn't slow down for a second. Up the sidewalk to the dog-piss patch of weeds, through the courtyard, that masking-taped crack in a bottom window. He pulled on the front door and it opened. Angel was following him, up the first flight of stairs, linoleum groaning under their feet, up the second, faster, past chattering television sets, closer now, and as they jumped to the final landing, he saw it there.

A welcome mat. A green-tufted welcome mat resembling ill grass. The cold lump had been right. Leon and Mama never had a welcome mat.

'Is it here? Here?' Angel bounced in excitement, anticipating the grand reunion. 'Come on,' she said, and he stepped on the mat that he knew wasn't hers and knocked. The same layers of brown paint, the same dents. He knocked again.

'Hello?' he said.

Under the door, behind the mat, appeared a slit of light. He heard footsteps and murmuring, and even if he knew it was hopeless, he pictured his mother standing in that light, Leon and Vivian and Michael behind her.

He shifted his backpack. The door opened.

'Yeah?' A short woman with wrinkled skin peered out through a gap, the chain still on.

Angel gasped.

'I'm Deming,' he said.

'Yeah? So?' The door began to ease shut.

'I used to live here. My family – do you know where they went?'

'I don't know,' the woman said.

A younger man with a goatee came up behind her. 'Ma, who is it?' The woman answered in Spanish. The man replaced his mother behind the chain. 'What's going on?'

Deming swallowed hard. 'I'm looking for my family. They used to live here. Did you know them?'

'Nah, this place was empty when we moved in.'

'When'd you move in?'

'September. You okay?' The man was closing the door. 'All right, kid. It's late.'

'What about Tommie?' Deming said. 'He still around?'

The door opened an inch wider. 'Yeah, Tommie got married. Polish girl.'

Polish? The door shut, the locks clicked.

'I'm sorry,' Angel whispered.

Deming walked downstairs to the waiting cab and crawled in, Angel beside him.

'Twenty-fourth and Madison,' Angel told the driver. 'Can you turn the music down?'

CHAPTER FIVE

Ten winters passed. On Rutgers Street in Chinatown, where Mama and Deming had lived pre-Bronx, there was a new high-rise on the corner, a white couple talking to a doorman in uniform, but farther down the block seemed unchanged, the same buildings with their reddish brown exteriors, fire escapes, and hanging laundry. The old apartment at 27 Rutgers had been smaller than Roland's place, but home to Mama, Deming, and their six roommates.

Daniel Wilkinson was two and a half feet taller, one hundred-fifty pounds heavier than Deming Guo had once been, with better English and shittier Chinese. Ridgeborough had made Daniel an expert at juggling selves; he used to see Deming and think himself into Daniel, a slideshow perpetually alternating between the same two slides. He wanted Deming to walk out of the building, for the two of them to do that little dance people did when they tried to pass one another on the sidewalk but kept moving in the same direction, over-anticipating the other's next move.

Deming wouldn't have the scar on his right forearm that Daniel had gotten from skateboarding with Roland in eighth grade. While Deming was growing up in Chinatown and the

Bronx, was Daniel hibernating, asleep in Planet Ridgeborough? Or had they grown up together, only parting ways after the city? Daniel had lay dormant in Deming until adolescence, and now Deming was a hairball tumor jammed deep in Daniel's gut. Or Deming had never left Rutgers Street; he'd been here all along.

The front door of 27 Rutgers squeaked open, and a woman with a bouquet of grocery bags walked out. Worried he might seem like a creep, Daniel took out his phone and pretended to text. He knew it wouldn't be Deming, couldn't be Deming, yet he felt wasted with disappointment.

Under the Manhattan Bridge, the sounds around him coalesced. The fruit and vegetable vendors here were speaking Fuzhounese, and he knew what they were saying, the words not nonsense sounds but sentences with shape and meaning. The words plowed in, discovered a former residence, and resolved to stay. He repeated them until he was confident they'd be the right ones, then moved toward the vendors.

'Hey, you,' called a man weighing vegetables in a saggy blue coat, knit hat, and jeans. He had tobacco-stained teeth, a gray beard, and one gold crown. 'What do you want?' he said in Fuzhounese.

'Hello,' Daniel said.

'Where are you from?'

'New York.'

'You Chinese?'

'Of course I'm Chinese.'

He fumbled for his wallet. The word for watermelon had swum up and emerged, and he concentrated until the rest of the sentence returned. 'Give me a watermelon. They're fresh right? Good watermelon, right?' He recalled enough to haggle, bumping the guy's price down twenty-five cents, and it felt like he'd been born again.

The man said, 'Go lower than that and my family will starve, thanks to you,' but there was laughter behind his scowl.

Daniel accepted the watermelon, triumphant. He pointed to a pile of greens. 'And those. Half a pound. Broccoli.'

He carried the groceries to Roland's apartment. It was one o'clock on a Tuesday, the winter sunlight so bright he had to squint; he had no plans for the rest of the afternoon. For years, he hadn't allowed himself to think of those days after Mama never came home, after Leon left and Vivian left him with strangers, and now he imagined his mother waiting for him on Canal Street with a cigarette, remembered her duck walk as she made her way across the ice, the firmness of her hand in his. He'd be taller than her now, but there would be safety in her hand. Once, when he and Angel had been talking about their birth families, she had asked if he still wanted to find his mother, and he said no, not anymore. It was enough for him to accept that she was gone. But he'd never had the chance to ask her why she returned to China – she hated Minjiang – or to understand why he ended up in Ridgeborough.

He stopped on a corner, took out his phone, and responded to the e-mail Michael had sent months ago, hitting send before he could change his mind:

you've got the right guy. what's up?

In Roland's kitchen, he steamed the broccoli and cut slices of watermelon. It beat eating another deconstructed burrito at Tres Locos, and was cheaper than eating out. His current credit card balance was $2,079.23, with eighteen percent interest, and that wasn't counting the ten thousand he owed Angel. Seeing the bill every month from the credit card company made him so anxious, he created an auto-withdrawal from his bank account for the minimum payment – last month it was twenty-two bucks. He hadn't talked to Angel for months, but now he would have to see her on Saturday, at her father's birthday party, along with Peter and Kay.

In high school, he'd played Texas Hold'em with other guys at parties and had a talent for noticing their tells while hiding his own, the years with Peter and Kay making him an excellent keeper of secrets. Sophomore year at Potsdam, he heard about online poker, and when he was procrastinating writing papers, he would play a few games, nothing big. Over the summer, living in Ridgeborough with a job painting new five-bedroom houses on the edge of town, he learned he had a knack for deciphering patterns online: the players who folded often and only bet when they had good hands, the action ones who bet foolishly and gambled too much. Back at school the following fall, he'd met a guy named Kyle who was winning real money, a thousand in one night, and Daniel started playing more, six, even ten hours a day, one sit-and-go tournament after another, winner takes all. Late one night he emerged from his dorm room to use the bathroom, hearing the sounds of chips and shuffling cards as he refilled his water bottle in the sink, then scurried back down the hall and resumed playing again, clicking to bet and raise and fold, betting thrice the big blind before the flop and watching his money tick higher. The hours blurred until he heard slamming doors and voices, his body cramped and sore. He'd played into the next day, or the day after. At some point, the overhead light had become painfully bright, and sunlight started falling across the keyboard. He drank Red Bulls, pissed into the empty cans. He bet the pot on a full house and realized he'd been panting out loud. The next day, he heard people shouting his name from a very far distance, and opened the door to see his hallmates there, checking to see if he was still alive. Cards moving across their faces.

When Peter and Kay called and asked if he was going to classes, he'd assured them he was. He could win $4,000 in one night of playing tournaments, then lose that much in thirty minutes. At one point, there was $80,000 in his account. It didn't seem like real money, but it was. He could have withdrawn it and cashed out, but there was always one more game, and one more after that.

All he needed was one good win, but the number that constituted a good win changed whenever he hit it. He shut down the account at zero then put it back up a day later. He went two whole days without playing, drove to Montreal with some friends to see a concert, and afterwards he wanted to buy himself a new guitar, new gear, get back into music. One more game and he'd be set.

He'd taken out a private loan to pay for next semester's tuition, since his grades had gotten too low to qualify for financial aid, and burned through the loan money in a day. He borrowed what he could from friends, twenty here, fifty there, opened new credit cards and maxed them out. The shakier he got, the more he lost, and the more he lost, the more of an action player he became. He borrowed two thousand from Kyle with a promise to repay him in two weeks, but knew it was over when he kept losing, got frazzled when he heard the warning beep that he was running out of time to bet. So he bet half the pot on a 7–2 off suit. This was a surprise: suicide was also a rush.

He paid Kyle back, two hundred dollars. 'Where's the rest?' Kyle said.

Kyle and his friends, two beefed-up brothers that looked like they lifted cars for fun, began to come by his room several times a day, asking for the money. Daniel stopped leaving his room or opening the door. Now he was $10,000 in the hole.

Angel was going to school in Iowa. She had waitressed all

summer and fall, working nights and weekends to save up for her spring semester abroad in Nepal, where she was going to teach at a school for girls, then spend the summer backpacking around Southeast Asia. She'd always loved architecture, geeked out on the layouts of cities, the differences in public transportation. Daniel had been dodging her calls for weeks, but he answered one night and told her about the losing streak, the money he'd borrowed from Kyle. 'I need a favor,' he finally said. 'I'll pay it back in a week.' She had been reluctant, but agreed to transfer him ten thousand dollars. He would get Kyle off his back, get his accounts square again, then take out another loan and use that money to pay her.

But after paying Kyle, he hadn't planned on his credit being so shot that his application for a loan would be denied. He decided to play one last time, so he could make enough to at least pay Angel something, but he hadn't planned on such a lousy beat – he'd been winning for most of the hand with a pair of aces for his hole cards, only to lose huge to a player named RichDanger who made two pairs on the river. And he hadn't predicted the extent of Angel's anger, or that when he didn't pay her she would call Peter and Kay and tell them about the gambling, though not the money he borrowed. By the time the letter from the dean arrived, he was already in Ridgeborough, attending Gamblers Anonymous in a garage in Littletown. He had told Angel he would make it up to her, that he was going to change.

'You mess everything up,' she'd said. 'Don't call me again.'

Now he wished he could tell her about writing to Michael, going to Rutgers Street. It wasn't just that she was the only person he knew who'd also been adopted (when he had mentioned his adoption to his ex-girlfriend Carla Moody, she had sighed, 'That's so *beautiful*'), but talking to Angel was unlike interacting with anyone else his age. She had no pretense. When he talked about music, she never pretended to know more than she did, and he never got bored listening to her, even when she was going on and on about the differences between the New York City subway system and the London subway system, or texting him pictures of cats she said she was going to get and never did, or telling him about the time she and her roommate had run out of gas on a long drive to nowhere and gotten lost in a cornfield. Maybe because they'd known each other all these years, she was almost like a sister.

One of the last times they had talked, Angel had told him that her parents had wanted her to be pre-med: 'But I'd puke if I had to dissect a dead body. So I told Elaine, sorry, okay, but you're going to have to settle for a social worker or something like that in the family. She said I was throwing my talents away. I mean, seriously, get a grip, Elaine.'

He had laughed and said, 'I'm a shitty professors' kid, too.'

'Then we're both black sheep. Even if that term is racist. Like the white sheep are supposed to be good ones.'

'Let's flip it and say white sheep as bad, instead. I'm the white sheep.'

'But you've always been so good to them,' she said.

'My parents? Nah. I'm not the kind of kid they want.'

Angel had sounded surprised. 'If that was true, you wouldn't even feel bad about it. I bet they're proud of you, even if they can't say it.'

She told him that in high school she had taken an overdose of sleeping pills, and Elaine and Jim had made her see a therapist who called her *hostile*. 'I've never told anyone about that before.'

Daniel hadn't deleted her phone number from his contacts list. There was still a record of all their text messages, the last one from four months ago. He opened a blank message and typed *i miss you*. He deleted the first and last words and changed it to: *miss talking to you. im working on paying you back. thanks for letting my parents know about the poker, for real.* He erased all that and replaced it with *you going to your dad's party saturday?* and pressed send. Now that they were no longer friends, he seemed to have lost the ability to be sincere, and in a single swipe he deleted all of his and Angel's texts, hundreds of them, then deleted her name and number from his phone.

He checked his e-mail. Michael hadn't responded yet, and when the phone did ring, it was only Kay. 'We'll see you on Saturday,' she said. 'Don't forget to bring the forms.'

He retrieved the Carlough College forms and smoothed them out.

> The Statement of Purpose provides an opportunity to explain any extenuating circumstances that could add value to your application as a transfer student to Carlough College. This is your opportunity to address the Admissions Committee directly and to let us know more about you as an individual in a manner that your transcripts and other application information cannot convey.

He started typing.

Michael wrote back two hours later and suggested meeting tomorrow at a Starbucks near Columbus Circle. The next day, Daniel showed up twenty minutes early and walked around the block three times before deciding to wait inside. He ordered a coffee and sat at a table near the door, looking up each time it opened.

One minute had passed since Daniel had last looked at his phone. 3:42 p.m. No missed calls, no new messages. Michael was supposed to meet Daniel at three thirty. Michael himself had suggested three thirty at this specific Starbucks on Sixtieth and Broadway. Daniel had agreed to meet Michael out of curiosity, but resolved to maintain a healthy suspicion. Whatever Michael had to tell him, it wasn't going to change his life. He sucked up coffee. If Michael didn't show in the next ten minutes, he'd leave, call it a day.

The door opened again. A beefy white man in a long T-shirt walked in, hand in hand with his similarly built daughter, but before the door could close all the way, a tall Asian guy in a navy blue coat, white sneakers, and a big backpack caught it and came inside.

Michael looked around, brightening when he saw Daniel, shoving his way through the tables and chairs. Daniel stood and his resolve fell away. They hugged, hard. Michael was an inch taller than Daniel, and they stood there, in the middle of Starbucks, slapping each other on the back.

'Deming.' Michael took off his bag and pulled out a chair. 'Sorry I'm late. My professor was talking to me and wouldn't stop.' Michael's voice was lower, no longer a kid's voice. Daniel had never heard this not-child Michael. Michael hadn't seen him past the age of eleven.

'No one's called me Deming in a long time.'

Michael scrutinized him. 'You look different. Your face is thinner, though your features are the same. I bet if we saw each other on the street we would've walked past each other.'

'You look different, too.' Michael's nerd exterior might be gone, but the core of who he was remained, and there was something familiar, visible only to those who had known him when he was a kid. 'But also the same.'

'It's weird, you having another name. Do you prefer Daniel or Deming?'

'Daniel, I guess.'

Michael folded his hands in front of him, as if they were in an interview. 'So, you must be in your junior year of college?'

'I was upstate at SUNY, but I'm taking some time off.' He was failing the interview already.

'Where are you living?'

'Down by Little Italy, Chinatown. I'm crashing at my friend Roland's on Hester Street. We have a band – I play guitar. We've been playing shows around the city.'

'I can totally see that. I remember you used to beg our moms to let us stop and hear the subway musicians and we'd stand there so long we'd miss the train.' Michael laughed. 'So what's your band called?'

'Psychic Hearts. I'm working on my own songs, too, just me singing and playing guitar. Real pared-down, almost confessional kind of stuff.' It was the first time he'd ever spoken about this out loud.

'Let me know when your next concert is. I'll come.'

'All right.' Daniel pictured a guy like Michael at a loft show, someone more out of place than himself. 'And you're going to Columbia, right?'

'Yeah. I went to Brooklyn Tech for high school.' Michael put his phone down on the table. 'I was late because I'm applying for this assistantship thing. I have to propose this genetics research project and I'm trying to decide between two of them. One's the kind of stuff that my faculty sponsor does – that's the professor I was talking to before. He's writing my recommendation, so if I go with that project I might have a better chance. But there's this other project that has less precedence, so less chance for success. It's the one I want to do.'

'When's the application due?'

'In two weeks. Wish me luck.'

Their eyes met for a moment. Daniel wanted to observe

Michael for as long as he needed, attempting to reconcile the guy across the table with the skinny kid who had tagged alongside him in the Bronx. For five years, they had shared a bed. 'How's your mom doing?'

'She's good, real good. She married my stepfather, Timothy, a few years ago, and we moved to his place in Brooklyn, in Sunset Park. I'm still there, commuting to school, but I'm hoping to move out soon.' Michael passed his phone over, displaying a picture of a family in a grassy yard, Vivian and Timothy with their arms around Michael. 'This is from last summer.' Timothy had a small potbelly and a receding hairline. Vivian's hair was short and permed curly.

Daniel peeked at the photo and passed the phone back. 'You still in touch with Leon?'

'Uncle Leon? Yeah, yeah, he's still in Fuzhou. He got married and has a daughter now. He works for a manufacturing company. We've talked a few times but he's not much of a phone person. But he's doing good.' Michael played with the strap on his watch. It was a chunky, silver watch, something a middle-aged man might wear. 'We didn't stay in that apartment too long after you left. We moved in with this family in Chinatown. Then we moved to Queens and my mom got this job in the building where Timothy worked.'

'Oh.' Some small part of Daniel had been hoping Leon and his mother had found each other and had been living together, and for some perfectly logical reason, though he couldn't figure out what that might be, they had been unable to get in touch with him.

'So I found these papers over Christmas break when I was helping my mom clean out boxes in our apartment,' Michael said. 'There was this form she signed, voluntarily transferring you to the care of social services. It said the placement would be for an indefinite period of time.'

Daniel said nothing, remembering the papers he'd seen in Peter and Kay's desk, the report from the permanency hearing. Hadn't it said something about Vivian signing a surrender form? He didn't remember anything about it being from an indefinite period.

'I know, I know, it's screwed up,' Michael said. 'And there was this other form, that said she'd gone to court for a hearing, a few weeks after you left. She approved a foster placement with Peter and Kay Wilkinson.'

On the Starbucks speakers, a woman was braying along to a strumming ukulele. Daniel was plummeting from the final board of a video game down to level one after accidentally missing the most elementary of jumps. Vivian and Leon had never planned on coming back for him. The thought of Vivian going to court after dropping him off with that Chinese couple, signing him over to the Wilkinsons without his knowledge, made him nauseous.

'I'm sorry. I wanted you to know.' Michael shook his head. 'I thought about you and your mom all the time. She was a cool mom. One time, I don't know where you were, but she took me to Burger King because she was craving fries, and she bought me fries, too, and on our way home we passed this empty lot full of pigeons and she said, super seriously, "Michael, in China we'd eat those bitches. But steamed, because their meat is tough." She was real funny, you know?'

'I know she was. How did you even find me?'

'I googled Peter and Kay Wilkinson and found a website with an article Kay Wilkinson wrote and it said in her bio that she had a son named Daniel. I found a profile picture of a Chinese-looking Daniel Wilkinson that looked like it could be you. It mentioned SUNY Potsdam, so I looked that up and figured out your e-mail address.'

'Shit. I'm glad you did.'

'I'm glad you wrote me back. When I found those papers, I thought you could've ended up with a bad family, anything could have happened to you.' Michael looked away. 'That morning, that last time I saw you? I would've tried to stop my mom if I knew where she was going. You guys went out and when she got home, you weren't with her. I was scared.'

After he and Angel took the cab to the Bronx and saw the family who wasn't his, Daniel had gone home to Ridgeborough and cried at night for weeks. Four months later, he and Peter and Kay had gone to court and a judge had approved his adoption. They'd signed papers. The judge congratulated them on becoming a forever family. He received a new birth certificate, listing Peter and Kay as his birth parents, and his name as Daniel Wilkinson.

'What did your mom tell you?' he asked Michael.

'Back then? She said she found another family for you to live with and take care of you. At first, she said it was only going to be for a little while. I was pissed, freaked out. Especially since it wasn't for a little while, you know? It never seemed right. But I couldn't do anything, I didn't know how to find you. So over Christmas, after I found the forms, I asked her and she didn't want to talk about it, but I kept bugging her, and finally she said she'd done it because she had no choice. We were broke. She said she did the best thing for you.'

'The best thing.' Daniel concentrated on reading the list of drink specials over the cash register. VEN-TI LA-TTE. The words seemed strange, like they weren't English. The smell of coffee and artificial sugar was overpowering and cloying. 'Does Leon know I was adopted?'

'I'm assuming my mother told him, but I can't say for sure.'

Daniel rested his face in his hands, pressing down on the spot between his eyebrows. Indefinite placement, he thought. 'I can't believe this.'

'You were like my brother, you know?'

'Yeah.'

'I tried googling you before but there were never any results for Deming Guo.'

'Well, that's no longer me.'

'Your parents – I mean, Peter and Kay Wilkinson. Were they good parents?'

'Sure. But I lost my whole family.'

'You never heard from your mother?'

'No. And I guess you never did either.'

Michael shook his head. 'But my mom wants to see you.'

'What?'

'She wants to have you over for dinner.'

Michael watched Daniel's face, awaiting Daniel's response. Like he used to when he was a kid, ready to pack up and run away to Florida without hesitation.

'Are you serious?' Daniel said. 'No fucking way.'

Friday night, Daniel took the subway out to Sunset Park, Brooklyn Chinatown, and as he walked down Eighth Avenue he recognized the neighborhood as where the Chinese couple had lived, where Peter and Kay had come to get him. He didn't know how he would get through this dinner without saying something terrible to Vivian, but the chance to say anything to her pushed him on.

They lived on one of the numbered streets off Eighth Avenue, in the bottom half of a two-family home, a two-bedroom apartment with a large front window that looked out onto the street. The house smelled like rice and pork and garlic. He removed his shoes and jacket, returned Michael's hug, and saw Vivian padding toward them in fuzzy purple slippers, plumper than she'd been ten years ago. He didn't remember her teeth being so bright before.

'Deming! You look the same,' she said in Fuzhounese. 'Big and tall and healthy. Exactly like your mother.'

How could she mention his mother after what she had done? 'Hi, Vivian.'

'Do you still like pork?'

'Of course.'

'I made pork and fish.' Vivian pointed to the kitchen. 'We'll eat soon.'

Michael and Daniel sat on a dark brown couch facing a wide-screen television and a shelf with glass figurines of unicorns. 'Remember that couch we had?' Daniel asked.

'That thing was busted,' Michael said. 'It had those giant flowers in puke colors. Remember that time that kid beat me up and you went and beat him up?'

'And then your mom went and beat me up.'

Michael laughed. 'Yeah, sounds about right.'

'I really loved that apartment.'

'You remember that kid Sopheap? I heard he's in jail. And there was that time those guys got killed in the park—'

'I don't remember that.'

Daniel ran names, tried to match them to faces, the kids of P.S. 33 with their giant backpacks. He tried to remember Sopheap, the park – *which park?* – and was alarmed at the inaccuracy of his memory, wondering what else had he forgotten, how much had he gotten wrong about his mother, Leon, even himself.

'Remember Tommie? Our neighbor? I used to think my mom ran away with him.'

'That guy?' Michael cracked up. 'No way.'

'I heard he got married.'

'God. I haven't thought about him in years.'

Timothy arrived, carrying a white bakery box wrapped in red string. 'You must be Deming,' he said. 'I've heard so much about you.' His English had Chinese-shaped tones, and his vowels were warm and curved.

Vivian had cooked a casserole of tofu and beef and mushrooms, greens with garlic, noodles, crispy pork, even a whole steamed fish. The smells were comforting, ones Daniel hadn't experienced in years. Timothy handed him a plate. 'You're in school, Deming?' he asked in English.

He wasn't sure if he wanted to be called Deming. 'I'm a Communications major, at SUNY. I play music, too. Guitar. I go by Daniel now.'

'Daniel. So you like the arts and the humanities. Michael is more into the sciences.'

'What kind of work do you do?'

'I'm a CPA. Accountant. That's how Vivian and I met.' Timothy switched to Mandarin. 'Vivian worked in the office across the hall.'

Vivian cut the greens. 'I cleaned the office.' It sounded like a script she and Timothy had recited before. 'Me and Michael lived with my friends in Queens. We had no money.'

'One day we met in the elevator at work,' Timothy said.

'That was a long time ago,' Vivian said. 'Things are so much better now. Michael's going to Columbia, and Deming is in college, too. Your mother would be proud.'

Daniel picked out fish bones, wanting to ask Vivian what she knew. His mother might have wanted him, after all. She couldn't have known that Vivian would give him away. He took seconds, thirds, fourths, trying to ignore Vivian's pleased expression as he loaded up his plate again, the credit she was surely taking for cooking so well, for feeding the starved orphan boy. He couldn't get sucked into how good the food tasted, how familiar it felt to be here.

Timothy passed Daniel the plate of greens. 'Deming, I mean, Daniel, you still speak Chinese?'

'Yes,' Daniel said in Mandarin. 'I still speak Chinese.'

'You have an American accent. I have it, too.'

'Michael still speaks perfect Chinese,' Vivian said. 'He can even write in Chinese.' She unveiled the contents of the bakery box, revealing a fluffy white sponge cake, a cloud of frosting studded with strawberry slices, and Daniel pretended he was watching a scene from television, narrated by the authoritative male voice of nature documentaries. *The female animal cares for only its biological young. It rejects any nonbiological children as a threat to the family unit.*

When they finished dessert, Michael collected silverware from the table. Vivian brought plates into the kitchen, and Daniel got up. 'Sit, sit,' Timothy said, but Daniel grabbed the dishes and trailed Vivian. He was much taller than her and could see the white roots in her thinning hair, a baby bald spot on top of her skull.

He spoke fast, in English. Vivian's English was much better than it had been ten years ago, but he still had the upper hand. 'Why did you do it?'

She transferred food to plastic containers and pressed down on the lids, double-checking to make sure they were sealed. 'Do what?'

He turned the faucet on and pumped soap onto a sponge. 'You said you'd be back for me soon, but you signed a form that gave me away to strangers. Indefinitely.'

'I don't know what you're talking about.' Vivian opened the refrigerator, restacked the containers, and pulled out other leftovers to make room. She removed a carton of orange juice, squinted at the label.

'You made me think my mother abandoned me, that she didn't want me.'

Vivian studied a gallon of milk. 'You could've been deported.'

'How? I'm an American citizen.' He turned to check that Michael and Timothy were still at the table. 'What do you know about my mother? Where is she?'

Vivian's face was hidden by the refrigerator door. 'I don't know anything.'

He scrubbed the dishes, scraped hard, making his skin sting. 'You actually went to court to get rid of me forever. You screwed up my whole life.'

'I didn't screw up anything. You wouldn't be in college, otherwise. You wouldn't be living in Manhattan and playing on your guitar. If you stayed with your mother, you'd be poor. You'd be back in the village.'

'That's where she is? Minjiang?'

Vivian's words were quiet and tunneled. 'I don't know.'

It didn't add up. There was no explanation for Mama's absence, her never getting in touch. Daniel looked at Vivian, staring hard, daring her to face him.

'Is she dead?'

At last, she turned around. 'No.'

'How do you know?'

'Because of Leon.'

He walked to the subway after hugging Michael and shaking Timothy's hand. 'See you soon,' Michael said. 'Don't forget to let me know about your next concert.'

In Daniel's pocket was an envelope that Vivian had given him as he was leaving. Less than half a block from the house, he ducked beneath a store awning and opened it. Inside was a hundred-dollar bill and a slip of a paper with a bunch of numbers that could pass for a long-distance phone number in China. *Leon*, it said.

Daniel put the envelope in his pocket and laughed, a hot jelly laugh, until he was shaking. As if one hundred dollars was supposed to make it all better. He walked until the block of shuttered storefronts dead-ended and took a left, reaching the entrance of Sunset Park. The air was warm, the trees in bloom. He made his way up a hill, above the streets and storefronts, a family trundling along the path below, the father pushing a stroller with a silvery red balloon tied to the handle. Daniel saw the Manhattan skyline, recognized the sketched spire of the Empire State Building, the sparkle of bridges, and from this vantage point the city appeared vulnerable and twinkling, the last strands of sunshine swept across the arches as if lulling them to sleep, painting shadows against the tops of buildings. No matter how many times he saw the city's outline he pitched inside. He had Leon's number. His mother was alive. Leon knew where his mother was; they had been in touch. The prospect made him rubbery. Knees quivering, he folded in half and burped garlic and strawberry cake.

Then he was cold. When Vivian pressed the envelope into Daniel's hands she had also said this: 'I paid your mother's debt. When Leon left, there was still money owed. Who do you think paid? If I hadn't paid, you'd be dead by now.'

Unable to decide whether to hate Vivian or be grateful to her, Daniel had only been able to take the envelope and say, 'Thank you.'

He dug his heels into the dirt and walked downhill, down the park's curved side, slow at first, getting faster, a grace note as his legs bounced upwards.

He would go home. He would call Leon. Propelled, he was almost in flight.

PART TWO

Jackpot

CHAPTER SIX

The night you came back into my life I was walking down the same old street in Fuzhou, from World Top English to the seafood restaurant where Yong always had his client dinners. He offered to pick me up but I said no, wanted those twenty precious minutes to myself. In my gray suit and leather shoes, I could pass for a city person. My life felt like a confection, something I had once yearned for, but sometimes I still wanted to torch it all over again, change my name again, move to another city again, rent a room in a building where nobody knew me. When I thought of all the seafood dinners I'd gone to and all the ones I had yet to attend, I felt an empty, endless DOOM.

Walking in Fuzhou: bicyclists, mopeds, trash bags, busted furniture, city people, migrants, all fighting for not enough sidewalk space. I walked to lose track of the life that had solidified around me when I hadn't been paying attention. I liked how close the past felt, how possible it might be to make up a new history. All the different routes I might have taken, all the seemingly insignificant turns that could change your entire existence. I could've become anyone, living anywhere. But let's be real, I was forty years old and most of my choices had already been made. Made for me. Not so easy to veer off course now.

Yong didn't see the need to walk when he had a perfectly good car, had no curiosity for exploring the city he'd lived in all his life. If he wanted an adventure, he said, he wouldn't walk around a couple of office buildings; he'd take a trip to Hong Kong or Bangkok or Shanghai, though he never did those things either.

Lately, Boss Cheng had been assigning my co-worker Boqing to do market research on expanding World Top to other cities, and I'd experienced envy so sharp I could smell it. Last week that chump Boqing had gone to Taizhou, and next week, he was off to Zhangzhou. *I* wanted to travel. But Boss Cheng hadn't asked me because traveling like that was supposed to be an inconvenience, a responsibility given to a more junior employee. Yong hated traveling for work but I would've jumped at the chance to even take the three-hour bullet train to Xiamen. I could sit by the window and watch the cranes and backhoe diggers, cement spreading like a cracked egg across Fujian Province. Fields flattening into housing foundations, villages shaped into towns, all of it whizzing by at two-hundred-fifty kilometers an hour.

There was a thick crowd outside Pizza Hut, waiting to get in. Yong and I had our first dinner there, seven years ago. We went after the last English for Executives class – he'd been one of my worst students – and he told me his wife had died young, of leukemia, and they hadn't had children, which was okay by him. He said he'd bought his apartment new, paid in full, in cash. 'I'm a self-made businessman,' he said, trying to play it cool. But I knew he wouldn't have been able to get the permits and licenses to start a business without urban hukou. It reminded me of those rich young people Didi and I used to see in New York, with their beat-up jeans and uncombed hair. I told Yong I had lived in America and he said, 'You must have studied English in university.' I didn't correct him; I neither confirmed nor denied.

He called me brilliant, hardworking, and kind, and we both

fell in love with this version of Polly. My office job and my English, that one suit I'd saved up for months to buy, that was enough for this city man to believe in my authenticity. So I wasn't about to let him down. And here we were, seven years later, the illusion and the reality one and the same. Polly: the woman who lived near West Lake and who had gone to university, decided to not have children. Yet it always felt temporary, like one day I'd be exposed, plucked out of the twelfth-floor apartment and deposited right back into Ardsleyville.

We got married six months after that first dinner. The marriage, the sex – they weren't as boring as I had feared. I got on the pill and figured I'd tell Yong about you eventually, say you were staying with relatives in America, but the months passed and then it seemed too late and too significant to reveal. A person could turn angry at any time. Telling him now? It would be worse than not telling him at all.

I was ten minutes late. When I walked into the banquet room, Yong said to the table, 'My wife was working.'

'Walking, not working,' I said.

Fu, a balding man Yong introduced to me as the Walmart buyer, sat between him and Zhao, Yong's partner at the textile factory. I took the empty seat next to Zhao's wife, Lujin.

Yong was wearing the silver cufflinks I bought him for our sixth wedding anniversary. Crevices bookended his eyes and mouth. He was handsome in a semi-ruined way; his beauty was that his beauty was behind him, his appeal reflecting what he had already survived, though he'd laugh at this because he was not into nostalgia. 'I can barely remember anything before the age of thirty,' he liked to say. Maybe he was lying. To his colleagues, he played like his success had been effortless, though before each big meeting he practiced what he was going to say in front of a mirror, wrote his lines down and memorized them. I helped.

The food came fast. A plate piled with prawns, another with scallops and vegetables. Jellyfish, conch, abalone. Lujin poured tea. 'How's business?' A smear of lipstick desecrated one of her front teeth. I didn't bring this to her attention.

'Our enrollment is at a record high.' I speared a prawn and tore off its head, laying it to rest on my plate. An eye looked up at me. 'Everyone wants to learn English.'

'I don't need English.' Lujin chomped on a large scallop. 'We're doing business in Shanghai.' Lujin was a northerner who'd never forgiven her husband for returning to his home province to run a factory, and Zhao liked to brag about her fluent Mandarin and Shanghainese, those pristine, elegant tones. Dinner parties at Zhao and Lujin's house in Jiangbin involved Lujin cooking complicated, flavorless meals as Zhao drank beer after beer and his belly got so bloated he'd have to loosen his belt one notch, then another. At these parties the men would complain about the Sichuanese who used to work for nearly nothing but were no longer migrating to Fuzhou in such large amounts, working instead at new factories in Shenzhen. Yong was the kind of boss who loved to complain about being a boss. His complaints were not actual complaints but well-crafted brags; Yongtex was doing well enough that he *had* things to worry about.

At these parties, the women's conversations were worse, because I was expected to participate. Ha! Which private schools were the best? Which housecleaners were cheap but honest? There'd be the circulation of a home renovation catalog, pictures of one disembodied kitchen cabinet after another, laid out and shot in flattering poses like swimsuit models. Pictures of empty pots on sparkling stoves and smiling mothers, fathers, and children, all of them black-haired and dark-eyed with improbably pale skin and long legs (where could such specimens be found in Fuzhou?). I'd flip through the pages and remember the plasticky couch in our Bronx apartment, those nights when hotdogs and instant noodles for dinner were more than enough. Or other nights, having left everything I'd known for a new city, thrilled and frightened at what I had done.

Yong was on his second beer, Zhao and Fu on their third. 'We have six million dollars in exports per fiscal year,' Zhao said. 'We delivered our Christmas orders early last year. The production cost for Walmart was one-fourth the retail price.'

Yong turned to me. 'My wife worked in New York City for a long time. She's an English teacher now, does international translation for Yongtex.'

Fu looked over. I channeled my teacher voice. 'I've seen the factories in America and they can't compete with Yongtex.'

'What are the buildings like in New York?' Fu asked.

'Tall. Beautiful. Majestic.'

Lujin looked down at her plate and scratched her thigh.

'And the weather?'

'Hot and sunny in the summertime, and snow in the winter.'

'Fuzhou could be a top-rate city, but it's being taken over by bad influences,' Fu said. 'Too many outsiders.'

'Cheap labor,' Lujin said.

'Twelve people crammed into one room,' Zhao said. 'You live like that, don't be expected to be treated any better than vermin.'

I hated hearing shit like this, but I held back. Yong had asked me here so I could make a good impression on the Walmart buyer. The one time I'd talked back to a client about Sichuanese workers, Yong hadn't gotten the deal. For weeks he fretted about losing the apartment, never being able to afford to move to Jiangbin like he wanted to, the potential collapse of Yongtex. 'I don't know why you're not worried,' he said, and I was about to tell him he was overreacting, that none of that would happen, when I saw how afraid he actually was, heard the tremble in his voice. Yong's worst fear was being exposed as a fraud, committing some fatal mistake that would result in a plunge in status. The city was full of people like this. It was easy to make money and easier to lose it. But because Yong had never gone without, he couldn't imagine surviving on less.

I took my phone out of my bag. The screen announced a new message from an unknown number; I hadn't heard it ring. I excused myself and walked out to the restaurant foyer, dialed the code to get my voice mail. *Hello?* said a man's voice. It was slow, almost hesitant, Fuzhounese laced with a weird, unplaceable accent. *This is a message for Polly Guo.*

At first I thought it was a client calling to complain about World Top, or another development in Yong's never-ending kitchen renovations.

This is your son, Deming.

My heart sped up. I listened to the message again. Your voice was a deep man's voice, but there was something recognizable in it, though your Chinese sucked: *I am good. New York is where I live. Leon your number gave me. Leon I found, Michael found me. You are good? I would like to talk to you.*

You left me a phone number and said I could call you anytime. I put my fingers in my mouth and bit. Pain darted down my arms. Were you okay? How did you find me? I hadn't spoken to Leon in years. When the hostess looked over, I took my fingers out and tried to smile. 'Business call,' I said.

For so long I had wanted to find you. Leon had told me you'd been adopted by Americans, that they were taking care of you, he insisted you were in good hands, and I tried so hard to believe him, because the only way to keep going was to act as if you were totally gone, that we were both better off staying put in the lives we had. But if I'd had a choice in it, and I hadn't, I would never have let you go, never! I played the message again, saved the number in my phone. If I ignored the accent and shitty grammar, you sounded okay, and there were no signs that you were sick or unhappy.

When I returned, the big plates of food seemed grotesque, indulgent. Zhao and Fu raised their glasses. 'To success,' Yong said. I repeated the toast, but my hand was shaking.

'Fu was impressed by your time in New York,' Yong said as he steered the minivan up the hill.

I checked my phone: no new calls. 'I hope the deal is signed.'

'I hope so, too.'

We parked in our building's garage, took the elevator up to the twelfth floor. The tiles, so nice and cool during the humid summers, felt chilly under my feet. I raised the heat on the digital thermostat. Cold was scratchy brown blankets, a chill that wrapped around my bones. I took a plastic bottle of water from a box in the kitchen and tried to ignore the drywall dust and construction tarp draped across the counters. A memory twitched, the Bronx kitchen. *Mama?* you said, standing there with your underpants over your face, you were six or seven years old and you laughed as you walked toward me with your arms sticking out like a monster's. Youyouyou – I clawed at the image but it bounded away. How swiftly it tumbled out of control, from your hand to Leon's mouth to nail polish to Star Hill and Ardsleyville.

I took off my makeup. We changed into our pajamas and sat on the couch, leaning against each other, and watched an episode of a Korean historical drama that took place in medieval times. Yong played with my hair; I rubbed his hands. This was

my favorite time of day, when we were home together, didn't
have to worry about how we looked or what we said.

In New York it was morning. Did you still look like me? How
tall were you? We used to play peek-a-boo in the boardinghouse
on Rutgers Street and you'd hide as I walked around, asking my
roommates, 'Did you see Deming? Where is he?' until you giggled and I'd go, 'I think I hear something!' Then you – chubby,
accusing, *mine* – would emerge from your hiding space and point
at me and shout: 'You lost me!'

Your adoptive family probably lived near Central Park in one
of those big-ass brick buildings with a gold-plated name on the
outside and a doorman in a uniform.

When the episode ended, the heroine and her lover hiding
from the king's army, Yong and I went to bed. We had a large, firm
mattress. Thick, soft sheets. 'Long day,' he said, laying next to me.
As soon as he fell asleep, I'd go out to the balcony and call you.

'Yes, it'll be nice to get a good night's rest.'

There was very little sound in our apartment, only the refrigerator hum and other vague whirrings that powered the constant
pleasantry of the place, keeping our life steady and moderate. I
looked at our high ceilings and clean walls, on which I'd hung
framed prints of paintings, abstract shapes in vivid blues and
greens. I loved the home we'd made together, the way we left
secret notes for each other – this morning I found one that said
Potatoes for dinner tonight inside my bag, an inside joke referring
to the shape of Zhao's head. I loved our wooden floors, the large
windows that overlooked the city. On a clear day, you could even
see a wedge of ocean. The first time I saw the water from Yong's
balcony I knew I had to live here.

What a relief it had been to find him, to have someone to
come home to, letting the everyday concerns take over: lesson
planning at World Top English and where to go to dinner,

filling myself up with tasks and conversation and possessions until there was no longer space to think about you. This was what could happen in a city like this. A woman could come from nowhere and become a new person. A woman could be arranged like a bouquet of fake flowers, bent this way and that, scrutinized from a distance, rearranged.

It was too much of a lie to reveal to Yong now, that I had a twenty-one-year-old son I'd somehow never mentioned before. You couldn't omit your own child from the story of your life, like it was no big deal. Yong disapproved of Lujin and Zhao putting their daughter in boarding school, and compared to that, what I'd done was unforgivable. I didn't want to think about it, didn't want to remember. If I called you, and if Yong found out I had lied about having a child, he would be so angry, and then he would leave me, and I would have to give up being myself.

I was tired. I took out my pill bottle, removed a pill. Without it I'd be dreaming of brown blankets and dogs, you waving to me from inside a subway train that leaves the station as soon as I get to the platform. But the pill would push me down and swiftly under, to safety, and every morning I woke up dreamless, the hours between getting into bed and hearing the alarm clock – an urgent beeping from the shore as I struggled to swim to the surface – a dense void, eleven at night and six thirty in the morning only seconds apart.

Yong wrapped his arms and legs around mine. We lay there together, like we had every night for the past seven years. I put my head on his chest. You and Michael would be laughing, Vivian and I talking at the table.

'I know it's a mess, but it'll be done soon,' he said.

'What are you talking about?'

'The kitchen.' His eyes perked. 'I spoke to the contractors about the cabinets. They're going to special order them.'

'Okay. Wonderful. Thank you.'

He kissed me. 'Good night.'

I tugged my sleep mask down. Yong could fall asleep in broad daylight, but I insisted on heavy curtains in the bedroom. Sometimes his ability to sleep soundly felt like a personal offense.

I listened to his breathing, deep and regular, as the pill began to take me under. I was too tired to talk now; I'd wait and call you another day. 'Good night,' I said. But Yong didn't say anything, he was already asleep, and it was only my own voice I heard, talking to myself in that dark, quiet room.

CHAPTER SEVEN

The house on 3 Alley had been as silent as our bedroom by West Lake. My father used to say women yapped too much, that some women would be better off not talking at all. So I'd grown up eating my words, and it wasn't until later that I realized how many had gotten backed up inside me. In the factory dorm, sentences spilled out of me like a broken faucet, and when I moved even farther away and saw children splashing into rivers spurting from fire hydrants, water pouring into the streets like it was endless, I would see my younger self in that hydrant, but tugged open, a hungry stream.

If you knew more about me, Deming, maybe you wouldn't blame me so much, maybe you would understand me more. I can only be as honest as I know how to be, even if it might not be what you want to hear.

My mother died when I was six months old. Cancer. I didn't remember her, never had a picture of her, nothing. In the two-room house where I lived with your grandfather, there were only two things that had belonged to her: a blue jacket and a gray comb. When Yi Ba was out on the river, I would run the comb through my hair and put on the jacket, a cloth coat that smelled weakly of leaves and scalp, the threads unraveling more each time I wore it, until one day the bottom button, dark blue, four tiny holes, tumbled right off. I found it trying to escape the room but clamped my fingers down and kept it safe inside the bag where I stored the comb.

'Was she smart?' I asked Yi Ba. 'Was she pretty? What was her favorite fish?'

He'd go, 'Sure, sure.'

I decided my mother had been a short woman with wavy hair, because I was short and my hair was a little wavy. There was this mother in the village who had a voice like a chiming bell – 'Come here, Bao Bao,' she'd say at the produce market, 'don't play in the dirt' – and whenever I was sad about not having a mother, which wasn't *that* often, I'd replay this chiming voice, pretend the woman was saying my name (Peilan, I was Peilan then) instead of Bao Bao's.

My father liked to say things like this: 'When I was a boy, my family was so poor, my brother and I shared a single grain of rice. People croaked all the time, but nowadays people are soft and spoiled. You don't know what it's like to suffer.'

Minjiang was a poor village in a poor province, but compared to some of my primary-school classmates, we ate pretty well. The fish Yi Ba caught supplemented the vegetables that our assigned plot grudgingly produced, and when there wasn't enough food, he'd push his portions on me. 'See what Yi Ba does for you?' he would say. I'd try to pass the food back to him, but he would say I had to eat every bite. You couldn't waste food when there were people starving.

On good days, my father took me out on his fishing boat. We got up at sunrise, long before the heat set in, so early that swirls of fog blocked our path. Yi Ba carried a container of tea as I padded beside him with a handful of beef jerky, the ground spongy beneath my feet. 'It's a lucky day,' he would say. 'See the way the clouds are like cobwebs? That means the water will be friendly.' On the western edge of the riverbank, the water was only visible between the clusters of long boats, and even the smallest waves would set off a series of wooden knocks, one boat bobbing against the side of the next boat bobbing against the side of the next, a string of hollow, mirrored noises. Yi Ba's boat was dark green; brown stripes exposed where the paint had peeled, a patched-over, fist-shaped dent at the helm, a punch from a hidden rock. I'd help him untie it and we'd push out into the current. 'Lucky, lucky, lucky,' I chanted, watching the waves lap at the wood like hundreds of tiny tongues. Then the shoreline would grow dimmer and the blue would shoot in all directions, filling the frame around me, the sky so big it could swallow me, and I cracked open with happiness.

On a less good day, the mountains would hem and corner me, everywhere another unscalable hill, the frowning clouds wagging their tongues: bad girl, bad girl.

Back then, leaving the village made you suspect. You might leave to marry a boy in another village and come home on holidays – look how fat and happy my kids are! – but otherwise, you stayed put. It wasn't as if Yi Ba had wanted to be a fisherman and remain stuck in Minjiang, but there weren't other choices for rural people, and he'd never gotten beyond grade four, though his younger brother had gone to grade seven and moved to a nearby town. So Yi Ba stayed in the same house where his parents had raised him. He told me about the paved streets of the town where his brother lived, the pictures of Shanghai he'd glimpsed in a magazine. I asked if we could go there, and he said no. Then who lives there? I asked. He said, 'Rich, lazy people.'

We had a chicken. It was my job to collect the eggs, scatter feed. I'd strut around the grass with my pigtails forming stiff horns, poking my head in and out. The neighbors' son, Haifeng, would abandon his own chores and run out to join me. 'Let's be like horses,' I would say, and we would gallop around, neighing.

I had two girl friends, Fang and Liling. We liked to play by the river after school and I would point at a speck and say, 'That's my father's boat,' even if I didn't know if it was his or someone else's or a big rock. We held our arms up as we ran beneath the tree in the village square, letting the leaves kiss our fingertips.

I always told you not to be like me. I quit school in grade eight. *Stupid*. I'd asked a boy who was an even worse student than I was, but whose parents were cadre members, to give me a cigarette. ('Girls don't smoke,' I heard him say, and that was a dare I couldn't resist.) The inhale made my lungs burn, but I held it in and forced down the coughs and exhaled so smooth and neat, letting the smoke exit my lips in a perfect curl. Teacher Wu paddled me but not the boy. I leaned over his desk as he whacked my butt with his wooden board, and as I faced my classmates' stunned faces, I laughed. I had seen boys cry when they got the paddle, but this smacking was no big deal.

I didn't go back after that, and the summer passed in the slowest ooze. My hair grew longer, my face sharper, and I swept the rooms until the floors were clean enough to lick. The whole village was sleepy that summer, a still pond on a humid day. The striped plastic tarps strung across the alleyway were faded and torn, and the vendors with their flip-flops, batteries, and scratchy panties in individually sealed plastic bags looked resigned to never selling anything. Our chicken's eggs were smaller, like she'd struggled to push them out.

For weeks it didn't rain. The grass got patchy and brown, Yi Ba complaining about the commercial fishing boats coming down the river from Fuzhou, with industrial-sized nets that could snatch up all the fish. He'd leased his boat to a younger fisherman and had gotten a job canning fish at a new factory, but the factory shut down and moved to the city and he had to refund the rest of the fisherman's lease to get his boat again. During the three months he'd worked at the factory there had been beef for dinner twice a week and even dried tofu to snack on and a new orange shirt for me, though I was clumsy and ripped the sleeve while climbing a tree with Liling and Fang. I missed the chewiness of the tofu – I'd marinate the chunks against the side of my mouth and be rewarded with a stream of salt.

Fang moved to town to live with an aunt. At Liling's, I'd ask her to let me look at this old book with pictures of national sites, black-and-white photos of waterfalls clouded in mist, giant sand dunes, Beijing's temples, the Great Wall. All the places I wanted to go. 'Turn the pages slowly,' she would say, watching me. After Liling passed the high school entrance test, she said I could have the book, she didn't need it anymore. But when I looked at the pictures at home they no longer inspired me.

One afternoon at the end of the summer, when I was fifteen, I was doing the laundry. Couldn't wait any longer for the weather to cool, and the clothes needed washing, though it was almost pointless to wash them in such humidity. I filled the plastic basins, wrung out the clothes and strung them, one by one, from the line, Yi Ba's underpants and my T-shirts, flapping squares of gray, red, and white. I heard a small squeak and looked up, and there was the neighbor boy, Haifeng, taller than when I'd seen him last, staring at me from atop a bicycle.

'Peilan,' he said. 'Want a ride?'

Yi Ba called him the Wimpy Li Boy. 'Soft like a pillow, that one,' he said, when we overheard Haifeng's parents ripping him a new one for failing the high school entrance test. I kind of felt bad for Haifeng. Plenty of kids in Minjiang wouldn't make it to grade nine. We all had as much of a chance of going to college and transferring out of peasant class as flying to the goddamn moon.

Haifeng's dark hair stuck to his face in the summer heat. He had a widow's peak that made him look older than he was. His limbs were gangly, but there were ropy muscles on his calves and forearms, tightly balled and hidden. Surprise!

It wasn't like I had anything important to do. I climbed on the bike's rack, balancing sideways, batting mosquitoes from my face, the tall grass tickling my feet. Haifeng pedaled, the sky gaping and bright, the wheels squeaking as we rolled through the fields. I sniffed him; he smelled like salt.

'Let's go to the river,' I said. We were already on our way.

The first and second days we went to the river, we talked about our families. I told Haifeng my father was pissed I hadn't bothered with the high school entrance test, though Yi Ba wouldn't say so. Haifeng said his parents were angry, but he had been relieved.

'I hate school.' It felt great to say it aloud.

'Me, too,' he said. 'I'm helping my father out with the crop planting. That'll be my land someday.'

Haifeng said he admired me for standing up to Teacher Wu. 'You were so brave. You didn't even cry when you got paddled.'

'It didn't hurt.' I couldn't remember Haifeng being paddled at school. He hadn't been a troublemaker, but he hadn't been a good student either. Actually, I could barely remember him in class. 'Aren't you friends with Ru?' I asked, though I had no memory of seeing them together. 'What's he doing this summer?'

'I don't know.'

'Who are your friends, then?'

'I was friends with Guang in grade four, but his family moved away.'

The third day he came by, I said, 'Let's do something different.'
I leaned over and kissed him. He didn't say anything.

'Did you like it?' I wasn't sure if I did. His lips had been a little sweaty, and I'd been hoping a kiss would spark a more significant feeling, like the frenzied mouth mushing I had seen on the shows I'd watched on Liling's parents' TV.

We tried again. Haifeng's face loomed over me, his features taking on a cartoonish quality. I closed my eyes and tried to channel the excitement of the TV actors. Still, no frenzy.

We pressed closer and I began to feel something. His mouth moved against mine; strands of my hair slipped between his lips. Now he was the one who seemed frenzied, and I had to break away, wipe the spit from my face.

He ran to my house each day after he finished work with his father. I liked the attention, but didn't have the same excitement about him. Haifeng had nice muscles, but he was too obvious and appreciative. There were days I turned him away, but by the time I finished my chores, the afternoon had barely started and I wanted someone to talk to. When Haifeng returned the next day, I'd hop on his bicycle without a word.

Lying by the river, I watched the sky, the drifting clouds, and saw myself launching into the sun. No other girls would do this; I was unlike all other girls. 'You're so pretty,' Haifeng said. He told me how much he liked my mouth, how my lips were shaped like the tops of two halved hearts. He even liked the mole on the side of my neck.

One morning, Haifeng's mother cornered me in the alley and grabbed me by the wrist. 'Stay away from my son,' she said.

I pictured Mrs Li squatting over a pit toilet and laughed. She took my earlobe and twisted it, and tears, sudden and humiliating, sprang into my eyes.

When he found out his mother had spoken to me, Haifeng

was livid. 'She had no right. No right!' He paced the riverbank and stomped on the weeds. He'd gotten a haircut, which made it clear how much his ears stuck out from his face.

'It's okay.' I missed being able to go to the river by myself, but the one time I told Haifeng I wanted to do that, just for one day, he had stalked away with a hurt look on his face, and I hadn't even enjoyed being alone.

'I'll see you whenever I want. She can't tell us what to do. One day, you could be her daughter-in-law, and then what will she say?'

I sat up and straightened my clothes. 'I need to get home.' He kissed me again, attempted to pry my mouth open with his tongue, but I broke away.

I was always home before Yi Ba returned from the boat, made sure Haifeng and I went to the part of the riverbank that was hidden behind trees and grass. But if my father caught us, or if Haifeng's mother told him that his daughter was messing around with her son, he might put a stop to it, or even send me away.

It started as a rumor: the city had stopped deporting rural migrants. Villagers couldn't get permanent urban hukou, but they could buy temporary resident permits and find better jobs than fishing and farming. Two older boys on 5 Alley left for Fuzhou, the provincial capital, and came home bragging about six-story buildings and women in hot pants. Then more boys left, finding jobs in the factories there. No girls from the village had yet to go to the city, but I knew that leaving in order to make money was less suspect than leaving to become a new person. I'd never been to Fuzhou, even if it was only a few hours away, and I wasn't sure what working in a factory would be like, only that I would make money, and I wouldn't have to sit through silent dinners with Yi Ba, watching his mouth as it grimly worked on his food.

When I asked Haifeng if he ever wanted to move to the city, he looked confused, then alarmed. 'No, I like it here.'

I told him I was thinking of going.

'To Fuzhou? Only boys can go.'

At the produce market, the parents of my former classmates talked about how their sons were sending home two hundred fifty yuan a month. One woman, whose son was still in school, said to the others, 'Aren't you worried with your sons alone in a big city? There are all sorts of girls living in the dormitories and no supervision.'

I ran home and rushed through the rest of my chores. At dinner, I announced, 'I'm going to the city to work in a factory.'

'Only boys work in factories,' Yi Ba said.

'They're hiring girls, too. At the factory where Mrs Jia's son works. They have separate dormitories full of girls and they make three hundred yuan a month.'

Inside the Fuzhou Garment Export Corporation, the rooms hummed with the motors of hundreds of sewing machines and the windows steamed with the blistering heat of flatbed irons. I was a snipper. On the south side of the fourth floor, I sat at a long table and snipped threads all day from piles of blue jeans. My hands cramped, but I worked hard, even if it was so hot I felt like vegetables frying in a pan. Sweat dripped into the fabric, no time to wipe it off. I couldn't put my scissors down for a second, to notice the way the sun streamed in through the windows, or marvel at how there were so many different shades of blue in a single square of denim. Those jeans kept on coming and if I was a second late, the girls down the line would curse at me and Foreman Tung would dock my pay.

The city was filled with girls like me, girls who swore we'd never go home again. I wanted to work my way up to a better factory, a bigger dormitory, and eventually, my own apartment, like my friend Qing's cousin.

Fuzhou didn't look like the pictures of Beijing in Liling's old book. The alleys split into streets clouded by moped exhaust, the highways were punctured with sinkholes, and the air was all chainsaws and hammering. We slept sixteen to a room, two rows of eight bunks each, decorating the walls with pictures ripped from magazines, actors and singers and landscapes of mountains and lakes. Stuffed animals dangled from the bed poles, teddy bears in shades of greens and pinks. In line for the bathroom at five thirty in the morning, we complained about our thirteen-hour shifts as if we were much older women, discussing aching shoulders and imitating Foreman Tung. I did good imitations. I would lean into the bunks and yell, 'Go, slowpokes, go, you turtles!' and emit a low snort my bunkmates agreed was exactly like his. 'Not fast enough! You missed a thread!' The other girls would double over with laughter.

I sent home two hundred seventy yuan one month, two hundred forty the next. 'You only made this much?' Yi Ba said on the phone. I said I'd try to send more, though the money I wired was twice what Yi Ba made on the boat. When I called to tell him that I'd made two hundred yuan in three weeks, he said, 'Guess I taught you well.' Later, the neighbors would tell me he bragged about me, said I was more hardworking than any boy. When they found out how much I was earning, they no longer said it was improper for girls to be living alone in the city. They let their own daughters go; they *made* their daughters go.

Soon Yi Ba had a television, the biggest one on 3 Alley, and when he came home from another crap day at the sea, there would be four or five children lying gape-mouthed in front of the screen, drooling at a fuzzy historical drama, and by night-fall this crowd would swell to nine or ten or eleven or fourteen children, splitting peanuts between their teeth and tossing the shells across the room. When Yi Ba walked to the outhouse, the shells would crunch and poke at his feet. 'Go home,' I pictured him saying, but not really meaning it, and he would be sad when other parents purchased televisions with money their older kids sent from the city and his nights were quiet again.

Two months after I left Minjiang, Haifeng's parents sent him to the city. As I snipped threads, he fit plastic spools into cassette tapes at an electronics factory on the other side of the highway, and we seldom had the same days off. When he first arrived he called the communal phone in my dormitory every week, though he rarely got through to me. I didn't think of him often, only missed him during the few times I was by myself, when I'd worry I wasn't doing enough for Yi Ba.

Mostly, I spent my free time with Xuan and Qing. The three of us had matching jeans, tight blue with a silver star on each butt cheek, and on afternoons off we paraded down the street arm in arm, moving in sync like the world existed only to watch us. We danced to cassette tapes Qing played on her Walkman, pop songs about true love and heartbreak. I memorized the words to the songs; I wrote them down in a hot pink notebook. There was a store that blared music from big speakers, with racks of colorful cassettes. My favorite songs were about girls who'd been treated badly by boys but were now happy on their own.

Xuan, who was the prettiest girl in our dorm room, with thick hair and puffy lips, had a city lover, a man who was nearly thirty. Her boyfriend, who had stayed in their village for high school, didn't know about the older man. I asked why she didn't leave her boyfriend, and she said she had to keep her options open because her city lover already had a fiancée who also had urban hukou, and she didn't want to marry him, anyway. He bought her sweaters and pointy shoes and gave her spending money she sent home to her younger siblings. I was impressed by how matter-of-fact she was.

'My boyfriend's ba wa is long and skinny,' Xuan announced. We were hanging out in the dormitory bunks before bedtime. 'And my city lover's is shorter, but fatter.' She ran her hands through her hair and pulled it over her shoulder.

'Shorter and fatter is better than long and skinny.' Qing wrinkled her nose and shivered elaborately. Her eyes were set far apart, and she was a little chubby. She had an older cousin who lived with four roommates in an apartment near downtown Fuzhou, and one Sunday the three of us had visited, taking buses across the city. Afterwards, I couldn't stop thinking about the apartment with its own flush toilet, the closet where the roommates kept their clothes and shoes. I wanted Yi Ba to visit me in my own apartment, remove a pair of guest slippers from my closet.

'My city lover has more experience,' Xuan said. 'He likes to do it standing up.'

'Oh,' said Qing, exposing the crooked incisor she usually tried to hide. 'That's nice.'

Xuan turned to me. 'What about you, Peilan? Which do you prefer?'

A checkered bedsheet hung over the edge of the top bunk. 'Long and skinny, I guess.' I hadn't had sex with Haifeng, but my friends didn't know this.

'You need to compare. What if you say you like long and skinny and you've never had short and fat? You'll never know which you'd truly like the best.' Xuan pursed her lips at the tragedy.

'Rural people don't shop around,' Qing said, though she was from a village so small it didn't even have a road. 'Shop around more, sister.'

'You could get a city man if you had this.' Xuan removed a lace bra from a bag printed with the name of the store: LOVERS. The bra had two heart-shaped cutouts, and the panties had a heart printed on the crotch. 'My city lover bought these for me.'

One night, when I was late getting back to the dormitory, Qing and Xuan went to eat without me, and I listened to my other dorm mates talk about getting jobs at newer factories. The room was hot and stuffy. It had been so long since I'd smelled clear air or seen the sea.

I went downstairs and waited for the phone booth. After being passed to three people on the other end of the line, I reached Haifeng.

'Peilan.' It had been months since we had talked. 'You called me.'

You *called* me. 'Can you meet me next week?'

We went to a motel Xuan recommended. Lied about our ages and bribed the desk clerk with my money. My initial excitement shriveled when I felt Haifeng's clammy fingers and saw, when he removed his clothes, that he was scrawnier than before. But I had already resolved to become a grown-up like Xuan.

The first time was over too quickly. We tried again.

'I missed you so much.' Haifeng kissed my cheeks and shoulders. 'My sweetheart.' I smoked one of his cigarettes as he slept and looked out the smudgy window at the construction scaffolding of another building in progress. Then I left early and returned to the dorm.

My period didn't come for two months in a row. How can I tell you how scared I was? My snipping grew sloppier, and Foreman Tung said he would fire me if I didn't shape up. In the motel room, Haifeng had said things like 'when we move back to the village' and 'when we're living together as husband and wife'.

I lay awake at night, saw the long march through the village in a rent-by-the-hour wedding gown, seamy with sweat from the armpits of the last bride and the bride before that, the neighbors snickering about the upcoming wedding night. If I told Haifeng I was pregnant, he would act like marriage was inevitable. He would expect me to be happy, or worse, grateful. I saw it written to the end, all the years of my life: village, 3 Alley, babies, me and Haifeng hating each other to death.

Payday. I borrowed Qing's Walkman and went to the music store, bought a tape with the money I was supposed to send to Yi Ba. I walked and walked and there was the highway. A bus came by and opened its doors and I climbed on. The driver asked where I was going and before the doors closed, I jumped off. Until now, I had done anything I wanted to, without repercussions. SHIT! I walked along the side of the highway. Trucks honked as they passed, kicking up clouds of dust. There were married women who brought their children to the factory with them, kids who napped in stacks of XXXL jeans awaiting shipment to American warehouses. But I wanted to go home to the village, have Yi Ba take care of me.

Sure, I'd been lonely, but I should have known better than to meet Haifeng at the motel. I knew we were taking a risk, but I hadn't thought I would end up pregnant. What were the chances? But I had walked into a trap, proving my father right. Yi Ba thought anything bad that happened to a woman was her fault. It made me sick. If a woman was unmarried it was her fault for being ugly or independent; if a woman was too devoted to her husband it was her fault for being mushy and desperate; if a husband had a girl on the side it was the wife's fault for driving him away and both the mistress and wife's faults for letting themselves get taken advantage of. If I told Yi Ba, then he and the neighbors would be satisfied that this was whom I'd always been behind my bluster, a girl who would do exactly what was expected of her.

By the time I returned to the dormitory it was dark and my feet were aching. Qing was angry with me, thinking I had stolen her Walkman. And so I broke down and told my friends.

'Get the procedure,' Xuan said. 'It's not that bad. I did it once. It hurts, but you'll only be out of work for a day. We'll come with you.'

'There's a hospital out on the highway,' Qing said.

Haifeng called the dormitory and asked for me. I didn't call him back. I never spoke to him again.

At the hospital, a woman with oblong eyeglasses sat at a desk obstructing the door to the examination rooms. 'ID,' she said. Xuan and Qing hadn't been able to get time off work, and I told them I would be fine going by myself. But I wished they had insisted on coming, even if they would miss out on a day's pay. I would have done the same for them.

I handed over my ID and the woman frowned. 'You're not eligible for medical care here because you're not registered as a city person. Your hukou is rural, so you can only go to a rural hospital. Go to the one in your village district.'

Back in the dorm, I slumped in my bunk and batted Qing's orange teddy bear with my feet. I couldn't remember the last time I'd been alone, though every day felt lonelier than the one before. My stomach flip-flopped at the reek of too many sweaty bodies in too small a space. I was sluggish and spaced-out at the snippers' table, like a window shade was being yanked over my eyes. I missed threads, cut accidental holes, letting the heaps of jeans grow larger, taller.

Then Foreman Tung fired me. Xuan and Qing were sure that if I took my ID to the rural hospital they couldn't turn me away.

I told them I would be back in the city next week to find another job, and on my last morning at the factory I snuck away to retrieve my bag while everyone else was working. In the empty dorm I slipped Xuan's heart bra into my pocket, even though it was too small and my boobs would never fit inside those tiny hearts. I left my notebook of song lyrics, my small collection of cassette tapes. I didn't have a tape player to listen to them.

I took a minibus straight to the rural hospital and flashed my ID. 'I'm a rural resident.'

'Is your fiancé meeting you here today?'

'I don't have a fiancé.'

'Boyfriend?'

'Sure . . .'

'Your ID says you're only eighteen. You can't get a marriage permit until you're nineteen and your boyfriend is twenty-one. And once you're married, you need to be twenty to get a birth permit.'

'Okay. Can I get the procedure done today?'

'Not without the father's consent. And without the proper permits for pregnancy there are usually fines. But since you're under the legal age for marriage—' The nurse glanced at the hallway and motioned to a door. 'Please, take a seat inside this room. I'll be back in a minute.'

I waited, but the nurse didn't return. The more time passed, the more worried I got. I had seen the family planning cadre drag pregnant women to the hospital, the women coming home smaller and subdued, but with no babies. I had also heard of married couples being fined for unauthorized pregnancies, forced to pay the equivalent of five years' worth of the average provincial salary. For an unmarried woman the fine would probably be steeper, though I had never heard of any woman in Minjiang declaring a pregnancy without a father involved. If I told Haifeng, I might as well get measured for a wedding gown.

I heard a telephone ringing, footsteps and voices, a running faucet. At the other end of the hallway, a pair of orderlies pushed a bed with a gasping figure strapped to it. I would step into the hallway and announce I had an out-of-quota pregnancy. They didn't need to come to 3 Alley and force me to go to the hospital. Here I was! Yet the nurse had mentioned fines, and paying even a year's worth of the average provincial salary would bankrupt me and Yi Ba. The only way to avoid the fees would be to apply for a marriage permit with Haifeng, even if we were underage. Or I could leave before the nurse got back.

The hallway was clear. I heaved myself off the chair and ran in the opposite direction of where the nurse had gone, down the stairs, out of the hospital, until I reached the bus stop. The sky was so clear and blue, so striking in its stillness that I wanted to cry.

After two years away, the village was different. Mansions had spurted up, built with the money of those who'd gone farther than Fuzhou, gone all the way to places like New York and Los Angeles, mansions with scalloped rooftops and fountains with plaster statues of goldfish, gates like metal doilies, four-storied balconies, windows as big as a lake.

'Everyone's gone to America,' Yi Ba said. I told him the factory had given me time off since we met our orders for the season. His eyes were more sunken, and his pants smelled, not faintly, of fish. Accustomed to eating in a room with one hundred people talking at once, I was no longer used to our quiet meals.

Three days passed. I cooked vegetables, gathered the chicken eggs, swept the floors, and scrubbed the laundry. I missed the city, especially during the sunny, unending afternoons, and knew I had to do something soon, but each morning I woke up frozen, overwhelmed. I could eat a spoonful of rat poison, but didn't want to die; I could go to the hospital and take my chances on another nurse, but what if I got someone who was even less sympathetic, who fined me six years' income or insisted on telling Yi Ba?

Minjiang was obsolete. The twisting alleyways, the fishing boats with their sagging nets, the peeling paint on the side of the houses, the faded green curtains hanging from our windows – like me, they were finished. On the wall of a building was a chalk drawing of one larger cat and two small kittens. I remembered a stray cat I had seen in the city, surrounded by a litter of blood-pink kittens, and how it had lay, defeated, accepting, as the kittens scrambled over one another in order to suck at its nipples.

I walked to one of the new mansions and pressed my face to the gate. The tiles smelled like rain and dirt. I backed away, a smear of dirt on my nose. At the river, I pushed a stick against the dirt, scratching an itch in the earth, trying to see what hid beneath the water's surface. The undersides of dead leaves. Fish. I passed the docks where the fishermen tugged at their crotches and talked about the girls they claimed to have plowed. One elbowed his buddy as I walked by, said he liked his chicks with extra meat. His friend shushed him. 'That's Old Guo's daughter, you idiot!' At the produce market, I saw Teacher Wu's wife, the head of the family planning cadre, haggling with a vendor over a cabbage, and I hurried back to 3 Alley.

One week passed. I slept all the time. I'd fall asleep at the table or standing at the sink, wake with a loud snore or when my feet wobbled. Sleep took over, sleep wiped me out, but in the moments before I succumbed, dark truths arrived. *I'm fucked. I'll have to give in and marry Haifeng.*

I awoke to the sound of Haifeng's mother and Yi Ba talking outside in the alley.

'She must be tired from all that work,' said Haifeng's mother. 'Haifeng says they work eight, nine hours at the factory.'

'Eight? That's nothing,' Yi Ba said. 'The city's too harsh for a young girl. But I knew she'd come home sooner or later. So many people are going abroad now, it's good she's come home.'

'She's grown up. She knows where she belongs.'

'The factory was only a phase. Testing her freedom.'

Haifeng's mother laughed. 'You can be glad that's over.'

I sat up in bed. Yi Ba had taken the money I sent home and never complained. I heard him say, 'Should I call you sister-in-law soon?'

'Not so fast,' said Haifeng's mother. 'I want a big dowry.'

'Hey, who says my dowry isn't big?'

Two weeks passed. An Incredible American returned to Minjiang and had a party. He hadn't been born an Incredible American but a mere villager like the rest of us, but had become an American by taking a train to Kunming, walking through the Burmese mountains, flying from Thailand to America, where he landed a job in a restaurant in Los Angeles, married an American – she was Chinese but had legit papers – and gotten naturalized, saved enough to pay off his debt and finally come home for a visit. His family was throwing a party at the mansion he built for them. I told Yi Ba I would rather scoop chicken shit than go, but he said it would look bad if every family showed up but us.

In school, I had known this Incredible American as Jing, a bully of a boy who'd been tight with the rest of the cadre sons and liked to sneak up behind girls and give them wedgies. At the party he did a poor job of pretending to not recognize me and Yi Ba. We stood in his mother's living room near a fake marble statue of a young boy petting a fawn, the statue rotating on a battery-operated disc painted gold. I saw his eyebrows go up, followed by a calculated removal of this expression of recognition, his features settling into a parody of blankness. 'Oh, that's right, Peilan! From primary school. Now I remember you!'

'How are you, Jing?'

'*John*. My name is John now.' He was only two years older than me but already had wrinkles around his mouth.

'How's America?'

'Oh, it's paradise. It's another world.'

'How much debt do you have?' Yi Ba asked.

'Very little, now. Started as twenty-five thousand, though the going rate is more these days. But the travel is easier, quicker. If you'd like to know more, I can introduce you. She's here today.'

Jing-John pointed at a woman with a faded caterpillar of hair on her upper lip, talking to some of the neighbors. Yi Ba had mentioned the lady with the mustache who arranged for people to travel abroad, and how she was responsible, indirectly, for the new mansions in the village. I said no thanks; didn't want to give Jing-John the satisfaction. But Yi Ba accepted a slip of paper from him with the lady's phone number.

Back at home, Yi Ba fell asleep. I noticed a hole in his socks, a pair he'd already mended several times. I walked around the room. Here were the bowls and chairs and pots from my childhood, which my mother had used before she died, the bowls now cracked, the pots burned on the bottom. I could stay here. Have the baby, take care of Yi Ba, have him take care of me.

Outside the window, I could see Haifeng's house. There was a light inside, the shadow of Mrs Li moving around in her own kitchen. I stepped away so she wouldn't see me. Soon Haifeng would have to come home, too.

I saw myself in a new country, with my own apartment, like Qing's cousin in Fuzhou. Xuan said in America, you could live anywhere you wanted to; it didn't matter if you had rural or urban hukou. They wouldn't care about things like pregnancy permits either.

Never mind the debt, so astronomical it was unreal, like the fake money burned graveside at Qingming holidays. Forget the grueling journey, which didn't seem real either, the distances and destinations nothing but nonsense words to me. I'd go where Haifeng would never go.

When I told Yi Ba I was leaving, he let out a long sigh. 'You too? Everyone's leaving except me. By the time you come home, it'll be for my funeral.'

'Don't say that.'

I told him I would send him money, and when I got settled, he could join me.

He waved his hand dismissively. 'I do well enough here.'

In the morning I made the phone call, and when the lady with the mustache asked if I was ready to leave at any time, I said yes.

It took me a few weeks to gather the money. At the riverbank I watched the lady count my down payment, the equivalent of three thousand American dollars, borrowed from relatives. They were sure that they'd receive an increase in status and income that came with having an American in the family. The rest, the forty-seven thousand, I borrowed from a loan shark. It would have taken me forty years, the rest of my working life, to earn fifty thousand American dollars in the village, but in New York, I hoped to pay it off in five or six.

A van drove me west on the highway to Guangxi. I took a train to Vietnam and another train to a packed apartment in Bangkok, where I received a fake Japanese passport that I would give back after getting to America. From Bangkok we flew on to Amsterdam, then Toronto, where I declared myself a refugee and followed two other women into a box in the back of a truck, which drove us to a house in New York. When they lifted the lid of the box, my pants were soaked with piss and my tongue raw from biting. I blinked at the lights and the shelves stocked with giant packages of toilet paper and bottled water, and the cars in the garage that were bigger than the biggest cars in Fuzhou, and the garage itself that was bigger than the main room in the house on 3 Alley, and I heard music playing and realized the words were in English. I tried to sit. 'I'm here,' I shouted.

Now I owed forty-seven thousand to a loan shark in China, to be wired in twice-monthly installments if I wanted to avoid a higher interest rate. I knew what happened to those who didn't pay enough, paid late, or didn't pay at all. One threat, one knife-blade flash from the loan shark's men, and it was pay now or disappear forever.

In New York City, I changed. For one thing, I was no longer Peilan. One of the other girls in the Bangkok apartment had suggested *Polly*, an English name that sounded a little like Peilan. So it was Polly, not Peilan, who was doing thirteen-hour shifts in a garment factory, the same work Peilan had done in China except for eight times more money, and it was Polly who paid too much rent for a sleeping bag on the floor, the spot given to the roommate with the least seniority. I hadn't thought I would live in a mansion like the one Jing-John built for his family, but I hadn't expected to live in a shithole like the apartment on Rutgers Street, a cramped block with such an inferiority complex that things never smelled right, and the wind blew a steady stream of bags, cans, and plastic bottles down the side-walk. The bedroom consisted of three bunk beds lined up so tight the women could only get out by crawling through the ends of their mattresses. I came home from work exhausted, ass throbbing from thirteen hours of sitting, and after a while I no longer noticed the jagged gaps in the walls or the floor tiles that had peeled away and exposed dirty crumbled plaster, or the cockroaches, or the drippy kitchen ceiling, and it didn't bother me that I had to put my hand in the tank when I wanted to flush the toilet. Jing-John must have worked for years to buy that mansion and marble fawn.

I'd arrived at the tail end of a New York summer. At intersections I would play a game, walking in the direction of whichever light went green first, and in this way, I zigzagged my way around most of Manhattan. When I got lost I tried to remain lost for as long as possible, making turn after turn until the street ended at a highway or river, or until I asked the closest Chinese-looking person for directions. No matter how tired I was, I always felt more awake when I walked. How varied the people of New York were, how quickly they moved, inches apart, while avoiding physical contact. On payday I splurged and rode the subway, and the best part was when I went up the stairs to the street and got to the next-to-last step, anticipating what I would see when I reached the sidewalk, if this neighborhood would be full of tall brown buildings or small gray ones, what kind of people lived there, what the stores were like. I saw myself in this neighborhood, that apartment building, that car.

New York was noisier than Fuzhou, and the sounds were different, car alarms and rattling subways, people blasting music out the windows of their apartments. There were so many restaurants, serving food I'd never heard of. My roommates and I took turns cooking. One put peppers in her beef, another fried her vegetables but barely salted them. I made fish balls and although the ingredients weren't as good as the ones back home, the taste made my chest hurt. My new life was unstable and unsure, but each new day was shot through with possibility.

Didi was the roommate I got along with the best. She was

from a village near Xiamen, had been in New York for a little over a year. She introduced me to the best places to buy vegetables, fish, and meat, took me to a tea shop on Bayard that sold sweet black sesame soup with chewy dumplings, which we slurped sitting next to American-born Chinese kids who teased one another in loud, slangy English. Didi didn't leave Chinatown unless she had to. 'We've got all we need here,' she said, 'so why are you taking the train to all those weird neighborhoods?'

All this time, you were with me. What I had hoped would work during the long hours in the box from Toronto had not. You were alive, stronger than ever, kicking harder. I was getting used to you, but I was so tired.

One of my roommates said to me, 'Girl, when are you due? Tomorrow?'

Maybe cold weather makes for cold people. But when I saw my reflection in a store window it looked like I'd doubled in size. This body definitely did not belong to me.

It was Polly, not Peilan, who went to the free clinic uptown, where there was a woman doctor who was Chinese and spoke Mandarin.

'Do your parents know?' She handed me a paper shirt.

'I don't have parents.'

The doctor's hair was cut short, forming a trim arrowhead at the nape of her neck, and her eyes were dark and kind. 'How old did you say you were, Miss Guo? Sixteen?'

I sat on a long metal table that was also lined with paper. My feet stuck out of the paper shirt and I stared at a ring of dirt on the floor. I'd told the doctor my name, address, and birthdate, which she scribbled on a form. 'Why does it matter how old I am? I don't need anyone's permission to be here.'

'You're right, you don't.'

There was a plastic figure on the counter with what appeared to be organs inside, and I wanted to remove them and tap them against the doctor's desk.

She looked at the form again. 'Eighteen. Sorry, you look a lot younger. How did you get to New York?'

'I came by myself.'

'That must have been hard.'

'No big deal. I wasn't scared.'

The doctor opened her mouth as if to talk, then closed it.

'Lay down. Scoot up a little,' she said. 'That's good.'

I was poked, first with fingers, then with a cold metal tongue. The doctor asked where I was from.

'Fujian. Where are you from?'

'Zhejiang.'

'And did your parents bring you here?' I asked her.

'I came here for university and stayed after medical school, to work.'

She ran a boxy device attached to a cord over my belly and pointed to a television screen with a black-and-white image of a shadowy blob. 'Looking good.'

'I don't want it,' I said, though I'd lived with you for so many months, it was hard to be entirely sure.

The doctor looked at the form again. 'Oh, you hadn't mentioned that.' She switched off the video screen. 'You can sit up now.' She walked around to face me. 'You're over seven months pregnant.'

I counted backwards, trying to recall how many months it had been since the motel with Haifeng, but I could barely recall his face.

'Twenty-nine or thirty weeks.' The doctor's face looked sad. 'We can't terminate after twenty-four weeks, or six months. I'm so sorry.'

'I'll go to another clinic, then.'

'It's the law. They won't do it either.'

My thighs were clammy against the table, my stomach smeared with jelly. Slime dripped from between my legs.

'I can give you some resources. I'd like to refer you to another doctor, so you can get the proper care.'

'I have to have the baby?'

My belly grew cold. The doctor lowered her voice. 'Listen, don't be afraid. They have good hospitals here.' Her Mandarin accent was citified, polished. 'I can also share information about adoption.'

'I didn't say I was afraid.'

The doctor backed away. There was a spray of gray hairs on her temple, a gold wedding band on her finger. I sat very still in that big paper gown. The screen was blank again. I had traveled thousands of miles just to learn there was no difference between the provincial hospitals with their IDs and age requirements and marriage permits and this clinic in New York with its stupid rules on twenty-four versus twenty-eight. Four measly weeks.

'Are you okay?'

I nodded, looking at my lap. She gave me a sheet of phone numbers and several pamphlets in English and Chinese. I promised to return for another checkup and to buy vitamins.

I walked out of the clinic into a cloudy and cool afternoon, fell asleep on the subway and woke at the end of the line, in Brooklyn, in a neighborhood full of white people speaking some language that wasn't English. I got off and heard seagulls and smelled salt water, and I walked to the edge of the city, removed my shoes, rolled up my jeans, and stepped into the ocean for the first time.

I stepped in farther. The cold water made me curl my toes and the waves lapped at my shins in a sharper, faster way than the dark blue of the river in the village, yet here the sea was cleaner, grayer, larger, more angry and thirsty and beautiful all at once, not unlike New York itself. I took another step. The water was up to my waist. My teeth chattered, but the cold felt good.

I had run out of choices; I was fucked. I had to have the baby. Or rather, *Polly* would have to have the baby.

I heard a voice calling from the shore. A man was waving at me and jumping up and down. A woman joined him. They yelled, their arms beckoning me to come back.

The water wasn't that cold. 'I'm not afraid,' I yelled in Mandarin.

Standing in the Atlantic, it grew into a challenge. For Polly, the girl who'd defy odds, the girl who could do anything. New York was a parallel gift of a life, and the unrealness of being here gave even the most frightening things a layer of surreal comedy. Peilan continued on in the village, feeding chickens and stray cats and washing cabbages, as Polly lived out a bonus existence abroad. Peilan would marry Haifeng or another village boy while Polly would walk the endless blocks of new cities. Polly could have a baby without being married. A baby might soothe the sharp edges of my loneliness, the loneliness that bubbled up when I saw couples and families and people laughing with their friends. I could raise my child to be smart and funny and strong.

I want you to know that you were wanted. I decided: I wanted you.

Yi Ba thought that only men could do what they wanted, but he was wrong. I stood with my toes in the ocean, euphoric at how far I had come, and two months later, when I gave birth to you, I would feel accomplished, tougher than any man.

I named you Deming. My roommates let me stay, despite their complaints that your crying kept them up at night, and in return I kicked in a little extra rent. I tried to hand you over to a stranger at a day care, but I couldn't, not yet, and instead I quit my job, called the loan shark, and took out an additional loan, one that enabled me to not work for six months.

No one had told me I could have such love for another person. When I thought of anything harmful happening to you the love burned a little, like a rash, but when I held you and you were calm, the love was beaming, like sunlight through the leaves of a tree. I was in love! I'd look down at you and get goo-goo-eyed and think, *This is a human being I made*. I no longer watched crime shows with my roommates; they made the world seem too dangerous.

Didi worked in a nail salon and said she'd try to get me a job there. She gave us her mattress and took over the sleeping bag. I don't know if you remember Didi, but she had a squeaky voice and fluffy bangs, and when you fussed, she would hold you and you would quiet down, discharging bubbles of drool that she blotted, nonchalantly, with the bottom of her shirt. After weeks of only sleeping an hour or two at a time, I responded to your screaming on autopilot. I'd hear your cries even when I was sleeping.

But it was grueling, how much a baby needed, how you would tug my hair and grab my shirt and latch onto my body because you owned it, too. Look how he wants his mama, my roommates would say, and a couple of them also got goo-goo-eyed, and a sliver of fear would present itself: what if I would always be required to offer myself up, ready and willing, constantly available? What had I done? And then: what was wrong with me? Didi loved kids, had grown up caring for younger siblings and nieces and nephews, and though she found it strange that I sometimes wanted to take off and walk around the neighborhood for an hour, smoking a cigarette – 'By yourself? And to nowhere in particular? But why?' – she always offered to watch you.

'When I get married,' Didi would begin her sentences, 'when I have kids . . .'

'How many kids do you want?' I asked, as we prepared dinner one evening.

'Two or three. Do you want more?'

'One's enough for now.'

'Only one?'

I told Didi about Haifeng. 'I guess I wanted more than just staying with him.' I poured oil into the pan and turned the knob that produced a gas flame.

'You're a free spirit, but practical. Like my sister in Boston. She'll marry this guy for a green card. Me, I'm more traditional. I'll marry someone I love.'

It pleased me, being called a free spirit.

Once a month, I called Yi Ba. 'How's New York?' he asked.

'Wonderful. How's Minjiang?'

'The same.' Then he'd tell me about a neighbor's new house with rugs that tickled his toes.

'I'll try to make more money so I can send you some,' I said.

'You need your money more than I do. I can take care of myself.'

Two of my roommates had given birth to children in New York and sent them to stay with relatives in China. 'They don't remember anything when they're babies,' said Hetty, a hairdresser with a shaggy bob. She was folding her clothes and stacking them into a box that she kept under her bunk. 'They don't miss us. What do you remember when you were his age? Nothing, I bet.' Hetty had a three-year-old son whom she hadn't seen in two and a half years, living with her parents in her village, her husband working in a place called Illinois. 'I'll bring my son here when he's old enough to go to school. Two more years.'

Ming, a chain-smoking waitress, hadn't seen her daughters for five years. They were living with her family near Nanping. 'You'll try to keep him with you, but you won't be able to,' she said in her raspy voice. 'I wanted to keep my daughters, too, but it's impossible. Who's going to look after them? We're all working. If you hire a babysitter you won't be able to pay your debt. You've got to concentrate on that, or you'll be screwed. Trust me.' She picked grapes out of a plastic bag, chewing as she spoke. 'Grapes?'

She held out the bag and I took several. 'I don't want to send him to the village.' I sat on Didi's bunk, holding you as you sucked on a bottle. 'It's only my father there, I don't have a mother to help out.'

Ming said, 'Grandparents treat them better than they treated you. They know the babies are going to leave again. Old age softens people.'

'Send him back,' said Hetty. 'It's the only way.'

'Free babysitting,' said Ming.

The two women laughed, but their laughter was the kind with no core, only loose edges.

In the tiniest spaces of time between naps and feedings, I explored the city with you bundled against me. We wandered to the bottom of Manhattan, where the sun warmed the river. There was a fence there, no way to walk directly into the water. That's because the city was insecure and wanted to contain itself, sticking up borders to keep its residents close. I didn't buy it. I believed we could leave whenever we wanted. Winter was coming, yet the sunlight heated my scalp, and I sang 'Ma-ma-ma' and my voice was as clear and sharp as morning birds. You squirmed against me. Love spun up like feathers.

Some days I would clean you, change your poopy diaper, put on your shoes and socks and hat and little jacket, haul you in the stroller down three flights of stairs, only to have you start howling the moment we turned the corner. Time to go back up with the stroller, three flights of stairs, change your diaper and clean you and put your clothes back on, and by then I would have lost any desire to go out. You poked me, wanting to show me the same thing for the tenth time, a roommate's pink shirt, a coin you'd found; you'd wail as you banged a spoon against the kitchen floor. I had only been Polly for such a short time, and Polly was already slipping away. There was so much of the world I would never see.

Weeks, months, drifted by in a haze, blending into one long, soupy day in which I never got enough sleep. Ice formed on the windowpanes and the sun refused to fully come up. It was too cold to go on walks now, too much hassle to ride the subway with a baby, so we stayed inside for days, moved between bedroom and kitchen and bathroom and bedroom, confined to our pen. I sang silly songs about chickens and goldfish and told you stories of fishing boats and banyan trees and Teacher Wu. I watched television when my roommates were at work. My closest friends were the actors on a Spanish show who fought and made up like clockwork, tiny lean women stuffed into high heels and short dresses and shiny men in collared shirts and pressed pants. I wanted a bedroom to myself like the actors had, to spread out in a bed big enough for four. The apartment got smaller and smaller.

Then it was spring, and then it was summer, and I'd been in New York for almost a year. You grew longer and heavier, energetic and curious, and once you were crawling I had to watch you all the time or else you'd be dipping your hands into the toilet and into your mouth, finding a rotten food dropping in a corner to eat, offering up a dead roach to me like a twenty-dollar bill. My money was gone. I didn't want to take out another loan, but if I returned to work, I would have to pay someone to watch you. My roommates were right. There was too much debt, and I was behind. I had yet to send Yi Ba any money. Yet Didi's nail salon salary fed her whole family in her village. Even Jing-John had bought his mother a house.

Didi asked her boss if she'd hire another nail technician, and her boss said they didn't need one, but maybe soon. I couldn't hold out for that. Had to pay off my loans, and that would take another seven or eight years, less if I got a higher-paying job, preferably one that didn't involve pulling on a ba wa. Waitressing was the best job, especially in a Japanese or Thai restaurant, which paid more than a Chinese restaurant, even though Chinese people ran all of them. But it was tough to get a waitressing job without the right connections.

I got a job at a factory with shorter shifts, sewing shirts for six hours a day, enough to meet the minimum payments to the loan shark. The interest had gone up, and I still owed so much. I'd fall asleep while giving you a bath, waiting until my roommates had used the bathroom first, days since I'd had a shower myself. I smelled like a foot. Except for Didi, there was no more cooing over baby toes. Now my roommates hurried out of the room when you began to cry.

Didi said she'd look after you when I was at the factory, and I tried to line up my shifts to coincide with the times she wasn't working, but when I couldn't, I had to stay home. Hetty had told me about a babysitter, and I visited her, twelve kids inside a two-bedroom apartment that smelled of mold, most of them crying, a few of them coughing. The woman had sat and smoked as one kid swatted another in the face. I wasn't going to leave you in a place like that. I couldn't even afford her on my salary. Imagine what a cheaper babysitter would be like.

Then it was fall. Didi's mother was sick. There were medical bills to pay back home, and Didi needed to take on more hours at the salon.

'It's not a problem,' I said. 'I can take him with me.'

As soon as I walked into the factory you started to cry. Can't say I blamed you – the room was packed and windowless, a quarter of the size of the room I'd worked in back at the Fuzhou factory. Your wails chorused along with the sewing machine motors, and I held you close, tried to avoid the other women's nasty looks.

I put a bag of diapers and bottles beneath my machine. 'What are you thinking?' hissed the woman to my left. 'That baby came out of your pussy last week.'

I placed some scraps of fabric inside an empty box and set you down in it, hoping the noise would mask your crying.

A mass of shirts awaited me. My job was hems. Fold the fabric, run it through the serger. A job that required focus and steady hands, things I'd always prided myself on, fold, press, sew, fold, press, sew. Each shirt bringing me closer to zero debt.

Today, the hours that usually passed with a numbing dullness were crawling by even more slowly than the longest day in the history of school. I kept thinking about when I'd have to feed you, and where I could go to do that. There were no breaks in a six-hour shift. The woman at the next machine shot me incredulous looks as you wailed ceaselessly – as if the noise and heat had given you permission to cry even louder – and my hand slipped. The thread veered sideways off the hem, the fabric violently bunched.

I tossed the ruined shirt and picked up a new one. My mind was running in half-time, hands twitching from not enough sleep, and again the needle staggered away from its path. 'Damn it!'

The woman next to me clucked her tongue. According to the clock on the wall, only ten minutes had passed.

'Looking at the clock instead of doing work,' my neighbor sang, firing off another shirt.

'Mind your own business,' I sang back. I did three shirts successfully, but the detours had thrown off my game. Again I looked at the clock. The woman next to me picked up a fresh pile of shirts, my first pile unfinished. Your sobs had sputtered out into hyperventilating hiccups.

I crouched down. When you saw me, you held your arms up.

'Little Deming,' I said. 'Mama's right here.'

It was hot down there. Dusty. Beneath the table, I saw feet pressing their machine pedals. One woman wore mismatched socks, another a sneaker with a hole in the side. I kissed you. 'Mama's busy now,' I said, in a soothing tone I hoped matched Didi's. 'Be quiet for a moment, and I'll feed you soon.'

I put you down and sat back in my chair. Finally, you were quiet. The woman next to me was already on her third pile of shirts, but at least I'd finished one.

Fold, press, sew. Fold, press, sew. You were crying again. I raced the serger to the end of the fabric and threw the shirt into the finished stack. 'Hold on,' I said, but you were screaming. I fumbled for a bottle, struggling to lift you while keeping you obscured inside the box, one hand behind your neck, the bottle in my right armpit. You tugged at the bottle. My knees hurt from squatting. You yanked, I lost my balance, and as I fell backwards my head hit the underside of the table. Ass to the floor, the bottle slipped from my hands and fell into the box, landing on your legs. You wailed. I rubbed my head. That was how the forelady found me, under the table with a crying baby and a box of fabric stained with spilled formula.

That's when I walked out. Down the block, past Grand, Pitt, Madison, Pike, Clinton, Henry, Essex, Cherry. Cars honked as

I zigzagged in the middle of the street with you strapped to my chest. Montgomery, Jackson, Water.

I didn't know where I was going. I paused at the chain-link fence of a playground, no children outside on this late September day, just crooked basketball hoops, a flag flapping in front of an elementary school and a row of tall buildings in the background. The forelady had given me the rest of my shift off without pay, said I could keep my job as long as I showed up tomorrow without a baby.

My brain returned to calculating how little I would make this month. Even if I worked fourteen-hour shifts there wouldn't be enough to pay rent and the loan shark and a babysitter. Didi's mother was sick.

To the water, then, with its choppy gray waves, the muffled thumping of cars on the bridge above. The row of benches deserted on a weekday afternoon. Barges floated along the river.

I was so tired. All I wanted was to be by myself in a silent, dark room.

Send him back. It's the only way.

You kicked me like you wanted to be freed. I don't want to tell you what I did.

Fast now, before I could change my mind, looking around to make sure no one could see me, I set the bag on the pavement under the bench and lowered you inside. The bag was taller than you, its sides a stiff, insulated plastic. When I got up I was lighter, relieved.

I ran.

'I'm sorry, I'm sorry!'

You sobbed. I squeezed your body against mine.

I'd gone almost two blocks before coming to a crosswalk.

The light was moving from yellow to red, but a bus was slowly making its way through the intersection. If the light had remained yellow a moment longer, if there'd been no bus, would I have kept running?

But I did return, and the bag was there, and you were still inside.

I stroked your hair. 'Mama,' you said again. '*Ma*-ma!'

I called Yi Ba and told him I had a son I was sending to the village until I paid down my debt and until you were old enough to go to school in New York.

Yi Ba made a sound like he was clearing mucus. '*Hrm*. Going all the way to America to end up pregnant.' He said he would take you, he'd accept any money I sent home. 'But to take care of your son. He needs the money, not me.'

Didi's sister, who'd married her American-born boyfriend in Boston, wanted to visit their mother in China. I took out another loan and offered to pay for the sister's flight if she brought you to Yi Ba.

I packed a bag with your clothes, pillow, and a photo of the two of us taken in a tourist booth at the South Street Seaport. In the photo my face was shadowed by sun and you looked cranky and hot. The background was a cartoon Statue of Liberty, a checkered yellow cab, and the Empire State Building all on the same block.

The night before you left, I stayed up and memorized your face. We fell asleep curled together. In the morning, my eyes pink and crusty from crying, I gave you to Didi's sister. You stayed asleep. Didi walked with you and her sister to the airport bus on East Broadway, but I didn't go with them. I couldn't bear to watch you carried off in another woman's arms and trust that you'd be okay, that I would see you again.

After you left I lay with my face against the spot on the pillow where you had slept. The spot, which had been so warm only minutes ago, was now cold.

Ming tapped my shoulder. 'Polly. Hey.' She shook my arm. 'You did the right thing.'

I didn't believe it, at the time.

CHAPTER EIGHT

In the end, he hadn't expected it to be this easy. Leon answered on the second ring, and hearing his voice felt like being petted by a pair of giant hands. 'Deming! You sound like a grown-up! I was waiting for your call. Vivian said she was going to see you.'

Daniel was the only one home at Roland's apartment at ten o'clock on a Friday night, bloated from the food he'd eaten earlier at Vivian's. In Fuzhou, it was Saturday morning, thirteen hours in the future.

'Did Vivian tell you she gave me away to a foster family? To get adopted?' He had looked up how to say the words in Chinese.

'Not until much later, when I'd been in China for a long time.'

'Because she knew it was wrong.'

There was a pause on Leon's end of the line. Daniel scratched the inside of his arm and listened to the anxious hiss of the radiator.

'I wish we could have stayed together,' Leon said.

'I wish you hadn't left.' He didn't call Leon Yi Ba. Leon said he had a daughter now, and it might creep him out to hear the word from Daniel.

Leon coughed. 'I have your mother's phone number. At least it was hers seven years ago. That's when I last heard from her.'

So the permanency hearing report had been right. She'd gone to China. 'You *saw* her?'

'She was about to get married then, was working in an English school.'

English? Married? 'What do you mean, you saw her?'

'I didn't see her,' Leon said, 'we only spoke on the phone.'

'Did she go to Florida?'

'She didn't really say. But I know she would have never left you on purpose.'

'Did you tell her I was adopted?'

'I did.'

Daniel lay on the floor, saw a ball of dust under the couch, a sock he'd been searching for. Ever since he spoke to Michael, he had constructed a new storyline – Deming and Mama torn apart by Vivian's evil machinations, victims of a family tragedy. Leon was saying his mother hadn't left him on purpose, but she hadn't gotten in touch with him either. She hadn't looked for him, yet she had looked for Leon?

'Come visit,' Leon said, 'I'll take you out for real Chinese food, none of that pretend shit they have in New York. By the way, your Chinese sucks. What happened, you forgot how to talk?'

'I'm just out of practice,' Daniel said. 'After you all left.'

He didn't call the number Leon had given him right away. He didn't want to call and have her not want to talk to him.

The next afternoon, Daniel ironed his one good shirt on the kitchen counter, pressed the hems and flattened the collars. He didn't have any pants other than jeans, but he put on his dark gray pair instead of the blue. His hiking boots would have to do. He put the Carlough College forms in his pocket, the statement of purpose he'd printed on Roland's printer.

For Jim Hennings' birthday, Elaine and Angel had rented out an Italian restaurant in the West Village, a neighborhood Daniel always got lost in, the streets west of the subway station switching from orderly numbered blocks to ones with old-fashioned names – Perry, Jane, Horatio. There were no chain stores in this section of the Village, only restaurants and boutiques with small signs in restrained fonts, and compared to Chinatown, the streets were nearly empty at five thirty on a March afternoon. As Daniel backtracked after taking a wrong turn, he passed a man walking a tiny white dog, both of them bent sideways against the wind, and a woman in an enormous dark coat, moving her walker, clunk by clunk, up the sidewalk. He wondered where his mother lived now, if she was still in the house on 3 Alley. The fire escapes here were painted matte black, a contrast to the glass high-rises downtown, and none of the buildings were over five stories tall. Inside these large front windows were chandeliers and tall bookshelves, kitchens with round wooden tables and hanging plants, and in one apartment, a room with nothing but a grand piano. Even the buildings' brick exteriors looked like they'd been given a scrubdown, preserved and buffed to a shine. Neither this nor the new luxury buildings downtown appealed to Daniel. They both seemed calculated, disingenuous.

The closer he got, the slower he walked, until he was standing outside the restaurant looking at a handwritten sign that said CLOSED: PRIVATE PARTY, the bottoms of the letters nudging in toward one another like he'd seen girls posing for photos, with pigeon-toed feet. Angel hadn't responded to his text message. He opened the door. The restaurant wasn't large, and the room felt crowded. He took one of the glasses of champagne lined up on a cream-colored cloth and saw Kay and Peter talking to Jim and Elaine. They were more casually dressed than the other guests, in slightly more formal versions of their usual outfits, a sports jacket instead of a cardigan for Peter, a skirt for Kay in place of corduroys. They waved at him, and Daniel thumped over in his hiking boots, feeling a surge of fondness for them.

He hugged them hello. That they didn't seem angry was a good sign. Angel hadn't yet told them about the money he'd borrowed. He hadn't seen Elaine and Jim for years, and Jim had gone bald, Elaine's long, curly hair all gray. Daniel shook Jim's hand and wished him a happy birthday, and Elaine kissed Daniel on the cheek, jewelry clinking under her pashmina scarf. 'You stranger, you've been in New York all this time and haven't let us know. We'll have to have you over for dinner as soon as possible.'

'Angel is by the appetizer table.' Jim pointed across the room. An Asian guy with a shaved head and thick eyebrows, handsome in a rugby player kind of way, had his arm around Angel, and she was laughing. This guy was too big, too handsome. His suit jacket stretched across his wide shoulders, and Angel's light blue dress had short sleeves and a matching belt. She was undersized, still, hair cut briskly below her shoulders. The guy looked like he could be Chinese, or Korean, but Daniel had never been good about guessing these things. 'That's Charles, her boyfriend,' Jim said, and Kay looked at Daniel.

'He's a senior, in the same program as her,' Elaine said. 'We met him for the first time over winter break.'

'Good head on his shoulders,' said Jim. 'Very polite, well spoken.'

He thought about the guys Angel had spoken about. There'd been an ex-boyfriend who was now one of her best friends; a co-worker she had a crush on.

'Angel,' Elaine called. 'Look who's here.'

Angel saw Daniel and said something to Charles, who scowled.

'Angel,' Jim called.

She crossed the room with Charles's hand in hers. When Daniel hugged her, she flinched. 'Hey,' he said. 'Good to see you.'

'This is my boyfriend, Charles,' she said, looking over Daniel's head.

Daniel shook the guy's hand, which felt like shaking air. His suit looked expensive. 'Nice to meet you. How long have you guys been together?' He heard a swell of voices behind him. Jim and Elaine greeted another couple and got pulled away in the crowd.

'We should head back to our table,' Angel said to Charles.

Kay touched Angel's arm. 'Angel, we haven't had a chance to catch up. How's school? We heard you were supposed to go to Nepal?'

'I was, but I had money stolen from me.'

'Stolen?' Peter said. 'In Iowa?'

'Even in Iowa.'

Daniel turned to Charles. 'So where are you from?'

Charles laughed, a sharp bark. 'Thieves are everywhere. You don't need to be in the same place as someone to steal from them.'

Daniel drained his champagne.

'How awful,' Kay said. 'Did they catch whoever did it? What happened, exactly?'

'Look, Mom, the food is coming.'

'What happened is that the thief knows exactly what he did,' Charles said.

'Oh, he does,' Angel said, her eyes meeting Daniel's.

Daniel took Peter and Kay by the elbows. 'We should sit down before the food gets cold.'

'It hasn't even arrived yet,' Kay said.

They walked to a table across the room. 'That's so strange,' Kay said. 'What Angel and her boyfriend were saying.'

Peter said, 'Something about a thief?'

Daniel took off his coat and hung it on the chair next to Kay's. He took out the forms for Carlough College and passed them to Peter.

'Good,' Peter said.

Kay's smile was so big, her whole face crinkled. Daniel smiled back. He was still full from last night's dinner at Vivian's, but ate marinated olives and arugula salad and linguine and lamb with eggplant, ordered a glass of red wine, another. As the servers cleared away the plates he saw Angel leave the room by herself. Maybe if he apologized to her in person, she wouldn't tell Peter and Kay who the thief was. He excused himself, taking another glass of champagne as he crossed the room. Angel stood in the front entrance with a short-haired woman in a white jacket, one of the restaurant staff, and he heard them talking about candles and cake.

'Angel,' he said.

She stopped in the middle of her sentence, astonishment flickering on her face.

'Is there a problem?' the woman said.

'No,' Daniel said.

'As I was saying,' Angel said, 'we'll dim the lights, then sing. He'll like that.'

He waited for her to finish talking, and when she turned to leave with the woman, Daniel blocked her.

'Okay,' she said. 'What do you want?'

'Did you get my text?'

She crossed her arms over her chest. 'What text?'

'I'm sorry about everything.'

'I'm sure you are.'

'Can you do me a favor? Please don't tell my parents about the money. Or your parents.'

She snorted. 'Why not? You're scared?'

'I don't want them to know. I'm working on fixing things. You've got to believe me.'

'You want them to think you're perfect? Then you shouldn't have screwed up so hard in the first place.'

'They already know I'm a fuck-up. I'm just trying to make things better.'

'You know you can't please everyone, right? Me included.'

'I swear I'm going to pay you back.'

'You need to figure your shit out, but don't expect me to do it for you.' She turned and left the room.

Elaine intercepted him as he made his way to the table, said they'd have to set a date for dinner, she would get his number later, at the apartment. His parents were staying over tonight, and they'd have coffee there after the party. 'You'll have more time to talk with Angel once we're all back at our place. Did you get to meet Charles, at least?'

'He seems nice.'

'He's planning on law school.' Elaine leaned closer. 'You know, I'm sure they wouldn't want me to say this, but I'm going to say it anyway, because you know me and my big mouth. Your parents are heartbroken that you're not going back to school. I know it seems like we're a bunch of old fuddy-duddies, wanting to control your *life*, but believe it or not, I was young once, too. I know how it goes. But in this case, I must say, your parents know what they're talking about. But, have you thought of suggesting to them a school in the city if you don't want to be upstate? I mean, I love your parents, but I get why a kid your age would prefer to be here rather than Ridgeborough. You could always stay with Jim and me. Think about it, will you?'

He heard Angel's voice across the room; heard her laugh. He'd have to text her again, keep trying until she gave their friendship another chance. She said he needed to figure his shit out, but wasn't that a sign of caring? 'I'm going to Carlough,' he told Elaine. 'For summer semester.' Saying it made his shoulders slump, but too late; he'd given Peter the essay.

Elaine clapped. 'Terrific!'

He told Kay and Peter he was sorry he couldn't join them at the Hennings', but he had to work early tomorrow, even though his next shift actually wasn't until Monday.

'We'll see you soon,' Peter said. 'Summer session is in two months, so plan on being home a few weeks before that, to get settled in and squared away. The first week of May would be best.'

Kay said, 'I'm glad you've decided to do the right thing.'

He had to do as much as he could in the city for the next two months, before he left, starting with tonight. He'd meet up with Roland and his friends. He deserved a night out.

He was almost at the corner when he saw Charles smoking a cigarette in front of a fire hydrant. Angel had always hated smoking, called it gross. She must have changed her mind.

'Hey,' Charles said.

'Hey, man.'

'I want to talk to you for a second.'

Daniel stopped. 'All right.'

Charles tossed his cigarette to the sidewalk, ground it out with his shoe, and took a pack of gum out of his pocket, popping a piece into his mouth.

'Can I have a piece?'

Charles tossed him the pack. 'Keep it. Seriously.'

'Thanks.' The gum was a green square, slightly bitter with artificial sweetener. Daniel immediately wanted to spit it out, but swallowed it instead.

'I know what you did,' Charles said.

'I've done lots of things. You see my show the other night?'

'I respect Angel's decision not to take this to the courts to try to get her money back, although I don't agree with her. But you better not try to talk to her again.'

'Wait. Hold on.'

'Are you seriously going to deny this? I know you stole ten thousand dollars from her. She's the kindest person I know and you took advantage of her.'

'I didn't steal.'

'So tell that to Angel's parents. They go on and on about what a good friend you are, how you guys grew up together like brother and sister. It's disgusting. You should tell them, or I will.'

Daniel took off, half-walking and half-running, toward the subway. He couldn't please anyone. But he wanted, more than anything, to not feel this terrible about himself.

When he emerged from the station at Canal Street, his phone rang. He scrambled for it, hoping it would be her.

It was Peter. 'Your mother and I looked at the forms. What is wrong with you? You know we can't submit that essay. *I don't even want to go to Carlough so I don't know why I'm writing this.* What is this garbage? We gave you another chance, which you clearly do not deserve, and this is how you repay us?'

Daniel reached into his coat pocket and pulled out a piece of paper. Under a streetlamp he unrolled it. *The small classes and liberal arts education that Carlough College offers, in particular its top-rate economics and political science programs, would allow me to pursue my professional career goals.* He felt disappointment, edged with relief. 'Sorry, Dad. It was a joke. Let me run over and I'll give the real essay to you now.'

'Not to mention, you were rude to Angel tonight at the party. Now, I know you feel like she betrayed your friendship because she told us about your gambling, but you could at least try to be civil to her. She was worried for you, Daniel. That's why she told us. To help you.'

'Where are you now? At the restaurant? At Jim and Elaine's? I'll come give you the essay. I have it, it's good.'

'Don't bother. You have made your decision loud and clear.'

'Dad!'

'This is the last straw. You have done enough.'

'Can I talk to Mom?' he said, but Peter had already hung up.

He ducked into a bar on Grand Street and ordered a whiskey. The bar was small and dark, nondescript, a jukebox playing AC/DC's 'Hells Bells' and a video slot machine glowing insistently at him from a corner. He turned his back to it and looked through his phone, went through a few messages and deleted them, saw a note he'd saved months ago, when he was still at Potsdam, with the name and address of an underground poker club in the city. Two hundred to buy in, Kyle had said. The address was on Lafayette, a few blocks away.

He deleted the note and finished his drink. He would go to Jim and Elaine's to give his parents the right essay, though he didn't know their address. He walked east, kept taking the green lights, staying on Grand, then saw a bank and went inside to get cash. His finger hovered over the button that said $50, but he hit $500, the bulk of his account, and watched the bills shoot out.

On the corner of Grand and Lafayette, the address for the poker club reverberated in his mind. He headed south to where Howard Street crossed over to Hester. It wasn't too late, he could turn and go right to Roland's, go right past the building, which was narrow, no doorman, only an intercom. He checked his phone; no messages. He was frightened by how much he was about to fuck up, by his lack of desire to stop himself, the rising anticipation at the prospect of falling down, failing harder, and going straight to tilt; he'd known from the moment he left the bar exactly where he would end up. He pressed the intercom button. 'What?' a guy's voice said. He provided the password, and for a moment, a feeble hope hung in the air that it would be the wrong one. But the door buzzed open.

The club was a one-bedroom apartment with two tables piled with poker chips. There was a large TV with a basketball game playing on mute, a counter with buckets of beer. Daniel gave his five hundred to a woman in a black suit and waited for a seat. The other players were all men, of different races and ages, and he was one of the best dressed. He approached a table, ready to play.

It was the deadest time of morning, before sunrise, when the street sweepers and garbage trucks had yet to emerge, and Daniel sat on a bench along the East River, wind blowing in an unsynced delay, hitting his face seconds after it rippled over his coat. At the beginning of the night, so many hours ago, when he left the restaurant, he'd had a hat, but lost it along the way. He'd lost the Carlough College essay as well, the one he had meant to deliver to Kay and Peter, though it was saved on his computer. He could e-mail it to them if he wanted.

He wanted breakfast, coffee, but was out of money. The men had been tougher than they looked. He'd known early on that he was in over his head, but kept playing despite their suppressed excitement. They thought he would lose so much he would break down, and they were waiting for the big show, his inevitable unraveling, but each loss felt like shucking off another weight and removing an uncomfortable article of clothing, so that by the end of the night he wasn't crying but grinning. When he left, he heard one guy say to the other, 'Wacko.'

He felt a savage euphoria. The night had confirmed his failures, and he'd freed himself from having to fight his inability to live up to Peter and Kay's hopes. He didn't want to go to Carlough, wasn't ever going to be the kind of guy Angel respected, some law-school-applying moral citizen. God, it was great to be himself again.

From his bench he could see winking lights on the water and make out flashes of ships as they moved toward the ocean. He heard the distant bellows of boats, purple, low and soothing, nautical mating calls. This was where he used to come with his mother, walking from the Rutgers Street apartment, and once she had told him that when she was a little girl, she had loved going to the river in Minjiang. 'We would watch how the waves went off into nothing and that was the place I wanted to go,' she said. 'Far, far away.' He never asked her who *we* was.

The sky pinkened at its edges, white clouds marbleizing into pastels, and the night broke into patches. Daniel's toes curled inside his boots. Well, she'd done it. She'd gone far away from him.

The sun tore the night into orange and yellow streaks. The river became blue and glassy. A wave of anger broke over him, and he wanted to talk to her, tell her how angry he was.

He dialed the number. The phone rang, but by the fifth ring he knew she wasn't going to answer and he relaxed. The woman on the recorded voice mail message didn't identify herself by name, but he recognized his mother immediately. Her voice was reedy and trumpety, yet her tones were clipped and plucked, a flawless-sounding Mandarin he didn't remember her having before.

He left a message with his name and number. If she didn't call him, it would be all the evidence he needed.

CHAPTER NINE

Daniel knew before they finished the first song that they would kill it, that he had arrived at the sweet spot when he was no longer conscious of being onstage. They had practiced plenty and he hadn't drunk tonight, but the secret was more than that, it was believing in it, even if the songs were crappy and over-wrought. At the end of the set he awoke to find himself onstage with Roland, covered in sweat, the room vibrating around him in sheets of violet and lavender, a roar of cheering and clapping.

When they returned to the floor, Daniel felt hands thump his back and shoulders. He heard voices he didn't recognize. 'Damn, you can play.' He followed Roland's head through the crowd, stopping every few feet to be complimented by someone else. Roland caught his eye and grinned. Daniel was a prizefighter, surrounded by his entourage after a landing a KO. He'd scored a comeback. He'd fucking showed them.

At the bar, waiting for Javier and his band to go on, Daniel recognized Hutch, the Jupiter booker, in a beige canvas coat and faded dad jeans. Someone else intercepted Roland, and Hutch said to Daniel, 'Didn't think you had it in you after the last time.'

'I'm full of surprises.'

'I like what you guys did with the sound. Maybe the vocals

and drums can be amped up even more. Push that distortion, up the reverb, you know.'

'We'll see. Thanks.'

Roland's friend Yasmin, of the theremin and melodica and strange, yowly songs, who always called him Darren or David, or one time, puzzlingly, Thomas, punched him in the arm and said, 'Daniel, great job.'

'First time you got it right,' he said, smiling.

People wanted to know what other bands he'd played in, how long he'd known Roland. One guy, whose pupils were so black and enlarged his eyes resembled marbles, told Daniel that Psychic Hearts sounded like pork chops. 'Hold on, my friend's here and I want to say hi,' Daniel said. 'I'll be back.' It felt good, being the one making the excuse to get away.

Within a week, everything changed. He and Roland lined up several more shows, and Hutch said he'd come to the one on May 15, at a space out in Gowanus, and that if things went well, he would keep them in mind for any openings later this year.

Summer was coming, the city delirious with warmth, the air damp and metallic, and Daniel's phone chirped incessantly with messages, what was going on that night, what had gone on last night, and even if the music he was playing was not the music he wanted to play, even if it meant he no longer had time to work on his own songs, at least he was playing something, going to shows and parties, charging drinks and car services to his credit card, wincing each time he swiped but telling himself he'd worry about it later, that right now, it was worth it to live a little. Because he had done it. He'd reached Peak Coolness. At a secret show in a Bushwick basement, watching a band who sang lyrics about animals written in this complicated sonnet-like poetry style, or drinking on a Sunday afternoon with Roland

and Javi and Nate while listening to a Lithuanian metal act, he would look around and think that this was no second-tier upstate wannabe party, this was the real deal, and it was only a matter of time before the life he had been waiting for would finally happen.

In the future, this would strike him as delusional. But lately, he was so rarely by himself he had no time to dwell on how he'd been ghosted by his own mother, or Peter and Kay, who also hadn't called – though he hadn't contacted them either – or Angel.

A writer from a music blog interviewed Psychic Hearts, e-mailing Roland a Q&A that he filled out and forwarded to Daniel.

Q: Roland, you're a veteran in the scene, having played in a number of different bands. What's it like working with Daniel? Do you both collaborate on songwriting and production?

ROLAND FUENTES (RF): Well, Daniel and I have been friends since sixth grade, so we've done some embarrassing projects together (I'll leave it to him to decide if he wants to talk more about our power punk days – LOL, straightedge 4-eva!) but the advantage of working with someone you've got such deep history with is that our communication onstage is practically second nature. It's like working with family. While I'm doing the songwriting and producing for Psychic Hearts, the songs also have DW written all over them – he does these insane key changes and melodies that are out of this world, and he doesn't even have to think about them, he *sees* them.

DANIEL WILKINSON (DW): Roland's a true visionary and a born front man. Anyone who's seen him onstage can vouch for that.

Q: The band's latest songs are more amped, more energetic
     than the earlier material. Has this shift in style been a
     deliberate one?

RF: It's been an organic decision to move in this newer direc-
     tion. It's what feels right for the project and it really plays
     to both our strengths.

Javier, who had an apartment full of cameras and video
equipment, took a picture of them on his rooftop at dusk, and
when the photo appeared alongside the interview, Daniel was
taken aback to see that Roland was in clear focus, while he
was in the shadows. Or was he being paranoid? At Tres Locos,
he passed his phone to Evan to show him the interview, who
agreed he did look out of focus. 'They're fucking you over,' Evan
said, 'and you should watch out.' That night, Daniel pulled the
link up on his laptop and looked at the picture more closely. A
dull, queasy feeling spread through him. He had often felt like
this that first year in Ridgeborough, and with Carla Moody,
whom he'd been with for a few months his freshman year at
Carlough, when he would wake up in the middle of the night
with her sleeping next to him and think, *You're only with her
because you don't want to be alone.* Most recently, he had felt it
last September, in the dorm room of a girl he'd been crushing
on for weeks – this was when he was still going to classes –
mouths moving together, skin buzzing from the weed they'd
just smoked. He saw her eyes move a little to the left, a quick
glance at the wall, and detected what he thought was her
waning interest. He got up and left.

When Roland came home, he said, 'You see the interview?'

Daniel looked at his friend's hopeful smile and closed his
laptop. He didn't want to be like Evan, yelling about being
fucked over. Psychic Hearts was blowing up. He and Roland

were on their way to something big. 'It's great. Great picture, too.'

Daniel sat with Thad and Roland on a rectangle of stained orange carpet, listening to the tracks they had recorded to tape. Thad ran a recording studio in the basement of a three-story house in Ridgewood, where he lived with ten other roommates. Daniel read the liner notes Roland had written for the cassette and saw the sentence: *All songs written by Roland Fuentes*.

'Listen.' Thad rewound. 'I like that.'

Roland nodded. 'That glitchy sound.'

The wall, a patchwork of plywood sheets, was lined with posters for performances by sound artists and video jockeys, bicycle repair workshops, an anti-gentrification rally in a nearby park. Tall shelves were crammed with mikes and amps, drums of all sizes, cratefuls of scavenged instruments – a dented trumpet, a silver harmonica, a plastic flute. A piano sat next to a TASCAM four-track and an Apple monitor with a screensaver of salamanders morphing into monkeys. While they recorded, a drummer visiting from Berlin napped on a couch by the piano, waking up periodically to smoke. 'It's good,' he said, when Daniel suggested that a recording studio might not be the best place to sleep. 'I've got the jet lag.'

Daniel put the liner notes down. A tangle of cables lay next to cardboard boxes full of cassettes by other Meloncholia Records bands. Later, when the only evidence of him having been in here was the Psychic Hearts demo, the cassettes would be filed away into one of these boxes, *All songs written by Roland Fuentes*.

'I'd like to bring in a fuller, more layered sound,' Roland was saying. 'Maybe even a drummer, another guitarist.'

Thad said, 'I can totally see that. Heavier, more guitar harmonies.'

Roland turned to Daniel. 'What do you think?'

Daniel picked at a callus on his index finger. He stared at the posters and imagined his mother watching an experimental noise artist manipulating sounds on a laptop, a what-the-fuck expression on her face. Why was he even thinking about her?

'Cool.' He was having trouble mustering up enthusiasm to match Roland and Thad's. Their friends read books about gentrification and food justice and spoke about the importance of *community outreach* and *safe spaces*, yet they were all college students or unpaid interns funded with credit cards paid for by their parents, and none of them had even grown up in the city. Thad's roommate Sophie, who had turquoise dreadlocks and cooked meals from ingredients scavenged from dumpsters, asked Daniel if he was familiar with socialist food models since he'd been born in China, and he told her he was born in Manhattan. Thad had said, 'It's dope that you left school and rejected your parents' boners for academia. It's such a scam, college, being a professor, all of that.' Uncomfortable at hearing someone else talk smack about his parents, Daniel asked, 'How'd you know they're professors?' Thad said, 'Roland told me.' Roland had told Daniel that Thad funded Meloncholia with the monthly allowance his parents gave him. 'I hear your dad's a hedge fund manager,' Daniel said. 'Yeah,' Thad said, 'he fucking sucks.' Daniel envied people who could take their origins for granted, who could decide to hate their parents.

Another roommate knocked on the door, shouting that there had been an explosion in the kitchen, a food processor malfunction. They were making pesto for Sophie's cooking podcast, and this guy's hand was bleeding all over the place. Did Thad know where the first aid kit was?

Thad stood, dusting off his jeans. 'I'll be back.'

'What do you think about the tracks?' Roland said to Daniel.

Daniel bit into the callus and tore off a piece of dead skin. 'Good, I guess.' He looked at the posters again. In high school, stoned at this party in Cody Campbell's barn, he had thought he was seeing bats, freaked out until Cody had to tell him that those weren't bats he was seeing up there on the ledge, but shadows of gardening tools. 'Chill-ll,' Cody had said. It was funny, ridiculous, the thought of barns and bats and Cody Campbell in this random basement in Queens.

'Hey, remember Cody Campbell?'

'What, that fat douche?'

He chewed on the piece of skin. 'I don't know if I can do this.'

'Of course you can. The past shows have been perfect. That first one was just a fluke.'

'I don't mean shows.'

But how could Roland understand? In Ridgeborough, Roland's last name and light brown skin had made him suspicious, but he was clearly a Lisio, too; he and his mother had the same pointy faces and thin, dark hair. Playing shows in towns where people didn't know them, there'd been a few guys who had heckled Roland in fake, singsong Spanish – the same sort of guys who'd throw *Konichi-waah!* at Daniel – and then there was the time a cop had pulled them over on the highway outside Ridgeborough, ticketed them for speeding, bogus charges as the old mail truck Roland drove could barely hit the speed limit. The cop had given Roland a sobriety test even though he and Daniel were sober, Daniel terrified in the passenger seat, noting the fear in Roland's back as he stood on the highway with his hands behind his head, the cop saying something about drunk Mexicans. When they were free to go, Roland had driven straight to Ridgeborough, and it was one of the only times Daniel had seen his friend at a loss for words. When Roland finally did speak, he said, 'We have to get the fuck out of here.' And Roland had, and so had he.

Still, Roland had never spoken any language other than English, never had any other name but his own, had known his whole life who his mother was and where she could be found. What had set him apart in Ridgeborough – the dead Latino father, the widowed white mom – Roland had used to his advantage. Looked as different as he could. Dressed like a freak, invited people's stares, ate it up.

'Were you taking me and Thad seriously? I was talking out of my ass. Thad's always talking out of his ass. We don't have to bring in more vocals or anything you don't want.'

'I'm not sure if this is the direction I want my music to be going in. I don't want it to be more layered.'

'So what do you want?' A sharper tone slipped into Roland's voice. 'This is a collaboration.'

'It doesn't feel like it. This is the sound you want to make, to please Hutch. You write all the songs.'

'You're more than welcome to write a song.'

Daniel was so mad, his leg was twitching. 'All you care about is being cool, people liking you.'

Roland looked stunned, like the time they were walking through Washington Square Park and a pigeon had shat on his shoulder. 'Like you don't care about that? Come on. I was trying to help you out.'

'Help me?'

'I could've found anyone to play in the band. Like there aren't any good guitarists in the city? But you needed a reason to leave upstate.'

Daniel pushed an empty coffee cup with his foot. 'I'm not your charity project.'

'Everyone likes you but you,' Roland said. 'You know how many times I've sung onstage? Every single time I get nervous. One time, I puked in the bathroom before sound check.'

Roland's chin bobbed as he talked, a vestigial trait from childhood, and Daniel had a flash of lost affection for the young Ridgeborough Roland. He couldn't bail on his closest friend.

'So we'll play with Yasmin on May 1, think of it as a warm-up, and then the big show on May 15, the one Hutch will be at. Two weeks to get it all ready.'

'Wait,' Daniel said, 'what day is it?'

'Monday.'

'I mean, today's date.' He looked at his phone. April 27. There was a missed call from an hour ago, from the person he'd been thinking of. 'Hold on, I'll be back.'

He wandered through a maze of hallways, past the kitchen, where he caught a glimpse of a countertop splattered with pesto and blood, Sophie and Thad bandaging a guy's hand, and found a door that opened onto a gravel lot. The night was cool, a slice of moon shining over the building's plastic siding. He unlocked his phone and called the number labeled 'Mom and Dad'.

He was glad it was Kay who answered and not Peter. 'Mom,' he said. 'Happy birthday.'

'I called you earlier, I didn't leave a message.'

'I know, I saw it on my phone.'

'Your father doesn't know a thing about this, and I'm not about to tell him, but I spoke to the dean at Carlough and she's willing to set up a meeting with you. You could still get in for the fall.'

'Wait—'

'She said to see her in two weeks, the Friday after next. May 15. You need to be up here by that afternoon.'

'I don't know – how's Dad? What are you doing for your birthday? Did he make you a treasure hunt?'

'We're fine. We did the treasure hunt this morning. The first clue came in the mail, he put it in an envelope that looked like a bill! Then he had me walking down the street to find a clue in the Lawtons' tulips. Now he's cooking me dinner.'

'Tell him I didn't mean it, with the essay.'

He heard Peter's voice yell, 'Honey?' and Kay said she had to go.

May 1, two weeks before the big show, Psychic Hearts played a few songs in an outdoor lot under the Brooklyn–Queens Expressway, opening for Yasmin. Daniel had invited Michael, and he came up afterwards and shouted, 'That was amazing.' Roland, Nate, and Javier looked over; Daniel had never had a friend appear at a show before.

He introduced Michael as his cousin, and Michael held his hand out to be shaken. Roland took it, while Nate and Javier nodded, then resumed talking.

'Your band rocked,' Michael said.

'Thanks for coming,' Daniel said.

Michael looked at Roland. 'How do you two know each other?'

Roland raised his eyebrows. 'We grew up together? Daniel's like my oldest friend.'

'We grew up together, too,' Michael said. 'We lived together in the Bronx.'

'You lived in the Bronx?'

'For a few years,' Daniel said.

'And your moms – your birth mom – they were sisters?'

'Something like that. Close enough.'

'Did you speak to her?' Michael asked.

'I left her a message, but I haven't heard back yet.'

'Hold up,' Roland said, 'you called your mom?'

'I got her phone number from Leon. Michael's uncle.'

'It could've been the wrong number,' Michael said. 'It was an old number.'

'It was her voice mail. I recognized her voice.'

'Then fuck it,' Roland said.

Michael's mouth hung open. 'Excuse me?'

'Sorry, I know it's your birth mom and all, but if she doesn't want to talk to you, it's her loss. I told you, if you called you'd regret it.'

'You told him not to call his own mother?'

Roland brushed his hair back with his palm. 'She's not his mother.'

Daniel said, 'She is my mother.'

'She didn't raise you. I mean, I never knew my dad, and whatever, you know?'

'I never knew my dad either,' Michael said. 'But Deming, I mean Daniel, he knew his mom really well.'

'Okay, do what you want then,' Roland said.

Michael's face flushed. 'Of course he will.'

Daniel said, 'Well, Kay's my mom, too.' He wished he could be cool; he wanted to not care. But instead he was like Michael; obvious, transparent. He asked Michael if he wanted to join them at a bar nearby, and when Michael said no, he had an early class tomorrow, Daniel felt relieved.

'It was good to finally see you in action, though,' Michael said. 'Seriously, you guys rocked. You were like a harder Maroon 5.' As he walked away, he said, 'Nice to meet you, Roland.'

'You, too,' Roland said.

As Michael turned the corner, Nate and Javier began to laugh. 'Did he say *Maroon 5*?' Nate snorted. 'Hey, Roland, does that make you Adam Levine?'

'Shut up, Nate,' Daniel said.

At Potsdam, he was never satisfied at parties, always thought he should be somewhere cooler, more exciting, with friends who were cooler and more exciting. Now he was surrounded by people who were supposed to be cool, yet that elusive sense of self-satisfaction and contentment – *love?* – hadn't materialized.

He went home by himself after the show, leaving Roland at the bar with his friends. Ever since he'd proved he could play, Nate had done a one-eighty with him, never forgetting his name, listening when he spoke. But Daniel didn't want to hang with people who were pretending to be his friend only when it seemed socially advantageous, who iced out Michael like they'd done to him two months ago. He was Roland's charity project and the guy in the background in Javi's photo, but Michael had always been loyal.

Maybe his mother had been busy, or traveling in a place that didn't have cell phone access, or she'd lost her phone or broke it and was in the process of getting a new one. Maybe his Chinese was so bad she hadn't been able to recognize it was him, even if he'd said his name and repeated his phone number twice. Maybe his tones had soured from disuse, and the words he believed sounded passable to the fruit and vegetable vendors were actually babble, non-language, guttural ranting. Or she was pretending to not understand him.

He needed to know. He dialed the country code and the numbers. There was a soft click and a ringing that sounded far away. Daniel paced Roland's living room and waited for her voice mail message to kick up.

He heard another click.

'Hello?' she said. 'Deming?'

'Hello?' he said in Fuzhounese.

'Hello?'

'It's me – Deming.'

'Hello, Deming. I'm glad you called again.'

Hearing her voice made his breath catch. 'Hello, Mama.'

'It's you. You sound like an adult.'

Now that he was talking to her, he didn't know what to say. She said, 'Are you okay?'

'I'm good.' The accusations he'd been poised to let loose remained stuck at the back of his throat. He sat on the couch, on top of his dirty laundry. Here he was, making small talk with his estranged mother. 'I'm living in New York City, in Manhattan, not that far from where we used to live.'

'You're twenty-one now.' Why was she whispering? 'Are you working? In school?'

'Both. In university. I have a job in a restaurant. I also play the guitar with my friend, in a band.'

'You always liked music.'

'How are you, Mama?' Each time he said the word, he got afraid. She'd change her mind; hang up on him. He removed a sock wedged between the cushions and flung it across the room. He wanted to ask why she hadn't called him back but didn't want to scare her away.

'I'm good. I live in Fuzhou, in an apartment by West Lake Park. I'm married. My husband has his own textile factory. I'm the assistant director of an English school.'

My life is perfect. That's what she was saying. Daniel switched to English. 'How did your English get so good?'

'I practiced,' she said in English, and her accent was so thick he wasn't convinced. She switched back to Fuzhounese. 'How did you get my phone number?'

'I spoke to Leon.'

'Ah.'

'He said he hadn't spoken to you in seven years.'

'Yes, it's been a long time. We were in touch before, but it's hard now. Work is busy, you know.'

Daniel walked to the window, returned to the couch. 'I found Leon because I saw Vivian. Through Michael. He found my e-mail address, which wasn't easy, because I don't go by Deming anymore. I go by Daniel Wilkinson.'

'*Daniel Wilkinson?*'

'My parents gave that name to me.'

There was a short silence. 'So you saw Michael.'

'I had dinner with him and Vivian. He told me she had gone to court as my guardian and given me away to a foster family.'

A longer silence ensued.

'Hello?' He should end the call. This had been a mistake.

'That bitch,' his mother said, but her words were too measured and quiet, lacking the fire he remembered. 'How could she do that?'

He wished he could see her face, wanted to be able to place her in a room. 'Mama?'

'Yes?'

'What do you see right now?'

'I'm in my apartment, in our office room. I see curtains, a desk. We're on the twelfth floor. If I look out my window, I see other buildings. Fuzhou is a big city these days, like New York. What do you see, Deming?'

'Some shelves. My computer, my clothes, my guitar. There's a window, but it faces another building.'

She asked if he remembered riding the subway, and he mentioned the time they had met their doppelgängers. In Ridgeborough, when Deming Guo was no longer a name that was said aloud, he used to picture the Other Deming and Other Mama, still living in Queens. It was a sort of comfort, bittersweet; at least *they'd* remained together.

'I have to go,' she suddenly whispered. 'I'll call you tomorrow.'

*

She called him the next day, Wednesday evening in New York, Thursday morning in Fuzhou. He was at work, didn't see the message until later. 'Hello, Deming,' she said. 'I wanted to say hello, but you're probably at school. Don't call me, we need to set up a time to talk in advance. But I'll call you again tomorrow.'

All next day he kept his ringer on high, but she didn't call. After work, he called and left her another message, asking her when they could talk next.

He went back to the apartment, ate takeout enchiladas from Tres Locos, and tried to work on a song, deciding against going out. He hadn't touched his own music in weeks. If he made himself unavailable, she would call, like bringing an umbrella for insurance against the rain. He took a long shower, changed into sweatpants, folded his clothes, did the dishes crusting away in the sink. Finally, he looked at his phone. She'd called, left him a message suggesting five thirty Friday morning, New York time. That night he slept well for the first time all week.

The next morning, he was ready. He got up earlier than he ever did, bought a cup of coffee and a bagel at a deli on Sixth Avenue, then sat at the kitchen table and dialed.

At first it was the wrong number and the call didn't go through. Panicked, he double-checked, dialed again.

She picked up. 'Deming?'

'Is this a good time?'

'Yes, my husband is out. I'm on our balcony right now.'

He'd made a list of things he wanted to ask. 'Remember the time you pushed me off a swing?'

'What made you think of that?'

'I just remembered it.'

'I never pushed you off a swing. You fell off. I remember when I asked the school to put you with another teacher. They wanted to move you to a remedial class.'

That had been Kay, wanting to put him in a higher grade. 'I don't remember that.'

'At P.S. 63. I even remember the principal. Spanish lady with lots of hair. You were having trouble, and I didn't want you to be in that class anymore. I got you transferred to Michael's class. He was in an advanced class, so it had kids from your grade in it, too.'

'It was P.S. 33, not 63.' Daniel put his elbows on the table and saw the outline of the principal's face, a memory of walking to her office with his mother, how strange it had been to see her in the hallway of his school, how relieved he'd been to sit next to Michael in another classroom. He saw another scene: his mother yelling at a woman. In the memory the other woman's son had made fun of his clothes or his lack of English and he had cried – yes, he saw it clearly now, Deming crying in the park and Mama running to him – and when the other mother defended her own son, said he'd done nothing wrong, Mama had let her have it, spitting in Fuzhounese. Fighting for him, being on his side. 'Damn,' he said in English. 'Tell me something else I should know.'

'When I came to New York, I was already pregnant with you. I had fifty thousand dollars in debt.'

'You were pregnant when you came here? Who was my father?'

'A boy in the village. My next-door neighbor.'

He waited for her to say more. As she told him about how she came to New York, he finished the bagel, chewing quietly, and the rest of his coffee. Then he told her he had grown up in a town called Ridgeborough, that his adoptive parents were named Peter and Kay, and he was taking a break from school.

The sun was coming up. Before she could end the call, he said, 'If you found Leon, why didn't you try to find me?'

'I did try.' She sounded hurt. 'I looked for years, even. Leon didn't know where you had gone. I was saving money to come back to New York. Even if it cost me sixty thousand dollars, I was planning on coming to find you. Even if the first thing they did when I got there was throw my ass in jail. When I heard from Leon that you'd been adopted I wanted to jump off a bridge.'

Her words retreated into a small, strangled space. Daniel's mind was a jumble of names and motives. It was Leon's fault they'd been torn apart, Vivian who had given him away. He stood against the counter, brushed crumbs onto the floor.

'But you're okay?' A hopeful note crept into her voice.

Daniel walked back to the living room. To acknowledge his mother's regret meant he had to think of what her leaving had done to him, the nights he'd woken up in Ridgeborough in such grief it felt like his lungs were seizing. Months, years, had passed like this, until he became adept at convincing himself it didn't matter.

'That doesn't excuse you going away,' he said. 'You have no idea what happened to me. You can't pretend you didn't mess up, that you did nothing wrong.'

Roland came out his bedroom. 'What's going on?'

'Nothing. Go back to sleep.'

'Everything all right?'

'Yeah.'

'Deming?' his mother said. 'You still there?'

Daniel waited until Roland returned to his room and closed the door. 'Yes.'

'There are so many things you don't understand,' she said. 'Ask Leon, you said you spoke to him, so why don't you ask him?'

He was silent. He heard his mother say, 'Yes, I'm in here.' She spoke in a loud, cheery manner, and he heard a man's voice in the background.

She whispered, 'My husband is home. I have to get off the phone. I'll call you.'

CALL ENDED, the screen said.

Daniel poured himself a glass of water and drank it in several gulps, then washed his face in the sink. As the cold water ran down his neck, he realized her husband didn't know about him, that she pretended he didn't exist.

CHAPTER TEN

Central Park was covered in a thick matting of leaves, and the smoky smell of October made me think of running through the temple courtyard with Fang and Liling. You were running around the village like that now. I flipped through an English-language newspaper a woman in an orange apron had given me in the subway. Couldn't read the articles, but I could make up stories. I didn't often feel self-conscious about being out by myself, but today I wanted you to be there with me, needed someone to play witness to my life.

Five years had passed since I sent you to Yi Ba and the pain of missing you had faded, become amorphous; it was like missing a person I no longer knew. After you left, Didi returned to her bed, and when another roommate moved out I was promoted to my own, the sleeping bag on the floor going to the next new woman that arrived. Now I had a top bunk. Most of the women I'd lived with when I first came had left for other apartments, even other cities. Didi spent a couple nights a week at her boyfriend Quan's apartment, but she and I remained on Rutgers Street, instructed the new arrivals on how to buy subway cards, where to get the best produce, which stores were rip-offs. I recognized the fear in these newcomers' faces, watched them absorb my recommendations with grave intention. They said I was brave; they were awestruck when I told them how long I'd been in the city. 'You'll get used to it,' I said. 'It gets easier.'

A few roommates had saved enough to buy into marriages of convenience. Didi and I went to City Hall for our friend Cindy's wedding to a gray-haired white man. 'I can introduce you to the woman I worked with,' Cindy said. 'Professional Chinese lady.'

'I don't want to sleep with a hairy American,' I said, then wanted to take it back, because that's what Cindy had to do.

'You can get a Chinese man who has citizenship. And you don't have to stay married,' Cindy said, 'only long enough for it to work. You don't even have to sleep with him if you don't want to. It's stupid to marry a guy without papers. It's a wasted opportunity. The way you're going, it's going to take a long, long time to get your green card.'

'If ever,' Didi added.

Since you'd left, I'd been working twelve-hour shifts. Sewed more hems than anyone else. On the wall next to my bunk, I taped a piece of paper with two columns, one with the amount I owed, the other with what I'd paid off, the numbers so small I could only see them when I was lying down, and slowly, the number in the first column decreased and the number in the second column increased. But with the months I hadn't worked after you were born and the money I sent to Yi Ba, it was taking longer than I expected. By the time you were five, I had paid off a little more than half the debt. More than twenty thousand remained.

I called you once a week. At first, Yi Ba would hold the phone to your face and ask you to say hello, and I would talk as you made gibberish sounds. Later, you were able to speak to me, and each time I called, your voice would sound fuller and you would know words you hadn't before.

'Are you listening to your Yi Gong?' I'd ask.

'Yes.'

'What did you do today?'

'Fed the chicken.'

'Do you remember New York?'

'No.'

You turned four, then five, old enough to go to school in New York, but Yi Ba made excuses. 'Why not wait until your debt is paid so you can have more time for him,' he said. 'Wait until you have enough saved to get your own place. He shouldn't be living with all those women. And you need to get a better-paying job, with better hours. Who will look after him when you're at work?' But Yi Ba had softened with his grandson. I'd told him that I'd met your father in New York, though your passport had your birthdate and anyone could do the math. Yi Ba hadn't demanded details, only accepted the money I wired. For Deming, he said. He told me you had grown three centimeters in a month, that you liked to sing along to music on the radio, had nicknamed the current chicken Feety. I was glad he treated you well; it made me feel less bad about sending you away.

He kept me up to date with village news, which we both claimed to not care about but I always looked forward to hearing. Haifeng was engaged to a woman from Xiamen, who his mother said was from a good family. I was happy for him, for landing a city woman, as well as for myself. I had escaped.

Visiting his parents on New Year's, Haifeng had seen you – you were too young to remember – and asked Yi Ba for my phone number. He called me several times, but I never called him back. But maybe I should have let him meet you; it might have made things easier.

It wasn't even noon yet, I had the day ahead of me, but I could no longer feel as good as I had when I left Rutgers Street for

Central Park this morning, wrapped up in a long gray coat Cindy had given me. When I wore the coat over my jeans and sweatshirt, I'd walk a little taller, blend into the crowds on Canal.

I took out my phone and called Yi Ba. It was past eleven at night there, too late to be calling, but I wanted to hear your voice. The phone rang for such a long time I thought I had dialed the wrong number. When someone answered, it was neither you nor Yi Ba, but a woman who sounded familiar. 'This is Peilan,' I said. 'Who is this?'

'Peilan,' the voice said. 'It's Mrs Li. Haifeng's mother.'

'What are you doing there?'

'I need to tell you. Your father died. He had a heart attack last night. I didn't know how to reach you and I was hoping you would call.'

A high-pitched ringing churned in my ears, like a train squealing to a sudden stop. 'No.' My voice sounded strange, but I refused to let it waver while talking to Mrs Li. 'I spoke to him on Sunday.'

'I'm sorry. It was quick. I don't think he was in much pain.' The ringing intensified. 'Deming has been staying with us. I ran over to your house as soon as I heard the phone inside. Will you be able to send him to America soon?'

Somehow, I was able to inquire about the funeral, which my relatives would arrange and which I could not afford to attend, and to walk to the subway and back to the apartment, where later Didi found me in my bunk with the newspaper spread over my face. My father and I had been apart for so long he only existed on the telephone, but I'd always hoped we would see each other again.

I cried into my sleeves when walking down the street, tried to sniff the tears away at work, and when I couldn't hold them back I let them drip, let my nose run onto the sewing machine.

I thought of how, when I returned to the village after working in Fuzhou, one of the neighbor women had pulled me aside and said, 'Your father is proud of you.'

I called Mrs Li every night so I could speak to you, to make sure you were still there. I cried for weeks, lay in bed on my days off. Mrs Li called and said one of Yi Ba's cousins was able to get a loan due to having a relative in America – I was the relative – and apply for a tourist visa. He agreed to take you with him on the flight to New York, as long as I bought the tickets.

Three weeks before you came back, six weeks after Yi Ba died, I went to a party at Quan's apartment. The men played cards while the women talked and watched TV.

I saw a man in the corner tip a bottle of beer to his mouth. Built like a block, he leaned back, mouth curled up at the ends, like he was daring me to come to him. He noticed me looking and unpeeled a large, open smile. There was a gap between his two front teeth, wide enough to slip a watermelon seed inside.

'You don't play cards?' He shuffled the deck in his wide hands. His Fuzhounese had retained the rural tones I'd been trying hard to sand down.

'No money for cards,' I said. A commercial blared on the TV, a deep voice narrating as a sports car looped the sharp curves of a mountain.

'You don't have to play for money.' He cracked a peanut shell in his mouth. 'We can play for peanuts.'

'I don't like losing.'

'Then you won't lose,' he said. 'Then you'll always win.'

I picked up a peanut and snapped it in half. 'So when did you come over?'

'Nine years now.' He cut the deck. 'You?'

'Six.'

He said the name of his village, which wasn't far from Minjiang. 'Better to be the one who leaves than the one who's left behind.'

'You think?' I saw the man's secret smile, his weighty brow, the eyes that tugged down at the corners, and wanted to unlock him. He was familiar to me, but nothing like Haifeng; he looked like if you got to know him, there might be something there. 'Working our asses off in America? Maybe it's better to be home, fat and happy in a brand new house.'

'And daydream of being here? You wouldn't stay there,' he said.

I smiled. He was right.

His name was Leon, and he worked nights at a slaughterhouse in the Bronx. It was demanding work, slicing and cutting cows and pigs, evidenced by his thick arms and shoulders, which I snuck a feel of when we kissed on the corner after leaving Quan's. When I opened my lips it was like being unraveled.

Sometimes, when I saw good-looking men on the street, I wanted to ask if they would take me home. Once I trailed a man for five blocks, admiring how he walked with his crotch pointed forward like a dare, moving with purpose while keeping his hips loose. Stopped when he stopped, stayed steps behind him, checked out his butt while he waited for the light. What if he didn't speak Fuzhounese, only Cantonese or another dialect I didn't know? He could be an American-born Chinese, or worse, he might laugh, shout that this crazy woman was propositioning him. I watched him walk off, my breath rushing out of me.

My third year in America, I slept with a guy from Anhui province a few times. He drove a produce truck and had a wife in his village, and I was relieved when he said she was coming to New York. Until Leon, abstinence was another sacrifice I could pride myself on: Look at all I've done. Look at all I've given up. But when Leon traced the star-shaped mole on my neck as we stood on the frosty little street outside Quan's apartment, beneath the fire escapes and perilous icicles, when he called me Little Star, there was a tug inside me in a place I had overlooked, like remembering a long-forgotten memory. Oh, that. How could I have forgotten that? Leon's mouth tasted like beer and peanuts. Leon's tongue nudged up against mine. There was a hard twist inside me, a knot of years loosened. This wasn't the village. A woman could kiss a man she just met, kiss him on the street in front of strangers, and nobody would care.

In three weeks, you were coming home to me. Because I had lived in the apartment for so long, my roommates said it would be fine if you stayed there, as long as I agreed to pay extra rent, though not as much as a new roommate would pay, since you'd be sharing my bed.

'We'll move out soon, to a bigger place,' I told them, though I didn't know how.

I mapped out the best route to the school on Henry Street and rearranged my hours at the factory. I was scared of being Mama again, having to care for a walking, talking, six-year-old boy that I didn't even know. I remembered how hard it was to be responsible for another person, how some days were like choking. What if I had forgotten how to be with you, or screwed you up by sending you away?

The day after I met Leon, he called to see when I was free. I told him my son was coming to New York next month. I didn't have to tell him, but I did.

'What's his name? How old is he?'

I told him you had turned six last month, that I hadn't seen you for five years.

Leon said, 'I can't wait to meet him.'

*

A cousin I'd never met before delivered you to me on a January evening. I patted your shoulders, but your arms remained at your sides. Your face was longer, your body meatier. 'Big boy,' I said, and you jutted your lower lip out at me. Fat clung to your face. You wore a green sweatshirt with an iron-on decal of a soccer ball, passed down from a neighbor or one of the other children on 3 Alley. Your hair stuck up in stubborn quills, like you had forced them out of your skin. Who had cut this hair?

Last Saturday, Leon's hands had pressed down on my hips. His sister, whom he lived with, had taken her own son to visit a friend, so we were alone and could make all the noise we wanted. He pushed into me with his eyes closed, and as I moved against him they opened. He said my name, I said his, and then everything was spinning and sliding. 'Say my name again,' I demanded, and he did and I laughed. This novelty, my hand on a new man's back. Such a nice, muscled back. Over five years in New York and this was the first time I hadn't been surrounded by people, just me and one other person in an apartment by ourselves, and afterwards I leaned against the sink in Leon's bathroom and cried, not only because of the sex and the beautiful man, but because of how good it felt to not hear sewing machines or honking cars or my roommates sniping at one another. *Savor this moment*, I told myself, *you may never get it again*.

'Deming,' my cousin said, 'you don't remember your mother?'

'Of course he remembers me. How could he forget?'

Three new roommates watched us across the room. One of them clicked her tongue and said, 'He forgot his own mother!'

'He's tired after such a long flight. It's not easy for a child to travel so far.' I reached for you again, but you turned and ran through the kitchen, and I raced after you and scooped you from behind, pressing my face to the back of your neck. You smelled stale, like old sweat, and at last you sagged against me.

My cousin was off to DC, where a dishwashing job awaited him. He didn't look that strong, with skinny arms and bad posture, so I slipped him some cash, hoped it would help him. He left, and I showed you the bathroom, gave you a toothbrush and a towel, and after you washed up you fell asleep without a word. I sat next to you hugging my knees and recalling your baby shape and squishy legs, all replaced by this much larger child. I didn't know if Leon would see me again, or if last Saturday would be our first and only time. I tried to concentrate on you, this boy who'd been gone so long he had no memory of my face. Leon liked my face. I should have been thinking about you, only you, but I thought, again, of Leon's hands, and my resolve to not think of Leon retracted like the electric cord on the vacuum cleaner, whipping into its hiding spot.

In the morning I made soup, alone in the apartment with you, and you glugged your food without talking, looking at the kitchen walls and plastic bags stuffed into plastic bags, the grease-splattered square of tin foil taped over the burners. 'Eat more,' I said. 'You don't remember when I used to feed you?' It was a dumb thing to say; I knew you couldn't remember, and I hated when adults spoke to children like they were idiots.

You shook your head. 'Soda?'

'You want soda?'

'Yi Gong gave me soda.'

So that was what he'd done with the money I sent him. 'No soda here.'

You crossed your arms, challenging me. The fat on your face jiggled and I could sense the heat coming off your skin.

'Talk to your mama.'

'No.'

'What did you say?'

'*No.*'

I'd sewed thousands of shirt hems to bring you here. 'Ungrateful brat.'

You got up and walked to the bedroom, pointed to a hump of laundry. 'Dirty,' you said.

'Listen to me. I'm your mother and this is your home. You were born here. You should be grateful I took you out of the village.' I shook your shoulders. 'Now wash up. We're going outside.'

You sulked, but went into the bathroom, and soon I heard the water running.

Snow had fallen overnight. Today it was fresh, sparkling in the sun, and you were hushed by the sight. Rutgers Street was bright and crisp, the kind of cold that went right up your nose. But it would soon morph into a muddy slush that melted into sad mounds dotted with dog poo. Around the corner were the hulking buildings that marched down to the river. We crossed over Bowery, making soft tracks. The city had unbuttoned itself and people walked slower, taking their time, and on Canal the cars were cowed by snow. The drivers steered hesitantly around corners, and at stoplights they didn't race to beat pedestrians. They sprayed slush, drifting, indecisive. I would teach you to love the city like I did.

We passed Elizabeth Street, Mulberry, Mott. Our steps were exaggerated and high, as if the snow had gummed our shoes. At a stall on Canal, I bought you a blue winter coat, haggled for a red hat and let you pick out a pair of boots with fuzzy lining.

Broadway. Sixth Avenue. 'Watch.' I took a deep breath and exhaled, creating clouds of frost. You seemed impressed. I took another breath and you took one of your own, blowing in the cold. We descended the stairs to the subway, I swiped my card twice, and when the train arrived you took the seat by the window, bobbing back and forth as you watched the tunnel stretch out, counting off the stops as we rode uptown, one-four, three-four, four-two, five-nine. At 125th Street the train would burst above ground, tearing straight into the sunlight, and I couldn't wait to see your face.

The nail salon where Didi worked was hiring. 'Don't sleep on this, Polly, or you'll be working at that factory until you're an old lady,' she said. She brought home old bottles of polish and I practiced on our roommates, so when I went to Hello Gorgeous to meet Rocky, the manager, I knew exactly what to do.

I gave Rocky a mani-pedi and got the job. Twenty-five hours a week to start, no pay until the three-month training period ended, though I could keep my tips. Took out a loan to cover rent, food, the black pants and shirts I had to wear, the fees Rocky charged for training, though the training itself consisted of watching my co-workers and cleaning up after them. But it was different from sewing, and there was the promise of more money.

To celebrate, I bought you a set of Legos and helped you construct the plastic pieces into a spaceship, which you held up in the air as you ran around the room. 'Crash landing!' you shouted, plunging the spaceship into a pillow. 'Boom!'

I rescued the spaceship and waved my arms over it, mimicking the sound of hammers and drills. 'They've made repairs. It's ready to fly again.'

'I want a tiger,' you said.

'A tiger?'

Getting to know you was strange. You wanted video games, but I bought you a box of crayons, which you pressed on so hard they broke in two. And now, a tiger. I watched you run around the room, the spaceship swooping and soaring. We had come into a large clearing. It no longer seemed we would never leave this apartment. I wished I could call Yi Ba and tell him.

As you filled out into a new person, so did I, and I tucked the years without you away as another triumph, another thing I'd survived; saved Leon's voice mails and replayed them on breaks, his messages brief and to the point, each word I coaxed out of him a victory or a challenge. *Leaving for work soon. Call me tomorrow. I'll be home by eight.* The same went for you. Victory when you ran to join your classmates before school and brought home drawings, when we took the train and I watched you call off the stops. At the playground, you were the first kid in your class to do a flip on the metal bars, the one who made the highest, most daring leaps between benches.

Didi called you Little Piglet, listened when you told the same stories for the five-hundredth time, indulged you in your favorite game, the excruciating one where you'd snatch your hand away whenever I tried to high-five it. 'Fooled you!' you'd say. 'Watch me again!' If I yawned or looked away, even for a moment, you would screech, 'Keep your eyes open, Mama, you have to keep them open!' But Didi could sit with you forever, unflagging in her response each time you took your hand away. 'Wow!' she'd cry. 'Little Piglet, you sure fooled me. Okay, let's try again, I'll high-five you – oh, wow, you tricked me again!' As I watched you and her, I would hear Yi Ba saying I was selfish and spoiled. Perhaps there was something wrong with me because I didn't have an infinite amount of patience for children's games. Remorse, dormant and persistent, flapped up. I'd abandoned my father; I hadn't mourned him enough.

Leon came to Chinatown from the Bronx, took us out to lunch on a street near the Manhattan Bridge. The cook knew him from his ship loading days back home, and the customers hunched over round metal tables that faced windows beaded with salty broth, steam eking onto the sidewalk. Three noodle shops on one short block, sweating and striving beneath the bridge's tail, each shop with its own specialty, beef broth, chicken broth, pork broth, lamb. Here there was only one dish, noodle soup with lamb.

'*Sst*,' Leon said, and a man in an apron stood up from behind the counter, dough stretched between his arms. Leon held up three fingers and pulled out stools. Spilled soup splashed our toes. The waitress set our bowls down with plastic cups of tea, wiping the liquid on the table with a dishcloth, and we slurped, sucking soft chunks of meat between our teeth. Chewy and thick, the noodles were perfect; the soup tasted like a favorite memory. Your face shone with pleasure. Leon burped and put down money for the meal.

'Where are we going now?' you asked.

Leon looked at his phone and calculated the time left before his shift. 'You like boats?'

'Yi Gong used to have a boat,' you said. 'Are we going fishing? Yi Gong used to fish.'

'You don't want to eat the fish in this river,' Leon said. 'The fish here comes out with two heads.'

The snow was melting, its surviving remnants peppered with dirt beneath icy top crusts. 'To the bottom of Manhattan,' Leon shouted. It was the Staten Island Ferry, a bright orange boat braying a hippopotamus honk. We stood on the deck as it shambled through the water, me with my arms around you, Leon with his arms around me.

Leon had been in America for nine years and his English still sucked. But the fees had been lower when he came over, so he had already paid off his debt. I kept asking myself if I should go for a guy who could get me a green card, or find one who liked to read newspapers and could help improve my English. It drove me crazy that Leon spat on the sidewalk, pushed onto subways as people were trying to get off, cut lines for cash registers like he was still in Fuzhou. But the way he strung his curses together in dialect, quick like running water, his striking familiarity, made me laugh and join in. He listened to me complain about work, and even if he didn't have a lot of money, he bought me food, spent time with you. I saw how happy he made you. We walked around Central Park, Battery Park, Madison Square, and he liked seeing trees and water, had also grown up around fishermen and farmers. Yi Ba would've liked him; he'd never be mistaken for soft. And look at the man. Who else – besides you – had made me feel wanted, singular, different?

On the boat, Leon whispered so only I could hear. 'What if you lived with me, Little Star? You and Deming?'

I wanted to remember this moment even as it was happening, to imagine it as already gone.

Spring was nudging in, the streets fuller, noisier, the city flung open with new colors and lights. We walked, hand in hand, after I picked you up from school.

'Can I have a plane?' you asked. 'There's a plane I saw, in a book.'

'You took a plane here, to New York. Did you like it?'

'I was sleeping.'

'One day, you'll take another one.'

'Where?'

'Anywhere. Around the world.'

The bakery had lime green lamps shaped like helmets. We ordered bubble tea in fluorescent colors and pierced the tops of our cups with oversized straws. 'Drink your tea,' I said. 'Don't blow bubbles.'

You made a farting sound with your lips. 'I like tea.'

'Do you like New York?'

You sucked up more tea and eyed me across the table as you blew a soft, loose bubble. 'Yes.'

'What do you like about it?'

'Subway.'

'Do you miss China?'

Shrug.

'Do you miss Yi Gong?'

'Yeah,' you said in English.

'Me, too.' I pushed my straw against the bottom of my cup. 'Do you like Leon?'

'He plays with me.'

'You can call him Yi Ba. He says he won't mind.'

You stared at me as if you were tasting the word, trying to figure out if you liked it or not.

'Next month, we're going to move to a bigger apartment and live with Leon and his sister Vivian. It's not far away, in a part of the city called Bronx. There will be another boy for you to play with, Leon's nephew. His name is Michael.'

'How old is he?'

'Around your age. I think he's five.'

You scowled. 'I'm *six*.'

'I know you are.' Thick shocks of hair erupted around your face, as if in protest. I walked to the other side of the table and squeezed into your seat with you. 'We're going to move in with Leon, but we'll always be a family, Kid, you and me.'

You blew bubbles into your tea, made another farting noise, and giggled. Your face became serious. 'Is Auntie Didi coming, too?'

The apartment was too small for all of us. Me, you, Leon, Vivian, and Michael. Michael's father, Leon said, had been a good-for-nothing Taiwanese with no papers who'd split on Vivian long ago.

My roommates had said the Bronx was dangerous and not

enough Chinese people lived there, but when we arrived on an April morning and I looked at the signs in English and Spanish – not a single Chinese character anywhere, not even at the takeout spot down the block – I felt like I'd been in rehearsal all this time and this was the real thing. It had taken six years, and I was still in the same city, but finally, I had gone elsewhere. Another woman was already waiting to take my bunk on Rutgers Street.

Leon and I slept on one mattress in the bedroom, you and Michael on the other, Vivian on the couch. It cost a hundred dollars more a month to live with Leon than it did to live in the boardinghouse, but I could take on more hours at the salon, since when you came home from school, Vivian or Leon took care of you and Michael.

Opposite-world Leon, he woke with the moon. The city buses would screech and hump across the Bronx, Leon slouched on one of their back benches, riding to the edges of Hunts Point. For a living, he dealt with the dead. He deboned ribs, pigs shrinking from whole animals into separate parts: belly, shoulder, intestines, from pig to pork. Boots coated in blood, gloves slippery with innards, Leon sliced at slabs, cleaved bones from muscle. On the kill floor, swinging from giant hooks, the hogs were stunned with electric shocks, their necks severed, scraped clean. The disassembly line. Sometimes I saw these animals in my sleep. The frozen pig, dazed and muted, the hog heads with their gaping mouths, all those groaning ghosts. Leon swore off sausage, ham, bacon. What separates the pig from the person? In bed he'd name my parts and chops, trace my cuts of meat with his fingers – leg, loin, ribs, rump; the skin around my belly – until I squirmed. 'Stop!'

We were all meat. Fat and gristle and tendon and bone. Cartilage and muscle, thighs and breasts. Leon had come over as a stowaway, washed ashore in New York on a garbage barge of old computers. The ship had sailed around the world, China to Thailand to Mexico, across the Pacific, but riding in the cargo Leon never saw ocean. Back when he came, you could enter without papers and customs would release you into the streets; there was nowhere for them to detain you. You'd get an order to appear in court and rip it up and throw it away when you hit the sidewalks, hail a cab to Fuzhounese Chinatown and fade sweetly into the crowd.

'Is it scary being with a man who kills?' Didi asked, and I said I supposed it would be, but Leon didn't kill, and despite how broad his back was, how his shoulders and arms could choke you, he was a gentle person. When he came home from work he took long showers, crawled into bed and dampened the sheets, climbed over me and onto me, pressing his weight into mine. It soothed me. He talked in his sleep, mumble-spoke, and at first it had confused me. 'No,' he would laugh, and I would say 'Yes,' clear awake, translating his mumbles to the language I wanted to hear.

Between shifts, we lay together, half-dressed. He told me the few memories he had of his parents, who both died young. Once, as a small boy, he had skipped into his house with a ladybug, excited to show off the colorful insect, and his mother, scrubbing pots, had taken the bug and squished it between her fingers. It was a story not intended to be sad, only true, but it made me so damn sad I couldn't find the right words to say, the comfort and sympathy that was supposed to come naturally to women. I wanted one memory, just one, of my own mother. I worried I couldn't be a good mother without having known my own.

I told Leon about Haifeng, the riverbank and the factory, the day I walked into the ocean. Our legs were intertwined, his foot brushing the inside of mine, an evil tickle, the sun forming a triangular shadow on the sheets. 'Do you ever wish you were with a woman who didn't have a child?'

'Of course not. I don't want to be with another woman.'

The more Leon comforted me, the less comforted I was. His solidity was so different from Haifeng's fawning, but it felt dangerous, it could be a trick, and I had to be careful. I was disappointed at Leon for not being able to properly reassure me and annoyed at myself for needing him to do so. I told myself I didn't want to be married, especially not to someone without papers. Told him I didn't care for weddings.

He said, 'I'd still like to marry you one day.'

Alarmed, I said, 'Let's wait and see.'

My old roommate Cindy had told me it was a waste to marry a person without papers. And Didi had hit the jackpot: Quan was American-born, so she had a good chance at getting a green card. I imagined being without papers for the rest of my life, unable to drive or leave the country, stuck in the worst jobs. No different than staying in the village. I didn't want a small, resigned life, but I also craved certainty, safety. I considered suggesting to Leon that we marry other people, legal citizens, for the papers, and after a few years we could divorce our spouses and marry each other. But I didn't want to marry anyone else, and I sure as hell didn't want him to either.

If I left him now, it wouldn't hurt as much as it would if I left him later. I lay beside him, watched him muttering in his sleep.

Nail polish fumes made me dizzy, made my nostrils burn and the skin on my fingers peel off in bright ribbons. When I returned to the salon after a day off, my breathing got shallow and my eyes stung, but after an hour, I no longer noticed it. The tips at the salon still weren't enough to cover my expenses. If I did nail art, I could get higher tips, but Rocky said I had to put down a $200 deposit to learn. I tried my English out on the customers who talked to me, asked their names, what they did for a living, where they lived in the city. I got accustomed to the awkward intimacy of holding a stranger's hand while trying to avoid each other's eyes. All the nail technicians spoke to one another in Mandarin. Joey liked to bake, brought in butter cookies for us to eat, while Coco, who was tall and skinny with a sleek helmet of hair, studied fashion magazines and knew the brands and styles of her customers' clothes and bags. 'That's a knock-off Balenciaga,' she'd say, 'you can tell because of the straps.' She spoke in a monotone, and people called her rude, but I found her refreshing. 'The women with the real bags that aren't knock-offs? They tip crap. They spent all their money on bags.'

Someday I would have enough money to spend on useless things. I wanted a better job, managing a salon like Rocky. There was a woman who used to work at Hello Gorgeous and had quit to run her own business in Queens.

Hana, who had the best English out of all of us, read phrase books on her breaks. 'You need to leverage the advantage of having a child who's growing up here,' she said. 'That's free English lessons daily. I learned the most English from my kids. I had them share their textbooks with me.' At home, I started to try out English words with you, tried not to let my frustration show when you laughed at my pronunciation.

'Let's look at this together,' I said to Leon, turning the volume down on the TV. Hana had given me one of her old books. 'I'm trying to learn twenty new words a week. The book says in two months we can be speaking at a third-grade level.'

'Third grade? That's for kids. Baby level.'

'If you don't try you'll be speaking at a fetus level. Silent.'

'Most of the people in the world are Chinese, but you don't see Americans trying to learn our language. You don't need

English at my job.' Leon took the remote control and raised the volume again.

Then you'll be in the slaughterhouse forever, I wanted to say. It was a young man's job, and when Leon's back pain got so bad he couldn't work there anymore, what kind of work could he get? I wasn't making enough to pay all the bills. When these thoughts kept me up at night I would smooth them over with color, the same way I could brighten a fingernail in a few short strokes. I'd think of Leon and me, talking in bed on a late morning as you and Michael laughed in the living room. You calling Leon 'Yi Ba', the five of us eating in the kitchen together. Our meals were never silent.

And I hoped Vivian would become an older sister to me, the two of us cracking jokes on Leon and taking care of each other's kids. Short and round, Vivian favored bright clothing, hot pink T-shirts with cartoon characters, pants with silver rhinestones down the sides. She took overflow orders from a factory, and some weeks there was a lot of work, other weeks nothing.

My first morning in the apartment, I told Vivian I liked her pants. She was snipping threads at the kitchen table, the floor crooked, the walls embedded with the remnant odors of past tenants, deep-fried, soggy with cooking oil. A moldy smell arose from behind them, more pronounced in hot weather, and if I could knock the walls down I might find mosses and vines, a trickling stream. Vegetation. Salamanders.

'Thanks,' Vivian said. One hand pulled the thread, the other angled the blade. 'Oh, I forgot to tell you. I bought pork for tonight.'

'Why, what's tonight?'

'For dinner. I was thinking pork dumplings. You like steamed or fried? Steamed is easier, right? But Leon loves fried, of course. Which do you make for him?'

'Neither. I have to work late, but I usually bring home take-out for Deming, so you don't have to worry about cooking him dinner.'

'There's plenty of food. Plenty for your son.'

'Get Leon to cook. He's doesn't have to go to work until after dinner.'

'Cook? Leon?' Vivian laughed so hard she started to hiccup.

She expected that I would cook, even if I had to go to work, that women just loved spending their free time standing in a hot kitchen mincing meat and vegetables, spoiling grown men as if they were children. But I didn't want to cause conflict. I wanted a sister. So Vivian and I cooked, after we finished our jobs.

She and Leon kept the apartment stocked with the soda you loved. One night, you and Michael sat on the couch with Leon, sucking down Cokes and seeing who could burp louder.

'That's enough, Deming,' I said. 'Stop it.'

'Oh, they're boys,' Vivian said.

As if he was proving Vivian right, Leon chimed in with a belch of his own. You burped again, and Michael stifled a giggle.

'Deming! Stop that!'

'But Auntie Vivian says it's fine.'

'Well, I'm your mama and you have to listen to me.'

You stuck your tongue out. A fizzy rage seeped through me like a poisonous gas. I was due back at the salon in the morning, it took almost an hour to get to Harlem on the bus and subway, and I'd already worked seven hours and stopped at the bodega to get food on my way home, where the owner, a nice man from South America, gave me discounts. There were dirty dishes in the sink, laundry to do, and you and Leon were burping while Vivian was trying not to laugh. You were all trying not to laugh at me. 'I said, stop it! And you—' I pointed to Leon. 'You're no better than a child.'

Vivian and Leon exchanged a look. Mortified at how you refused to obey me, I ladled out the soup Vivian and I had made. You and Michael balanced your bowls on your laps. 'Thank you,' Michael said, looking at Vivian and then at me, as if he was waiting for permission to eat. His eyes were large and watery, and I realized he was afraid of me.

Didi and I were in the alley behind Hello Gorgeous, splitting a cigarette on our break. A pigeon circled the trash cans.

'I've been leaving hints for Quan,' she said. 'The other day, I showed him a picture of an engagement ring in a magazine.'

'What did he say?'

'He just nodded.' She shook her head. 'Do you think I'm wasting my time?'

I didn't mention that Leon had suggested marriage. 'If he doesn't want to marry you, then he's a fool,' I told her. 'You could find a better man, someone who will.'

Her face relaxed. 'I know. And you could, too, Polly.'

I did know that, though I didn't tell Didi how I daydreamed about men with money and papers. I'd hear our neighbor Tommie talking about visiting family in the Dominican Republic and wished I could travel like that. Living with Leon and Vivian, I found myself slipping back into a village accent, but envied how easily they could talk to one another, how Vivian bought Michael books and DVDs when she made even less than I did, and I worried I would never get better at English and you would grow up to be a meat cutter. There were other cities out there with other opportunities. Riding the bus downtown, I'd think: *I could keep riding. I could never get off.*

'Ignore Vivian,' Didi said. 'Ignore Leon's nonsense. Act like a woman who likes to eat dried squid out of the bag for dinner. The world's not made of magic.'

'I like dried squid,' I said, passing the cigarette to Didi.

'All right, squid breath.'

'And I never said the world was made of magic.'

'It's an expression.'

'I've never heard that expression before.'

Didi passed the cigarette back, green eyeshadow glimmering. 'That's because I made it up. Don't worry so much, okay? Either stay with Leon or move on.'

'You, too,' I told her. 'Don't worry so much.'

I linked my arm in Didi's. It was good to have a friend.

Vivian was the oldest of Leon's three siblings. 'She was the first to come to America,' Leon said, 'then she married that cocksucker who ran off on her. Had another woman on the side. Now she needs us to help pay the rent. But inside she's a soft woman, like you.'

'I'm not a soft woman.' Then I wondered if Leon had asked me to move in with him only to help Vivian with the rent.

'Yes, you are.' He rubbed the knobs at the top of my spine. 'Your boobs are soft. Your ass.' I grabbed his waist and he pushed me onto the bed, kissing my neck, my earlobes, my shoulders.

He bought me gifts, an itchy yellow sweater covered in yarn balls that resembled pimples, a stuffed unicorn, a plastic kitten to hang from the antenna of my cell phone. When he presented them to me the hopeful look on his face reminded me of you, gifting me, pictures you'd drawn at school, lopsided scratches in jiggly colors. I kissed and thanked him. Leon bought gifts for you, too, a softball, a big leather mitt for catching. The three of us walked to the park on a summer Saturday, and I watched him throw you the ball. When you missed, he was encouraging. 'Good try!' Then he'd toss it again. When you caught it the two of you would leap up and down, like you had won an Olympic medal. Leon let you high-five him again and again.

'Come play, Mama,' you shouted.

'Polly, join us,' Leon said.

I got up and watched, my son and my man, your comfort with one another, your laughter. All that I had once wanted, this big life, my exciting life, seeing the places in Liling's old textbook, the promises I had made to myself when I called the lady with the mustache, were in danger of drying up. Or had they been a young girl's fantasies? I walked with Qing and Xuan outside the factory. I stepped into the Atlantic Ocean and decided to have a baby. Maybe it wasn't about moving to new places, but about the challenge of staying put.

Leon tossed the ball. You caught it and lobbed it back. How did I get here? A flock of birds flapped over the trees, but the sun was shining so hard, it hurt to see.

Second grade turned into third grade, third grade into fourth, and your English grew from timid to fluent, you and Michael learning how to keep secrets from Vivian and me. At P.S. 33, the kids were Cambodian, Mexican, Filipino, Jamaican, Puerto Rican, Vietnamese, Guyanese, Dominican, Haitian, Ecuadorian. They were all from other places, or at least their parents were.

Michael was skinny on the bottom but wider up top, shaped like a bobble-headed toy, with an array of similarly undersized friends who also became your friends, Hung and Sopheap and Elroy. The year you were in fourth grade, you and Michael talked about something called Power Rangers as if they were actual people in the neighborhood.

'Who is this Timmy? A kid from school?'

You and Michael writhed on the couch, slapping your thighs,

clapping your hands. 'Tommy, not Timmy! He's not a *kid*. He's the Black Dino Ranger.'

'Black . . . die?'

'What?' Vivian said. 'Who's dying?'

You and Michael shrieked. '*Dino*, not *die*! Dino, dino, dino!'

When I watched you and Michael play catch in the park, I was proud because you could throw the ball harder, faster. Still, while you were stronger and more fearless, Michael was the A-student, and you were bad at school, like I'd been – I could memorize lyrics to pop songs and figure out the precise mix of colors to make a certain shade, but never the multiplication table – and neither Leon nor Vivian were scholars, which made Michael's grades a fluke, random enough it might as well be you who was the good student, you the one who said things like 'when I go to college.' I knew it was unfair to compare you two when Michael had never lived anywhere except New York, but when he chose to read a library book as you sat in front of the television – and yes, I was likely right there next to you – watching a rerun of a rerun you'd already seen four times, claiming to have lost your homework yet again, I felt exposed for my own lack of interest in books, unless they were the books on art and painting Coco brought to the salon; those I liked to read. You'd been slow to learn English. Your sweat had a cabbagey odor that I was convinced was Haifeng's genetic bequest. You always took the biggest piece of candy, gorging yourself before others took a bite, banged chicken wings on your plate and pretended you were playing the drums. Chunky and padded from the food you ate, your shirts rode up around your waist, and you teetered on fat, outgrowing new pants overnight. As if I had money to buy new clothes all the time! I worried it was my fault when you acted impolite or selfish, that it reflected a deficiency in myself.

Hana had left Hello Gorgeous to run a dry-cleaning business

with her husband and brother, but I remembered how her two children were going to high schools in the city, ones they had to pass a test to get into.

'You're too hard on him,' Leon said. 'He's not doing so bad.'

I had been in New York for ten years and often reminisced about those early months on Rutgers Street, a time so desultory I would wake up in my sleeping bag each morning startled by where I was and what I had done. Back then, the passing of each day had felt inconsolable, as if there would be no end to the uncertainty – the baby, the job, the debt – but I revisited that first year in New York more than any other time in my history, loved to flip it around, marveling at my youth, how scary and exciting it had been, how so much had changed since then. Even the time I took you to the factory seemed safe enough to remember, though I always backed off when I pictured what things would have been like if I hadn't returned to the bench where I had left you.

There was this one Sunday, about a year before we were separated again, that we rode the subway to a point you picked out on the map. It had been a long time since we had done this. We ended up downtown, at the tip of Manhattan, walking on a winding pathway that overlooked the water. I missed it, the water.

'We used to come to this park when you were a baby.'

'I don't remember,' you said.

You were looking more like me, the same eyes and mouth and nose, the broad shoulders and bony legs, though when I saw your face in profile, I'd see how much you could also resemble Haifeng with the point of your chin and your bushy eyebrows. Then you would turn another way and look like me again.

We sat on a bench and put our feet up on the railing. The water sparkled. I pointed into the distance, to a large boat moving away from the city.

'I have a new nickname at school,' you said. 'Number Two Special.'

'What does that mean?' I felt self-conscious, like when I took you and Michael to that carnival and you made fun of me when I mistook the English word *octopus*, the name of a ride that spun you around in circles, for *lion*.

'It's a joke. You know, from a Chinese takeout menu? That's how they order the dishes. Number one special, number two special. Get it?'

I watched the boat until it became a white speck, fading into the skyline. 'You don't work in a takeout restaurant.'

'Yeah, but I'm Chinese.'

'You better tell them not to call you that.'

'It's a joke, Mama.'

I took out another loan to cover fees for nail art training. Intricate designs became my specialty. I could draw palm trees, diamonds, and checkerboard patterns, even a recognizable depiction of a person's face on a thumbnail, though I didn't know why people wanted that. On a good week, I made more in tips alone than I had earned working at the factory. Rocky called me a customer favorite, and everyone said I had a steady hand, an eye for the best color combinations.

I was gratified when I heard Rocky's laugh, several soft puffs out her nostrils, but when her voice was strained, her face worried, I pushed myself to learn more new designs and act extra nice to the customers, not only for tips, but because I recalled the story of the woman who had gone on to manage her own salon. Once, I overheard Rocky saying to a friend in her office: 'I bet Polly could run this place as well as I could.' Didi said Rocky had been talking on the phone about taking out loans and speculated she might be opening another salon. A new salon would need a new manager, and if Rocky hired me to be one, she might also sponsor me for a green card.

The nail techs gossiped about Rocky when she was out. 'She lives in a mansion on Long Island,' said Joey. 'Her husband runs an import–export business for fruit.'

'Her husband doesn't work. He stays home and takes care of the house and cleans,' Didi said. 'He takes care of their son and drives her around, too. Haven't you seen him pick her up from work?'

'I heard she married him because they were in love, but he was illegal and about to get busted by Immigration,' Coco said. 'They were going to throw him in one of those immigration jails.'

'What immigration jail? I thought her husband was Chinese mafia,' I said.

Joey snickered. 'Mafia would explain a lot about her personality.'

On a slow Tuesday morning, I sat on one of the pedicure chairs and flipped through a magazine.

'You're here until two, right?' Rocky stood in front of me holding a ring of car keys, eyeliner on her right eye, but not her left. 'I have to run home for a minute because I forgot something. Come with me?'

It turned out Rocky didn't live on Long Island, but in north-eastern Queens, which was almost in Long Island. The drive took half an hour, over highways and bridges, and she talked about her bad ankles and high blood pressure. 'Getting older is a bitch, Polly, you know that?'

'You're not old,' I said. She was probably ten years older than me, in her forties.

'You're so good to me. But seriously. High blood pressure! I'm going to have to give up coffee, red meat, fried foods, you name it. Take pills. And I'm forgetting things right and left. I have these forms I was supposed to bring in today and I left them at home. I even wrote myself a note to remember.'

Rocky's house was at the end of a block of similar-looking houses, with two stories and a front yard and an attached garage. The outside was brown brick, with a dark red roof, a low gate separating the yard from the sidewalk. It wasn't a mansion; the new houses in Minjiang were far bigger. But it was a real nice house. I followed her into an entranceway with a full-length mirror on the wall and into a living room with a nice leather couch and two tall windows. There was an electronic keyboard in the corner with paper piled on top, and a school picture of Rocky's teenage son, whose smile exposed a mouth full of plastic braces.

'You want water?' She gave me a plastic bottle of Poland Spring from a cardboard box. 'Take a seat on the couch. I have to run upstairs to find this form.'

I sat, but as soon as I heard her walking on the floor above me, I got up. Down a short hallway was the kitchen, which had a dishwasher and a microwave, boxes of cereal and bags of chips on a round table. The sink was full of dishes, and the counter stained with dried sauce and crumbs. On the other side of the kitchen was a small room. I heard voices, the sound of a motor revving.

It was the television. I leaned closer to the open door and saw a man in a reclining chair, dressed in striped pajama pants, slippers, and a baggy white undershirt. One hand gripped the remote control, the other rooted inside a bag of Cheetos. He crunched in a mechanical motion and sighed, content.

Rocky's husband was home in the middle of the day, eating Cheetos and watching action movies in his pajamas. He didn't look like the owner of an import–export business, or even a househusband who cooked and cleaned.

'What does your husband do again?' I asked Rocky on the drive back to the salon.

'Oh, he's in between jobs right now, so he spends too much time at home. Let me tell you, I'm glad I have this salon. Speaking of which, I wanted to talk to you. Where you live, in the Bronx, are there a lot of nail places?'

'A few,' I said. 'Smaller places. I've never been to any of them.'

'Are they nice?'

'They aren't trying to be spas.'

'Is your neighborhood near Van Cortlandt Park? Riverdale?'

'No, those are north of where I live.'

'I'm going there later today.' Rocky turned onto the highway. 'There's a space for lease in Riverdale and I think there's a market in the Bronx, especially in those higher-end neighborhoods. Lots of people with money who don't mind paying for a clean nail space.'

We got to the bridge entrance and Rocky slowed down at the toll. The E-ZPass sensor clicked to green. I took a breath and counted from one to ten. 'If you do open another salon,' I said, 'and you are looking for a manager, I would be good at it.' I tried to catch a glimpse of Rocky's profile without looking directly at her, and thought I saw her nod.

She looked over her shoulder as she changed lanes. 'Yes, I'll let you know, of course.'

I took you and Leon out to dinner at a Mexican restaurant, the room cheery with red and yellow streamers, and told you it was too premature to say for sure, but there was a good chance I might get promoted to become the manager of my own salon. A man fed a dollar into the jukebox and a raucous chorus of trumpets kicked up. You kicked your legs under the table and I didn't tell you to stop.

*

Later that summer, Didi and Quan got married. Quan had proposed after winning big one night in Atlantic City, kneeling on the carpet of the casino hotel and presenting a diamond ring. I stood with them before the judge at City Hall, sat next to Leon at a restaurant table, clapping as the newlyweds posed for photos. Didi applied extra coats of fuchsia lipstick. Quan's spiky hair fell over his eyebrows.

One of the other women at our table said I should inquire how much the meal cost in case I wanted to have my wedding here, too. I didn't. Didi was marrying a man who gambled his paycheck away. Sure, she loved him, but even Leon agreed she was getting the shit end of the deal.

Meanwhile Leon's back was giving him trouble. At work, his pay remained the same, though he'd been there longer than most of the other men. 'You've got to ask for a raise,' I said, but there was always another excuse. His boss was in a bad mood. His boss quit and he got a new one. That boss was out that day. Then he was in pain and couldn't get out of bed, so he missed three days of work, not to mention pay. Vivian and I kept telling him to see a doctor before his back got worse, but he refused, said we were overreacting, he was fine with ice packs and Tylenol.

A former co-worker named Santiago was starting a moving company, and when Leon said he was thinking of joining, I was so happy I pounded my fist on the kitchen table and said, 'That's a great idea!'

Whenever he mentioned it might be nice to have a baby together, I'd say I didn't want to while I still had debt. But each month I paid only the minimum. I just didn't want another child. You were almost eleven, and in a few years you wouldn't need me to look after you all the time. I could work more, get a better job, learn English. Not take care of a baby.

Two months after Didi's wedding, Leon met me after work,

and as we were walking in Riverside Park, he slowed down as we approached a big tree. Then he stopped.

'What's wrong?' I asked. 'What, your shoelace got untied?'

He rooted around his pocket and removed a box. My heart started to pound. He fumbled with the lid, finally opening it to reveal a gold ring.

'Do you want to get married?' he asked.

Eyes pleading, brow furrowed, Leon leaned forward with his chest. We stared at each other, and every second that passed, he looked more nervous, and it became clear that whatever I said, I wouldn't be able to take back. But I couldn't say no; I couldn't hurt him. So I said yes.

Vivian and Didi threw us a party to celebrate, and we put on the radio and danced – Vivian loved to dance, had great rhythm, and even you and Michael joined in.

'Now Leon will be my real Yi Ba,' you said.

Vivian raised a bottle of beer. 'To my brother and sister!'

All my life I had wanted sisters, and now I was so glad to have Vivian and Didi. Leon wanted to go to City Hall right away, but I said let's wait until spring, when it was warmer, and we could afford a proper banquet.

That Monday, I woke up alone in the apartment on my day off. You and Michael were at school, and Leon and Vivian were visiting a family friend in Queens. I walked through the apartment, not bothering to pick up your clothing or a pair of Leon's boxers, lying plaintive on the bedroom floor. I made a cup of tea and let the rare quiet settle over me. On Rutgers Street I had felt alone all the time, even with so many roommates, and now I was rarely alone, though there were times when I was so lonely, like when you and Michael spoke to each other in too-fast English as I sat next to you, or when Vivian and Leon reminisced about their parents and siblings.

For the first time in months, the day was all mine. I got dressed, walked outside into a sunny morning, early October, and boarded a nearly empty 4 train, the rush-hour crowd already at work, the kids already in school. I stayed on as it went underground, through Manhattan and into Brooklyn, got off at a stop I had never been to before, climbing the stairs up into a quiet street with large trees. The buildings, though not too tall, were wide and regal, with wrought-iron fences, brick walkways, and arched entrances. I waited for the light to change alongside a young woman pushing a stroller, shoulders shaking to a secret song, headphones in her ears, the baby girl in the stroller dressed in a miniature jacket and denim pants with pink cuffs. I smiled, the baby gumming back at me, and saw myself at nineteen, pushing you in a stroller I'd bought at a secondhand store on the Bowery. That was my first year in America. I would look down as I walked and see your tiny sneakers poking out in front of me. Now your feet were bigger than mine.

I was often fatigued by the city, its bad breath belching through vents in the pavement, a guy testing his cell phone ringtones on a packed subway, but this neighborhood felt peaceful. Leaves crunched beneath my shoes, and the breeze didn't bite. I turned at the next block, onto a street with narrower buildings. A delivery man, Chinese, bags dangling from his bicycle handlebars, cut me off at the corner.

I looked up at the rows of fire escapes and air conditioners, the barred windows and scraps of curtains. In two weeks, I would be thirty years old. My own mother had been dead at my age. One day Yi Ma had been alive, and the next, gone.

A door opened onto the sidewalk, a bell jangling from its handle. The deliveryman walked into a takeout joint, and I followed him and ordered a plate of chicken and rice, taking the container to eat at one of the two tables.

The food was salty. I asked the man if I could have a cup of water.

'We don't have water,' he said.

'Who doesn't have water?'

The woman at the other table held out a plastic bottle. 'Here, you can have mine,' she said in Fuzhounese.

I hesitated, not wanting to share a stranger's bottle.

'Take it, it's fine,' she said.

I was so thirsty I didn't care if I was being rude, so I uncapped the bottle, wiped its rim on a napkin, and took a long swig. 'Thank you.'

'No problem, sister,' said the woman. Her clothes were well-made, tall brown leather boots, a long skirt printed with purple flowers, and a loose, chocolate-colored sweater. An empty food container was on the table in front of her. She had a wide, pretty face. 'How long have you been in New York?'

'A long time,' I said. 'Ten years.'

'I've only been here for three. But I'm leaving soon.'

The woman smiled and exposed a crooked incisor that seemed familiar, as if I had seen it in a movie or on a relative I'd only met once.

'Leaving for where?'

'California. San Francisco. I hear it's beautiful.'

'You been there before?'

'I've only seen pictures. I knew a man that moved out there, but he's somewhere else now.'

'So you're going out there by yourself.'

'Sure, why not? It's time for a change. New York is hard.' The woman tossed out her container. 'So long, now.'

'Good luck to you, sister.' I watched the woman walk out, skirt swishing, hair hanging down to the middle of her spine. Once I might have become this woman, free to move across the country because she heard a city was beautiful. Instead I had become a woman like Vivian, watching TV, cooking for you and Leon, making sure the dumplings were fried and not steamed, unsure if I should marry my boyfriend but not wanting to lose him either. An uneasiness settled into me. This October would be followed by another winter, another spring, until it was time for October again.

It wasn't until I was on the subway that I realized whose crooked tooth the woman's had reminded me of: Qing, my old friend in the factory dormitory in Fuzhou. The more I ruminated on it, the more I was convinced. This woman was Qing, ten years later. They spoke a similar dialect; they were around the same age. She had called me yi jia, big sister. Qing, I remembered, had wide-set eyes and a wispy voice that sounded like she had a little spit in her mouth. The woman in the takeout joint had wide-set eyes, and her speech could've been a little wispy. She hadn't recognized me, but perhaps I no longer resembled my younger self.

The subway went express through midtown Manhattan. I leaned against the door, absorbing each bump on the tracks. I knew I should get back on the train to Brooklyn, leave a note in the restaurant asking Qing to call me if she ever returned. But I remained inside, locked down by indecision, as if I was allowing something valuable to slip away.

When I got off at Fordham Road, the sun was already low. I walked up the stairs to our apartment, passing Tommie from next door. 'Not-bad-not-bad-not-bad,' he said. Flustered, I dropped my keys, and he bent down to retrieve them for me.

For days after seeing the woman who might have been Qing, I slept poorly. Eight-hour shifts at the nail salon seeped by in a haze, and Leon only registered at the periphery of my vision. To your delight, I heated up frozen pizza for dinner. You asked if you could have money to buy bootleg DVDs from the lady who sold them in the Colombian restaurant and I handed the cash over without a word. When I came home from work to find you and Michael and Vivian engrossed in a movie about a man blowing up people with a machine gun, I went into the bedroom and shut the door. It was too much effort to protest. Soon it would be winter again.

I sat at the window, looking down at the block, the darkening sky filling me with a strange terror. I saw a man with a cane making his way across the street, Mrs Johnson walking arm in arm up the hill with her daughter, the two women talking close to each other. I went into the living room and joined you in front of the TV.

The bus to Atlantic City smelled like feet, its upholstery dusty, faded into uniform shades of beige and brown, and its seats were at capacity, rows of heads protruding from ski jackets, topped with baggy knit hats in primary colors. Leon and I sat in the back, half the age of the other riders, eating pork buns from a bag emblazoned with a yellow happy face. The bus emerged from a tunnel onto a garble of highways. The high-rises flattened and spread into parking lots and concrete dividers, dim and gray in the winter light. Only the signs were bright green, the names of New Jersey towns I read aloud to myself: Hacken Sack. Pah Ramus. Old people snored against the windows, some coughing and hacking and rattling, as if they were running low on batteries. My sneakers produced kissing noises as they moved against the floor. I took the last pork bun, sinking my teeth into the sweet, spongy dough.

Atlantic City was a gift from Quan, who'd bled so much money at the casinos they gave him vouchers for free hotel rooms, dinners, drinks. Didi had accompanied him in the past, but this time gave a voucher to me and Leon, though we weren't gamblers. 'You need the time away more than I do,' she said. 'It's a pre-wedding gift.' Besides, Quan had quit gambling. Now he was attending weekly meetings for people who gambled too much.

So Leon and I checked into Caesars for free, a carpet-padded casino of ringing noises and lights. We bought a bottle of Hennessy and drank too much, which gave me a headache. Yet the freshness of being out of the city, even in this too-bright room that felt like the oxygen had been sucked out and run through a machine and pumped back in, made me reach for more Hennessy. Two shots, slammed fast, and the heaviness receded. Four shots and Leon was reshaped into the man he had been when I first met him, a prize I had wanted to win, whose attention was sudden, precarious, instead of this man whose aging sometimes took me by surprise, like when he was putting money on his card at the subway station and I noticed how his body was stiffer, his neck thinner, the skin around his throat loosening. There were days his arms hurt so much he couldn't work. And I was different, too, though I lived in the same body that had once slept with Haifeng, been packed into a box, delivered a baby, craved Leon so much its hands shook. A body changed in increments, and while this shifting seemed slow, it was unstoppable. The flesh got weightier, the skin coarser. Hairs in places they hadn't been before. But it was the same body, even if there was no visible sign of its past. Like muscle memory, a body could recall things on a hidden, cellular level.

'What happened to the moving company?' I asked Leon, and he said Santiago had changed his mind.

'He's going into landscaping now. He says there will be a job for me there. So I'm going to work in landscaping.'

Leon's optimism was ridiculous, even harmful. 'But does he

have a plan?' I doubted he would ever work for Santiago. 'Is he taking out a loan? Does he have a business partner?'

'Oh, Santiago is Santiago. He'll figure it out.'

I was irritated at Santiago, at Leon, even at Rocky. Nearly six months had passed since I had gone to her house, but when I asked how the visit to the space for rent in Riverdale had gone, she chirped, 'We'll see!' I was still a nail tech, still working for the same lousy tips.

At the lower-limit blackjack table, tugging choppy pieces of hair around my ears, I tried to remember the rules. Twenty-one was bust. Dealer stood on seventeen. Coming straight from work, I hadn't had a chance to wire my pay to the loan shark, and my payday cash was inside the pocket of my denim jacket. I parted with a crumpled twenty-dollar bill, the dealer delivered an ace and a five, and I signaled for a hit. The dealer gave me a four, totaling nineteen, and stood at eighteen.

'Look, I won.'

'Let's win more,' Leon said, and we wandered to Palace East, where the old people from the bus pressed hungrily on slot machines. Fueled by Hennessy, Leon bet big, and when we won at blackjack, we moved on to poker. The couple across the table was pointy and pale, the woman's low-cut dress displaying cleavage dotted with sunspots, bisected by a large diamond dangling from a chain. Leon gave the dealer so many chips I had to look away.

When I looked back at the table, the couple's faces were pinched and the dealer was pushing the pile toward us.

'Three of a kind,' Leon said.

'Yes!'

We jumped up and down.

'It's a game,' I said. 'It's all a *game*.'

He thought I was talking about cards.

'No, no, nonono.' It wasn't real money. Nothing was real. Twenty could become two hundred in a minute. I wanted to hear the bells go off on the slot machines, see the walls fill with the reflections of flashing lights. I wanted, badly, to win.

We drifted out to a hallway, the carpet so fluffy I wanted to rub my face across the fibers. No one else was around. 'I mean, us. Me. Leon!' I grabbed his arm. 'We're living in a game.' Not only the card tables and slot machines, but our lives. We lived as if we were still villagers, forbidden from changing jobs or moving to a new place, but all this time, we could have been playing and winning.

He poked my nose with his finger. The lines around his mouth deepened. 'You're drunk, Little Star.'

He flashed that gap between his front teeth, I nibbled his ear-lobe and the floor swayed. I had forgotten how much I loved him. How could I have forgotten, why was I so serious, what was there to worry about? I would marry him. He was more than enough.

He steadied my shoulders. 'You should go lie down.'

'Aren't you going to come with me?'

Leon looked at the money in his hands.

'Okay, go play.' I took the skin on the back of his elbow and twisted it. 'But come to the room soon so you can be with me.'

'Yow,' he said, jumping a little.

I squeezed his butt. 'Hurry.'

He moved down the hall away from me, walking backwards, blowing smacky kisses.

At home we slept facing opposite sides of the bed, exchanging the occasional peck on the cheek. It had been months since we'd had sex, and instead of frustration I felt nothing and wanted nothing, like I had outgrown that part of me. Only rarely did I think of how it had been when I had first moved in with Leon. When you and Michael were at school and Vivian took a shower, we used to run into the bedroom. Standing up, palms hard against the wall, Leon's hand over my lips, his fingers crammed into my mouth. But ever since I saw Qing, I'd been noticing hot men on the subway, on the street.

In the hotel room, upstairs from the casino, I flopped across the bed and called the apartment. You answered.

'What are you doing?'

'Watching TV.'

'Be good and listen to Vivian. I'll be home tomorrow and have something for you.'

You answered in English. 'A present? I love presents.'

'I know you do.'

Buzzed, liquored, I folded myself into the blankets and floated on visions of my hair pulled up in an elaborate froth of curls like Didi's, Leon in a suit and tie. The money he was winning could pay off my debt and pay for a wedding banquet, one bigger than Didi and Quan's.

Didi was taking English classes at a school in Midtown. She told me how good the teachers were, how much she was learning. Her teacher had published a newsletter with his top students' essays, and she brought a white pamphlet to the salon and pointed to an article on the front. 'Look, I'm a published author.' All the nail techs had gathered around as she read the article out loud, a paragraph about how she and Quan had visited her sister in Boston. Didi had used the wrong word in one sentence, 'wake' when she meant 'woke', but there were so many other words I didn't recognize.

I was being left behind. I saw Leon injured, unable to work, eating chips in an undershirt like Rocky's husband, while I worked longer shifts to pay his doctor's bills. I rolled from one end of the giant bed to the other, then off the bed and onto the floor, spooning myself against the legs of a chair. I raised myself up, grabbed my jacket, and stumbled out to the boardwalk. As I walked away from the hotel, the wooden slats squeaked beneath my feet.

For over a decade, ever since I'd come to New York, I hadn't left the city. I had gone to Queens, Brooklyn, and Staten Island, to beaches and parks, taken subways and buses in all five boroughs, but I hadn't gone beyond the city's borders until now, though nothing had been stopping me except a vague fear of the outside, whispered warnings about how you could be picked up by police, deported. But there was nothing to worry about. The farther I walked from the hotel the darker it got, and when I looked up I could see stars, so many more than I remembered, showering the sky with light. Stars were obscured in the city, but here they were, still bright and beating. The ocean waves, somewhere beyond the boardwalk, crashed and echoed around me, a distant, salty smell. Minjiang.

My feet were sandwiched around a loose plank. An entire country existed, a world. There was another life I should be living that was better than this. Reeling down the boardwalk, I felt it, a small, familiar friend: the pinch of freedom, a dash of possibility. I had become too complacent, accepting.

I walked back to the hotel and went up to the room, hoping Leon had returned so we could fall asleep together in that giant bed. I didn't want to see him in the casino diminished by the noise and colors, engulfed by his old brown coat. But the bed was the same as I had left it, the covers rumpled, the sheets halfway down. No sign of Leon. I got undressed and pulled the blankets over me, no longer drunk, and fell asleep in minutes.

Morning. The sun was straining through the curtains, and Leon was on the bed.

'Little Star,' he said. 'I'm sorry.'

I rubbed my eyes, the hotel room coming into focus. It was

so quiet. How strange it was to wake up without you nearby. 'What time is it?'

'First I won so much, you wouldn't believe it. Five thousand dollars!'

'Five *thousand*?'

'I should've stopped then.'

'But you didn't.'

'Okay. I should tell you. I used your money, too.'

'What money?'

'The three hundred and eighty in your wallet. I came back to the room, but you were asleep, and I was on a roll. '

'That money's supposed to go to the loan shark.'

'I got greedy. Thought for sure I'd win it back.'

My eyeballs felt like they were swimming in paste. 'How could you do that?'

'I'm sorry. It was wrong of me.' He lay down and his face curled. 'My shoulder.'

'You can't do your shift tomorrow.'

'Who's going to pay rent? The salon treats you like shit.'

'Then who told you to lose my money?' I threw a pillow against the wall and watched it slump onto the carpet. All the fingernails I clipped and sanded, the hours of gluing on rhinestones with tweezers and drawing palm trees and hearts until my wrists ached, to make that three hundred and eighty dollars.

'How could you think we could win money for free?' I said. 'Nothing is free.'

We slept on the bus ride back to the city. We unpacked our bags. We went to work.

'Look,' Joey whispered to me from across the manicure table.

I saw one of the new girls spreading wax on another girl's arms. She ripped it off. The second girl yelped.

Coco had quit. She simply didn't show up for her shifts. When I finally got her on the phone, she said, 'It's good to do something else.'

Rocky was no longer in the office every day, and whenever I tried to talk to her, she would say she was in a rush, she was out the door, she had to make a phone call. Michelle, a cousin of Rocky's, seemed to be taking over as manager. To replace Coco, Michelle hired four new girls, which meant our hours were capped. Like Rocky and Michelle, these new girls were Vietnamese Chinese, sullen-faced younger girls who arrived and left together in a van driven by a man with bronze highlights in his hair. The receptionist made no efforts to hide her distaste for them, not bothering to even address them by name.

'Hair removal,' Didi said. 'Next they're going to try Brazilians. Be glad you don't have to rip off crotch hair.'

'For now,' Joey said.

Four nights after Atlantic City, I told Leon I'd heard of a good job that wasn't in New York. 'It's the only Chinese restaurant in town and they want a waitress. Joey told me about it. That Hunanese girl at the salon. She's from the same village as the restaurant owners. You know how rare it is to find a good wait-ressing job.'

Leon stood, naked and dripping, in the bathtub after his shower. 'Okay.'

I gave him a towel. 'So, let's go.'

He dried his hair off. 'Go where?'

The steam was soothing on my face. 'Florida. Are you even listening to me?'

'Why would you want to do that?'

'It's a good job. Great money.'

He removed the towel. A drop of water fell onto his shoulder. 'It was only a couple hundred dollars.'

'Three hundred eighty dollars of my money. Which you stole from me without my permission. No big deal to you, I guess.'

'Of course it's a big deal to me. I screwed up. Said sorry. It doesn't mean you've got to go to waijiu. We can make up that money fast.'

Beyond the cities was waijiu, the outside, America's backwards villages. Everything that wasn't New York. I bent closer to Leon and inhaled his soapy smell. 'Florida has cities, it's not all waijiu. Come on, you know that new manager is about to can my ass. I can make more in a month waitressing than I would in a year back home.'

'You're just going to leave Deming? And me?'

I watched him step into his boxer shorts and thought of Qing, the boardwalk, the fat stars over the ocean. 'Of course you'll come. We can have a big house, all three of us. With a restaurant job, you eat for free. Joey said they might need men in the kitchen, too.'

'Yeah. Dishwashers.'

'Nothing wrong with dishwashing.'

'If it's such a great job, why doesn't this Joey go do it herself?'

He opened the bathroom door, releasing clouds of steam. On our bed, he stretched out and whispered, 'It's not safe. Look at that man in the Chinese papers. Robbed and killed delivering food. Lost his life for fifteen bucks.'

'Well, that wasn't at a restaurant, and it's always dangerous going into strangers' homes.'

'Look at the one who was shot at the takeout spot. Through bulletproof plastic!'

'That won't happen. Waitressing is safe.' I picked a pair of your pants off the floor. 'Listen, I want to go. It's time to try something different. Don't you think?'

'I think it's time for me to go to sleep. Forget about Florida, I'll make the money back for you next month.'

'Leon.'

'If you want money so bad, find a rich guy with papers who doesn't have to take care of his sister, too.'

'Stop it.'

It wasn't about the money. I could do better than Hello Gorgeous. Leon could do better than the slaughterhouse. You needed to go to a school where you weren't called Number Two Special.

I floated the idea to Didi. She socked me in the arm. 'Waijiu? Are you crazy? You might as well take the subway to the moon.'

We were standing in the same damn alley, smoking cigarettes like we'd been doing for years, facing the same brick wall of the same building. Didi's plan was to move to another salon downtown, and when her English got even better, get a job that didn't involve painting nails. 'I don't understand why you won't come with me to the other salon,' she said, addressing the bricks. 'She wants to go to Florida but she won't go to Thirteenth Street.'

'I told you I don't want to.'

'Rocky's never giving you that manager job. She's stringing all of us along, even if we've been working for longer. They're going to cut our hours down to nothing and keep these new girls on for cheap. Michelle's taking over and Rocky will manage the Riverdale salon herself. If you don't leave, they'll make you leave.'

She was right, but it hurt to hear. A police car drove down the street, sirens wailing, and I was agitated and weary at the same time. 'Don't you get tired of being in New York?'

'Not really. Things are good now.'

This was true, at least for her. When Quan was going to Atlantic City regularly, sometimes I'd reassure myself: at least I'm not Didi. But since Quan had quit gambling, Didi had the money to go to English classes instead of fronting him rent, and now she was trying to convince him to have a baby. And you couldn't try to sponsor me for a green card until you turned twenty-one, but after Didi got married, she'd applied for papers. Soon she would be legal and could work anywhere.

'You have a place with your man and your son, and you want to give it all up.'

'I just think this isn't the best I can do. And they'll come with me.'

'But you know what it's like here. Anything can happen in Florida.' Didi looked at her cell phone. 'We should go in before Michelle breathes her dragon breath on us.'

'Right, anything can happen. That's the exciting part.'

'You're angry about Leon and the money, but it's nothing.'

'It's not about the money. You and Quan should come, too.'

'Stay in New York. Get married, have a baby.'

I saw how much Didi would miss me if I left. I would miss her, too, though I already missed her, the way we had been when we only had each other, believing that being the oldest residents at the boardinghouse was a thing to be proud of, when the ambiguity of our lives was terrifying and enthralling, when each new day was equal parts fear and opportunity. My solitary walks through Central Park, the streets so new I could still get lost easily. Riding the subway and watching the lights of the city rear up in front of me, wondering if this would be the closest I would get to love.

It snowed, again, heaping inches of slush, and none of us could remember what it was like to be hot enough to need a fan. Leon cleared a path down the front steps of our building with his boots. 'Florida sounds nice right now, doesn't it?' I said.

'Will you stop with that? I told you, I'll pay you back.'

'You don't think I'm serious.'

'I have to go to work. I'll see you later.'

'Can you say that you'll consider it, think about it a little bit?'

'Okay, okay,' he said as he walked away.

I went upstairs and called the restaurant in Florida. I told the manager that I knew Joey and was interested in the job, answered questions about how long I'd been in America, said a few English phrases. The manager explained that the restaurant was in a small town called Star Hill, an hour outside of a city called Orlando. 'Don't wait too long,' she said. 'We need a waitress soon.'

I said I'd call again, in a day or two, after I bought tickets for a bus from New York.

My Wednesday shift had been shortened, so later that day I was able to meet you when you got out of school. The building seemed like it was always under construction, metal scaffolding attached to its sides for as long as you'd gone there, and the few times I had been inside, I had been struck by the stale, mildewy marinade of sweat, glue, and floor cleaner. It wasn't safe for children to go to school in a construction zone.

'I'm not going,' you said, when I told you about Florida.

'Deming, I'm your mother. You have to go with me.'

'You weren't with me when I was in China.'

'Yi Gong was with you. I was working so I could save enough money to have you here. It's different now.'

'Different how?'

'You'll love Florida, too. You'll have a big house and your own room.'

'I don't want my own room. I want Michael there.'

'You've moved before. It wasn't so hard, was it?'

You answered in English. 'I'm not going! Leave me alone!'

I knew the proper words to respond, but didn't say them, didn't want to give you the power of making me switch languages, to talk only on your terms. A dense heat rose in my face and arms, like I was fighting against being shoved into a bag.

We were outside the bodega. I saw Mrs Johnson from our building watching us. Your face was wrinkled and hurt, so I hugged you, hard, and you squeezed out of my arms and ran ahead of me, arms sticking out the wrist holes of your coat. Deming, I loved you so much. I made a note to buy you a new shirt. We wouldn't need coats in Florida.

That night, I stayed up as you slept, waited for Leon to get home from work. You asserted yourself even while unconscious, flopping on your side, while Michael slept on his back with his arms and legs straight. I hadn't been that much older when I had left home. It was good for a child to experience new things, learn how to be brave and independent. Like when you had fallen off a swing. It was scary, but I was proud of you for being strong. I wasn't going to baby you. I wanted you to be smart, self-sufficient; to never be caught off guard.

When you were a baby, small enough to fit on top of a pillow, I couldn't bear to be away from you, craved my skin against your skin. The city had seemed too harsh and loud for a child, and I wanted to protect you from the outside, ensure you'd be safe. I still did. I wanted to give you the chances I hadn't taken for myself. Show you that you didn't have to settle, stay put.

Streaks of light appeared in the sky. I drifted in and out of sleep and woke to Leon's weight next to me. I curled into his shoulder, pressed myself against him, and he patted my back. 'Go back to sleep. It's late.'

'If we were both working at the restaurant, we'd go to sleep together every night, wake up together every morning.'

'Mm,' he said.

'Don't you want to go with me?'

'I can't leave my sister. She's my family.'

'Vivian and Michael can come with us.'

'She doesn't want to leave New York.'

'How do you know? Maybe she does and you don't know it.'

'She called me today. Thought I was leaving without telling her. I didn't know what she was talking about.'

'I don't either.'

'You told Deming we were moving to Florida. I didn't agree to that. And he told Michael, of course, and Michael got scared and told Vivian, and she called me. She was so upset.'

'I didn't tell Deming we were moving.'

He pressed his finger to my lips. 'Be quiet. You'll wake the boys.'

I pushed his hand away. 'You be quiet.'

'You want to take your son away from here, but what about what he wants?'

'Deming is a child, he doesn't get to decide.'

Leon snorted. 'A mother is supposed to sacrifice for her son, not the other way around.'

'You better take that back.' This man I had slept next to for years, this man I was supposed to marry – he'd never known me. 'Take that back right now.'

A mother was supposed to lay down and die for her children, and Leon got to be called Yi Ba because he watched TV with you several afternoons a week. If he bought you a cheap toy, Vivian would crow, 'How thoughtful!' and when he took you to the park the neighbors complimented him for being such a good daddy. But no one called me a good mama when I did those things. And now Leon was blaming me for wanting a better life?

I smacked the bed, hard, with the edge of my hand. 'You think I don't love my son? Go fuck yourself.'

You grunted in your sleep. Leon pulled me up and led me out of the bedroom.

We sat at the kitchen table in the dark and whispered as Vivian slept on the couch.

'You've never liked her, have you,' he said.

'Vivian? Of course I do. She's my sister.'

'You wanted her to accept you without question.'

'Is that so wrong?'

Leon looked as if he was coming to realize an unpleasant truth.

'I was the new one,' I said. 'You have each other.'

We were so close I could feel his breath on my face, warm and sour. He couldn't meet my eyes, even in the dark. 'You're not a nice person sometimes.'

'I'm nice to you. I'm nice to Deming and Michael and Vivian, too.'

'You only want to go to Florida for yourself. Not for Deming or me. It's always all about you.'

'No, you've got it all wrong.'

Across the room, Vivian snored, and in the bedroom you continued to dream steadily, perhaps of Power Rangers, or maybe that was last year's fad. From behind the curtains the sun struggled to rise, and I said I wouldn't go. We would stay in New York with him and Vivian. I would forget about Florida. But Leon's warmth did not return, and it was as if his opinion of me had already altered beyond repair.

So many times in the years after, I would revisit this night: plot a different path, see myself with Leon at the kitchen table, and the next day, instead of going to work, I would stay home and pick you up from school, take you out for donuts and tea. Didi would get her papers, and eventually, so would I.

But that didn't happen. What I did was go to work. Thursdays brought a steady stream of customers to Hello Gorgeous, refreshing their manicures for the upcoming weekend, chipped polish wiped away and replaced with new coats. Some women debated over what color to choose, like it was as important a decision as picking a name for a child, while others came in already knowing the name of the shade they wanted, the same red their friend had, the same bronze an actress wore in a magazine picture. Brittle tips were shaped into triangles, feet that smelled like spoiled milk soaked, buffed, and scrubbed. Calluses, tough and hardened like mean nuggets of tree bark, were sanded down, dead skin scraped away.

After two mani-pedis and one pedicure, my next customer only wanted a mani. She chose a purple polish and held her hands out, primed for service. She was chewing gum, her mouth moving beneath a coat of brown lipstick.

Base coat, first coat. I dared my customer to look at me. Her bare nails were thin and yellow, a sign of too many manicures. I finished her right pinkie and twisted the bottle shut, glad I hadn't been roped into waxing mustaches like the other girls. I switched on the hand dryer and motioned to the customer. 'Wait to dry, okay, then we'll do the second coat,' I said in English.

I checked my cell phone, which Michelle frowned upon. I yawned; I'd barely slept. In the morning, Leon had sought a truce. 'I'll think about Florida,' he said. 'It's a good opportunity for our family. If we have another child, we'll have space for him.' Startled, I agreed. 'We can talk more tonight,' Leon said. But when I embraced him, he didn't hug me back. He kept his arms at his sides and presented his cheek for my kiss, not his lips.

The new girl at the next station was struggling to keep her brush steady. 'It's easier if you do it fast, or else the polish gets sticky,' I said. 'Flick the brush, one-two-three, don't give yourself time to think.'

The girl scowled. Her ponytail hung like a mouse tail against the back of her shirt. She bent closer to her customer, her body rigid, too nervous to do good work. Her customer tapped her feet.

I began my customer's second coat. One of the new girls was smearing hot wax onto a woman's upper lip. The new girls chattered to one another in Vietnamese and to the customers in limited English, and the speakers in the front of the salon played a radio station with American songs while Michelle watched Korean movies on a TV in the back office. I could hear operatic crying and swelling string music.

I would finish this lady's nails, and if nobody else came in, take my break. Didi was off today, at her English class, and I thought again about Star Hill, the house you and I and Leon could live in.

My customer's hand twitched. I'd painted her skin by mistake. 'Sorry,' I said.

She met my gaze at last, sucking her teeth in one long intake. I wiped the blob of polish off. The second coat was glossy and dark.

I finished the left hand, picked up the woman's right, concentrating so hard on applying the polish that I didn't notice the men who had come in, not until the customer had yanked her hand away and the girl at the next station had jumped up and there was a clatter, voices shouting in English and Vietnamese.

Men were yelling. 'Down! Down!' They were policemen, uniformed.

Customers grabbed their purses and ran out with their nails still wet. One woman left with a stripe of wax above her lip. My customer fled without paying. 'Stop her!' I yelled, and then I was shoved into a mass of bodies.

The new girl with the ponytail spat out words that sounded like curses. 'What is going on?' I shouted.

Static voices buzzed over the men's walkie-talkies. 'Stay down,' one of them said, and pointed at me.

The door was closed now, guarded by another uniformed man. A third man had handcuffed Michelle, who was cursing in English.

The first man turned to me. Years ago, riding in the truck from Toronto to New York, bumping over potholes, stiff with fear, I had thought, *This is what it's like to be dead*. Now, as I felt my arms pulled back in a decisive motion, like trussing a hog, I thought of you. It was you that I thought of. Always, it's been you.

CHAPTER ELEVEN

Yong was practicing his speech again. 'I come from humble beginnings.' He looked at his notepad. 'Like so many of you.' His gaze traveled to a point over me, landing on the wall behind the couch. 'Many, uh, obstacles were met.'

'Wait.' I leaned forward. He stood before me in a pair of boxer shorts and a white undershirt. 'It sounds a little braggy.'

'But how can it be bragging if I say I grew up poor?'

'That's the thing. You didn't.'

'Sure I did. We lived in an apartment. One bedroom for three people.'

'But you always had enough to eat. You were a city person and you could go to school wherever you wanted.'

'This is the Fuzhou Business Leaders Forum awards. Everyone makes speeches about being from humble beginnings.'

Seeing him there in his underpants made me want to shower him with clothes. 'I guess it just seems dishonest.'

'I don't even want to give this speech. I'm no good at speeches.'

'Take a deep breath before you talk. I do that when I'm teaching a class. Or you can pretend you're speaking to your friends, like you're telling me and Zhao a story.'

He tried again. 'I come from humble beginnings.'

'You have to project, talk louder.'

He took it from the top, louder this time, his words forced and exaggerated. 'I come.' He swept his arm in front of him. 'From humble. Beginnings!'

My cell phone buzzed and I grabbed it, saw a string of numbers, the kind I'd been hoping to see every time it had rung over the past month. Five weeks had passed since you called me and I hadn't called you back. I was scared of what you would say to me, that you'd be angry. I was scared of a lot of things I hadn't been scared of before.

'Hold on,' I told Yong. 'I have to take this. It's a business call. Keep practicing, I'll be back in a bit.'

I took the phone and walked down the hall to our guest room, which we used as an office. Shut the door, locked it, and sat on the floor by the window, against the one wall that wasn't shared with the living room.

'Hello?' I tried to even out the nervousness in my voice.

'Hello?'

'Hello, Deming. I'm glad you called again.'

'Hello, Mama,' you said.

'It's you,' I whispered, delighted and anxious.

From the living room I could hear Yong repeating the first lines of his speech, varying the intonations of the words. *I-come-from-humble-beginnings. I come, from humble . . . beginnings. I come from humble beginnings?*

You told me you were in school, that you had a job and played guitar. Your adoptive parents had insisted on changing your name, not only your first name, but also your last, so there was no longer any trace of me. What the hell kind of name was Daniel Wilkinson? I could never call you that. You told me Vivian had gone to court so that you could get taken in by a white family, but I already knew.

'Deming,' I said, and each time I said your name I felt a tiny thrill, 'remember the times we used to ride the subway together? That was fun.'

'We went to Queens and met the other mother and son and pretended they looked like us.'

'They did look like us, didn't they?'

'Sure.' You paused. 'Do you remember what you told me that day?'

My little Deming, freshly returned from China, both of us still without English. Your stubby legs and fat cheeks and over-sized winter jacket. Gripping my hand as we crossed the street, afraid of all those fast cars.

'No.' I couldn't remember; it was so long ago.

There was a knock. The doorknob jiggled, and I heard Yong say, 'Polly?'

'I have to go,' I whispered, then said, loudly, 'Thank you for your phone call. I'll call you tomorrow.'

I opened the door. Yong was in the hallway. 'Can I run the speech by you again? I think I've got it now.'

I nodded, wiping my sweaty palms on my thighs. My smile was taped onto my face.

'Why'd you lock the door?'

Yong was so unsuspecting, it pained me. 'A phone call from a client. Aren't you cold? Let me get you some clothes.' I took a pair of his pants out of the closet, tucking a note into the pocket. On it, I had written: *The award for best speech goes to you.*

In class the next morning, I wished I'd followed my own advice to take a deep breath before speaking when I stopped in the middle of a sentence and couldn't remember what I wanted to say next. My students stared as I glanced at the screen behind me. The word *toward* glowed in English. My mind churned; the word meant nothing to me.

On my way to work, I had noticed boys your age, young men scurrying with briefcases to office buildings, or dressed in jeans, balanced on construction scaffolding. You could be one of my students. Instead, you had been raised by strangers. You called an American woman *Mom*, someone who had never had any indecision about motherhood, who wanted it so badly she had taken another woman's son as her own. When I thought about this I wanted to scream; I wanted to kill someone. I was afraid that if I let myself cry, I would never stop.

A student in the front row raised her hand. 'Teacher, you were talking about prepositions.'

'*Toward* is a preposition,' I said, in hope that it would spark the next sentence. 'Can anyone tell me what a preposition is?'

The same student raised her hand. 'Prepositions work in phrases to give additional information.' She flipped through her notes. 'Common English prepositions include *under* and *after* and *to*.'

'Thank you, Mindy.' I pressed a button on the projector and advanced to the next slide. 'Let's review more vocabulary words.'

According to the clock on the wall, it was ten thirty in the morning. In New York, it was nine thirty the night before. New York, and all of America, was taking place in the past.

As the vocabulary words flashed on the screen, I took my phone out and scrolled down to the number I had saved in my contacts list, under your name: DEMING. Your Chinese name, your real name, not this *Daniel Wilkinson*. The name I gave you. My chest squeezed. I stepped into the hallway, called you, and left a message.

That evening, I bought a pack of cigarettes for the first time in years and chain-smoked on a bench in the park until I was dizzy. I thought of your new voice, your new name, and wanted to talk to you more. A lump remained in my chest, a raw, welling feeling that I needed to kill. I smoked more; then hurried home to shower, brush my teeth, and wash the smell of cigarettes out of my hair before Yong got there.

Later that week we arranged a time to talk, an early evening when I was home alone, and I took the phone out to the balcony to wait for your call. When I had first moved in, Yong and I would sit here on humid nights and make up nicknames for the towers busting up across the city. Silvertop. Boxyred. Uglygray. Week after week, these buildings grew upwards until their construction scaffolding was removed like post-surgery bandages, followed by a buffing and a filing and a final layer of paint. These days, I could no longer recognize Silvertop and Uglygray from the balcony, as they'd long been absorbed into a mass of other buildings, the skyline so cluttered I couldn't tell which buildings were new and which were less new. But it was comforting to know that nothing stayed the same for too long, that each day was a new opportunity for reinvention. A person could be transformed by a fresh wardrobe or a different nickname, like the ones I gave my Speed English Now students – Kang, a sour-faced boy with orange-streaked hair, became Ken; Mei, the girl with glitter eyeliner, was Mindy.

I waited. At 6:35, the phone rang, and I answered before the first ring was finished.

'I called a little late,' you said.

'I'm always a little late, too.'

'Is this a good time?'

I looked through the sliding glass door, into the apartment. Yong wouldn't be home for another hour, but I'd have to dress quickly for the awards banquet.

'Yes, my husband is out. I'm on our balcony right now.'

It wasn't hard, talking to you. I told you how I had come to New York. You told me about Ridgeborough, the town where you had gone after the Bronx, and your American parents, whom you called Peter and Kay. I didn't want to know their names. It should have been me who had gone to your high school graduation, who called you on your birthday, whose house you returned to at Christmas. I should have been the one to take credit for raising you. But all you could remember was me leaving and not finding you again.

You were angry. I couldn't blame you. I was angry, too. I wanted to find a way to fix it, but didn't know how, not without telling you about Ardsleyville. I didn't want to think about Ardsleyville. Instead, I said all the wrong things.

Leon was the only person I had ever told, and though enough time had passed that it probably didn't matter – no one would fine me now or give me prison time for how I left America – it wasn't information I wanted to share. Telling Yong would ruin everything. There were still nights I would wake up thinking of the concrete floor, the Styrofoam bowls of lukewarm oatmeal – I couldn't look at oatmeal now; I'd never eat it again – and the din of hundreds of women talking in different languages. I hated that Leon knew this, how fully I'd exposed myself to him. Because if he knew, then it had been real, not a nightmare I could just write off as my imagination. Like how talking to you reminded me of the nightmare of losing you.

Leon was the one who had left on purpose, not me. *I* didn't leave on purpose. *I* loved you more than anyone. You could call another lady 'Mama', but I was your mama, not her. I knew I had forfeited the right to say that, but it was never going to change.

There was a knock on the window, and I jumped in my chair, saw Yong pointing at his watch. I told you I had to go.

*

The Fuzhou Business Leaders Forum awards dinner was in a conference hall with small windows near the ceiling. It was May, warm outside, but inside I was shivering as Yong fidgeted next to me. Onstage, a real estate tycoon was rambling about his childhood in a village north of Fuzhou, running ten minutes past the five-minute time limit. 'I learned the lessons of hunger as a child during the famine years,' the tycoon said in an oddly cheerful lilt, 'when my mother would feed us a thin paste of rice and water. Our stomachs growled, but we never complained.'

Chopsticks clinked against the insides of bowls. Metal spoons scraped against serving plates. Yi Ba had said his family had been so poor that he and his brother had shared a single grain of rice, and I felt annoyed listening to the tycoon claim the same. He was rumored to never eat leftovers or use a towel more than once, his servants whisking away his bath linens immediately after he used them, the excess food disappearing as if it had never existed. I wanted to duck into the bathroom and call you, share the absurdity.

Between speakers, I tried to pay attention to the conversations around me. Lujin and Zhao wanted to buy a small country home in the mountains, while Zailang said he'd prefer one by the sea. I said I preferred ocean to mountains. I told the couple next to me about our kitchen renovations, gave them the names of the workers Yong and I had used. 'Good craftsmanship,' I said, comforted by my city accent, the confident way I talked. These were characteristics of Fuzhou's Polly, not the Polly who had lived in New York and wore five-dollar jeans and used the same soap to wash her face and body, who let her son watch TV all day.

'Hong Kong will be our next vacation destination,' Yong told Ning and Zailang. 'And after that, Singapore and Tokyo.'

'Tokyo?' Zailang said. 'Have you booked the tickets yet?'

'I haven't gotten around to it,' Yong said. 'Work is so busy.

But perhaps a winter trip to Hong Kong. It's so easy to get there. What do you think, Polly?'

'Sure.' I took a second helping of broccoli, but could barely taste the food. 'Wonderful.'

'Let me know when you go, and I'll send you a list of my favorite restaurants,' Ning said.

'That sounds great. Tell me more about what it's like there.' But as I watched Ning's mouth move, I was unable to concentrate on the words. Tomorrow, I would call and let you know I hadn't meant to end our call so abruptly.

Our table was full of our friends, Zhao and Lujin, Ning and Zailang, and Yong's other colleagues and their wives. I looked around the room and saw the same table duplicated, over and over: fat men in dark suits, lipsticked women in tight dresses, plates and plates of food, empty beer bottles. I didn't look out of place. My purple dress had been tailored to fit, and I wore a pair of diamond earrings and a matching ring, a gold bracelet with oval loops that resembled a chain. My hair had been dyed and highlighted. Earlier tonight, after I got off the phone with you and changed into my dress, Yong and I had admired our reflections in the bedroom mirror. 'Look how we match,' I said. I couldn't tell him about you or Ardsleyville, destroy the illusion we built for ourselves.

Another round of dishes arrived, and the Forum's president, a man in a pinstripe suit, introduced Yong, who made his way to the stage. He tapped the microphone to make sure it was on, even though it had been working fine when the president had spoken.

'I come from humble beginnings,' he said, 'like so many of you. I met many obstacles and challenges along the way, but overcame them through perseverance. And now, I am proud to lead Yongtex. We are truly the future of business, because we're not only a factory, but we work for the social good. First, by providing job opportunities to the needy.' He looked down at his notes and up at the crowd. I silently pleaded for him to keep talking. 'And – second, we promote trade. Third, we are spurring economic development in the region and elevating the status of Fuzhou business.'

His words petered out, but he finished strong. Our table clapped, followed by the rest of the room. 'Thank you,' Yong said. When he returned to the table, I could see how relieved he was. I placed a hand on his knee. We needed each other. I belonged here.

'You did good,' I said.

After the dinner, we had coffee at Ning and Zailang's apartment. The women sat along the end of an L-shaped sectional couch, the men at the long dining table. Ning and Zailang had blocked off part of the living room and constructed a new wall to create a bedroom for their son, Phillip.

Lujin and Zhao's daughter was taking grade nine English, even though she was only in grade eight. 'She was falling behind, so we decided to push the teacher to place her in a higher class,' Lujin said. 'That's what you have to do, force them to do better.'

'Children don't function that way,' I said. 'They also need encouragement.'

Ning smiled. 'You have to encourage, but you also have to be firm. They need to learn on their own.'

'But what are we telling our children if we set them up for failure?' I saw Ning exchange a look with Lujin. 'We could be harming them, affecting them later in life.'

'On those TV shows the parents are always giving their children empty praise,' Lujin said. 'But real life is different.'

'I am talking about real life,' I said.

'Real-life children aren't like the ones you see on television.'

'I'm not talking about television. What, I can't have an opinion about raising children, too?'

Lujin raised her eyebrows. Ning stood up and pulled down the front of her dress. 'Excuse me, I need to check on Phillip. It's his bedtime and I bet he's still up.'

The room felt airless. 'The weather has been so warm lately,' I said to Lujin.

'I hear it will rain tomorrow,' she said. 'What a relief that will be.'

I went to the kitchen and rinsed out my coffee cup. I wanted you to call again, but you were right: I had messed up. I had given up on finding you so that I could sit at parties with people like this. Keeping you a secret, as if you were the thing that was wrong. I dried my hands on a towel that hung from a hook on the side of the refrigerator, and the cloth snagged on the bracelet Yong bought me last year. When I pulled the towel away, the bracelet seemed too large and gaudy for my wrist, like the chain was mocking me.

In the living room, Zhao was talking about Sichuanese migrant workers, his favorite topic. 'That's why we pay tuition to send our daughter to a private international school. The public schools are overrun with outsiders.'

I sat across from him and said, 'But they can't even get into state schools.'

'Exactly. And they should stay out.'

'They have schools in the countryside they can go to,' Lujin said.

'You just said they're taking over the public schools in the city, and then you said they can't get into these schools. What are you saying? You can't have it both ways.'

Zhao scoffed. 'Public, private, what's the difference. The bottom line is, they don't belong here.'

Yong shifted in his chair. 'But you hire them,' I said. 'To do your renovations, paint your apartment, work in your factory. You're contradicting yourself.'

When I saw Yong's smile fade, I kept talking, trying to drown out Zhao and Lujin, until Ning came back and changed the subject. I hadn't given you up to agree with such hateful things. I was a good person. I am a good person.

'That's why you can't see anything. It's because of those damn sunglasses.'

Getting into our apartment, Yong banged his knee against the door. Sometimes his dark lenses made him look sleek, even a little dangerous, but at other times, like tonight, they seemed desperate.

'I'm glad it's over,' he said. 'The speech, the dinner, the whole thing.'

He looked tired. I decided to be kind. 'People loved your speech.'

'See, I told you it was what they wanted to hear.'

Tomorrow was Saturday, and Yong didn't have to go to work until after lunch. We could sleep in, have sex. I washed my face and brushed my teeth, checked to make sure the door was locked and the lights were off in the living room. We'd skip watching TV tonight.

I thought Yong had fallen asleep, but as I got into bed, he spoke up. 'So, who's Deming?'

I shut the light off so he wouldn't see the alarm on my face. 'Who?'

'Your phone rang when you were in the bathroom. It said *Deming*.'

My phone was lying face up on the night table. The screen displayed a missed call from you, a new voice mail message. I would listen to it later, when Yong was asleep.

I spoke at the ceiling. 'Deming is one of Boss Cheng's Xiamen clients. He's traveling abroad right now, calling at odd hours. He must have forgot the time difference.'

'Okay,' Yong said. He didn't sound convinced.

I pulled the sheets over my shoulders. 'Good night.'

A minute later, Yong spoke again. His voice sounded far away, even if he was next to me. 'When I came home earlier tonight, you were out on the balcony, on the phone. As soon as you saw me you ended the call. You were acting strange.'

I was glad he couldn't see my flushed cheeks or hear my rapidly beating heart. 'Are you accusing me of something?'

'No.'

'I haven't done anything wrong. You have nothing to worry about.'

'I'm not worried. But you seemed upset with Zhao.'

'I can't stand it when he talks about migrant workers that way. Why don't you ever say anything? Yongtex has your name. You got the award tonight. Tell him to shut up, once and for all.'

'I just don't let it bother me.'

'Could we go to Hong Kong instead of talking about it?'

'After the holiday season. There's a lot going on at work.'

'That's more than six months away.'

'Not so long, right?'

'I'm tired of these parties. Don't you get tired of it, too?'

'I don't mind.'

Yong didn't fight me. He wasn't angry. Again, I felt let down. I imagined leaving him, or being left. Losing this companionship, the comfort of being with someone you knew so well. I thought of the nights I had lain awake at Ardsleyville and in the workers' dormitory, even in the bunk on Rutgers Street, and how long they'd been, how endless the days. All I'd wanted then was to not feel alone. Last year, when Yong had been away for three weeks on business, I'd been glad to have the apartment to myself, didn't pick up my clothes or clean the dishes or take out the trash. But when I came home from work the apartment felt empty, and when I finally slept I would dream about you, a ten-year-old reciting New York City subway lines, then wake up unsure of where I was, expecting to see you across the room.

Yong touched my arm. 'I did good tonight, didn't I?'

'You did great.'

I knew that I should wait, hold off on telling Yong the truth and on calling you until I was stronger. I didn't want to upset you more. Yi Ba believed that to give in to your cravings was a sign of weakness. *Be strong*, I told myself, though I wasn't sure what that meant anymore. *Think it over before you say anything.*

But I couldn't stop myself. 'I have a son and I lost him.'

The words hung in the air for an awful, extended moment. 'A son?'

I couldn't answer.

'What do you mean, lost?'

'I had him when I was nineteen. Got pregnant by my neighbor in the village. I left him in America, because I couldn't take him back to China with me, and then he was adopted by an American family. He recently got in touch with me. That's who Deming is. That's his name. Deming Guo.' I wanted to say it again, so I did. 'Deming Guo.'

Your name echoed in the bedroom. Yong took his hand off my arm.

'He lives in New York, now, and he just found me. We spoke on the phone twice.'

Yong shook his head, as if he was trying to clear water out of his ears.

I looked at my husband and tried to will him to look back at me. Years ago, as a student in my class, his English had been clumsy, halting. In Chinese he could talk and talk, but in English he was nearly mute, and I had felt like I was somehow responsible.

'You left your son?'

'It's not like that.'

'I don't understand.'

'I was deported, okay? That's why I left America.'

'Why are you telling me this now?'

'I didn't want you to worry.'

'I can't believe you didn't tell me before.'

'I can explain.' He didn't respond. 'Are you mad at me?'

He wasn't mad. He didn't yell, or leave the room, or ask me to leave. Instead, he let me rest against him. He leaned into me. He took my hand and held it close.

But hadn't I always known he would do this? He had never been the yelling type.

In the moment before I told him about you, I had imagined I was ready to be left, to hear the slamming door, feel my anticipated punishment. That was the reason I'd kept you a secret for so long; why I had given up looking. But Yong was staying, and I would stay, too. In the end, what surprised me the most was my relief.

CHAPTER TWELVE

Roland's roommate Adrian had been home for days. Dumped by his girlfriend, he was no longer moving in with her at the end of May, and now Daniel had to wait for Adrian to finish taking a shower before he could get to the bathroom, which was two hundred percent hairier, the guy being both bearded and long-haired, a shag carpet of a man. Adrian was as silent as Roland was talkative, lumbering out of his room each day with a towel wrapped around his waist and greeting Daniel on the couch with a single 'Hey.'

On the morning of May 13, two days before the big show, Roland couldn't stop talking about who had RSVP'd and who hadn't, changing the set list for the twentieth time. Later tonight, they would run through the songs again.

As Adrian entered minute fifteen of a marathon shower, Daniel brushed his teeth in the kitchen sink. 'Thirty percent chance of rain today,' Roland said, pacing the living room. 'Think it'll make a difference in the turnout? People don't want to go out in the rain, though what's wrong with them, are they allergic to life? But there's also the humidity factor, since it's a new space to us, and that could affect the sound.'

Daniel rinsed his mouth and spat. If he didn't leave the

apartment in the next five minutes, he was going to be very late for work. He heard his phone ringing and dashed across the room to find it, knowing it wouldn't be his mother, yet hoping it would be. A week had passed since they had last spoken, and yesterday, tired of waiting for her to get in touch with him, he had called and left a message telling her to not bother calling him again. And she hadn't. He'd beat her to it.

It was Kay. He let it go to voice mail, and as he searched for a matching pair of socks he listened to her message, reminding him about the meeting with the Carlough dean, the day after tomorrow.

'Bad news?' Roland said.

Daniel found the missing sock. 'I might have to go upstate the day after tomorrow. For a meeting.'

'You're fucking with me, right? We have a *show* on Friday.'

Daniel poked through a lump of T-shirts and towels and found his right shoe, but not his left. 'A meeting with the dean of Carlough College.'

'You don't want to go to Carlough College.'

He pulled on the right shoe and laced it, hobbled around with his left foot in a sock. 'Maybe I do.'

'Who's going to play the show with me, then?'

'Get Javi to do it. I don't know. The guitar parts are easy.'

'Easy?' Roland mimed tearing his hair out. 'Make up your mind for once! You've been here for what, five months, and you haven't gotten a better job so you still can't afford to rent your own room.'

'I thought Adrian was moving out. I was going to take his room.' Daniel turned to face Roland. 'Do you want me to leave?'

'That's not the point. The point is that you're never going to get anywhere if you keep on doing what your parents want. You don't even know what you want. You don't think you deserve better.'

'Don't psychoanalyze me and don't tell me what to do.'

Daniel found his left shoe under the couch. In the bathroom, the shower shut off, Adrian crooning Christmas carols.

Roland looked disgusted. 'You know what? Don't bother coming to rehearsal tonight.'

'Come on. I've got to go to work.' Daniel opened the door, still holding the shoe. He'd put it on in the hallway. Right now, he needed to get out of the apartment.

Eight hours of burrito-making produced little relief. 'I'm going to your show Friday,' Evan said, as they sliced bell peppers. 'We used to have raves in Gowanus back in the day, these warehouse ragers. Now it's all gentrified and ruined.' His co-workers Purvi and Kevin were going, too. All afternoon, Daniel's phone buzzed with messages. Of course he'd play the show. Of course he wasn't going to Carlough.

When he left Tres Locos, it was after seven. He went back to the apartment to get his Strat, rode the train out to Bushwick, ran up the block to the building and took the rickety service elevator to the seventh floor. Outside the metal door, he heard a Psychic Hearts song playing, thought Javi might be at the rehearsal, too, but when he pushed the door open he saw Nate, strumming a guitar as Roland sang and pressed buttons on a sequencer. Nate's floppy hair bounced as he bobbed to the beat. He was hitting the right chords, but the song sounded even flatter than it already was.

Nate and Roland saw Daniel and exchanged a look. The song stopped.

'What's going on?' Daniel said. 'We're getting a second guitarist?'

'You're out and I'm in,' Nate said. 'That's what's going on.'

Roland walked over and said, his voice lowered, 'I can't have a band with someone who isn't reliable.'

'I'm going to play the show tomorrow.'

Roland shook his head. 'You'll change your mind again.'

'I won't, I swear. I'm not going to Carlough.'

'Too late,' Nate sang in a falsetto.

Roland glared at Nate, then walked Daniel out the door and started to close it. 'Sorry.'

It took less than ten minutes to scoop up his things from Roland's living room and shove them into his backpack. He left the Strat behind and grabbed his acoustic, walked up Lafayette, past the poker club, and turned onto Broadway. He put on his headphones and inched the volume up, let the music make the world louder, a glorious reverb of lights popping on like candy-coated solar flares as he listened to Bowie and Freddie Mercury's voices bursting out in 'Under Pressure':

> *why can't we give love*
> *givelovegivelovegivelove*

Without music, the world was flattened, washed out, too obvious. Daniel cranked the volume up even more, until he was awash in colors and sound and there were only lights and possibility and flying, the way it was when the guitar was translating his brain. He walked through Union Square, through the Flatiron, past people eating outside restaurants, a group of skateboarding teenagers, tourists clutching subway maps, laughing couples. Herald Square, chain stores; Times Square, more tourists. At Columbus Circle he sank onto a bench and put his guitar case down. He'd blown it.

He spent the night sipping watery coffee in a diner booth, typing angry texts to Roland and deleting them before sending. He sent a text to Angel, saying *hi, hope you're well* – he texted her every few days, but she never wrote back. Port Authority wasn't far away; he could buy a bus ticket and be in Ridgeborough in a couple hours. But Roland's accusations had stuck with him. He didn't know what he wanted, and he didn't know how to figure it out.

In the morning, he took the N train out to Sunset Park, had a bowl of pho at a Vietnamese spot, killed a few more hours in a café, then headed to the only people he knew in the city who might let him stay with them.

Vivian was on her porch, watering a planter of yellow and red flowers. 'Deming?' She eyed his bag and guitar case.

'Hi, Vivian.' Her eyes were shadowed by a lime green visor with VIRGINIA BEACH printed across the top, and Daniel couldn't read her expression. 'Is Michael here?'

'He's at school right now,' Vivian said in Fuzhounese. 'He'll be back later. You want to come in?'

'I need somewhere to stay. For today, tonight.'

'Okay. Put your bag in the living room.'

This was how he ended up cooking with Vivian. Timothy and Michael would both be home by dinner, she said. Daniel looked at the clock on the wall. It was just past two. Dinner was a long time away.

He chopped garlic and ginger on a cutting board, seated at a wooden table, as Vivian browned chunks of beef. On the table was a stack of mail, fliers for local businesses, printed in English and Chinese, the one on top advertising an immigration lawyer with an office on Eighth Avenue, the accompanying photo of a woman with aggressively airbrushed teeth. This was what his life would've been if he had remained Deming Guo, if his mother and Leon had stayed together. They would all be having regular family dinners with Vivian and Timothy.

'Leon said he spoke to you,' Vivian said, as the meat sizzled. 'He said he was happy to hear from you.'

'He gave me my mother's phone number.' When Vivian didn't say anything discouraging about his Chinese, he decided to press on, taking the time to remember and choose the right words. 'I called her. I spoke to her.'

He told Vivian about how his mother had remarried but hadn't told her husband about him. 'I still don't know where she went after she left New York, if she went to Florida.'

Vivian flipped the pieces of meat with a pair of metal tongs, then removed them onto a plate lined with a paper towel. 'I don't think so. Here, give me those.'

Daniel gave her the cutting board and she slid the garlic and ginger into the pot with the edge of the knife and stirred them with a wooden spoon. The room grew fragrant. 'But why did she end up in China, then?'

'I don't know, but she wouldn't have left without you. You were all she could talk about, all the time.' She returned the cutting board to him, now piled with carrots. 'Chop these into small pieces.' She put the beef back into the pot, filled it with water, clapped a lid on top. 'We would talk about the plans we had for you and Michael. She'd be smoking—' Vivian mimed taking a cigarette from her lips and holding it out with her elbow, gaze to the side, like his mother used to do. 'Always smoking, and she had that big old voice. And we'd have these giant mugs of tea in front of us in that little kitchen. We'd say Michael was going to become a doctor and you were going to work on TV.'

'TV?'

'She saw you working with the sound on TV or movies. Because you liked music. And TV. We weren't so wrong, were we?'

'You were pretty close.' Daniel sawed away at the carrots. An orange disc flew off the cutting board. He got up, hunted for it at the other end of the table.

'Here,' Vivian said, taking the knife from him. 'Cut like this.'

He angled it the way she showed him, slicing the carrots more loosely. She checked on the soup, adding salt and pepper. 'There was that nail salon. You remember the name?'

'Hello Gorgeous.' He'd looked it up, too, but it was no longer there.

'You remember your mother's friend there? Woman with a high baby voice.'

'Didi.'

'Right, Didi. So after your mother disappeared, Didi called Leon. Turned out someone ratted their boss out to ICE. Immigration. They came and arrested a lot of people at the salon. Your mother was supposed to be at work that day.'

He could remember overhearing Vivian and Leon talking about Didi, a lawyer. But not this. 'Nobody ever told me anything.'

'It happened to a woman I knew who worked in a restaurant. Someone crosses the wrong person, makes a call to ICE and they come take the workers away.'

'Take them where?'

'Deport them. Or they have these camps, these jails, for immigrants. We always heard rumors about them. I knew a lady whose husband had been sent to one, though. He went out driving to the grocery store and never came home. She found out he was in a jail in Arizona or someplace like that, and then he was on a plane back to their country, somewhere in Central America.' Vivian shook her head. 'So your mother's friend Didi figured out the restaurant in Florida where that job was and called them. They said your mother was buying a ticket for Florida, but never showed up. But Didi and Leon called ICE and they said she wasn't there either.'

She bought a bus ticket to Florida, but had told him they

weren't moving. It made no sense. 'So she wasn't in jail? I always thought it was another man. Though she was going to marry Leon.'

'I don't know.' Vivian picked up the junk mail and tossed the fliers into a plastic bin. 'We waited and waited for her. You remember, all those months. I wouldn't have paid off her debt if I knew she was coming back. I wouldn't have given you away.'

Had his mother been in jail while he was listening to records in Ridgeborough, when he and Angel had taken the cab to the old apartment? But she'd also known about his adoption? Daniel put the knife down. He had once stood with his mother and Leon on the Staten Island Ferry, both of them with their arms around him, their love sure and shining, the kind of gesture Kay and Peter tried to offer up but he could never bring himself to fully accept. He had lost so much, and he was lost. The distance between then and now felt enormous.

Now he was nervous that Michael and Timothy's arrival home would puncture the unexpected calm he had felt, being alone with Vivian all day. But when Michael did come home, after Daniel had taken a shower and a long nap, Daniel's dread disappeared. It felt good to be with people who didn't know him as a fuck-up.

After dinner, after his second helping of soup, then a third, Michael said, 'Want to play pool? There's a place in Bay Ridge.'

At the pool hall they got beers and played eight ball. Daniel made the break and called solids. 'I spoke to my mom again, by the way. Your mom thinks maybe she got caught up in an Immigration raid and thrown in jail and deported and that's why she ended up in China.'

'Damn. Did you ask her about it when you talked to her?'

'I didn't have the guts. She didn't seem to want to talk about it.' He aimed for a side pocket and missed. 'Thanks, though. You helped me get in touch with her.'

'Yeah, of course, of course. So are you going to talk to her again?'

'We'll see.'

Michael leaned onto the table and into his cue stick. 'Twelve to the ten. Corner pocket.' He made the shot.

'You're good,' Daniel said. 'Where'd you learn to play like that?'

'I play a lot with my friends. Some of them like to bet, but I don't. Hey, remember that research assistant job I was telling you about? I turned the application in. I decided to go with the project I wanted to do, the riskier one. Guess I have you to thank.'

There were video games across the room but Daniel didn't see video poker. 'What did I do?'

'You inspired me.'

'I don't know anything about science.'

'I mean, you're doing music, you're in this amazing band, you're living with your friends in the city. I can't even afford to move out of my parents' apartment unless I get this grant. I have to commute three hours to school and back and my mom grills the hell out of me if I stay out late. Instead of doing the safe thing, you're like – free.'

After Michael knocked down four balls in one round, Daniel managed to drop a solid ball. 'I'm not an inspiration. I got kicked out of the band. I owe my friend ten thousand bucks and she won't talk to me anymore. I got kicked out of school.'

'You did? Why?'

'You know how you said some of your friends like to bet? I guess I do, too.' Daniel finished his beer. He told Michael about the poker, the expulsion.

'Shit,' Michael said. 'I'm sorry that happened to you.'

'I kind of wanted to leave anyway.'

'Are you going to go back?'

'My parents want me to transfer to the school where they teach, upstate.'

'Do you want to go there?' The kindness in Michael's question gave Daniel déjà vu.

'No. Though sometimes it seems like I don't have a choice.'

Michael adjusted his watchband. 'I remember what you were like after your mother left. You thought she left because of you. You blamed yourself.'

'I was a kid. I didn't know what was going on.'

'I know it was a long time ago.' Michael laughed a little. 'But I just want you to be okay. And if you're not okay, I guess that's fine, too.'

'I am okay.' As he said it, he knew it was true.

'I miss her,' Michael said, 'your mother. She was always real nice to me.' He picked up his cue and studied the table. 'Eight ball, side pocket.' Daniel leaned against the edge, trying to distract Michael from scoring the winning shot, but Michael sank the ball and Daniel whooped, high-fiving him.

The apartment was quiet, everyone asleep except Daniel, who was on the living room couch. He looked at a picture of Michael in a cap and gown at his high school graduation, framed and hung on the wall over the television, along with a large department-store studio portrait of Vivian, Michael, and Timothy posing against a blue backdrop. Peter and Kay had one like it in their living room, with Daniel in the middle, taken several Christmases ago at the JCPenney's at the Littletown Mall. They had a framed picture of him from his high school graduation, too.

On the bottom shelf of a cabinet below the TV, Daniel found a row of photo albums. He removed one and flipped through the pages, saw pictures of Vivian and Timothy's wedding, faded portraits of people he didn't know, a younger Timothy with a full head of hair. He knew there wouldn't be any photos with himself in them but he kept looking, album after album, as if the next page would be the one where he would finally see Deming.

PART THREE

Tilt

CHAPTER THIRTEEN

'If we plot the supply curve and the demand curve on the same graph, we see that, in an efficient market, they intersect at an equilibrium price and quantity.' Professor Nichols pressed a button and the PowerPoint advanced, displaying a black-and-white graph. Fifty students sat at long tables arranged bleacher-style up the back of Peterson Hall, most studying their laptops, multiple chat windows dotting their screens like hungry mosquitoes. One woman in the back had headphones on, not bothering to hide her laughter as she watched a movie on her tablet.

'We call this p and q, respectively,' Professor Nichols said, twisting the end of his gray ponytail. Daniel Wilkinson sat in the next to last row, to the right of Amber Bitburger, watching the guy in front of him play online poker. The guy's neck was pink, his back set in a hard line. He kept betting too much on terrible hands and losing, and Daniel couldn't look away. The software that prevented him from playing was still installed on his laptop, and he hadn't seen a game in months. Unable to stand it a moment longer – the guy's back was so close he could almost touch it – he leaned until he was halfway over the table. The guy was wearing headphones but Daniel could hear the exact sound the cards made as they shuffled, a decisive, brassy bronze. He leaned closer. 'Hey,' he whispered. Amber glanced over. 'Don't do it,' Daniel said, as the guy's finger hovered over the bet button on an eight of clubs and a three of hearts. 'Damn it!' Daniel said out loud, as the guy clicked.

The guy twisted around, his ears reddening. 'What the fuck?' he hissed.

Professor Nichols said, 'Gentlemen, is there a problem up there?'

Daniel slumped down. Amber looked at him and mouthed, 'What was that about?'

After four months in New York City, Ridgeborough seemed smaller, shabbier, and more remote. The teenagers in the Dunkin' Donuts appeared younger than he'd looked when he was their age, and the Food Lion, with its wide, empty aisles and piped-in Lite Oldies music, evoked gloom. There were so many cereals, so many brands of toothpaste, and yet so few people; you could practically see tumbleweeds rolling down the floor past the sodas and chips.

Summer session was a four-month semester crammed into six weeks; he was in classes weekdays from nine to five. 'Good training for the working world,' Kay said. Mornings, Daniel felt like he'd been dug out of the ground and had to relearn how to walk. He would fall asleep in class, jerk awake, obsess about Psychic Hearts and the acclaim Nate was receiving that was supposed to be his.

On May 15, he had left the city at dawn, arriving in Ridgeborough in time to meet with the dean. That night, as Nate and Roland played for Hutch and Daniel's co-workers, Daniel had apologized to Peter and Kay. 'We can't take you seriously until you take yourself seriously,' Peter said. Kay had been able to get him into two classes, in her and Peter's departments: Comparative

Politics and Microeconomics 101. Eight hours of daily lectures felt isolating, and Daniel felt aggrieved, but also committed, superior; it was good for him, like going to the dentist or holding the door for a slow-walking stranger when you were in a rush.

After Econ, Amber Bitburger, whom he used to sit behind in Mrs Lumpkin's sixth-grade class, walked out with him into the full heat of a June afternoon. The onslaught of sunlight made his eyes sting after a long morning inside the windowless lecture hall, where the air conditioning always seemed to be set to fifty-five degrees. He removed his sweatshirt, and, in a green Meloncholia Records T-shirt with a picture of a cantaloupe on a turntable, bared his arms for the walk across the quad.

'What was that about?' Amber asked.

'That dude was losing hard. I wanted to help.' Daniel had looked for the guy after class, but lost him in the shuffle to leave Peterson Hall.

'A bunch of us are getting drinks on Saturday at the Black Cat,' Amber said, in her shaggy but upbeat voice. She still lived at home, still hung out with the same friends she'd had in high school, and was taking summer classes so she could finish college in three years.

'That sounds fun.' On Saturdays, Daniel would join Amber, Kelsey Ortman, and their other friends for beers at one of the two animal-named bars on Main Street in Littletown, down the hill from the Carlough campus: the Black Cat and the Spotted Cow. One week, there'd been an off-campus party, a near-duplicate of the parties he had gone to at Potsdam, white people dancing badly to corny hip-hop in a ramshackle house, beer bongs and screaming guys in baseball caps, someone barfing on the front lawn.

'They have an Open Mic there on Thursdays. Didn't you used to be into music in high school, with Roland Fuentes?' Amber pronounced it *Fen-Teez*. 'Wasn't he, like a little off in high school, with the green hair? He wore eyeliner.'

'I used to play guitar. We had a few bands back then.'

Amber's white-blonde hair was almost transparent in the sun. 'A bunch of us should check out the Open Mic one night.'

'Sure, that sounds good,' Daniel said, though he couldn't think of anything he wanted to do less.

'Harry's class will be a good entrée for you into the world of economics,' Peter said at dinner, 'a solid foundation for your future. There are so many ways that knowing economic theory can help enrich your life, from tracking your budget to knowing how to manage your stock portfolio. If only they made it a required class for all undergraduates.'

Kay asked him how Melissa's class was today. Melissa was Professor Schenkmann, a heavyset woman who wore long dresses in eighties prints, geometric overlapping shapes in hot pinks and lavenders. Daniel remembered going to her house as a kid, summer barbecues with other faculty families.

'Good,' Daniel said. Professor Schenkmann always made it a point to call on him, as if she was doing a favor to Kay, ensuring he got his tuition's worth.

They were having broccoli and chicken Parmesan. At least Kay had ceased her efforts to cook Chinese food. These efforts flared up periodically, once after they'd visited the Hennings and Elaine had given her a cookbook, and another time after he'd gone to a weeklong camp for Chinese adoptees, where the college-aged counselors, also adoptees, talked with such bare emotion that he felt embarrassed for them. Angel had learned how to make oddly sweet won tons that summer, but he was the only kid there who had been adopted past the age of infancy, who remembered anything about his birth mother.

Kay had become careful around him, overly solicitous. He knew she worried when he went out for drinks, so he made sure to be home by midnight, which wasn't hard; there was only so much time he could stand being around Amber and her friends. He could see how it reassured her. All it took to make her and Peter happy was to come home and go to Carlough, say he was going to GA meetings.

After dinner, Peter called Daniel upstairs to the study, where he was kneeling on the carpet with a mess of computer cables, whistling softly. 'Where does this go?' Peter peered over his reading glasses.

'Here, let me.' Daniel took the cord and tried several slots before a green light flashed on the speakers.

'Aha. Take a seat.' Peter cleared some old bills from a folding chair, typed in a website address and pulled up a YouTube screen. 'Look at that, you can get all kinds of music for free online. The other day, I watched footage from a concert I attended in 1978. Aerosmith at the War Memorial Arena in Syracuse. I was twenty-one – your age. Can you imagine, a concert you go to today, seeing it online in forty years?'

This was the most Peter had said to him in months that wasn't lecture-based. 'Is that what we're going to watch now? Did you see yourself in the audience?'

'No, you can only see the stage, and barely even that. Video technology was primitive back then.' Peter pressed play. 'But here, listen to that.'

It was video footage of an actual record spinning as it played Jimi Hendrix's '1983 ... (A Merman I Should Turn to Be)'. Daniel and Peter sat in their chairs and listened as the track slowed to a break and picked up again. Creeping, plodding. 'That backwards tape, it's a slow burn,' Peter said. 'They didn't need computers to make good music in those days.'

'It's a good track, Dad. One of his best.'

'I used to listen to this song when I was a kid. The age you were when you came to live with us in Ridgeborough. I had a few of my older brother's records that he left behind when he took off for college. We used to share a room, and after he left I'd sit on his bed and listen to his records. That's where I got my music taste from, your Uncle Phil. They say you always maintain a fondness for the first records you listened to. Like you and Hendrix.'

'I listened to music before Hendrix.' There'd been music in the city, plenty of it, and even Hendrix seemed kind of childish to him now.

The song transitioned into red-tipped sparkles, feedback and clanging bells. A shift in keys felt like the sun peeking through the clouds. 'I'm working on some new music,' Daniel said. 'Trying to, at least. You'd like it, it's just vocals and guitar, no computers. It's really different from what Roland and I were doing.'

Peter delivered a few soft slaps to the back of Daniel's shoulder. 'I'm glad you're back in school. Glad you're back at home.'

How easy it was to make Peter proud, how hungry he was for Peter's approval. 'I know.'

At the Food Lion, picking up groceries for Kay, he heard a voice go, 'Hey! Wilkinson!' and saw Cody Campbell in a cashier's uniform, waving to him from one of the registers. Cody looked mushier than he'd been in high school, where he had played football; he was still bulky, but his muscle had converted to fat.

Daniel got into Cody's checkout line. 'Hey, Cody.'

'I heard from Amber and Kelsey that you're back in town. Thought I'd see you around.'

'What have you been up to?'

'Same old, same old.' Cody scanned a package of frozen peas. 'Hoping to get out to Colorado soon. Couple buddies of mine are there. Bryan Mitchell and Mike Evans? They're going, too. Mike's brother lives out there, says they legalized weed. You can walk into a store and pick up edibles there, like you're going to the grocery store. You can buy it with your credit card, get stoned, like right there.'

'Wow. Colorado, huh?'

'Yeah. You coming out to the Black Cat tomorrow?'

'I think I'm busy,' Daniel said.

The next night, the phone rang on the landline and Kay called up the stairs. 'It's for you, Daniel.' He was staring at his notes for Professor Schenkmann's class. Their final assignment, three short essays, were due tomorrow, and he hadn't begun. When he tried to work on them he would end up googling Psychic Hearts, which was how he found out they were playing Jupiter at the end of August.

He picked up the extension in the study.

'Hey, it's Cody. You want to grab a beer?'

'I would, but – another night.'

Daniel was about to hang up when Cody said, 'Hey, you still smoke?'

They drove out to the pond at the bottom of Cedar Street, where they had hung out on summer nights in high school. Cody pulled his Jeep into a clearing at the edge of the woods and parked.

'You still live with your folks?' Daniel asked, as they passed a bowl back and forth. He couldn't see anything outside, the darkness vast, the silence eerie. He switched on the radio, which was tuned to a classic rock station. Pearl Jam flew out.

'Yeah, but—' Cody flicked the lighter. 'I'm getting out soon. Got to save up.'

Daniel took another hit. Several moments passed, and the familiar, grateful fuzziness arrived. He leaned back in the passenger seat, thinking he should buy weed off Cody and go to class high. 'For Colorado.'

'Right. I have to get my cash money in order, you know? I have some debt I have to pay off, but I'm working on it.'

'I have some of that, too. Debts.'

'Sucks, man. Fuck a debt.' Cody packed another bowl. The car was choked with smoke. 'Hot-boxing in the front of my Jeep,' he sang to the tune of 'Party in the U.S.A'. His voice wasn't half bad.

'Nice. You should record an album. Roland and I recorded one a few weeks ago, with this record collective in the city. Meloncholia? You know it? The band, Psychic Hearts, we're playing a show on August 18 at Jupiter. This club down in the city.'

'In Colorado,' Cody was saying, 'there's mountains everywhere. You can live on a mountain and ski to work. That's what I'm going to do. I don't know how you could live in New York Shitty. It's fun to party in, but it smells like a bag of assholes. Anyway, I couldn't live in one of those little apartments that cost nine thousand bucks a month. I want a house in a mountain. A whole house in a whole motherfucking mountain.'

'It doesn't cost nine thousand bucks. That's only for celebrities. So where are you going to live?'

'What? I said, Colorado.'

'I mean, in Colorado. Where are you going to live *in* Colorado.'

'In a mountain! I said that. You're not listening. Where Mike's brother lives. The – I forget the name of the town. His name's Chris.'

'When did you visit him?' This was ridiculous. Daniel wanted to tell Roland about getting faded with Cody Campbell at the pond at the bottom of Cedar, about going to Econ every morning with Amber Bitburger, but he hadn't spoken to Roland since getting kicked out of the rehearsal space. It wasn't like Roland had contacted him either, but he missed Roland, damn it, missed him like subways and rooftops and singing, even if being back in Ridgeborough was an unanticipated reprieve. He had eliminated the possibility of feeling out of place by banishing himself to *no place*, stoic nights alone in his bedroom or flipping through news magazines with Peter and Kay.

'I haven't gone there yet, Wilkinson, I saw pictures. I told you, I've got to get my money in order, pay off that debt, but I'm working on it, I'm figuring it out. Like you. Gonna make our dreams happen, right?' Cody held out the pipe. 'More?'

'Yes, please.'

Cody's phone chirped, signaling a new text. 'It's Amber. She wants to know if we want to go to the stupid Open Mic at the stupid Black Cat.'

'Let's go.' Daniel wanted to be around other people, even if they were Amber and Kelsey. He rolled down the window and heard crickets and frogs over the radio, but the woods seemed sinister, foreboding. One time in high school, Mike Evans had driven his brother's moped into the pond.

'You serious?'

'Come on, we can grab a beer, chill.'

Cody considered this. 'I am kind of parched.'

In the back room of the Black Cat, the only business open on a block of boarded-up storefronts, four middle-aged men were playing a cover of Guns N' Roses' 'Paradise City'. Amber and Kelsey waved Daniel and Cody over from a table near the stage.

'You guys found each other,' Amber said. 'You smell like a bong.'

'Like Colorado,' Daniel said.

'How's all that studying going for your test tomorrow, Wilkinson?'

'What test?' Daniel poured himself a glass of beer from the pitcher on the table. The band broke into a guitar solo and the lead singer, bald and stocky, started headbanging. Daniel laughed. 'These guys suck.'

'They're not that bad,' Kelsey said.

'They'd last half a song in the city until they got booed off stage.'

'Guns N' Roses is all right.' Cody screwed up his face and played air guitar. His fingers weren't even in the right places for the imaginary frets and strings. '*You're in the jungle now!* I don't care if they suck. I don't care.'

Kelsey shrieked. 'Oh my God, you guys are twins!'

Daniel looked down. He was wearing his hiking boots, even in the middle of the summer, because he didn't have any other shoes. Cody was wearing a pair, too. Both of them wore blue jeans and black T-shirts.

'You're like the Asian version of Cody,' Amber said, and everyone laughed.

Kelsey took a picture with her phone. Cody said, with a fake lisp, 'We planned our outfits together.'

The singer screeched. The band, at least, looked like they were having fun.

He came home at midnight, his buzz long gone, and lay on top of the same quilt that had been there when he'd first become Daniel. Those early months in Ridgeborough had been suspicious, begrudging. But at some point it had become easier to play along; it had become second nature. The doubts had burrowed deeper until he barely felt them at all. By his last year in high school, thinking of Deming or Mama was like remembering a terrible band he had once loved but now filled him with mortification. Only once, in high school, after he saw the Chinese woman in the mall, had he let things slip. When Kay and Peter had told him that he had to stay home and study for the SATs instead of going to see a band with Roland, Deming had said his real mother would've let him go. It had popped out, unbidden, *real mother* an abstraction; Mama would probably have made him stay home. He hadn't meant to hurt Kay and Peter that much, but he was angry at the injustice – if he missed this show he might never see this band again! – and Kay had winced and told him it wasn't the end of the world. 'We are your real family,' Peter had said.

Back then, the mystery of what happened to his real family had been too enormous to solve. But now he had found them, and nothing had changed.

He'd have to pull an all-nighter to finish the essays. Schenkmann had returned his last paper marked up in red pen. He typed his name out on a blank Word document, followed by the date. The cursor blinked back at him as he read the first question again.

> Discuss two major theories that characterize the role played by interest groups in U.S. politics. Describe the insights these theories can offer regarding the operations of the legislative process.

He sighed. He had never seen the guy who was playing poker in Econ class again; Amber said he might have dropped out. Daniel closed his laptop and decided to take his guitar out instead. A new thing was forming, not the essay he was supposed to write, but the song he'd been working on before he left the city.

Two hours later, when he returned to the essay, he saw an e-mail from Angel. He'd been sending her the occasional message, but this was the first time she had responded.

> Daniel, PLEASE don't text me anymore. I wish you
> the best.
> ~ A

He read it again. She had wished him the best. It was proof she still cared for him, otherwise she wouldn't have bothered to write at all. He recalled her clear, low voice, devoid of shrillness or forced emotion, and craved her decisiveness, her competence; he would keep writing her until she understood. Because here was a way he had changed: he'd lost his mother and Roland, things that should have made him feel worthless and rejected. Yet it hadn't destroyed him.

He'd do it for Angel, then. School, grades, career, show her he could get it together. She would have to forgive him. He hit reply, a streak of hope:

> i'm going to do better for you

CHAPTER FOURTEEN

The front of the card was pastel blue plaid. 'Dear Dad,' he wrote. 'Happy Father's Day. Love, Daniel.'

'I was thinking,' Kay said, sitting next to Daniel at the kitchen table, 'since it's Father's Day and all.'

He folded the card into the envelope, licked and sealed it, wrote 'Dad' on the front.

'About how Mother's Day has always been a little uncomfortable for me. I appreciate how you always give us cards. But I can guess that maybe these aren't the most comfortable holidays for you either?'

'I don't mind.'

'I mean, when you were younger I thought I didn't deserve to celebrate the holiday, that it was, I don't know, inauthentic for me to do so as an adoptive mother. Elaine was the one who told me, just embrace it. It didn't do you any good to have a parent doubting her ability. You needed a mother, and if I wasn't a mother, then who was?' Kay ran her fingers along the edge of the table. 'I had those doubts a lot when you first came to live with us.'

Daniel pushed his empty sandwich plate around in a semi-circle. Peter was upstairs in the study; he should go spend more time with Peter. It was Father's Day.

Kay's eyes flipped from Daniel's face to the wall to the kitchen window. 'We were so afraid of doing something wrong. We thought it would be better if you changed your name so you would feel like you belonged with us, with our family. That you had a family.'

Daniel never knew if Kay wanted him to apologize or reassure her. Either way, he always felt implicated, like there was some expectation he wasn't meeting.

'Mom.' He didn't want to see her cry, especially if it was on his behalf. 'It's okay.'

Kay got up, and he heard her opening the drawer of the dining room cabinet. She returned, placing a fat manila envelope on the table.

'What's this?'

'It's all the records we have concerning your adoption. The correspondence with the foster care agency, the forms we filled out. I've been meaning for you to have them.'

Daniel opened the envelope and flipped through the stack of paper, saw the forms and e-mails he'd read that afternoon ten years ago. 'Thanks.' There would be nothing in here he hadn't seen before.

'Your father didn't agree with me about doing this. He said it would only stir up bad memories, but I insisted.'

Daniel bent the envelope's metal clasp back and forth. 'I do know some things, actually. I should tell you. I found my mother recently – I mean, my birth mother. She's in China.'

He told Kay about how his mother had gone to work and never came home, how Leon had left for China six months after. How Vivian had gotten him fostered. That his mother might have been deported.

Kay looked like she'd been punched.

'I spoke to her,' he finally said. 'Twice.'

'What did she say? What was it like?' Kay's smile was trembling at the sides, so strained it looked like it hurt.

'It was good, though a little weird, and my Chinese is rusty but we managed to understand each other. She lives in Fuzhou, and she's married and working as an English teacher.'

'Are you going to talk to her again?'

'Maybe.'

Kay picked up the envelope and tapped the bottom of it against the table, straightening out the papers inside. 'By the way,' she said, 'I received a curious phone call the other day. From Charles, Angel's boyfriend.'

'Oh?'

'He said you borrowed money from Angel and haven't paid her back. I asked him why he was calling me about it and he said I should ask you. So, I'm asking.'

Daniel tried to detect whether he heard an accusation in Kay's statement, whether she was still assuming the worst from him, if he was the Daniel that fucked up or the Daniel who needed to be cared for. 'She must have been talking about this one time we met up in the city. I didn't have any cash on me and I had to borrow some to pay for dinner.'

'It sounded like more than that. What Charles said, it sounded serious. And wasn't she talking at Jim's birthday party about a thief?'

'It's not serious. He's making it up.'

'But why would her boyfriend call me and make something like that up? Please, explain.'

'There's nothing to explain. For all I know, he might be jealous. Of me and Angel being such good friends. Some guys get like that.'

Daniel saw, in Kay's expression, the same mix of hurt and suspicion as when she learned about his expulsion from

Potsdam. He got up, taking the envelope. 'But you reminded me that I forgot to pay Angel back. I'm going to go do that now, on my computer.'

He passed both his classes for the first part of the summer term, a C+ in Comparative Politics and a B in Microeconomics. The second part proceeded in the same joyless vein, Macroeconomics in the mornings, an American History course in the afternoons. In late July, a lone text message appeared from Roland, asking Daniel how he was doing. Daniel wrote back, congratulating Roland on the Jupiter gig and wishing him the best, echoing Angel's wish to him in her e-mail – which had been insincere, as she'd sicced Charles on him.

That night, he borrowed Peter's Volvo and drove around by himself. He had missed driving while in the city, the steering wheel hard beneath his palm, free hand floating out the open window with air thick between his fingers, the easy slide down the curving two-lane roads. He remembered driving through the night with Roland their senior year, all the way to Boston, drinking gas station coffee and singing along to mix CDs. They'd been driving to a friend's house when they decided to get on the highway and keep going east, couldn't bear another Saturday night in Ridgeborough, and when they got to Boston they had breakfast at a diner, waffles and pancakes and Western omelets, a bright winter morning with flurries of snow. Daniel had watched the joggers in their thermal outfits crossing the bridge over the Charles River, college students in sweaters and scarves toting large cups of coffee. He had dreamt about leaving home and being on his own, about the life that awaited him once he left Ridgeborough. When he could be free, in the way Michael thought he already was.

Now, looping around town with no destination, his phone

plugged into the car's speakers, skipping from song to song and album to album and growing bored with each track after a few seconds – he was sick of all his music, five thousand songs and not a damn thing to listen to – the music went silent.

He pulled over to the shoulder. Either his phone's battery had died, or the cable needed to be replugged. He rolled down the windows and heard layers of chirping crickets, opened the door and walked out to the street. There were houses in the distance, the occasional light, and a swath of tall grass on the corner he pushed around with his feet. He and Roland used to practice wheelies on their dirt bikes near here. He stood still, absorbing the night.

For so long, he had thought that music was the one thing he could believe in: harmony and angular submelody and rolling drums, a world neither present nor past, a space inhabited by the length of a song. For a song had a heart of its own, a song could jumpstart or provide solace; only music could numb him more thoroughly than weed or alcohol. With Roland, he had wanted to fill other people's silences, drown out their thoughts and replace them with sound. It was less about communication, more about assault and plunder. That was how he'd preferred it. But standing on the dark street, a pressure released inside him, the crickets a consolation for his remorse over leaving the city, that he had pushed his mother away before she could tell him the truth.

Most nights Daniel began to stay in. He did homework, wrote music, used an old condenser mic to record several tracks onto Peter's computer, which ran a pirated version of Pro Tools faster than his laptop. The songs he was writing weren't anything like the ones he and Roland played. They lacked structure, didn't cohere in a predictable way. They were too bare, too vulnerable, they cared too much to be cool. He no longer wanted to make music that forced itself on you, or tried to be something it wasn't. The challenge was not to overstate, but to be honest, unguarded. In class, he worked on lyrics as Professor Nichols droned on about X and Y variables; it felt like he was defrosting a windshield, that the fog would eventually reveal clear glass.

In the back of his closet, he found a stack of cassettes. One of them had a label drawn in marker: NECROMANIA: BRAINS ON A *spike!!!!* He remembered recording it on Roland's mom's old tape player one afternoon, his first year in Ridgeborough, the two of them wailing along to a three-chord backing track they had downloaded online. He put the tape in a padded envelope along with a note that said, 'Remember when we used to jam?' and mailed it to Roland's apartment.

He was at Cody's on a Friday night in August, in the Campbells' basement, watching an MMA fight. Cody was the only person he talked to these days, besides Peter and Kay. Amber wasn't taking classes for the rest of the summer and had gone to visit family in Connecticut.

The match ended, the guy in the red shorts standing over the prone body of the guy in the black shorts. Blood ran down both their faces.

Daniel had transferred the tracks he'd mastered from Peter's computer to his phone. 'You want to hear something I'm working on?'

Cody looked over.

'Will you turn the volume down for a second?'

'Hold on.' Cody waited to see if the announcer was saying anything important. When the match switched to a commercial, he hit mute.

Daniel took out his phone. He heard the familiar first

notes, the guitar, his own voice, tinny and monotone on the microspeaker. The sound was too poor to make out most of the words.

'That you?' Cody said.

'Yup.' The song didn't need any more changes or rewrites. It didn't matter if he'd ever perform. It was exactly what he wanted it to be.

'You've changed, Wilkinson,' Cody said, after the song ended.

'How so?'

'In high school, you were all like—' Cody hunched over, curling his shoulders in and looking down at the carpet. '*Reave me arone,*' he said. 'You barely spoke English! Now you're all American.'

'What the hell are you talking about? I spoke English.'

'You called that English?'

'Fuck off, Cody. Fuck you.'

'You need a drummer,' Cody said, as Daniel headed toward the door. 'Like those guys at the Black Cat Open Mic. They rocked.'

He couldn't sleep; he decided to sit on the porch. Looking for his phone, he spotted the manila envelope from Kay, grabbed it and then went outside. Beneath the porch light, he examined the printout of the permanency hearing report. *Foster parents plan to petition for termination of mother's parental rights on grounds of abandonment.* He held the envelope upside down and shook it hard, until the rest of the contents fell into his lap.

There was the surrender form, with Vivian's signature. *Placement: Indefinite.* Another form she signed, authorizing his foster placement. There was a smaller envelope, too, tucked into the papers, which contained a transcript of his grades from P.S. 33. He'd gotten straight C's and D's in fifth grade. A note from his teacher, a Ms Torelli, that said he should take remedial classes. Another note that said he had been in detention on February 15. He had forged his mother's signature on the required line and must have neglected to return it to school after she disappeared.

There was a black-and-white photograph of him and his mother paper-clipped to one of the forms, the bottom half of the picture a printed illustration of the Empire State Building, the Statue of Liberty, and a yellow cab driven by a googly-eyed giraffe, along with a caption for the South Street Seaport. He was a baby, fat cheeks and a swirl of dark hair, and his mother looked like a child herself, younger than he remembered her. It was the only baby picture of himself he had ever seen, the only picture of her he had. Why hadn't Peter and Kay given it to him before?

He pulled it closer to his face, pictured Vivian packing his clothes for him, finding the detention form, calling the school for his transcripts, going through his mother's things and digging up the photograph. She had put it in the pile for him to have, a single memento of his mother, dumped it all in an envelope and handed it over to Social Services. But had Vivian done these things, or had Leon? Or was it his mother, had *she* had a hand in it? He examined the possibilities. His mother had been in jail. She'd been deported. She loved him. She didn't care. You could play it one way and play it another, the same note sounding different depending on how you decided to hear it. You could try to do all the right things and still feel wrong inside.

He found her number, still in his phone, and called one last time. She didn't answer.

The next day, he registered for the fall classes Peter and Kay suggested, and when Kay said, 'You paid Angel back, right?' he said he had.

*

To celebrate Daniel finishing the summer with passing grades, Peter and Kay took him out to dinner at the Ridgeborough Inn, where they had gone for his high school graduation, the publication of Kay's book, and Peter's promotion to department chair after Valerie McClellan had retired. The Inn was a dimly lit cave with wooden beams and obsequious elderly waiters in heavy maroon-and-gold uniforms, a matching menu listing steaks and chops and French onion soup in ornate cursive font. It was the only restaurant near Ridgeborough where you didn't look out of place in a jacket and tie.

Peter ordered a bottle of Malbec. The waiter filled their glasses, and Peter raised his. 'To Daniel, for being back on the right path. To the beginning of the rest of your life.'

Daniel had borrowed a tie of Peter's and wore the one suit jacket he had, the sleeves now short on him, but the shoulders loose. He kept adjusting the tie, pulling down on the cuffs. Even his pants were tighter than they had been a few months ago, now that he drove instead of walking.

The right path was veering off the side of a cliff. Peter and Kay were beaming. 'We're proud of you,' Kay said.

He blew on his soup to cool it, used his spoon to break up the bread on top. A tendril of steam escaped; still too hot to eat. He placed his spoon on the table, its round face shining up at him like a query.

The waiter hovered over them, offering pepper for their salads. Small candles twinkled on the tables, but the maroon wallpaper and thick curtains made the room cold and dark. Paintings with baroque brass frames hung from the walls, portraits of men in military uniforms, women in long dresses, their expressions pinched and severe. Landscapes of rolling hills and weeping willows, white farmhouses in the distance.

'That's the famous Ridgeborough oxbow.' Peter squinted at a painting of a meadow with a river on one side.

'I don't see any oxen,' Daniel said.

'Ox*bow*. The river is making an oxbow there. See, it bends this way and that. This must be former Wilkinson land, here in the painting. My grandfather mentioned it in the family history he wrote before he passed.' Peter's voice rose. 'Your great-great-grandfather owned that land once. He grew vegetables, he had horses. He was an enterprising man. Jacob Wilkinson.'

Daniel pressed his spoon into his soup again. There was a quiet sorrow about the weighted silver cutlery, the paintings of bygone people and places. He was the last of the Wilkinsons, the only grandchild. His only cousins were on Kay's side of the family, and they had his Uncle Gary's last name. The way Peter spoke about it, being the last of the line was a great responsibility; he had to do something special to live up to Jacob Wilkinson's legacy. This man he looked nothing like, whom, if he had been alive, would probably never accept Daniel as a true Wilkinson.

The spoon peered up at him and he looked down at the metal, hoping to see his reflection, but it was too dark to see anything but drops of soup.

The night before the first day of fall semester, Daniel edited a track on Peter's computer. His voice sounded strange, pitching sharp, too forceful for the melody.

The shelves in the study housed an overflow of books, with somber covers and lengthy titles about democracy and open markets. Copies of Peter and Kay's own books filled half a shelf. He'd looked at them before, had seen the author biographies and photographs. Peter's book was dedicated to Daniel and Kay; Kay's to Daniel and Peter. The wall above the computer show-cased their diplomas: bachelors', masters', and doctoral degrees for both of them. Framed proof of their other accomplishments, awards, articles, book reviews in academic journals, surrounded him. He took his headphones off. The song wasn't working.

He walked past Peter and Kay's room to make sure they were still asleep, then came back to the study and shut the door. Telling himself it wouldn't work, that he was only trying because he wanted to make sure it wouldn't work, he typed *BigPoker* into the browser. Breath quickening, he typed *.com* and hit return. He remembered an old account, one he'd barely used and hadn't told Peter and Kay about. The homepage loaded, and seeing the green background and digital cards felt like running into an old girlfriend. There was fifty dollars in this forgotten account. He would play just one game and log out, then cancel everything.

He started on a table of chumps, like that guy in his Econ class, and someone named AardvarkTexas went all in with a pair of queens – Daniel called, holding pocket aces – but then he couldn't quit while ahead. One game turned into two, which turned into a sit-and-go, and another, and his account was up to a hundred dollars, then three hundred, then five. He danced in the chair, listening to the clinks and chimes of chips and cards, woozy from the rush, until he felt a hand on his shoulder.

'I knocked,' Peter said.

'Dad?' His heart pounded, but he couldn't help it; he turned to the screen to confirm his winning hand. His account ticked up. As Peter watched, Daniel pumped his fist in the air.

This time, Peter was calm, like he'd been expecting this. 'All right. That's enough now.'

It was seven in the morning. Daniel packed his backpack, the same one he had brought with him to the city, but left his guitar in his room. He'd have them send it to him later, wherever he was going.

Kay sat at the kitchen table, drinking a cup of tea. There were half-moon shadows under her eyes, which were puffy from crying.

'You're not going to ask me to stay?'

She shook her head. 'I got an e-mail from Elaine.'

He pulled his bag onto his shoulder. 'I'll let myself out.'

CHAPTER FIFTEEN

He remembered nothing about the flight, only darkness, rocking, then waking nineteen hours later to sunlight slamming through the window, walking off the plane and into a humid afternoon, one full day disappeared. The lone runway was surrounded by potholed streets, a long line of dirt and rocks, like the airport had been dropped into a sandbox. Language flew around him at warp speed, harsher and throatier than the same dialects he'd heard in New York.

Motorcyclists circled like vultures. 'Fuzhou!' they barked. 'Fuzhou!' He took a step forward, and three motorcyclists braked and shouted. 'Get on, quick,' the first man said, and Daniel balanced himself on the seat and was fixing the straps of his backpack when the driver accelerated and he flew forward. 'Grab on,' the guy said. He wrapped his arms around the man's waist, coughing back exhaust as they shot through the streets. He saw other motorcyclists and passengers wearing smog masks.

'Where you going?' the driver asked.

'Fuzhou,' Daniel yelled.

'*Where* in Fuzhou?'

'Downtown?'

'Wuyi Square.'

'Yeah,' Daniel said.

They careened down a long road, empty except for the occasional passing truck. Daniel spat out gravel and dust and the wind blew a glob of saliva back onto his jeans. He couldn't let go of the driver's waist, so the spit sat on his thigh, taunting him, spreading into the fabric. Green fields and hills were punctuated by clusters of buildings. With their knobby trunks and feathery leaves, the trees seemed older, friendlier, than the pines and oaks of upstate New York.

'Where you from?' the driver asked, as the fields gave way to taller buildings.

'America.'

'Ha!'

'New York.'

'Chinese?' the driver asked.

'Yes.'

'Cantonese?'

'Fuzhounese.'

The driver made a sound like *pshaw*. 'No.'

'Yes. My mother is from Minjiang.'

'*Hrm.*'

The four-lane road was clogged with cars and buses. The driver slowed to a standstill, surrounded by a solid mass of traffic, all of it honking in unison, then lit a cigarette, the smoke drifting directly into Daniel's face. The light changed to green and the driver threw the cigarette onto the ground and accelerated, Daniel bouncing hard against his back.

He was dropped off on a busy street near a Pizza Hut and a shopping mall.

'You know a hotel around here?'

'Over there,' the driver said, gesturing to the other side of an overpass and a traffic circle. He had a small, pimpled baby-face, and Daniel saw that they were around the same age.

'How much for the ride?'

'One hundred fifty yuan.'

Daniel took out two hundred-yuan bills from the money he'd gotten at the airport currency exchange.

'You speak funny.' The driver handed Daniel his change. 'You've got a Cantonese accent.'

It wasn't until Daniel was paying for a room at the Min Hotel, a six-story building with wall-to-wall orange carpet, that he realized the driver had given him only ten yuan in change.

His room was on the third floor at the end of a long hallway, a double room with two queen-sized beds, more expensive than the singles. It was the only room they had available, the clerk said, and Daniel had been too tired, too humiliated by his accent, to argue. He crawled into the bed closest to the window, the sheets and pillows smelling like cigarette smoke, though he'd requested a non-smoking room. He would call her when he was more coherent. Maybe then he would sound less Cantonese.

He woke up three hours later, head aching, the room dark. According to the clock it was early evening, and when he opened the curtains, it was still light out. A line of buses idled in traffic below. A crowd of people were standing outside the Pizza Hut. Overwhelmed, he sat down on the bed. He calculated what time it was in New York, how long it had been since he'd eaten. He turned on his phone and dialed his mother's number, but it wouldn't go through. He tried again and got the same result. There was no wireless Internet in the hotel, so he couldn't get online to see if he had to dial a special code. He tried again using the phone by the bed, but it only produced an automated recording that said he was unable to make this phone call. It was Planet Ridgeborough all over again.

'You'll have to dial this code,' the clerk said, when he went down to the front desk.

'Even for a – nearby call?'

The clerk's eyebrows resembled subtraction signs. 'Your cell won't work here,' she said. 'If you use the phone in your room and punch in this code, you should be able to complete the call. We can charge any phone calls to your account if you give us a credit card.'

Daniel tried to decipher the clerk's rapid words as he grasped for a response. He took out his credit card. He'd already charged the flight; a couple phone calls wouldn't make a difference.

He returned to the room and called his mother's number again, using the phone by the bed. This time, he got her voice mail.

'Mama, it's Deming. I'm in Fuzhou and I want to see you. I'm staying at the Min Hotel in Wuyi Square, room 323. Please call me.' He left the phone number for his room and went out in search of dinner.

Fuzhou smelled like a barbecue in autumn. The buildings had windows that reminded him of eyes, tracking his winding journey. Some buildings were wide and curved with long strips of windows like slices of gray masking tape, others tall and skinny with sharp or circular rooftops. Some buildings looked like an open greeting card, set on a table with arms flung out to embrace him. Others were only partially constructed, their tops a skeletal cage of scaffolding, and from a distance they resembled a band of mismatched toys. There was an architectural incongruence, but it made sense. Daniel preferred disorder to order, liked the trees in the spaces between buildings, leaves touching the low roofs of older homes. The city looked like it was trying to build itself up but would never fully succeed. This was an underdog's city, ambitious and messily hungry, so haphazard it could collapse one night and be reassembled by the following morning.

The sounds of Fuzhou were deep yellows, blues, and oranges. Fuzhounese and Mandarin banged out around him, the playlist of his unconscious, and even the words and phrases he didn't recognize were like falling into a warm bath. There was not one scrap of English, not anywhere; not in the street signs and bus stops and billboards, not in the voices he overheard, nor in the music sliding out of taxis. It was trippy, surreal, the swirl of familiar sounds on such unfamiliar streets. He'd never been to Fuzhou before but it was a place he already knew. His brain struggling to stay alert, he repeated to himself in English: *I'm in China! I'm in China!*

He turned to avoid a moped careening down the sidewalk and a bicyclist nearly swerved into him. When he stopped, the woman behind him yelled, 'Move it!' He ducked into the nearest store to get his bearings. After a little effort he recalled the word for map and bought one of the city, but when he unfolded it the street names were in Chinese characters and he couldn't read a thing.

He saw a family heading onto a crooked side street, nearly hidden in the high-rises, and followed them along a stone wall plastered with signs exhorting the importance of washing your hands after you sneeze. Stepping over puddles with an oily sheen in the center, he walked into a courtyard. The noise from Wuyi Square had disappeared, and the buildings reminded him of the houses on 3 Alley, two-story homes with brick walls and hanging laundry. Children played as old women sat on plastic stools and fanned themselves with newspapers, talking about how so-and-so's daughter was marrying so-and-so's son. Inside the houses he saw families cooking and eating dinner. A lump formed in his throat.

He found a noodle stall tucked between two of the houses and ordered a bowl of vermicelli noodles in pork broth with vegetables, glad nobody commented on his Fuzhounese. The food appeared and he scarfed it down, drank cups of watery tea until his headache subsided. On his way back to the hotel he got lost, went the long way around a construction site of eerie half-demolished structures, and by the time he found Wuyi Square, it was dark.

No new messages for him in the hotel room. Daniel took a long shower, filling the bathroom with steam clouds. He called his mother again, left her another message, then lay down. He woke at seven in the morning with the light streaming through the open curtains. She still hadn't called him. A heavy stinging grew behind his eyes. He had made it here, but she didn't want to see him, and he had no one to go home to.

Two mornings ago, he had left Ridgeborough with nine hundred and sixty bucks in his bank account. During a lull in the middle-of-the-night drama with Kay and Peter, he quietly cashed out of the game, charged a ticket to Fuzhou leaving from the Syracuse airport the following afternoon, and deleted the poker account. On the corner of Oak Street at seven in the morning, he called Cody.

'Can you do me a huge favor?' he'd said. 'I need a ride to the airport.' Cody arrived in his Jeep with a good-bye present, a baggie of Vicodin from his recent wisdom teeth removal, for Daniel to take on the flight. When Daniel checked in at the airport and cleared security six hours early, he sat at the empty gate and realized he was shaking. In the end, he hadn't been able to do what Peter and Kay wanted. Three more semesters of classes, followed by graduate school. Staying upstate. He hadn't been able to do what Roland wanted either, play the music Roland wanted him to play. If he could just talk to his mother in person, maybe he could figure out who he should be.

Now, in the hotel, he wished he had her address. All he knew was what she'd told him on the phone, that she lived in a neighborhood called West Lake and worked in a school that taught English. He called and left her another message, took the elevator down to the lobby. 'Can you look up an address for me?' he asked the clerk. 'A Polly Guo. Or Peilan Guo. She lives in West Lake.' She might have changed her last name when she got married, but he didn't know her husband's name, only that he owned a textile factory.

The only phone book the hotel had was five years old. The clerk flipped through the pages. 'Guo ... Guo.' She ran her index finger down the pages. 'I don't see a Polly or Peilan. Here's a Peng, Pan ... There are Guos with a P sound for first name, but the addresses are nowhere near West Lake Park.'

'Do you know of any English schools nearby?'

'You want to learn English?' the clerk said.

'Um – sure.'

'My friend goes to an English school near the highway. I can ask her for you.'

'Is that in West Lake?'

The clerk opened a drawer and took out a bus map. 'Look, we're over here.' She pointed to a spot. 'West Lake Park is up here.' She traced a line across the city, her finger stopping on a square of green. 'You can take this bus, the stop is two blocks away.'

Daniel asked if there was any way he could check the Internet. He could try looking up English schools, use an online translator to convert the Chinese words into English, call around and see if any of them had a Polly or Peilan working there. The clerk said there was an Internet café not too far away, but it wouldn't be open for another hour or two. 'Do you want breakfast?' She gestured to the far corner of the lobby, where there was a group of tables behind a partition, and said breakfast was included in the price of the room.

At the tables were men and women in matching green shirts. Daniel took a seat next to a guy with a stringy goatee, across from a couple talking in Mandarin. A hotel employee came over and asked what room he was staying in, checked a notepad and deposited a tray with a bowl of watery congee, small plates of salted peanuts and pickled vegetables, and a box of soy milk with a tiny straw. Daniel peeled away the plastic wrap on top of the congee and ate a spoonful. It tasted like boiled cardboard.

Nobody else at the table had finished their food. 'Are you part of a school?' he asked.

'We're on tour,' said the woman across the table. 'We're doing ten cities in fifteen days.'

The guy with the goatee looked at Daniel's congee. 'Don't eat that bowl of hemorrhoids. There's a bakery down the road. We're going there after this.'

Daniel laughed. 'This congee tastes like ass.' He loved cursing in Chinese, the breadth of options unavailable in English. He had trouble remembering the words for map and computer, but curses, those he knew by heart.

He pushed his tray away and got up. In his preoccupation with finding his mother, he'd forgotten to call someone. 'Have a good tour,' he said. He went upstairs and called the second most foul-mouthed person he knew, second to only his mother.

'What are you doing in that crap hotel?' Leon shouted on the phone.

Following Leon's directions, he took a bus to a neighborhood on the other side of the highway, walking through streets less populated than the ones in Wuyi Square. Leon lived in a block-shaped building with concrete siding, five doors across each of the four stories, metal railings along the edge of the walkways, one big rectangular grid. Daniel walked through the gravel lot and up the stairs. The walkways were crowded with bicycles, plastic coolers, beach balls, and flowerpots. In front of one apartment was a giant stuffed teddy bear with bright blue fur, crammed into a child-sized lawn chair.

He rang the bell for apartment number nine. A pink tricycle was locked to the railing opposite the door, decorated with stickers of cartoon characters. He heard footsteps, the sound of a latch lifting.

'You're here!' Leon's hair was choppy and grayer, his chest and shoulders thinner, but his grin was the same.

'Hi, Leon,' Daniel said, unable to suppress his own smile.

Houseplants hung from the ceilings, on shelves and tables and windowsills, their long green tresses stretching lines down the walls. Daniel followed Leon through the main room to the kitchen, where a woman was reading a newspaper at the kitchen table.

'This is my wife, Shuang,' Leon said.

'Hello, Deming,' Shuang said. 'I'm glad to finally meet you.'

A little girl was at the table, too, with Leon's wide mouth and Shuang's narrow face. Her legs swung in opposite directions, alternately tapping the metal chair legs in two–four time. She was bent over a coloring book, ponytail swinging as she gripped her blue crayon with concentration.

'Yimei,' Leon said to the girl. 'Say hello to your cousin, Deming.'

She looked up. 'You're my cousin?'

'Hi, Yimei,' Daniel said. 'What are you drawing?'

'A princess.' She took a sip from a box of apple juice. 'She's eating a sandwich.'

'You had no trouble on the bus?' Shuang motioned to the chair next to her.

'It was easy, no problem.'

'I told Leon to go pick you up in a taxi. I said, he's come all the way here and you're making him take a bus? He could get lost.'

'Deming's good with buses.' Leon leaned against the door-frame. 'He lives in New York City. Why take a cab when it'll be faster and cheaper with a bus?'

Shuang shook her head, but Daniel could see her laughing. 'You'll stay for dinner and sleep in Yimei's room. She can sleep in our bed.'

'I can?' Yimei said.

'Yes, you can sleep with Yi Ma and Yi Ba.'

'It's a treat for her,' Leon said.

'I don't mean to be trouble. I've already paid for the hotel room.'

'Are you kidding me? It's not every day Number One Son comes to visit from America,' Leon said. 'You stay as long as you want.'

Daniel's face flushed. 'Don't be such a bad host,' Shuang said. 'Offer our guest something to drink.'

Leon opened the refrigerator, took out two bottles of Tsingtao, and gave one to Daniel. 'Come on, I'll show you the rest of the apartment.'

It felt strange, drinking around Leon, but Daniel was grateful for the beer. Leon led him out of the kitchen and into a hall-way with three doors. 'The bathroom's here.' He pointed to the left. The other two rooms were the bedrooms, the smaller one Yimei's, decals of cartoon animals on the wall, bedsheets printed with yellow ducklings. The back bedroom, where Leon and Shuang slept, had a window that opened up onto a small balcony the size of a fire escape. Leon lifted the screen and

Daniel stepped out after him. The balcony's view looked onto a dumpster surrounded by empty plastic bottles and bloated trash bags, a whiff of garbage in the air. In the distance you could see the outlines of mountains.

A planter with fuchsia flowers hung from a hook on the railing. 'Shuang's good with plants,' Leon said. 'She works in the new Walmart. Gardening section. You like the apartment?'

Pastel sounds drifted from the windows of other apartments. A running faucet, clanging pots and pans, a baby crying, a radio announcer.

'It's nice,' Daniel said. 'How long have you lived here?'

'Two years. The construction isn't flimsy, we're on solid ground. I researched the foundation. My cousin knew a guy who worked for the landlord. My cousin owns the company I work for. We do import–export, I work in shipping. Better than cutting meat.' Leon put his bottle down. 'Now tell me. You didn't come all the way to Fuzhou to pay me a visit?'

'I was planning to see you.'

Leon laughed and Daniel blinked fast, tried to focus on the outlines of the mountains.

That night, he fell asleep in Yimei's room in the shadows of the animal decals – a donkey, elephant, cow, and lion – and when he woke up he heard the sound of the television. He looked at his phone. It was ten in the morning. If his mother called him at the hotel, he wouldn't be there to get her call.

In the front room of the apartment, Leon was eating toast.

'I need to get to the hotel,' Daniel said. 'My mother might've called me there, and I should check my messages.' He had paid for his room through tonight, hadn't officially checked out.

'You want toast?' Leon held up his slice of bread.

'You don't work today?'

'Taking today off.'

Daniel put his shoes on. 'I'm going back to the hotel.'

'No, we're going to West Lake.'

Daniel walked to the window and lifted the blinds. He could hear birds outside. 'Why?'

'We're going to find your mother. What, you want to sit on your ass all day waiting for her to call you?'

'I should go to the hotel,' Daniel said.

'We can call the hotel from here and ask if you have a message. After that, we'll go to West Lake.'

'But we don't know where she lives.'

'You said she told you she lived there. That's enough for me.'

'We're going to walk around and call her name until she comes running out of a building?'

'Don't be silly.'

Daniel played with the leaf of one of Shuang's plants. 'We could find her and she could slam the door in my face.' Imagining it, having the final, definitive answer to so many years of not knowing, made him slump.

'Come on, if you show up at her door she's not going to do that. You're her son.'

There were no potholes on the streets near West Lake Park, and fewer pedestrians, and with its large trees and single-story storefronts, the neighborhood resembled a wealthy American suburb. The bus passed the entrance to a park and a row of high-rise apartment buildings, and Leon signaled for the driver to stop. 'You said she told you she lives in an apartment with a balcony,' Leon said. 'These are all the apartment buildings. They overlook the park.'

'There must be hundreds of apartments.'

'They have directories. We'll go up and read them and see if your mother's name is there. Or we can ask the guards. These rich people, they always have guards.'

It felt treacherous, referring to his mother as *rich people*. The first building they saw with balconies had a security guard outside the gate. When Leon asked if a Polly or Peilan lived there, the guard said he couldn't give out private information about tenants.

They walked around a bend in the road. A bus whizzed past, honking. The second building with a balcony had two guards and no gate. 'There's no one named Polly or Peilan here,' the younger one said.

The third building they found had no guards, but a tall gate and no directory in sight. The fourth, fifth, sixth, and seventh buildings had neither guards nor directories.

When Daniel was Deming, he had thought his mother was invincible. She was louder, funnier, faster, and smarter than other adults, and he could never keep secrets from her, about his grades or if he'd been having regular dumps or if those were his crumbs that had spilled on the floor. She wasn't particularly strict, or cruel, but she was sharp, one step ahead. She was competent, she worked hard, and no matter how tired she was, there was always concern or vigilance left over for him. Yet at some point, this had changed.

To their left was a railing, and below was the park. Daniel stopped. 'She doesn't want to talk to me.'

Leon stopped, too. 'Your mother, she's complicated.'

Daniel wished he knew how to say *understatement* in Chinese.

'You meant more to her than anything. Whatever's making her scared to talk to you, it doesn't erase that.'

'She never even told her husband about me.'

'Is that so.'

They stood against the railing, watching cars pass. It was past noon. The sun was searing and Daniel wished he had sunglasses. He'd left his in Ridgeborough.

They began to walk again, more slowly. 'When I saw her, after she got back,' Leon said, 'there was something broken in her. She didn't want anyone to know.'

'You saw her? You said you only spoke to her on the phone.'

'We did see each other. It was when Yimei was a baby.'

'But you told me—'

'Don't blame Vivian or your mother. Blame me. I left on my own. If only we could do it over again, Deming, we could still be there, on that ugly couch your mother hated.'

'We'd have bought a new one by now.' A black SUV with tinted windows barreled down the hill. 'Did you know I went back to the apartment about a year after you left? A new family was living there.'

'Sometimes,' Leon said, 'when Shuang and I are tucking Yimei into bed, I think, this is the way it turned out. This is my life, the woman who wanted to marry me, the child we had. How could I give this up now?'

Daniel thought of playing a show, coming to and hearing the cheers of the crowd. 'I think the same thing sometimes.'

'So maybe she thinks the same thing, too,' Leon said.

Daniel saw two apartment buildings across the street, half hidden by a clump of bushes. His mother, with her new life – it wasn't the same thing. He needed to tell her she couldn't just walk out on him, pretend he didn't exist. 'I still want to find her.'

Hours later, they had gone to all the visible buildings in the neighborhood with balconies and the heat had become sweltering. They chugged bottles of water they'd bought at a convenience store, where Daniel had seen a woman his mother's age and had a flash of hope it would be her, though the woman looked nothing like her. They reminisced about New York, and Daniel told Leon about Ridgeborough, how he was taking a break from school.

He was getting more comfortable speaking in Chinese, no longer caring so much. Even if each sentence took effort, and even if he felt more like himself in English, hearing and speaking Chinese was like replaying an album he hadn't listened to in years, appreciating how solid the sound was.

'Should we go back to the buildings without guards, see if there's a way we could get in?' At Leon's apartment, there would be beers waiting. He could come back here another day, but doubted he would.

'Maybe,' Leon said.

'You want to go back?'

'Soon.'

They turned up another street, steeper than the last, the park only slightly visible below. 'Let's go back.'

'Here, let's try this building.' Ahead of them was a six-story structure with a silver gate, balconies protruding from the sides. There was a list of names on the outside. 'There's a Gao, but no Guo.'

'Let's go back,' Daniel said. 'I'll try the Internet café tomorrow, find English schools.' But he had lost steam for the search. It had been enough to spend the afternoon with Leon. He could always tell himself that he had looked, that he'd tried.

'Wait.' Leon pointed. 'Over there.'

Daniel followed Leon's finger and saw a speck of water, so far down he could barely tell what it was. 'Yeah, you can see the ocean. We must be pretty high up.'

'Deming. Where did your mother like to go when she was a little girl? Where did she like to go in New York City?'

'To the river. But we're in the middle of the city. There's no river nearby.'

'If she was going to live in an apartment with a balcony, what would she want to see from there? Water! This is the street she lives on,' Leon said. 'It has to be.'

They continued up the hill. The next two buildings had no balconies, so they skipped them. At the end of the block was one last building. It had balconies.

'This is where she lives,' Leon said, and Daniel wished he could match Leon's conviction.

The security guard was an older man with a jowly face, reading a paperback inside a narrow booth. 'Can I help you?'

'We're looking for a Peilan or Polly that lives in your building,' Leon said. 'Would it be possible to ring her apartment?'

'There isn't anyone by that name here.'

'Are you sure?' Daniel said. 'She's about average height and weight, with a loud voice and a mole on her neck.' She could have lost weight or gained it, gotten plastic surgery for all he knew. But this was the last building, their final chance. 'Her last name might not be Guo, but her first name is Polly, or Peilan?'

'Nope.'

'She's married to a man that owns a textile factory? She works in an English school?'

The guard returned his book. 'Told you. Nope.'

'Okay,' Leon said. 'Thank you.'

They walked down the sidewalk. 'Well, we tried,' Daniel said. 'We tried.'

'Let's go home now.'

'You hungry? I know a restaurant we can stop at. Not in this neighborhood, the food is too fussy here. But this place, they have soup with lamb, and the noodles are handmade.'

'Can't wait,' Daniel said. 'I'm getting hungry now.' He hadn't booked a return plane ticket, but he could find one that left in a few days. Leon and Shuang were nice to him, but he didn't want to push it. You couldn't show up out of nowhere and expect to be treated like a real son.

Compared to downtown, the sidewalks by West Lake were spotless. There was no gum or litter marring their path, no mysterious orange puddles or booby traps of dog poop like in New York. A pebble rolled down the sidewalk, its trail unobstructed, and Daniel kicked it, watching as it veered to the right.

'Stop,' Leon said.

Daniel saw a gap in a hedge and a short path that led to a wider lot. Beyond that was a building. When he craned his neck up, he saw a beige high-rise. Rows and rows of balconies.

'We must have missed that one,' Leon said.

They turned onto the path. In front was a security guard, dressed in black pants and a dark gray shirt. He was putting a cigarette out into a metal ashtray.

They asked the same questions they'd been asking all afternoon. The guard shook his head. No Polly Guo in the building. No Peilan.

'No Peilan?' Leon repeated, like he couldn't believe it.

'She's an English teacher. Director of an English school.'

'Oh! You should have said that. I know the teacher lady you're talking about.'

'Polly,' Leon said.

'Polly *Lin*.'

'You said there's no Polly in the building,' Daniel said.

The guard lifted a telephone receiver and pressed numbers on a hidden keypad. 'I'll ring the apartment for you.'

Leon paced along the path. The back of his T-shirt was covered in sweat. The guard put the receiver down and said, 'He's coming down to meet you.'

'He?' Daniel asked.

'Yong. Polly's husband. She's not home right now.'

Leon raised his eyebrows. The guard lit another cigarette. Daniel needed a drink of water, but they had run out, their bottles empty. He didn't know what he was going to say to his mother's husband.

Five minutes later, the front door of the building opened and a man emerged, dressed like a gangster, black suit jacket over black button-down shirt, dark sunglasses. As he came closer, Daniel noticed his silver cufflinks and jade ring.

The man nodded at Leon and Daniel. 'I'm Yong.' His voice was gravelly yet soft, his hair a shade of jet black that only occurred out of a dye bottle. The wrinkles on his face put his age a little north of Leon's. 'Can I help you?'

'My name is Deming. I know your wife – from New York. This is Leon.' He was unsure of what to say next. Yong wasn't big, but looked like he could be a scary guy, if you insulted him or said the wrong thing. If Mama had never told her husband about him, he might be putting her in danger, putting himself in danger, by revealing who he was.

Yong took off his sunglasses and studied Daniel's face. 'What did you say your name was again?' Two of his teeth had gold caps.

'Deming ... Guo.'

'Oh, you're her son! You look so much like her. I can see it, the nose, the mouth, the jawline! How incredible. She mentioned she spoke to you recently and you lived in New York?'

Daniel caught Leon's eyes and laughed. 'Yes, I'm here visiting.'

'She's going to be so upset when she finds out she missed you.'

'Where is she?'

'Beijing. The school she works for is looking to expand their branches, so she's traveling to research the markets. There's a conference there this week on education, so she's there for that, as well.'

'I've been trying to call her for days. I've left her so many messages.'

'Her cell phone was stolen on the train. She called me from the hotel yesterday.'

'When is she coming back to Fuzhou?'

'This weekend.' Yong passed his cell phone to Daniel. 'This is the name, the Conference for English Educators. At the Park Hotel.'

Daniel gave the phone to Leon to translate. 'I can't read Chinese,' he said. The noodles and lamb were as delicious as Leon promised, especially washed down with cold beers. When they returned to the apartment, Yimei and three other kids were riding their bikes around the parking lot. Shuang and another woman sat in lawn chairs, drinking cans of iced tea.

'Guess who's going to Beijing tomorrow?' Leon said.

Daniel listened as Leon described their day. As the conversation shifted into talk about a family who'd recently moved out of the building, he excused himself and walked around the lot. There was a slight breeze, and the sweat on his arms and scalp was drying. The sky was a light purple, and the garbagy smell had faded with the day's heat. The other children abandoned their bicycles to toss a ball, and he heard Yimei say to her friends, 'That's my cousin from America.'

He waved in her direction. 'Deming!' Yimei said. 'Catch.'

He saw the ball bound across the air, a swift yellow blur, and lifted his arms, letting it nestle against him. 'Heads up, Yimei,' he shouted, and threw the ball back.

CHAPTER SIXTEEN

Beijing was a city of circles. Six ring roads, each one larger than the next, a series of concentric donuts. The train station was in the third ring. The high-speed train out of Fuzhou took twelve hours, and Daniel had only managed to sleep in spurts, his legs sore from sitting. He ignored the throng of motorcyclists outside the station and instead hailed a cab to the Park Hotel, and the closer he got to the inner rings, the more intricate the architecture, whether it was neon high-rises or older buildings with scalloped rooftops. Thick smog hid the upper stories of the tallest buildings, and some people on the sidewalks wore masks or scarves wrapped around their mouths. Frantic techno music leaked out of the radio, spasming reds. 'Turn it up,' Daniel asked the driver. The cab filled with overproduced vocals, a guy rapping in Mandarin. 'Louder, please.' The driver complied, the colors deepened. 'Louder.'

The Conference for English Educators was taking place on the ground floor of the Park Hotel. Daniel paid the driver and said thank you in Mandarin, got out on the corner carrying his backpack. The street was full of shops selling fake jade jewelry and Buddha figurines to tourists, and he heard one man say in English, 'Goddamn I need a nap,' the long vowels funny and exaggerated, almost painful to hear.

He walked through the revolving doors of the hotel, through the lobby, past the front desk, and around a corner, where two women with white nametags sat at a table with books and magazines. A conference schedule, in both Chinese and English, was displayed on a metal stand, and he saw his mother's name, Polly Lin, listed as one of the speakers on a panel called Teaching Young Adult Learners, from 10:30 to 11:30 a.m. He looked at his phone. It was 11:05.

A man in a blue suit, whose nametag announced him as Wei from an English school in Suzhou, intercepted him. 'Do you have your nametag?'

'I'm sorry, I must have left it in my room. Should I go and get it?'

Wei turned to check with the two women at the table. As the three of them conferred, Daniel slipped into the auditorium and into the first empty seat he saw, two rows from the back, his view partially blocked by a pillar. Two women and a man were sitting onstage, and one of the women was his mother. A third woman, the moderator, was in a separate chair. His mother had the mic. 'That's what I mean,' she said, her words clear and forceful. She was making emphatic gestures with her right hand as she held the microphone with her left, and Daniel was glad to see she still spoke with her hands. 'You cannot apply the same methods to younger learners that you do with older ones. It's not a one-size-fits-all solution.' Several people in the audience clapped, and Daniel joined in, making his claps extra loud and resonant.

The moderator asked the man a question about creating an English-language curriculum with Chinese references. His mother passed the microphone. She wore glasses with small gold frames, a snug brown blazer, a cream-colored blouse with an energetic ruffle, and a silk paisley scarf. Her hair was short, puffed, and wavy. She didn't look ten years older, he couldn't see any wrinkles or gray hairs, at least from afar, but she looked neater, polished. Not like the professors at Carlough with their former hippie stylings, not like Peter and Kay in their L.L.Bean, but like a real estate broker or a bank teller. She was wearing a skirt. She looked like someone else's mom.

The man handed the microphone to the woman who was next to his mother. After she spoke, his mother spoke again, and Daniel felt himself puffing up, proud at how confident and intelligent she sounded, how smooth her Mandarin was. The man stuttered, the microphone amplifying a catch in his voice, and the other woman's sentences were peppered with excruciating pauses, but his mother spoke without hesitating.

The moderator asked the audience if they had questions. A woman near the front rambled on about a program she had created until the moderator cut her off. Daniel raised his hand, and the moderator walked over. He'd played enough shows to know his mother wouldn't be able to see the back of the auditorium from the stage, not with the pillar in the way. He spoke in his best imitation of a northern accent, trying not to crack up because it was a terrible caricature of Mandarin. 'I'd like to learn more about bilingual education in Chinese schools. Do you teach Chinese and English at the same time? What about students who can speak both?'

The man onstage answered the question, talking about an initiative at the college where he worked, but Daniel saw his mother look around the auditorium, trying to find him, as the rest of her face struggled to remain still. He suppressed a laugh.

She found him after the panel ended, pushing past people waiting to talk to her.

'Deming! You scared the shit out of me!'

Her eyes widened. They stared at each other. She was wearing makeup – he didn't remember her wearing makeup before – and her skin was powdered and oddly even. He was relieved to hear her curse, to know a part of her remained the same beneath this new exterior polish.

'Hi – Mama.' His face and hands grew warm. Why did saying the word feel so embarrassing? It felt like he was claiming something that didn't belong to him.

Her mouth wobbled. His heart was beating so loudly he could hear the blood thump in his ears. People were trying to move past them, but Daniel and his mother could only stand there, looking at each other. He felt the intensity of her stare and had an urge to duck and hide. He wanted to apologize to her for growing up, for also becoming unrecognizable from his former self.

The moderator rushed over. 'We're going to get lunch, Polly, with the group from Shanghai.'

'I can't,' his mother said, not taking her eyes off him. 'My son is here.'

The moderator turned. 'This is your son? You must be a bilingual education teacher, too.'

'Something like that,' Daniel said. He wanted to tell the moderator to leave them alone. Couldn't she see that they didn't want to be bothered?

His mother linked her arm in his and he could feel her trembling. 'Let's go,' she said, and they walked across the lobby and out of the hotel. She wore high heels, black and spiky, and there was a sense of overcompensation to her movements, her features carefully set to a neutral expression. She kept her arm in his, steered them onto a busier street and into the backseat of a cab, directing the driver in rapid Mandarin. Then they were stuck in what appeared to be endless traffic.

'You came all the way from New York,' she said.

'I flew from New York a few days ago.'

Her voice got high and choked. 'You traveled so far!'

'Well, today I just took the train from Fuzhou.'

She took a handkerchief out of her purse and blotted her forehead, then her eyes. 'I don't like being onstage like that, being watched.'

'But you were great.' He noticed the muscles working in her face, the labor it took to hold herself together. 'What about when you're teaching, up front in a classroom?'

'That's not so bad. I don't teach much these days, though. My work is more administrative. Are you hungry? Yong e-mailed me to say you came by the apartment.'

'I wanted to surprise you.'

'Some asshole stole my phone on the train. I had to get a new one, change my number. Such a pain. I hope you still have yours with you.'

He touched his pocket. 'Right here.'

'You've never been to Beijing before, have you?'

'No.'

'This is the second time I've been here this month. I've been traveling more for work.'

'Do you like Beijing?'

'There's a lot of change happening here.'

'There was construction all over Fuzhou when I was there.'

'Here, too. The government rips down these homes where families have been living for years. They say they're going to compensate them properly but they get shoved out to a crappy apartment on the outer ring.'

'That sounds like New York. There are big new buildings in Chinatown, now, with doormen and white people.' Daniel watched the traffic clear, stop again. They were moving up the road in ten-second increments. Wherever his mother was taking him, they'd get there next year.

Trucks bumped along in the next lane. 'Ten years ago, that would've been a bicycle lane.'

'You'd rather be riding a bicycle?'

'Never.' She laughed.

'In Ridgeborough, the town I lived in after you left, you need a car to go anywhere. One time I told a friend I'd hop on the train to see him, but then I remembered there's no train.'

'Your Chinese has gotten better. You don't sound as illiterate as you did on the phone.'

He basked in her barbed teasing, recalled her toughest, most resilient love. How different it was from Kay's exposed emotions. His mother had never demanded his reassurance.

'I've been in China for almost a week now.'

'You don't lose a language,' she said. 'You need to be exposed to it again, and the brain remembers.' The cab rolled forward. 'It's elastic, the brain.'

'Would that be the same for you and English?'

'If you heard me, you'd laugh. But compared to the other teachers, I'm practically fluent. Very few of them have gone abroad, so they learn from watching movies and listening to recordings. It's not the same.'

'I'll help you practice if you want.'

'It's all right.'

'When do you need to return to the conference?'

'Not until tomorrow. I'm going to skip the rest of the day, spend it with you.'

He felt his shoulders loosen. The cab stopped at a group of old buildings with elaborate rooftops.

'This is the Summer Palace,' his mother said. She led him across a bridge and down a long pathway, the ceiling an intricate mosaic of blues and greens. Suddenly it was quiet, and Daniel was mesmerized at the colors. They crossed into an open space where tour groups gathered, the guide speaking into a megaphone in Cantonese, and entered a quieter corridor, passing through another pavilion until they arrived at an expansive lake. Daniel stopped, taken aback by the sight of so much water at once.

They sat on a bench, next to each other. 'This is my favorite place in Beijing,' his mother said. 'The Empress had her summer vacations here, in the Qing Dynasty.'

He saw an arched bridge, small boats with yellow roofs. Fatigue rippled through his body. He was fried. Four days ago, he'd been in Ridgeborough.

'It's a man-made lake. Like West Lake Park in Fuzhou. I go there when the walls start to come. Did you go when you were there?'

What did she mean by *walls*? 'Leon and I just walked around the neighborhood.'

'And Leon, he's doing well?'

Her fingers knotted over one another like pigeons fighting for a discarded hotdog bun. Daniel did the same thing when he was nervous, played with his hands. He wanted to separate her fingers and calm her down.

'He's good. I met his wife and his daughter. They have a nice apartment.'

'Yong said in his e-mail that my son and his father came to visit and for a minute I didn't know who he was talking about. I thought he meant Haifeng. Your real father.'

'Haifeng?' She'd never mentioned his name.

'I haven't spoken to him in years. Before you were born, even. I hear he's in Xiamen now.'

'Yong seems like a good guy.'

His mother's expression brightened. 'He is. When I told him I wanted to travel more for my job, he didn't like the idea at first. He said he'd miss me. But eventually he understood.'

'What do you mean?'

'I don't like to stay at home for too long. The same walls and roof. I get a bad feeling. I get nightmares.'

'So he knew about me. Even before I saw him.'

'Yes, he knew.'

Daniel smiled. His eyelids patted open and shut.

'Where do your parents work?' his mother asked. 'The ones who adopted you?'

'They're teachers. In a university.'

'They must be smart.'

He didn't know when he would see Peter and Kay next. He dreaded the prospect of talking to them again, yet he was scared they wouldn't want to talk to him either. This woman next to him, his mother, a stranger, was the only true family he had. 'They want me to be like them, to go to college and study what they study.' He struggled against his impulse to defend them. 'I'm not sure if it's what I want, though.'

They watched the boats float. Daniel needed a nap. He wondered when they would talk, really talk. His mother picked up his hand, squeezing so hard he nearly pulled away. But he held on and sandwiched his hand between hers. He remembered how trapped he used to feel when Kay kissed his cheek and told him she loved him, as if he was supposed to respond in the right way. He didn't feel like that now.

She released her grip. He wasn't sure when the Qing Dynasty had taken place, only that it was long ago, and he imagined the Empress being rowed across the water on a long, gliding boat, the pavilions and temples full of people. Now the rooms were empty and the only sounds they heard were shouting tour guides. It was a sad place, a palace of ghosts.

'Are you hungry?' His mother let go of his hand and tapped his arm. Did they look as alike as Yong had said? 'I want to take you out to eat.'

He wasn't that hungry; he'd eaten a big breakfast on the train. But he let her take him to a café in a neighborhood where the storefronts were glass and chrome and people carried shopping bags and leather handbags. The café had a French name.

'Take a seat,' his mother said. 'I'll go in and order.' Daniel found a table on the patio and watched her walk inside, a slight shake in her heels. She rubbed her temples and shut her eyes, then opened them, her features rearranged into a blank pleasantry.

It was like being at a Starbucks in SoHo. He leaned back in his chair and was drifting off when his mother came out with a tray full of food.

'This café is famous for sweets.' She passed him a plate with a slice of chocolate cake, the icing already melting, and a plate of egg tarts. Two coffees, one for her and one for him, and a pile of sugar packets and plastic pods of creamer.

'Thank you.' He took the spoon she offered and a bite of the cake. The frosting was so sweet it made his tongue curl.

His mother watched him. 'Is the cake good?'

'It's good.'

She took a small piece and washed it down with coffee. He could see a smudge in her eyeliner, and she'd drawn in her eyebrows with a pencil that left a tiny clump in the hairs. 'Have an egg tart.' She nudged the plate toward him.

He picked up a pastry and took a bite. 'It's good,' he said, though it was a little stale.

'You always loved sweets.'

He pressed cake crumbs beneath his spoon, self-conscious under her gaze.

'Have more.'

He took another bite. It was true, she had his eyes and mouth. Their lips had the same curve and dip in the middle – he'd always thought his mouth was a little too delicate for a guy's – and their eyes the same large pupils and thick eyelids. Whenever he had looked into a mirror during the past ten years, it had felt like nobody resembled him. But she had been with him.

She rested her palm against his cheek. Just held it there. Her hand was warm, and he couldn't move. Like if he twitched, the ground would open up beneath him.

When she took her palm away it left a hot patch on his skin. He said, 'I'm here, Mama' and she made a long sighing sound.

They walked through an old hutong neighborhood, wandered through the Forbidden City, each building more marvelous and intimidating than the next. As the day progressed, his mother showed no signs of impatience, didn't act like she was in a hurry to get back to the hotel. But when he said even the most innocuous things about the Bronx – remember Tommie? Mrs Johnson? The bodega, the 4 train? – or mentioned Leon or Vivian or Michael, she would change the subject, steer them back to the present, talk about Beijing, architecture, teaching.

They had roast duck for dinner in a fancy restaurant with thick white tablecloths, and he ate as much as he could, which seemed to please her. By the time they got to the Park Hotel, it was nine at night. His mother's room was on the fifth floor, a double room like the one he'd had in Fuzhou, but cleaner and less shabby. He took a shower as she wrote e-mails on her laptop, and after toweling off and brushing his teeth, he studied the reflection of his face in the bathroom mirror. Before he left, he would take a picture of the two of them together, for proof.

She sat on her bed in her pajamas, removing makeup with a cotton ball. 'We each have our own big bed. So different than how we slept in New York. I always say I could never go back to living like that, but we never saw ourselves as being deprived, did we?'

'We weren't deprived.' He unzipped his backpack and took out the old photo of them at the South Street Seaport. 'I wanted to show you this.'

His mother held the photo by the corners. 'How'd you find this?'

'Kay. My adoptive mother.'

'How did *she* get it?'

'Vivian, I think.'

His mother kept staring at the photo. 'You were so small. And look how young I was.'

He had to ask her. She wouldn't kick him out of the hotel this late at night. He coughed up the first sentences that came to him. 'You were going to never talk to me again? You were good with that?'

She passed the photo back to him. 'I didn't know if you wanted to speak to me, after everything I did.'

'Of course I did. I called you first, remember? And I called you, again. Twice.'

'You told me to never call you again on your last message.'

His face grew hot. 'I didn't mean it. I was angry.'

She waved a hand at him, cutting him off. 'You were right when you said I couldn't pretend I didn't mess up.'

She went to the bathroom, then returned to her bed. It was late. She had an eight o'clock meeting tomorrow morning with teachers at the conference, and after that, she would leave him. At any moment she could switch off the light and he would never find out what happened.

He got under the covers yet remained sitting. His mother checked to make sure the blinds were down, the curtains shut. She removed an eye mask, lined in pink fabric, from her bag.

'I can't have any lights on when I sleep, so if you want to stay up, I'll wait for you to sleep first.'

Then he would keep her up for as long as he needed. 'I don't remember you being like that in New York. We always slept with the blinds open.'

She uncapped a bottle of pills. 'I have nightmares,' she said. 'One time, Yong got up to use the bathroom and forgot to turn the light off in the hallway, and I woke up screaming. Then he screamed, too, because he heard me scream, and we were both scared. It was funny.'

It didn't sound funny. 'You have these nightmares a lot?'

'As long as I take my medication, I'm okay.' She shook out a pill and reached for a glass of water. 'They help me sleep.'

'Wait,' he said. 'Can you not take it yet? Just wait, please?'

She hesitated, then put the pill back in the bottle. 'I have to make sure it's dark.' She switched the light off next to her bed, so the room was lit solely by the lamp next to his. 'In Ardsleyville, it was light all the time, dogs waking you up in the middle of the night. You can't sleep like that.'

'Ardsleyville. That was—'

'The name of the camp, the detention camp.'

A chill ran up his back. He studied a framed picture on the wall, a print of the same lake they'd visited today. 'Tell me about it.'

She laughed, nervous. 'I can't.'

'I won't be mad. I promise.'

'I can't, Deming. It's too much, I don't want you to know.'

'I want to know the truth. How did you get there? What happened to you when you went to work that day? Please, I deserve to know.'

She put her head in her arms. 'There was a van. They raided the nail salon.' He leaned forward, holding his breath. 'There were no phones there, no way to contact anyone. When I got out, they sent me to Fuzhou. I wasn't myself anymore.' She stopped. 'If I tell you, you wouldn't get it.'

'Please try.' He touched the wooden headboard behind him. He was in Beijing, China. New York and Ridgeborough and Daniel Wilkinson had fallen away and the world consisted only of him and his mother, their voices in the hotel room.

She told him she remembered being in a crowded room, looking at the numbers on a telephone.

'In Ardsleyville?'

'No, this was still in New York.'

CHAPTER SEVENTEEN

The van that took me from the salon had no windows so there was no way to tell if we were five or fifty blocks away. I couldn't see any of the other women from Hello Gorgeous, only shouting strangers, more officers in uniforms. One of them passed me a phone and said I could make a call.

My finger hovered over the keypad as I tried to remember Leon's number: 347, that part I was sure of. 453-8685. Or was it 435? 8568? 445? His number was programmed into my own cell phone, but that was in my bag.

'Where's my bag?' I asked in English. The officer didn't answer.

I dialed. 347-453-8685. The phone rang. Leon might be at work, but I could leave him a message.

It kept ringing. There was no message, so I tried again. 347-435-8685.

Two rings and a man picked up who wasn't Leon. I asked for Leon, but the man said something in another language.

The officer reached for the phone. 'One call only.'

I ignored him and dialed again. 347-453-8658. After several rings came a recording, a computerized one that repeated the number, followed by an instruction to leave a message. It wasn't what Leon had on his phone, but I spoke fast. 'It's Little Star.

The police took us from the salon. I don't know where we're going, but find out and come get me. Hurry.'

Later I'd feel certain that the number was 435-8586. In the tent, there was a single telephone that hung from the wall, but it had no dial tone. Each morning, for the next four hundred and twenty-four days, I would pick up the phone in hope that there would be one.

'But there never was,' I said. 'That damn phone never worked.'

'You were there for four hundred and twenty-four days?' You sounded like you didn't believe it.

'I counted.'

'That's almost two years!'

'Fourteen months. See, I told you, it's too much to hear.'

'It's not. I need to know.'

I wanted to stop talking, but also I wanted to tell you. I said, 'The hours in between lying down and getting up were a nightmare.'

The plane had touched down in darkness and sand. In the distance, swollen tents were boxed in by barbed wire, big white boxes in a harsh sprawl of nothing. Texas, though I didn't know it then. The endpoint, the ultimate waijiu. Too cold in the winters and too hot in the summers, a mean, scorchful hot that grasped for rain.

Heavy white plastic stretched over the tent's metal frame. Uneven concrete floors, like the cement had been poured in a hurry. The food looked sickly: waxen bread, pasty oatmeal, noodles with fluorescent cheese, and because the dining area was next to the toilets, it all tasted like piss and shit. The sharp tang of urine eventually faded, leaving only hunger, and I ate milk and cheese that left me cramped on the toilet.

The lights never turned off, so my eyeballs ached and

throbbed. I'd lay in my bunk and hear Leon sleep-talking next to me in the bed we had shared, you and Michael next to us in the bed you had shared, and I'd curse at the guards in Fuzhounese. *Fuck your mom. Fuck yourself.* The worst part was that you would think I abandoned you.

When sleep did come, it was jagged and soundless. I'd wake to voices, not sure if it was hours or minutes later, and see a guard standing over me, marking a piece of paper.

Bed check, the guard would say.

I'm here, I'd respond in English.

The tent was the length of a city block but narrower. Two hundred women slept in two-person bunks grouped into eight rows of three bunks each. We wore dark blue pants with elastic waistbands, baggy blue shirts. Shoddy sewing; sloppy hems. None of us had any money and we couldn't get any, unless our families knew where we were. We could work on the cleaning crew, sweeping floors, scrubbing toilets, taking out trash for fifty cents a day, but there was a long waiting list to join, seventy-three names ahead of mine.

The toilets and showers were in a large open stall ringed by a low wall that came up to my waist. Most days there wasn't any soap and often, no water. Hives broke out across my face and a rash oozed up my arms, and my skin got raw and dry. In the middle of the tent was a glass octagon with tinted windows, where the guards watched us. They could see us but we couldn't see them. I'd stand under the octagon's stepladder and wave.

I asked the guards for a lawyer, for Immigration, but they told me to wait. No one offered advice or answers. Some women didn't speak any English, and others spoke in such rapid English I couldn't keep up. Any day now, I kept telling myself, Didi and Leon would find me and get me out of here.

*

On the twelfth day, a Chinese woman with freckles came up to me in the oatmeal line and said in Mandarin, 'Come eat with me. I'm Lei.' I was so happy to talk to someone I wanted to kiss her.

Over oatmeal, I found out Lei was originally from Shandong and had been in the tent for almost eighteen months. She'd gotten a speeding ticket in Chicago and was shipped off to ICE.

'*Eighteen months?*' I'd been trying so hard to tamp down my panic by picturing myself back home with you, these twelve days just a blip in our regular routines. Thinking of these routines comforted me. Cooking dinner with Vivian. Riding the train to work. Telling you and Michael to shut the TV off and go to bed. Now that hope of returning was being yanked away. 'I can't be here for that long. I have a family and they don't even know I'm here.' I looked around at the tables of women scooping up clumps of oatmeal with their hands. There were never enough forks or spoons.

'There are some women who've been here a lot longer,' Lei said. 'There's a woman named Mary who's lived in America since she was six months old. Born in Sudan. Was in college, had a travel visa, got arrested at the airport after coming home from studying in France. The government says her parents never adjusted her immigration status when she was a baby and she needs a physical examination to complete her application to change her status. Of course, an exam costs three hundred bucks and they won't give it to her at Ardsleyville. And she can't access her bank account because ICE put a hold on her name.' Lei shook her head. 'Typical.'

Nobody knew anything. There were too many cases in the immigration courts, Lei said, and we didn't get things like lawyers, only a judge who decided if you would stay or go. None of us knew when we would see this judge, if the authorities would release us from custody, where we would end up.

*

I was sleepy, so sleepy all the time. My legs ached from not walking enough. Once or twice a week, the guards let us out into the courtyard for an hour, a rectangle ringed by barbed wire, large enough for us to stand no more than arm's length apart. Beyond that was a giant American flag, flapping in the hot wind, and an open yard surrounded by more wire, which housed a separate prison that Lei called the Hole. The men were in other tents beyond that, tents we couldn't see.

There were days I stayed in bed, itching under the blanket. I assumed the sun was still swapping seats with the moon every twelve hours, though for all I knew the sky could've become green, the sun now square, the stars extinguished and smeared like mosquitoes on the underside of a slipper. De-ming, Deming – your name hammered a drumbeat between my eyes. I had wanted to move and now you would think I left on purpose.

I scratched my arms so hard the skin broke into angry red snarls. You might forget my face. The next time I saw you, your voice might be lower. Leon might find another woman. I had the ring he gave me, and I twisted it around my finger, felt it pinch my skin.

Starry night. Grassy field. Cricket chorus. Clucking chicken. You. I tried to visualize all the things I loved. If I produced more saliva, I could pretend I wasn't so thirsty. Glass of water. Cup of tea. Wet kisses. Leon. I tried to relax, hoping for a few hours of sleep before the first bed check. Warm hands. Loud music. You.

I told Lei about you, how good your English was, the way you took care of Michael. But every day I worried more. Were you doing okay in school, was Vivian feeding you enough, and were your clothes clean? You needed a new pair of shoes, your feet were growing so fast, you couldn't walk if your shoes were too tight, and who would buy you shoes, how could you walk?

*

Weeks, then months passed. I lay on my back in the top bunk. There wasn't enough space to lie in any position except on my back and perfectly still, a lesson I'd learned when I rolled off the bunk and fell onto the floor. I pulled the blanket over my face, exposing my feet. Then I got up and went to eat with Lei.

She was sitting with a woman named Samara, who was from Pakistan. The three of us could communicate using the spotty English we knew.

Some of the women were planning a protest, Samara said. There were church people who held a vigil outside the tent, and somehow Mary, the woman who'd lived in America since she was a baby, had gotten in touch with them.

'The guards won't care if we protest,' I said.

'I saw what they did to people who protested before you both came,' Lei said. 'Three guards kicked these women until they bled. Then they got deported. What makes you think it's going to be different now?'

Day 203. Sunlight blazed onto the tent roof. I sat on my bunk, reached under my shirtsleeves, applied nails to skin, and scratched. I knew my arms were already inflamed and split red, but scratching produced the sweetest pain, the most exquisite fire. When I scratched, I could dig my fingernails into all the unspoken words of the past months.

I began to hate Leon and Didi, to want to forget them. Had they even tried to find me? Maybe it was better this way, to pretend they didn't exist. Missing them was worse. So was waiting.

We made a plan. When the guards let us into the courtyard, we weren't coming back in. One woman would deliver a list of our complaints. The church group had gotten in touch with journalists, who would come and film us so that Americans would learn about the tents. The government would shut down Ardsleyville and we could go home.

I didn't think it would be that easy, but we had to try something. It was better to participate than to acknowledge we had no options.

Lei refused to be a part of it.

After lunch, the guards unlocked the door to the yard and we walked outside. After a few minutes we began to move around, changing from bunches to lines and corners. We spelled out letters. H-E-L-P. So that the news helicopters could see us from above.

I stepped behind Samara, rolling my sleeves up in the heat.

'Your skin is broken,' Samara said. 'It looks painful.'

I pulled my sleeves back down. 'It's nothing,' I said.

We stood for a long time, waiting for something to happen, for the church people, the journalists. But nothing happened except the guards got angry, yelling at us to go in. Lei and the other women on the opposite side of the yard returned to the tent. Samara and I stayed standing. The sky remained blue and still. There were no birds in the desert, no cars driving on a nearby highway, no cool ocean lapping my ankles, only hot sky. Then I heard it, a buzz slicing the air. The buzz grew louder and I saw a shape circling the clouds, a blue dot no larger than a bird, and the bird grew bigger and the buzz was thundering.

But when the plane flew away the silence was monstrous. 'We haven't figured out what to do after this,' I said to Samara.

Guards with helmets and plastic shields pushed into the yard, and as the air filled with burning, my eyes seared and my tongue became bitter. I could only see clouds and helmeted men. I felt a stick in the side and hit the ground hip first.

The length of my new room was eleven footprints up and eight across. All those months in the tent waiting in line for the toilets and now I could spend a week sitting on a toilet by myself. There was a mattress on a concrete shelf, a chair shaped from a concrete block, and a little light that was forever on.

Three times a day, the steel door on the front wall would open and a tray would push through the slot like a tongue protruding out a mouth. *I am breakfast,* I imagined the mouth saying. *Hello, I'm lunch!* The tray contained a brown slab. Breakfast or lunch, a slab. Dinner a slab. It tasted like mush. I talked to the mouth as I shoved the empty trays back. *Do you like how that feels, Big Mouth? You like it. You love it.*

Three times a week the guards would thread a chain around my ankle, another around my waist. Three hours a week I was allowed outside, in a cage inside a yard surrounded by tall walls, my legs and arms sore from not moving, my eyes sore at having to focus so far, unused to seeing anything farther than eleven footprints up and eight across. Sometimes I'd see traces of others. Was that shape Mary? Samara? But I never saw anyone close enough to be sure.

Against my will I'd think of your smile ripping open as we rode the subway, of the words that had dripped and skipped so easily on Polly's tongue, delivered without having to strain or translate. I thought of Peilan kissing Haifeng, how Peilan's body had been so new that she would catch a glimpse of herself in a window and think, Yeah, that's *me.* When Peilan was supposed to be doing the wash she would brush her hair for hours until it shone, linger outside so her hair could catch the light and drink it in.

The walls were a lie, a trick. I could pull them apart with my hands, gentle and determined, like pulling a shirt over a child's head, blow on the floor until it fell away and then I would be in the grass, sunshine rolling up my body, lapping at my fingers. The sun would have a tongue, nice and fat, licking slow and lazy, and the grass would smell like worms and dirt. My body would pick up speed as I rolled, bouncing into the air, soaring over hills and oceans. There was my house, Yi Ba in the yard with chickens. I'd arch up, kick my legs, and coast.

Because I wasn't really here. This was the life of another person I was watching in a movie, saying, *What a pity, oh that poor woman, oh I'm so glad that isn't me.*

I pushed at the walls with my head. I'd crack them open so I could return to you. Keep you with me.

They bandaged my skull, clucking at my head and scratched-up arms, and for days it felt like my brain was sprouting nails.

In a room with long rows of chairs and tables, I listened to a young man in a suit talk through wire mesh, his collar damp with sweat, his words muffled through the grating. I couldn't tell what language he was speaking. The last person I had spoken to was a guard, the person before that a guard. The man in the suit said *lawyer* in Mandarin. As he spoke he gestured with his hands and I imagined them wrapped around my neck and I screamed. I don't know how many days later, I was in a van as it moved down a highway, and my eyes watered at the sudden sunlight. Then I was in a room with windows, the space so long I could sense myself falling. One by one, men in blue pants and shirts walked to the front of the room to speak to an older man who introduced himself as the judge. When it was my turn, the judge spoke to me, but he talked so fast, I couldn't tell what he was saying.

A white woman was next to me in a brown suit, waiting for a reply. I dredged up one word and turned to the woman: *why?*

The judge slammed his hand on the podium. *You don't. Talk.*

'What is your name?' the judge asked in English.

'Guo Peilan,' I said. 'Polly Guo.'

He slammed his hand down again. The woman in the suit spoke in Mandarin. 'You need to wait for my translation.'

'What is your name?' asked the judge again, and again I answered before the woman had spoken.

'You need to wait for my translation,' the woman repeated. 'You can't answer his question until I translate it.'

'But what am I doing here?'

'They want to deport you, but they need to get the right documents first.'

'They can't do that. Where's my lawyer? I have a son here, he's an American citizen.'

The judge said something I couldn't hear.

'Dismissed,' the woman said. 'You spoke out of turn. He's going to issue an order of deportation that says you didn't show up today because you spoke out of turn.'

'But I showed up!'

The ride back to Ardsleyville was hot and shaky. A man in an officer's uniform asked me to mark a paper printed with English words. I wrote my name on the line.

Back in my room, the walls dissolved and I stepped outside. I was becoming someone else again.

I remembered a solitary light blinking on the tip of the plane's wing, the man in the next seat jiggling his knees like he was about to jump out of his pants. It was night. I shivered, sweating, couldn't remember the last time I'd eaten, and then I leaned over and vomited on my shoes.

Two uniformed men ushered me off the plane with a twenty-yuan bill and a newly issued ID. There were people around me speaking in Mandarin, Fuzhounese.

'Where are we?' I asked one of the men in Mandarin.

'Fuzhou. Changle.'

'There's no airport in Changle.'

'There is now.'

I found a door and pushed it open. I stood on the curb, nauseous, as mopeds and cars roared around me, the noise deafening, thunderous, and as I took a step forward a moped zoomed past, nearly knocking me over. The uniformed men had said I could go, but where? There could still be guards watching.

It was a cloudy morning in November, or January, and the air was packed with smells I recognized, memories of the village: burning wood and paper ashes, roast meat and salt, a brackish odor, swampy and thick with a tinge of rot. The scent of the riverbank. Was this for real, or was it a trick? I needed to find you.

A minibus for Minjiang pulled up. The driver, a woman whose hair was arranged into long, curly ribbons, opened the door. I stared at her. She said, 'You're getting in, or what?'

I paid for a ticket with the twenty-yuan bill, sat by the window, and watched the road disappear behind me as we drove away from the airport. Nobody was following. For weeks, months, years, whenever I turned a new corner or opened a door, I'd expect to be ambushed by guards. Even now I can't trust that they won't come for me someday.

The entrance arches of the village were far wider than they'd been twenty years ago, extensions built onto the top and sides, and there were new street signs and lampposts. The dirt roads were all paved. I passed chickens and trucks and bicycles, plastic sheeting strung between poles, posters on the walls announcing new development projects. I searched the face of each person I saw, dreading the moment I'd recognize someone and wishing someone would recognize me, but although some people looked familiar, I couldn't identify anyone I knew. After twenty years away, nobody looked the same.

At a newspaper stand I picked up the morning paper and saw the date on top. It was April, but the year was different. I had counted the days correctly. Fourteen months had disappeared while I was at Ardsleyville.

I felt faint. My head spun. I searched the newspaper vendor's face, hoping for a sign of recognition, but none appeared.

On 3 Alley, the lane was cleanly swept and there was a fresh coat of paint on my old house. I tried to open the door, but it was locked. I knocked, and Mrs Li answered, dressed in a lavender sweatsuit printed with dark flowers.

'Peilan? What are you doing here?'

'What are you doing in my house?'

'We've been using it. My cousin and his family live here, though they went home to the countryside last week for the holiday. Are you back for the holiday?'

'What holiday?'

'Qingming.' Mrs Li drew her words out slowly, eyeing my Ardsleyville uniform.

'You're using my land? My house?'

'You were in America. We couldn't contact you.'

'I didn't give it to you.'

'You can stay if you want.'

'It's not for you to decide.'

I pushed past her. The inside of the house had also been repainted. My old room was full of the belongings of Mrs Li's countryside cousin and his wife. Mr Li had died eight years ago, and Haifeng and his wife had a son of their own, a five-year-old whose photographs Mrs Li showed me. I was relieved to notice he didn't resemble you.

Neighbors came by, though I couldn't remember most of their names, and they looked shocked when they saw me. Had I changed so much? I told them I'd come home because there weren't many jobs in New York, that you were staying with relatives until you finished school. To have been detained for over a year was embarrassing, like I'd been caught out of stupidity, and I couldn't let anyone know.

Mrs Li gave me a pink sweatsuit to wear. I roamed the village without hitting a fence or a wall, swinging my arms and legs, gulping in the clean air. At the temple I saw my name next to Yi Ba's on a plaque with the names of villagers who'd given money for repairs. Yi Ba must have donated with the money I sent home. I ate meat and rice and vegetables and not oatmeal, heard music and cars and people, walked for hours without guards ordering me inside. I tucked blades of grass between my toes and pressed my thumbs against leaves and bark. The dirt smelled sweet and the breeze was as soft and clean as freshly laundered sheets. But the house was no longer my house. Mrs Li's cousin had a little girl, and her books and clothes were strewn across the room downstairs. Yi Ba's television was gone, a new one in its place. I found, hidden in a corner beneath the bed, one of your old shoes. I had bought them for you that first winter in New York, before sending you here. I held the tiny gray sneaker in my palm, remembered slipping it onto your little foot, pulling the laces tight. You must have been wearing it on the flight from New York. Dirt had settled into the creases, and the sole left my palm blackened with dust. I couldn't find the other shoe.

That night, I slept in my house. The next morning, I took a bus to Fuzhou with five thousand yuan that Mrs Li had given me for taking over my house. Later, I would learn that the house was worth at least fifteen thousand, even twenty, but by then it wouldn't matter.

Downtown Fuzhou looked nothing like it had twenty years ago. Fountains spurted in a square, surrounded by statues of men and women with their arms raised, with faces that looked oddly European. People walked past me in business suits. In a telephone booth, I called the number for the loan shark, which I'd gotten from a neighbor on 3 Alley, and told the man who I was, my birthdate, how much I had paid off before leaving New York, that I was in China and wanted to know the balance.

'One moment,' he said. 'Let me check.' I waited. Then the man got back on the phone and said, 'Your debt has been paid. Your balance is now zero.'

I bit my fingers. Leon must have wired my payments, month after month, when I was in Ardsleyville.

I bought an international calling card and dialed Leon's number, the one I thought I remembered. The phone rang twice and disconnected, no answer, no voice mail. I tried again and again and again and again. I stayed in the phone booth, attempting different combinations of phone numbers, all the numerical combinations that could possibly be Leon's, but none of them was the right one. I even dialed my old cell, a number I did remember, which was answered by a teenage girl. I had never memorized the numbers for Didi or Hello Gorgeous. With each dead-end phone call, my optimism receded, until I was crying into the sleeve of Mrs Li's sweatsuit. You were lost; my family was lost. Fourteen months had disappeared, and I didn't even have a place to live.

It was hunger that finally drove me out of the phone booth and into a nearby food stall, where I ate until the shakiness retreated and my despair hardened into ambition. Mrs Li had mentioned a nail salon, one of the first in Wuyi Square, and I found the address and introduced myself to the owner, a woman whose French manicure was flaking at the tips. 'I worked in New York,' I told her. 'Give me ten minutes and I can draw your face on your thumbnail.' By nightfall I had a job and a rented bed in a building full of Sichuanese workers.

CHAPTER EIGHTEEN

A door slammed down the hotel hallway, followed by the sounds of footsteps. I stopped, mid-sentence, and heard two women talking, their voices fading as they walked toward the elevator, and felt like I had woken up from a trance. You'd asked me to tell you the truth, and now that I had, you looked like you wished I hadn't.

'You couldn't call me because I was already in Ridgeborough,' you said.

'I know that now. But back then, I was so worried.'

'But you found Leon. You even saw him. Didn't he tell you I was adopted?'

I tried to figure out what I should say.

'You *knew*, and didn't do anything?'

'I didn't find him,' I said. 'He found me.'

Every week, on my one day off, I looked for Leon's family. If I found them, they could put me in touch with him, and he would put me in touch with you. I had to keep believing this. So I took a minibus to Leon's village and went to the homes of all the Zhengs in the phone book. Imagine how long that took. But nobody knew who he was.

To get to the district government office, I had to take two city buses followed by a minibus and then walk through a wasteland of parking lots. Then I waited outside a squat building in the humidity, sweating through my one clean outfit. The door was always closed, the blinds pulled tight. The silence was eerie and there was no shade, only sunlight on bare asphalt. Finally, the door would open and an official would walk out.

'Excuse me,' I would say, as they walked past me. I'd wait until they got back from their breaks. It could be five minutes, or two hours, and I had to intercept them fast, before they disappeared into the building. I learned to bring a bag of peanuts for lunch and a bottle of water, to speak politely yet forcefully, smiling to evoke both urgency and empathy. 'I'm looking for the family of Leon Zheng. I'm his wife. We got separated. I need to find his family.'

After the first few visits the officials recognized me, and they'd flinch when they saw me waiting, avoiding my eyes. 'Miss Guo,' one man said, 'I told you last week that family registration records were classified. Unless you found your marriage certificate . . .'

'I'll come back again. I'll call tomorrow.'

I went each week and called every day until a man said if I didn't stop asking, they would arrest me.

For months, I only spoke if I had to, avoiding the other women at the boardinghouse, who treated me with suspicion and spoke to one another in Sichuanese. I had two outfits and washed each one in the sink at night after wearing it, hung it to dry on a rack I'd constructed out of dowels and rubber bands. I worked as much as I could, until I was too tired to be overrun by guilt, fury, and crushing sadness. Sometimes, painting a woman's nails, I'd suddenly want to scream, and on breaks I'd go into the bathroom stall and do exactly that, stuffing my fingers into my mouth so no one could hear. The weeks melted by. Days off were the worst, because there'd be no work to distract me, and my mind was fresh enough to cough up memories of you and Leon and Ardsleyville. The hours spent waiting outside the government office were an opportunity to berate myself until I wished a bus would swerve off the street and flatten me. I started working seven days a week. I did a double take in the bathroom mirror when I saw the mournful, wounded expression on my face – like I'd been permanently punched – but it also seemed a fitting punishment.

One afternoon, after I had been in China for about six months, I was painting some lady's toenails when I noticed a strange man in the salon. I returned to the toenails, but could sense him walking closer, and when I looked up I saw the gap between his front teeth and let a blob of polish fall on my knee.

'Little Star?' he said.

I finished the pedicure as fast as I could, asked a co-worker to take my next customer and led Leon outside and down the block. He said that one of the Zhengs in his home village, a man I'd left the salon's address with, had run into him in Mawei.

We found an alleyway and put our arms around each other, and when I pressed my cheek to his, the smell of his skin was exactly the same. Musty and sweet, so beautiful, familiar. When was the last time anyone had held me? Too long ago. It had been Leon, before I'd been taken to Ardsleyville. I held him tighter, spoke into his neck. 'Where's Deming? Is he with you?'

'I need to tell you something.' Leon spoke at the wall. He told me how you had been adopted by a white couple, Americans in New York. Vivian had arranged it. She hadn't known how to get in touch with me, and they'd thought I was never coming back.

'I should have never left,' he said. 'If I hadn't left, he would still be with me. It's my fault. I don't know how to get in touch with him.'

I heard Leon sniffle, and then the sound of my own crying. I yelled at him, blamed him, called him the worst names I could. For the past six months, I'd been alternating between holding out hope that I would find you and trying to accept that you were gone.

Leon drove me to the boardinghouse and I got my things. We went to a small apartment on the eastern edge of the city, which belonged to a friend who was out of town. I asked him why we weren't going to his apartment, and he said, 'I need to tell you something else.' And he did.

The first night we were together, I jolted awake. Fluorescent lights, a guard with a notepad – I felt a hand on my arm and shouted out loud.

'Little Star, Little Star.'

I saw Leon's face. It was a repeating nightmare, the screaming in my sleep that my roommates complained about. The walls of the Hole, the weight of the handcuffs around my wrists and ankles.

Leon kissed me. 'You're here with me now.'

We only left the apartment for food, takeout meals we ate at the kitchen table naked, taking quick showers only to end up in bed again. Leon's cell phone rang occasionally, but he rarely answered, and when he did, he was considerate enough to take the call in another room. The third afternoon, he went out and came back with a bottle of pills, and that night my nightmares were blotted away, sleep reduced to a dark, blank square.

It was only five days, a fever dream, and by the end we were exhausted but still coming together, like two tired magnets that gravitated toward one another out of habit, or lack of choice. As long as we stayed in this room, time wouldn't go on. We could pretend that two years hadn't passed since we'd last seen each other, that we weren't avoiding questions. That you weren't missing.

You being gone like that, given over to another family like a stray dog, was too much to comprehend, and it hovered, like the rest of the world, just out of reach. I'd heard of a rural couple who had tried to get their daughter back from a family who had adopted her, but had gotten thrown in jail. I thought of taking all the pills at once, took them out of the bottle and counted them (there were thirty-five), and put them back inside. Maybe you could still find me.

As long as we stayed inside, your adoption would not be real. But Leon's friend was coming home the next day and we would have to leave the apartment.

'I could come with you,' Leon said. We were eating breakfast in a bakery, had gone out to wash the sheets and towels. 'We could be together again.' He held his arms across the table, his fingers wrapping around mine.

An ambulance drove past, and I jumped at the sound of the sirens. The past five days had been a delusion. He was asking me to stay with him because he thought it was what I wanted to hear, but he already had a family. I could see the relief in his face when I told him no.

Because being with Leon made your loss real. 'Go home to your wife,' I told him. The first day we had been together I thought I could make him choose, but by the fifth day, I no longer wanted to. 'Go home to your baby girl.'

You slid down the wall until you were buried under the hotel sheets.

'And that was it?' you said. 'You forgot me?'

'I didn't forget. I just survived.'

*

I took a class in business Mandarin so I could bury my village accent and get a better job. When the teacher heard I had lived in America, he said he was also opening up an English school. I told him I'd studied in New York and gone to America on a student visa. Even if my English wasn't good, it was better than some of the other teachers'.

'Working for World Top can't get you an urban hukou right now,' Boss Cheng said, after I moved into the teacher dormitory, 'but we'll see about the future.' I decided I would work this job, make a lot of money, and figure out a way to go back to New York so I could find you.

I'd been teaching at World Top for almost a year, working and saving as much as I could, when Yong appeared in my class. He didn't manage to learn much from me, but on the night of his last class, he said in English, 'I'd like to see you sometime.'

He started to take me out to dinner twice a week, a few hours during which my grief would retreat, a momentary break. I liked his steadiness, his ambition and kindness; I'd forgotten what it was like to have someone pay attention to me, to have someone to talk to. Here was someone who could be a partner. And this was my chance to marry into an urban hukou, to get a permanent city residency permit. Without one, I'd always be a migrant. The city could kick me out any time. Those five days with Leon, the feeling of the floor dropping out from beneath me? That could never happen again.

After two months, I kissed Yong. Six months later, we had our wedding at a hotel in Wuyi Square. Twelve courses were served, eight of them seafood.

'There wasn't anything I could do,' I said. 'I couldn't go back to America after being deported. I couldn't go anywhere. If I thought about you too much I wouldn't be able to live.'

I knew how it must sound to you: I hadn't tried hard enough, I didn't love you enough. But I could have kept looking forever. I needed you to understand.

'You forgot me,' you said.

'No. Never.'

'You didn't even tell your husband about me.'

'I did tell him. You met him. You know.'

'You didn't tell him until I called you.'

My head sagged. You were right.

'I thought he'd be angry, and then he would leave me.' But that, too, was a lie. I'd only told myself that. I had never believed it.

'I thought you went away because I did something wrong. I was a kid!' You pounded the mattress with your fists. You must have wanted to punch me, too.

'You didn't do anything wrong,' I said. 'When I returned to China and learned Leon had paid off the rest of my debt, I knew you were okay. Even if I hated the idea of you calling a white lady "Mama" or "Mom".'

You snorted. 'Leon didn't pay off the loan shark. *Vivian* did.'

Now I felt like I had really been punched. 'But you were safe, weren't you? With your adoptive parents?' I could hear the pleading desperation in my own questions, how badly I wanted to believe you'd been fine, that I had done all I could.

There was a long silence. Finally you said, 'I never call my adoptive mother "Mama" or "Mom".'

You shut off the light. For a moment we lay together, on our separate beds, as your words pulled a warm blanket over us and made us less alone.

CHAPTER NINETEEN

He hadn't expected to like teaching so much. Today he split his students out into groups of three for role-playing: ordering at a restaurant, asking for directions in English. The other instructors, even his mother, laughed at him for making work harder for himself and not teaching the workbook. But his students were awake, engaged, and he was willing to be held up for their amusement and curiosity. When he said they could ask him anything they wanted, as long as they asked in English, they shouted out questions. What kind of clothes did people wear in New York? What did they eat? Did he have a girlfriend? Boss Cheng had reprimanded him, said his class was too noisy, but when Daniel's students told their friends about him and these new students enrolled and requested to be in his class, Boss Cheng stopped bugging him. 'Boss Cheng doesn't know his head from his ass,' his mother said, cackling her old laugh. He leaned toward her compliments, always craving more. 'You're the best teacher at that school. You should be director.' That was her new plan for him. He'd stay in Fuzhou, follow her footsteps. It made him feel proud, yet also unsure. He didn't know if he wanted to be the director of World Top English. But then she would look at him and smile and he would smile back, thinking, *Yes, this is where I belong.*

He had been living in China for three months, hadn't spoken to Peter and Kay since leaving Ridgeborough in August. People no longer laughed at his accent; his Mandarin and Fuzhounese had slipped back into native-speaker levels, and the gaps between translating and speaking had grown smaller and smaller until they were nearly imperceptible, his brain automatically shifting into Chinese.

His tourist visa was expiring soon, and his mother was in the process of sponsoring him for a real work visa. The forms had been in his room for weeks, and he needed to fill them out. Until then, he couldn't legally receive a salary, wasn't on the official payroll at World Top English, but Boss Cheng paid his mother extra money, which she then deposited into his bank account.

After his morning class, Daniel went out for lunch with two of the other teachers, Eddie and Tammy. They usually insisted on McDonald's or Pizza Hut, places where he would never voluntarily eat. Today they were going to a spaghetti restaurant that Tammy said was sophisticated, though Daniel would have been fine going to a noodle stall and slurping down a cheap bowl of soup. They walked the three blocks from World Top to the restaurant, Daniel familiar with most of the streets in downtown Fuzhou, accustomed to mopeds coming at him in all directions. The summer in Ridgeborough, the liminal New York winter that had preceded it, seemed like another lifetime ago. It was astounding to think that that had been him, tromping across the ice on Canal Street, not knowing that by the end of the year, he would not only have seen his mother again but be living with her, seeing her every day.

Inside the restaurant, an old song was looping on the speaker, the moon hitting the singer's eye like a big pizza pie. The waitresses wore red, white, and green uniforms. It was a

Macaroni Grill on steroids. Eddie climbed into the banquette next to him. 'Is the menu authentic?' Outside of class, they spoke Fuzhounese.

Daniel flipped through the pictures of pastas drowning in red and white sauces. If it wasn't a Chinese restaurant, Tammy and Eddie always made him order. 'Yes,' he said.

Tammy brushed her bangs away from her eyes. Unlike Eddie, she avoided eye contact at all costs. 'Restaurants where the waitresses wear uniforms are always authentic. Deming, you order for all of us.'

Daniel asked the waitress for three bowls of spaghetti and meatballs and a platter of garlic sticks. Eddie's unblinking gaze felt like being cross-examined. Tammy said she'd heard that the restaurant served the best American food in Fuzhou.

'This food isn't American,' Eddie said.

'Well, it's Italian,' Daniel said. 'But the dishes are more of an American style. They would call it Italian American.'

Tammy said, 'But is it Italian or American?'

'It's both.'

'But Italians aren't American,' Eddie said.

'Sure, they can be Italian American. Like if your parents were born in Italy, but you were born in America.'

'Then you'd be American,' Tammy said. 'Because you were born in America.'

'Well, you can be Chinese American. I'm Chinese American because I was born in America.'

'But you have a Chinese face so that makes you Chinese,' Tammy said.

'Americans can have Chinese faces. They aren't only white people.'

Tammy and Eddie glanced at each other and Eddie muttered a quick sentence in Fuzhounese that Daniel couldn't catch.

'I'm right here, you know,' Daniel said. 'I can hear you talking about me.'

'We're not talking about you,' Tammy said.

The tomato sauce was too sweet, the pasta overcooked, and Daniel ached for a proper New York thin slice, folded in half and chowed down while standing at an oily pizzeria counter. Tonight, he'd pick up food on the way home and eat in front of the TV. If he was in Manhattan or Ridgeborough his friends would be buying him shots, but instead he would return to an empty apartment. His mother was supposed to be coming home late, on the bullet train from Xiamen, where she had spent the last two days for work. She no longer watched him so carefully, like he was in danger of vanishing, and on weekends they spent hours walking around the city together, having long, easy meals, and he would feel warm and full. But when she made plans for him, mentioned people she wanted him to meet or a trip they might take in the future, he would feel a sticky dread, like he had overslept on a winter day and woken up to discover it was already dark.

He didn't want to be alone, not today. 'What are you two doing tonight?'

They exchanged another glance. 'We have dinner with our families,' Eddie said.

He waited for the bus to West Lake Park after his last class of the day. Yong would be working late tonight, or at a business dinner. One night he had taken Daniel to his factory, and Daniel had looked down from the executive office at rows of women at sewing machines. 'Your mother doesn't like to visit me at work,' Yong said.

Once or twice a week, Daniel took the bus out to Leon's place to eat with him and Shuang. He played with Yimei in the park, showing her how to toss a Frisbee and do wheelies on her bike, and wished she were his real sister, or at least his real cousin. When he mentioned these visits to his mother, she said, 'Maybe I'll come with you sometime.' But tonight Leon was also busy; he'd said he had to work late.

Now that Daniel was making money again, he had started to pay Angel back, little by little. He had cut up his credit card and was chipping away at the balance, but whatever extra he had left over, which wasn't a lot, he sent to her. She never responded, but deposited the money.

He hadn't heard from Roland either. The last time he had googled Psychic Hearts, several weeks ago, he had read a review of their latest show with the headline 'Don't Believe the Hype':

While guitarist Nate Lundstrom – a former member of a number of Meloncholia projects – is technically and stylisti-cally astute, Psychic Hearts' new, dancier configuration lacks the claustrophobic, manic-depressive, and almost mystical cohesion of its original pairing. The looping beats have gotten frayed and agonizingly repetitive, and Fuentes' howls grown stale, like a fifth-rate Lightning Bolt meets bubblegum pop . . . How can something so heavy sound so damn minimal? Sure, it's cool, kids, but there's no *there* there.

The bus arrived. Of course, all the passengers were Chinese. It had taken him weeks to not find it surprising that everyone around him, including the people on TV, including the hottest girls, were all Chinese. Being from America made him an object of desire, which was both flattering and strange; girls flirted with him when they found out he was from New York. Even Tammy, who had a boyfriend, walked a little too close when they went to lunch. He'd hooked up a couple times with a girl who'd gone to high school with one of the other World Top teachers, a sales manager at a company that manufactured plastic slippers. There was another girl, too, a friend of a friend of Eddie's, who lived in the suburbs with her parents and texted him sporadically.

There was a comfort in belonging that he'd never felt before, yet somehow, he still stood out. The bus driver eyed him for a beat too long when he bought the ticket, as did the woman in the seat across the aisle, a bag of groceries on her lap. Yong and his mother assured him his Chinese sounded close to normal now and not as freakish as it had when he first arrived, but Daniel figured it was his clothes, his bearing, or the way he looked or walked or held himself, something that revealed he wasn't from here. Even if he encouraged them to ask questions, he often grew tired of the students and other teachers at World Top finding him a source of perpetual fascination. His students asked him why he was so tall, even if Eddie was taller than him, and prodded him to sing songs to them in English. When the other teachers asked what he did for fun and he said he liked to walk around and listen to music on his headphones, they laughed.

He called his mother to see if there was a chance she would be home for dinner, and when she didn't pick up, he didn't bother to leave a message. He shouldn't have to ask her to be home tonight. If she forgot what day it was, he would know what to do. God, he hoped she hadn't forgotten.

He plugged his headphones into his phone, feeling rubbery as the music kicked in, a mix of old favorites, Suicide, Arthur Russell, Queens of the Stone Age. His phone buzzed and he expected to see his mother's name, but it was a wrong number, a guy who said in Mandarin, 'I thought this was someone else.' It was stupid being here again, waiting for her. Disappointed by her.

He had thoroughly searched the apartment when he was

there alone, combed through the drawers and cabinets, even scoured beneath the beds and leather couch (finally, his mother had the nice couch she'd always wanted), but found only clothes, folded and neat, a binder with documents pertaining to work and the apartment. He was looking for hidden facts, a sign that would point him toward what he should do next. Yet there was not a single photograph in the apartment, no squirreled-away shoebox of sentimental keepsakes, no hidden diaries or items that could confess any aspects of his mother and Yong beyond what they portrayed to him. They existed only in the present, their lives as brand new as their apartment. He had hoped this would allow him to trust them, but still, he worried, didn't want to be left the fool.

The woman across the aisle was staring at him openly, and he noticed the tension in his jaw, how tightly he was squeezing his hands. He turned the music louder, but couldn't regain that initial rush. Apprehension lingered, the fear he was letting somebody down, that he was the one who was being let down.

At the apartment gate, carrying a bag of takeout from a restaurant near the bus stop, Daniel greeted Chun, the security guard. 'Have a good night,' Chun said, and smiled. Daniel used his key to open the front door of the building and rode the elevator up to the twelfth floor.

He stopped before switching on the light, was in the process of using one foot to loosen the heel of the other shoe when he heard a scuffle along the floor. 'Who's there?' he said, and a second later the lights were blazing and there was a chorus of people shouting 'Surprise!' His mother was at his side, and Yong, and a blur of other faces.

She hadn't forgotten his birthday. Not only had she remembered – of course she'd remembered; how could he have thought she hadn't – but she had filled the apartment with everyone he knew in Fuzhou: Eddie and Tammy and the other teachers at World Top, his Speed English Now students, her and Yong's friends. Even Leon and Shuang and Yimei were there. The living room was crowded, balloons tied to the chairs, and there was food on the counter, platters of fruit, grilled meat, and noodles. Music was switched on. Someone put a beer in his hand.

It was a real party. 'Were you surprised?' his mother asked. 'People thought it was strange when I said we were having a surprise party. I remember seeing it in a movie once.'

'Tammy and Eddie kept it a surprise when I had lunch with them. And my students didn't say a thing.'

She laughed. 'I said I'd get them fired if they said one word to you.'

Daniel looked around the room again. People sat on the couch, eating chips and peanuts, while others drank beers in the kitchen.

'You don't like crowds, though,' he said.

'I don't mind.'

'You don't like parties.'

'That's not true. I used to love parties.'

'Used to.'

'Now, too.'

'You invited Leon.'

'I wanted everyone here who's important to you. He called me the other day and we talked for a little while. I met his wife, his daughter . . .'

She sounded genuinely glad about it. 'Thank you,' he said.

'Happy birthday, Deming.' She patted his arm. 'My son, the future director of World Top English.'

'Well,' Daniel said, 'it's true, I don't see Boss Cheng here tonight.'

He wandered around the apartment, stopping to talk to people. Pop music with autotuned Mandarin shot out from a pair of portable speakers. Shuang and his mother's friend Ning were dancing with Tammy, the two older women following Tammy's more intricate steps.

Leon and Yimei were talking with Yong in the kitchen, and Yong waved him over. 'Let's take a picture.'

Daniel grinned, hot and buzzy. 'Send me a copy,' he said, and put his arms around Yimei, Leon behind him, as Yong snapped pictures with his phone.

'Do you have anything to draw with?' Yimei asked.

He wondered if they looked alike in any way, even if they weren't related. 'I don't have crayons, but I have paper and pens. Let me go look.'

In his mother's guest room, which had become his bedroom, his laptop was furiously dinging. He pressed a key and the screen came to life, flooding him with messages from Ridgeborough and New York City, even Potsdam. Michael had sent a video of him and Timothy and Vivian singing 'Happy Birthday' in their kitchen in Sunset Park. Roland e-mailed: *Happy birthday, D. Miss you.* Even Cody messaged: *when r u coming home?*

Daniel read the messages, one by one, read them again. There were so many of them, and seeing them made him giddy with sadness. He hadn't been forgotten.

From the living room came a round burst of laughter, and he remembered why he had come into the room. He rooted through a pile of papers, pushing aside the visa application he had promised his mother he would fill out by last week, and found a notepad and a few pens for Yimei. He was about to close his laptop when a new window popped up.

pkwilkinson is calling, the window announced. Another window appeared with an accompanying message: *daniel are you there?*

The window pulsed and glowed. He crossed the room and shut the door, muffling the party, then sat on the bed and clicked. Kay and Peter's faces appeared, squinting into their computer screen. They were in the study in Ridgeborough. He recognized the bookshelves, the blue wallpaper, the framed diplomas and awards.

'Daniel?' Kay said.

'Where are you?' Peter asked.

'In Fuzhou. China.'

They were talking over each other. There was a split-second delay, so Daniel saw their mouths moving before he heard their voices, and their motions lagged a little, pixilated smears of color trailing their faces. He heard Kay say, 'China?' and Peter say, 'Happy birthday.'

Daniel shouted into the screen. His English sounded knotty, peculiar. 'I'm staying with my mom – my birth mom. I'm fine, I'm working. Teaching English. I haven't been gambling. My Chinese is great now, I mean, it's back.'

Kay's face was on the verge of crumpling. 'We wanted to wish our son a happy birthday,' she said.

He felt his eyes well up.

'What time is it over there?' Peter asked.

'Eight at night.' Daniel could hear the music from the living room. He wanted to stay and talk, but he didn't want to miss out. 'They're throwing me a party here. How are you guys doing?'

Kay said she had run into Cody at the Food Lion the other day. Peter said he had watched a Tom Petty concert from 1980 on YouTube. Daniel told them he was the favorite teacher at World Top English.

'You may have found your calling,' Peter said.

'Are you going to come home? To America?' Kay asked.

'I don't know.'

'You know you're always welcome here,' Kay said.

'Christmas is coming up,' Peter said.

He swallowed. 'I'll have to see.'

He heard footsteps outside. 'Deming?' his mother called from the hallway. 'Where are you?'

'Just a minute,' he said in Fuzhounese. But the door opened and light and voices spilled into the room, and it was too late to cut the call short. He turned and saw his mother in the doorway.

'The cake is ready,' she said. As Peter and Kay watched, she picked up the visa form, which had fallen on the bed. 'You still haven't filled this out?'

She looked over him, at his computer, and Daniel could see her face on the small screen that reflected what Peter and Kay saw on theirs. His face, and her face, next to each other, looking into the camera together. He saw Peter's expression move from confusion to recognition. Kay's mouth hesitated for a moment before she caught herself and smiled.

'Kay and Peter? This is my mother, Polly.'

'Hello,' his mother said in English.

'It is very nice to meet you, Polly,' Kay said, pressing her lips together. He thought he detected a slowness in her words that wasn't usually there. The three of them studied one another as Daniel tried to think of the right thing to say.

'You do look alike,' Peter said. 'I can see it.'

'Thank you for taking care of Daniel,' Kay said. 'He must be having the time of his life in China.'

His mother nodded, staring at the screen, and Daniel noticed her teeth clench. He wanted to protect her, but from what? When she had told him about Ardsleyville, he'd remembered what Leon had said: that there was something broken in her.

He wasn't sure if she didn't understand Kay and Peter, or if she didn't have the English words to respond, or if she didn't know what to say, but he wanted her to say something, anything, for her to be as loud and demanding and opinionated as she usually was. He hated that he could see her the way Peter and Kay must be seeing her, a mute Chinese woman with a heavy accent. Their tense smiles were making him angry.

'I should get back to the party,' he said in English.

'Okay,' Kay said. 'We'll talk to you soon, Daniel.'

'And maybe we'll see you at Christmas,' Peter said. 'Maybe we can help pay for a plane ticket.'

His mother leaned over, blocking his face on the screen, and said, in English, 'His name is Deming, not Daniel.' Daniel nearly laughed out loud; he bit the inside of his lip. Then Kay's smile dropped, and he felt the need to apologize to her and Peter. Or should he apologize to his mother instead?

He said good-bye and logged out of the program. In the living room, his friends were waiting with a cake, and his mother lit the candles and he blew out the flames, then looked up to see Leon and Yong, Eddie and Tammy, Shuang and Yimei. The sound of their clapping was a shimmering yellow, and the sound of his mother saying his name – *Deming!* – the warmest gold.

He collected plates and spoons, empty bottles of Tsingtao; tied up the trash bags; vacuumed crumbs from the rug; swept the kitchen floor. If he kept busy he could ward off the possibility of his mother asking him about Peter and Kay.

He didn't want to go to Carlough. He didn't want to present papers at the Conference for English Educators. Peter and Kay had supported him, in their own way, so why did he feel angry with them? But he couldn't let his mother down either, because while he had been playing video games with Roland and listening to Hendrix, she had been in a prison camp. She still had nightmares. At the very least, he didn't want to make her feel bad.

Everyone had stories they told themselves to get through the days. Like Vivian's belief that she had helped him, his mother insisting she had looked for him, that she could forget about him because he was okay. In the hotel room in Beijing, he had wanted to hurt her when he told the truth about Vivian paying off her debt, so then he had gifted her with a lie: that he never called Kay 'Mom'.

'I saw this in your room.' She came into the kitchen in her pajamas, holding the visa form. 'You must have forgotten to fill it out.'

'Leave it on the table,' he said, scrubbing at a stain on the counter. 'I'll take care of it later. Wasn't it funny when Eddie and my students sang that happy birthday song and wrote new lyrics so it had my name? I didn't know Eddie had such a good voice, or that Tammy was such a good dancer.'

'Stop scrubbing. I'll clean up later.'

'We drank so much beer! No wonder the neighbors were telling us to keep it quiet.'

'Sit down. Let me do it.'

'You threw me a party.'

'Because I wanted to. You don't have to repay me.'

She took an orange from one of the plates of leftovers and brought it to the kitchen table. He put the sponge down and watched her peel it, rubbing the rind away with her fingernail, separating the wedges onto a plate, half for her, half for him. He stood over her shoulder and hugged her from behind. Surprised, she held his arms in her hands. Over the years, he had thought about what his life would have been like if Mama and Leon hadn't left, if Vivian hadn't taken him to the foster care agency. It was like watching water spread across dry pavement, lines going in all directions. Peter and Kay might have adopted another boy. He could be living in Sunset Park, or in the Bronx or Florida or some other place he'd never heard of. He had imagined his doppelgängers living the lives he hadn't, in different apartments and houses and cities and towns, with different sets of parents, different languages, but today he could only see himself where he was right now, the particular set of circumstances that had trickled down to this particular life, that would keep trickling in new directions.

He sat down. His mother passed him the visa form and a pen. 'I'm going to send it out tomorrow.'

He took an orange slice. All this time, he'd been waiting for his real life to begin: Once he was accepted by Roland's friends and the band made it big. Once he found his mother. Then, things would change. But his life had been happening all along, in the jolt of the orange juice on his tongue or how he dreamt in two languages, how his students' faces looked when they figured out the meaning of a new word, the wisp of smoke as he blew out his birthday candles. The surge and turn and crunch of a perfect melody.

'You're going to New York for Christmas?' his mother said. 'To your adoptive family?'

'No, of course not.'

'They call you all the time?'

'I haven't spoken to them since I came here. This was the first time.'

'They want you to come home, though.'

He was like Tammy, unable to meet his mother's eyes.

'This is my home.'

'So you're going to stay? With me?'

It was a funny thing, forgiveness. You could spend years being angry with someone and then realize you no longer felt the same, that your usual mode of thinking had slipped away when you weren't noticing. He could see, in the flash of worry in his mother's face as she waited for his reply, like he had heard in Kay and Peter's shaking voices when they said good-bye to him earlier, that in the past few months, his fear of being unwanted had dissipated. Because Mama – and Kay, and Peter – were trying to convince him that they were deserving of his love, not the other way around.

He ate the bite of orange, took the visa form and uncapped the pen, scanning the paper for where he was supposed to sign.

PART FOUR

The Leavers

CHAPTER TWENTY

In the spring, four months after you left, I left, too. Not just Fuzhou, but my life – Yong, my job, our apartment, everyone I knew. I decided to move to Hong Kong. While you were staying with me I had pretended we had never been apart, that Ardsleyville had never happened. But when you left Fuzhou, I understood that I could also leave, and maybe it wasn't too late.

It was a short flight to Hong Kong, less than two hours, and by the time I had gotten used to being up in the air, the flight attendants were already preparing to land. At the airport I rolled my suitcase, a small one containing all I had packed, through Immigration, then onto a train that took me into the center of the city. I exited onto a street outside a mall, where the cars drove on the left side of the road, not the right. It took me several tries to cross. Even at night, there were still crowds out, people talking in Cantonese, signs flashing in Chinese and English. I had the address of the one-room apartment I'd rented, sight unseen; and tomorrow morning I would start my new job at a school in Kowloon.

At the ferry terminal I bought a ticket, then found a place on the upper deck. The boat rocked in the waves, and as I saw the lights of Kowloon come through the fog, I held the railing, breathless with laughter. How wrong I had been to assume this feeling had been lost forever. This lightheaded uncertainty, all my fear and joy – I could return here, punching the sky. Because I had found her: Polly Guo. Wherever I went next, I would never let her go again.

The breeze blew my hair back, then forward. The water was Minjiang, New York, Fuzhou, but most of all it was you. I thought of the last time you and I had gone to the water together in New York, the summer before I was taken to Ardsleyville. Late August, afternoon edging into evening, the heat lessening its grip, we had walked to a bridge over the Harlem River, spanning the Bronx and Manhattan. The air was soft and thick, and the walkway swayed as cars drove past. The river below was brown and muddy.

We'd stood in the middle of the bridge. You were ten, almost eleven; already you preferred your friends' company to mine. I'd had to bribe you with a candy bar to get you away from the TV.

I pointed to a building on the Manhattan side. 'Can you see who lives there?' I asked, remembering one of our old games.

You shook your head and rolled your eyes.

'Maybe it's a mother and son,' I said.

Finally, you said, 'No, a baseball team.'

'The whole team? Or just a few of them.'

'Everyone lives together in the same apartment. It's a big apartment.'

'They play at night,' I said. 'They sleep during the day.'

You broke into a smile. 'They eat French fries. Play catch on the roof.'

'But they never fall off.'

Far below us, the water moved, revealing an umbrella, a mass of plastic bags. The river looked tough, decisive, but it always gave up its secrets.

Now the ferry engine slowed as it approached the dock. A man tossed a rope overboard. 'This is Kowloon,' I heard a woman say. We floated to a stop, and I lifted the handle of my suitcase, letting myself be pushed along with the crowd. Soon I would be walking onshore to a new place. The beginning, I knew, was always the best part.

On the bridge above the Harlem River, an ice cream truck had tinkled its song, followed by the snort and stop of a bus. A car had rolled down its window, music pouring out, a woman singing, *Some people want it all . . .*

We had stood and listened on the verge of a summer night. Then you'd cupped your hands around your mouth and leaned over the railing, shouted your name into the air. I joined you, shouting mine, and we let our voices rise, leaping and echoing, flying over the city. My heart unclenched. You were growing fast, and soon you would be taller than me, but there was always this game, this song.

We started toward home, the sun coming over the rooftops, and when you began to run I followed, feet pounding the sidewalk, only a moment behind.

CHAPTER TWENTY-ONE

The third time he played was on a Tuesday night. The opening act out of four, he sat onstage with his acoustic guitar and looper station, which had the back-up tracks he'd recorded at home in his room. Outside, what seemed like the twentieth snowstorm of the season was grinding up to its chorus, and inside, only one of the tables was occupied, and by members of the next band. A couple had wandered in from the main bar in search of the bathroom and left ten seconds into Daniel's first song. He'd heard them talking during his short introduction (his name, a hello; he nixed the obligatory quip about the weather), and when they walked out he had wanted to run off stage after them.

He hadn't invited anyone to his shows, though the last time he played, two weeks ago, Roland had happened to be walking past the bar and had noticed Daniel's name on the blackboard outside, alarming him by shouting 'Daniel Fucking Wilkinson!' after the last song. 'Why're you being so secretive?' Roland had said afterwards. 'We hung out two days ago and you didn't say anything about playing.' It wasn't about being secretive; it was about self-protection. 'Just say the word and I'll let Thad know and you can put this out. But don't wait too long. No one else is doing stuff like this.'

Christmas lights were strung up along the bar's walls, points of blues and yellows and reds. Daniel heard the guys from the next band talking to one another, caught a glimpse of the bartender playing with her phone.

The first two songs came out wobbly, his voice still froggy, the pacing rushed, but by the third song, the one about Deming and his doppelgänger, the initial terror had mostly burned off and his playing was steadier, his voice stronger, and he started to feel the words he was singing. Between songs, he paused for enough time to elicit a trace of dry applause from the next band, which made up in enthusiasm what it lacked in volume.

What was the compulsion to expose himself so fully, to keep doing something that scared the shit out of him? It hadn't been scary when he'd been playing other people's music, or performing with other people. This was different. Roland had called his songs fresh, crazy honest, the real deal, and after each gig Daniel thought, *May I never have to do that again.* But a few days later he'd be sending out links to his webpage, trying to book the next one.

He made it to the final verse when he looked up at the near-empty room, the fear barging in. *Do the audience a favor,* he thought. *Cut the set short.* He stumbled, forgetting the next line. The song hung in freefall. He wanted to flee, to safety and also to humiliation, but knew these were good songs, that he was worthy of being heard, and he hated, more than anything, not being listened to. He remembered the line and the song righted itself, regained its balance.

When he finished his set, no one congratulated him. It was the end of another winter, more than a year after Psychic Hearts' first show at the loft party, and Roland and Nate were recording a full album. Toward the end of February, several days after Angel had deposited his sixth money transfer, she had e-mailed him, one line, which made him laugh:

The white sheep comes home to roost.

~ A

He was rarely home these days, working at Tres Locos and teaching private guitar lessons to middle-schoolers on the Upper West Side. He met up with Roland a few times a week, and on Wednesday and Friday afternoons taught an after-school music class at a community center in Chinatown, where most of his students' families came from Fujian Province, and more than a few had also been sent to live with their grandparents until they were old enough to go to school. The Upper West Side kids got frustrated when Daniel tried to teach them how to hold the guitar, and their parents wanted them to be the next Jack White (in their spare time, grades came first), and he looked forward to the days he taught in Chinatown, how the kids there called him Yi Go and got excited when they nailed the rhythm of a song. They hadn't yet learned how to be afraid of not looking cool.

It was less than ten blocks from the bar to the subway but felt farther, carrying his guitar and gear in the sleet, boots skidding along the sidewalk. Across from the subway station was a pizzeria, and he was hungry, but he would wait until he got back to Manhattan. There was food in the refrigerator, and he was becoming a good cook, trading meals with his roommate, perfecting a soup that was a decent rendition of the one at Leon's spot back in Fuzhou.

One month after his birthday, eating dinner by himself while his mother and Yong were at work, Daniel had come across a picture in an article he was reading online, Lower Broadway on a spring afternoon, delivery vans and cabs, halal food carts and fire escapes. That night, for the first time since he had come to China, he listened to the songs he had written over the summer.

The music shot through his headphones in silver waves; it was the familiarity of feeling perfectly like himself. He wanted to tweak a few lines, so he typed up some notes, wishing he had his guitar.

After he decided to leave, he told his mother that it wasn't about Peter and Kay, that he wasn't choosing them over her. She had cried. The visa form had already been submitted. 'But we'll see each other again,' he said. Leon came with them to the airport, and when Daniel turned at the ticket counter he saw them from a distance, his mother in her suit and heels, Leon in his sneakers and windbreaker, talking and laughing like old friends. He wasn't sure if he was making the right decision, didn't know how long he'd stay. Maybe he would come back to Fuzhou after New Year's. Either way, it was incredible to decide something. He had never allowed himself to fully trust his choices before.

Three stops and more than twenty-four hours of travel later, he arrived at the Syracuse airport the morning of Christmas Day. English clanged out around him in fraught copper lines, and nobody looked Chinese. Outside, waiting for Peter and Kay, it was freezing, and he didn't have a jacket.

They parked and got out of the car. 'You must be tired,' Kay said, hugging him tightly. 'All that flying!' Peter hugged him, too, thumping him on the back.

On the drive to Ridgeborough, fighting jet lag, he'd entertained them with light observations about the differences between Fuzhou and New York, talking about traffic and smog, the menu at Pizza Hut, his Speak English Now students. How it didn't snow there, it was that far south. He felt bad, offering Eddie and Tammy and Boss Cheng up for amusement, but it seemed easier than having the spotlight on Mama or himself.

Back in the house, he skipped out on church and took a nap, and when he woke up he took his guitar out of the closet.

After months of not being played, the strings were still in tune. Moving between chords, his fingers and wrists loosening, he elicited color shifts he'd forgotten about: brown and aqua, ranges of mauve and pink, the squeakiest of greens. Shit, it felt great. Though he could have sworn there used to be these tiny cracks in the fingerboard that he had wanted to fix but never got around to. Or had he fixed them before he left and forgotten?

Peter knocked on the doorframe. 'Reunited at last,' he said.

Daniel looked up. 'Yeah, it's been a while. Still works, though.'

'Do you notice anything different?' Peter pointed to the fingerboard. 'I took it to the Music Department at Carlough and one of the professors recommended someone he knew, a guitar repairman. I thought it could use a little TLC.'

He helped Kay chop vegetables and peel potatoes for dinner. 'I haven't had potatoes in ages,' he said, as she poured canned pumpkin mix into a pie shell. She was wearing a lavender sweater he hadn't seen before; Peter had a matching one in green. 'We had rice, though. Lots and lots of rice.' Hearing himself in English still felt strange.

How easy it would be to say it: *I learned so much when I was there – let me tell you about her. She had wanted me.* But every time he started to say something, he stopped.

Kay passed him the pie shell and told him to put it in the oven. He set it down on the rack and closed the door. When he stood up, she was watching him, and he was afraid she would start talking about him going back to Carlough, or GA meetings.

'Was it hard?' she asked. 'Being in China?'

He removed the oven mitt. 'It took a while for my Chinese to come back, but once it did, it got a lot easier.'

'But still, it must have been pretty foreign for you.'

He didn't know why, but he didn't want to tell Kay about

how he had always felt a little different there, even if he could speak the language. 'Fuzhou's a big city, though, real modern.'

'Your father and I were reading an article about how women in China are still second-class citizens. It makes sense, I suppose, with the cultural bias against girls.' Kay shook her head. 'Polly, your birth mother? She must be very brave to have the kind of career she does.'

'It's not really like that,' he said. Though she *was* brave, and in ways Kay didn't know about. And sure, it could be hard for women in China, harder than it might be for women here. But it bothered him, talking about Mama like this, when she wasn't here.

'It's a shame, really, when you think of the ways these women might have flourished if they'd had access to the right opportunities and education. They could be doing so much better, so much more.'

'She's doing great. A lot of women in China have college degrees.'

'Oh, I just had an idea. Maybe I'll talk to someone at Carlough about starting a scholarship for a female Chinese student.'

She wasn't listening to him. He recalled how she and Peter had insisted on English, his new name, the right education. How *better* and *more* hinged on their ideas of success, their plans. Mama, Chinese, the Bronx, Deming: they had never been enough. He shivered, and for a brief, horrible moment, he could see himself the way he realized they saw him – as someone who needed to be saved.

No. He felt queasy, terrified. He balled his hands into fists, pushed them into his pockets.

Kay leaned over the oven, checking the timer on the pie. 'Do you want to make the whipped cream? You always loved doing that. Licking the bowl and all.' She took down the mixing bowl from the cabinet. 'It's good to have you back. I mean, I'm glad you had the opportunity to explore your roots, but I'm also glad you've come home. The house felt lonely without you here.'

The oven warmed the kitchen, filling it with the scent of baking, sugar and butter and cinnamon. In the living room Peter had lit a fire, and Daniel could hear the crackling flames, classical music on the stereo. His guitar was upstairs, restrung and repaired, his bed piled with favorite quilts. 'It's good to be here,' he said, and got the cream from the refrigerator.

He slept: for twelve hours, waking up at four in the morning, taking long naps in the late afternoon. At dawn he lay awake in bed, the room slowly sharpening, and remembered walking around Fuzhou with his mother, biking in the park with Yimei, his bumbling first days in the Min Hotel. All of it so peculiar and distant, like someone else's life.

He spent the week watching television, barely changing out of his sweatpants or bothering to go outside. On New Year's Eve, Kay and Peter were asleep by eleven, and Daniel fell asleep in front of the TV after watching the ball drop in Times Square, pop stars singing to crowds of drunken tourists. He woke up to an infomercial for acne medication.

His footsteps muffled by wool socks, he walked around the house in the dark. Even with his eyes closed, he knew he could put a hand out on a wall in any room and have it land exactly on the light switch, that he had to veer to the right of the bookshelf in the living room in order to not bump into the corner of the end table where Kay kept her magazines, that there were fourteen steps up to the second floor. Every floorboard, every square inch of the house remained with him. Yet there was so much that this house, that Peter and Kay, would never know. He stood against the kitchen wall, listening to the hum of the refrigerator, the sound of his own breathing. If he couldn't feel at home in China, if he didn't belong in Ridgeborough, then where did that leave him?

Three steps to the dining room, left turn, wall. His growth chart was still here, sketched against the doorjamb. There was a dent near the floorboard, made from a basketball he'd once bounced. Five steps to the china cabinet, its top drawer stuffed with envelopes and postage stamps, old checkbooks, a desiccated rubber band ball. He reached out a hand and closed his eyes. It was home, a home, but he knew he would have to leave here, too.

It was a long ride to Harlem from where he had played the show in Brooklyn. Daniel and Michael lived uptown, not only because the rent was more affordable, but because it was closer to Columbia, where Michael stayed late, after his classes, to work in the lab. With the grant money he received, he'd been able to move out of Sunset Park.

Daniel trudged up the stairs of the subway station, down the four blocks to his building, and up the five flights to the apartment. When he unlocked the door, he was glad to see the lights on, and that the place was warm and smelled like food. He unlaced his boots, took off his coat, and put his guitar on his bed.

There was no couch, TV, dining room, or kitchen table. They ate on the floor, using a blanket as a tablecloth. Each of the bedrooms was large enough for a twin bed and nothing else, with space on only one side of the bed to squeeze in and out, and there were no closets, so Daniel had put his box spring up on concrete blocks and stored his clothes in plastic bins underneath. Over the past three months he had replayed his memories of Fuzhou until they lost their potency, leaving only a sense of awe: I went there. I did that.

Michael's door was open. Daniel knocked on the wall and said, 'What's up, brother?' in Fuzhounese.

Michael was sitting against his bed, eating out of a large bowl. 'Long day at the lab. I'm beat. How was work?'

Daniel switched to English. 'I didn't work tonight. I had a show. I mean, I played a show.'

'You did? Where?'

'At this bar in Brooklyn.'

'How'd it go?'

'Actually, it was really good.'

'Why didn't you let me know? I would've come.'

'I'll let you know about the next one.'

Michael held up his bowl. 'I made food. It's on the stove.'

'Thanks, I'm starving.'

The kitchen, on the opposite end of the apartment, consisted of a two-burner stove, a sink, and a small refrigerator. The dish rack sat on top of the microwave, the cutting board sat on top of the stove, and the rice cooker was on top of the cutting board. Daniel lifted the lid. Steam floated out, along with the sweet, garlicky odor of pork sausage, which Michael had cooked so that it would flavor the rice below. A fried egg awaited him as well.

He took out the other bowl, filled it with egg and rice and sausage, and topped it with a spoonful of hot sauce. Sunday nights, he and Michael went to Sunset Park, where they did their laundry in the basement and left the house armed with condiments. When Daniel helped Vivian make dinner, he would think of his mother, in her new apartment, looking at the harbor in the distance. 'I'll visit you in New York,' she had said in last week's video chat, and he told her he would like that, though he wasn't sure if she could get into the country after being deported.

For now, this was where his life would be. This apartment with Michael. This city. His best home. The heater clanked, a siren ripped up the block. He placed the lid back on the rice cooker and took his bowl into the bedroom so he and Michael could eat together.

ACKNOWLEDGMENTS

When you work on a novel for years and years, you don't do it alone. My gratitude is immense.

Thank you, Barbara Kingsolver. Thank you, PEN. Huge thanks to my agent, Ayesha Pande; my editor, Kathy Pories; my publicist, Michael McKenzie; and the fantastic team at Algonquin Books for their hard work in putting this book out into the world. I couldn't be more grateful.

Big love to the VONA/Voices diaspora. I'm especially grateful for the wisdom of Elmaz Abinader, David Mura, and Junot Díaz. Thanks to Emily Raboteau, Linsey Abrams, Judy Sternlight, and my novel workshop-mates for seeing the possibility in the early days, and to the Asian American Writers' Workshop, where I first found community.

This novel wouldn't be what it is without Sunita Dhurandhar, Serena Lin, and Melissa Rivero, who read drafts, wrote with me, and shared their generosity and brilliance. Thank you to Lorelei Russ, Amelia Blanquera, Zohra Saed, Melissa Hung, Glendaliz Camacho, Grace Lee, and all my friends who encouraged, listened, and laughed with me while I was writing this book, as well as everyone who tolerated my many questions in the name of research, including Vin Ferraro, Howard

Myint, Brendan Crosby, Michael Maffei, Retha Powers, and Linlin Liang.

To my parents, Alfonso and Lilian Ko, my original entourage: thank you for so many things, including your grind, heart, exuberance, love of music and dancing, and teaching me how to see life as narrative and the importance of asking tough questions.

To Julman Tolentino, whose love and understanding changed everything: thank you for a building a home with me, and for long talks about Daniel and Polly.

I never could have written this book without the support of the fellow artists I've met through the Lower Manhattan Cultural Council's Workspace Residency (which finally saw me over the finish line), Hawthornden Castle, the MacDowell Colony, the Blue Mountain Center, Writers Omi at Ledig House, the I-Park Foundation, the Anderson Center, the Constance Saltonstall Foundation for the Arts, the Paden Institute, the Kimmel Harding Nelson Center, the Van Lier Fund, and the New York Foundation for the Arts.

Xiu Ping Jiang, Cirila Baltazar Cruz, Encarnación Bail Romero: I am in your debt. Nina Bernstein's 2009 *New York Times* article 'Mentally Ill and in Immigration Limbo' provided the spark. Numerous other sources offered guidance in shaping this novel, including *Outsiders Within: Writing on Transracial Adoption*, edited by Jane Jeong Trenka, Julia Chinyere Oparah, and Sun Yung Shin; *Factory Girls* by Leslie T. Chang; *Smuggled Chinese* by Ko-lin Chin; *Golden Venture*, directed by Peter Cohn; *Last Train Home*, directed by Lixin Fan; *Wo Ai Ni Mommy*, directed by Stephanie Wang-Breal; the Transracial Abductees website; and articles by Patrick Radden Keefe, Ginger Thompson, and Kai Chang. I've taken fictional liberties with the material, and any inaccuracies in the novel are purely mine.

Bringing a book from manuscript to what you are reading is a team effort.

Dialogue Books would like to thank everyone at Little, Brown who helped to publish *The Leavers* in the UK.

Editorial
Sharmaine Lovegrove
Jennie Rothwell

Contracts
Stephanie Cockburn

Sales
Sara Talbot
Ben Green
Rachael Hum
Viki Cheung

Design
Helen Bergh
Duncan Spilling

Production
Nick Ross
Narges Nojoumi
Mike Young

Publicity
Ella Bowman

Marketing
Jonny Keyworth
Kimberley Nyamhondera

Proofreader
Jade Craddock